For my sister and cousins,
who taught me how to use my imagination
and pushed me to write that first story.

Gyre: whirl; gyrate; a spiral; a vortex.
—Oxford Dictionary

Chapter One

Trevor

The crowd swallowed me whole, and I welcomed the invisibility. I leaned my head against the wall and savored my freedom while I still had it. Hopefully the military wouldn't find this place. Eighteen-and-up venues were rare in Boston, so that'd narrow it down. *Please, luck, don't fuck me over tonight.*

A rock band played through their set list to the tune of hundreds of fans screaming out every lyric. Phoenix and Lobster's lead singer sported a wicked grin, her hazel eyes lit up from the cheering and applause. Her honey-colored hair bounced as she jumped and strummed her guitar. Despite the music's violent tone, she moved with a grace I'd never seen before. Her allure cautioned that danger could follow, all while hinting that the plunge was worth the risk.

She enraptured me, but paranoia clawed at my insides. I ripped my eyes from her perfect face and plastered them to the venue's main entrance. *They're gonna find me for sure.*

The door swung open, and my breath hitched. Crap. That quickly?

A herd of teens piled in and I heaved a sigh, dispersing the clawing beast as if it were cigar smoke spiraling into the air. People pushed against me, but I ignored them. They could rub their sweaty, flailing arms all over me, and I wouldn't care so long as that discomfort meant safety. Anonymity.

I lifted my eyes to the lead singer again. She was already watching me, smiling as she sang. Her eyes bore down on me like no one else existed. It could have been my imagination, but my skin heated like all the stage lights had been swiveled to focus on me. My pulse pounded under her gaze, as if my mind had come alive long enough to cling to her like a lifeboat. Because she noticed me when I tried to stay hidden. Freedom blazed around her like a veritable burning bush, bright as a campfire in the middle of the woods. Wild and fluid and everything I craved. She didn't need to hide; it was obvious from the set of her jaw, the purpose in her presence. This was a girl who faced things head-on, a girl who had the freedom to do so.

Lucky her.

She turned away, breaking our connection, and finished her song without looking back, breaking our connection. A weight fell down my throat to my chest.

The rejection hurt, but my own stupidity offended me more. Maybe she'd only checked to make sure I hadn't passed out drunk like the people at the bar. Slouched against the wall during a rock show, I'd call myself a drunk, too.

The show ended, and the room cleared out. I wandered through a door near the stage that led out back. Darkness swept the alleyway with little reprieve. Clouds puffed out from my mouth with every exhale, spiraling upwards. I shivered into my hoodie. Next time I ran from the military, I'd be sure to wear something heavier. Or pick somewhere warmer to run to.

Shuffling sounds pervaded the alley, followed by the sharp *ting* of a can getting kicked against a wall.

"Get the fuck away from me!"

"Shut up, bitch!"

My chest tightened as I turned a corner to find two people mid-scuffle. A man shoved a young woman against a brick wall, her head connecting with a *thwack*. His baggy hoodie obscured everything except his height, a feature that left this girl without a hope of fighting back.

"Hey!" I shouted.

They both spun toward me, and my fists clenched when her face met mine. The lead singer. The girl who had pinned me with an electric stare then glanced away like she hadn't allowed me a deep glimpse into her being. She swiveled, slammed both open palms against the wall, and kicked outward, sailing the man straight across the alleyway.

All the way across. To the other brick wall fifteen feet away.

What the hell?

Maybe she didn't need saving after all. I sure as hell couldn't do better than *that*.

I sprinted forward, intent on putting myself between them, but the man jumped to his feet. He charged forward a few steps then froze. His head cocked to the side, like a dog investigating an intruding noise.

"Back the hell off!" I shouted at him, my words way off my mark. I'd never been in a fight in my life, never had a reason to jump into one. But something about this girl, how she *saw* me, sent my feet moving five steps quicker than my head. An ache started in my chest and flowed to my arms and hands. For all the confidence she'd exuded on stage, and despite the strength that allowed her to kick the guy away, she needed help.

The way the streetlight fell from the road, I couldn't see his face. But an intricate tattoo covered his hand in an endless stream of swirls, a dark-inked infinity contained on his skin. Four tight curls of ink stayed the center of the tattoo, anchoring the lines that floated outwards. The design seized my attention—and my breath. I'd seen it before, hundreds of times. It was the mark my parents made me memorize as a kid. Their company's logo. The symbol broadcasting my parents' and this man's shared belief in a fantasy so ridiculous they'd advertise such conviction on their skin—that time travel was possible, achieved through connections forged in man-made objects.

My chest dropped, so heavy my legs threatened to buckle beneath me. Had he targeted her because I ran, because he needed a way to draw me out? Was it a way to get me to go back and be a good Lemurian spy? Some part of my mind was disgusted that could be true.

But why attack *her*? Why would Lemurians even come to Boston? *The Fine Art Museum*, my brain offered. Artworks, artifacts, everything they'd need to be set up for a while. Every tool they'd need to travel through time for at least a month.

The man didn't back down. Mom probably sent him after me when Lieutenant Weyland—unaware of my ancestral predicament, along with the whole of the Navy—failed to find me quickly. I barreled forward, tackling the man to the ground. The singer gasped and backed against the wall. It was the only good hit I'd likely get on the guy, and I took it.

We tumbled and rolled. I got in a punch, but I couldn't avoid one he threw in return. His fist smashed my jaw. Reality swam around me in a stunned sea of confusion. He yanked me up by the collar of my shirt and reeled back. I tore into his grip, trying to make space between my neck and the fabric accosting it. *Air. Need air.*

The man froze again, cursing under his breath before shoving me against the ground. His footfalls died off as he ran away.

Kill me now. My head pulsed and my jaw ached like it'd been completely unhinged. I ran my fingers across the bone. It didn't *feel* broken. Tender and bruising fast, but not broken.

"Shit," the singer said. "Why the hell did you do that?"

The singer. She was still here, standing over me with a hand on her head and the other wrapped around her waist.

"Trying to help." I stood, grunting with the effort, and wiped my mouth. My sleeve came away red with blood.

She backed off a step and glared. *I jump in to save her, and she's pissed. Figures.*

"That was kind of stupid." Her eyes softened. "Thank you."

I shrugged off the thanks. "Are you okay?"

"Just peachy. Perfect day, you?"

The light masked her face, but caught enough to reflect off the tears on her cheeks. "Sure you are. I can tell you were crying. Did he hurt you?"

A stupid question because I *watched* him pitch her into the wall.

"No," she said, cradling her head despite her words. Then again, she wasn't hurt enough to not defend herself. She'd kicked him clear across the alley.

Impossible things, Abby had said, right before—

"You sure you're okay?" she asked, pointing to my face. "Come inside. I'll get you ice or a drink or something."

And god dammit, almost every part of me reached out for that invitation. But something held me back, a nagging in my brain that clawed its way out. It said to run. Now. Away from this Lemurian attack if I ever wanted to get out for good.

I didn't move. Either toward her or away from the alley.

"You hit your head pretty hard," I said. "Is there someone you can call?" My eyes wandered to the door we'd both exited from. "Someone from your band?" If I had a phone, I'd call 911 *for* her.

"I will."

But she didn't retreat. So I didn't either. I wished she'd at least pull her hand away from her head and check for blood. The sound her skull made as it struck the brick echoed in my ears.

She dropped the arm she had wrapped around her chest. The tension in my ribs, squeezing my insides together, released when she relaxed, leaving behind only the pain in my face.

"Thank you for stepping in," she said.

"Looked like you handled yourself." I wiped my lip again. Still bleeding.

Her eyes darted past me to where the man collided with the brick. "Yeah. I don't know about that."

Impossible things.

Her face fell, eyes darkening like there'd been more to the exchange than I'd seen. What'd he do to her before I'd gotten there? I wanted to comfort her, to wrap my arms around her to prove she'd be safe now, but I wasn't sure she'd let me. She barely let me stand three feet away from her. I shoved my hands into my pockets so I wouldn't be tempted to reach out.

Silence fell into the space between us. It wasn't enough to fill the void, and it wasn't enough to press me to leave. My feet wouldn't comply even if my mind gave them orders. I wasn't leaving until I knew she'd be okay, the girl who'd given me a glimpse at what pure freedom looked like.

"Well, thanks anyways..." She trailed off, as if waiting for something more.

I offered all I could think of. "Boncore. I'm Trevor Boncore."

A smile edged her lips. "Like James Bond or something? I think you're taking this saving me thing a bit far, don't you?"

I let a smile crack through the unease threatening to engulf me. I ran from the military to escape my parents' absurd war with ancient civilizations, not run into a girl with unnatural strength. Maybe the whole incident was a coincidence. Maybe she held a black belt, or the mugger was pathetic. I couldn't tell anymore. My jaw throbbed in time with the bass leaking through the walls of the venue.

"I didn't do much," I admitted. *Aside from getting punched in the face.* Not exactly the best way to win a girl over.

Her penetrating, wild stare begged to differ. Like she believed without a doubt I'd done it all.

"Still, thank you. I'm Chelsea." She tucked hair behind her ear. "I... wish we could have met under different circumstances."

I chuckled, but it wasn't funny. "Yeah, me too."

Just about *any* other circumstance might have been better. On the run from the military, I'd found her being attacked by a Lemurian who's probably related to me somehow. I didn't know for sure. But she probably just saw me as a stranger willing to take a beating to save her. Maybe she didn't remember our exchange during her band's set at all.

"What'd he want with you?" I asked.

She shrugged and wrapped her arms around herself. Her lip quivered, but she covered it up with a sharp inhale. "Money, probably. He didn't talk a lot. Then you showed up." Her eyes wandered to the door. "I should go inside now. Are you sure you don't want to come?"

"I'm sure." I didn't know why Mom had targeted her or how many others were nearby. I had to get out now and never stop running if I wanted to stay free. "Have someone check out your head, Chelsea." God, just saying her name aloud propelled jolts up my spine.

"I will. Get ice for your face." She wandered to the door but, instead of opening it, her hand hovered over the handle. Her eyes flitted to mine. "Thank you."

"You're welcome."

I turned for the street without looking back and sucked air into my lungs to calm my racing heart. Ice sounded good. My jaw ached for numbness.

I couldn't stay here, but Boston was the only endgame I'd planned as it'd been a big enough city to get lost in. Maybe New York City would be better. I hadn't exactly thought this "running away" thing through.

The harsh sound of breaks squealing to a stop froze all thought. A black SUV pulled up on the other side of the road. Dammit. Boston wasn't a big enough city to get lost in? How'd they even find me? I popped up onto the balls of my feet and shot my gaze up and down the street. I could run, return to the club and race out the front door. Maybe I could even get a few blocks down the street before they figured out where I went.

Two guys emerged from the vehicle, navy blue sweaters standing in for their Navy uniform jumpers. Exhaustion and annoyance marred their faces. I tipped back onto my heels and slouched. Running now was pointless; I couldn't blame any of the war on them. And making Lieutenant Weyland chase me after I'd disappeared on shore leave hadn't been fair. I'd made him look bad, and I hadn't intended to do that. Being my parents' pawn in a clandestine war between Atlantis and Lemuria had taken its toll, and I hadn't agreed with them. So I'd run. Simple as that. But you can't hide from the military when you're the head of a civilian department in the most classified operation to date.

The soldiers didn't cross the street. Weyland stood there, arms across his chest, eyebrows raised like a parent scolding their child. I imagined him saying: *Get over here and get in the car. Now.*

I sighed and followed the unspoken orders as any civilian would: with heavy feet and sagged shoulders. Working for the military had some perks. My problems consisted of things they didn't know about. Like their station being a subversion for a higher purpose.

Before I climbed into the backseat, something in the alleyway caught my attention. I squinted through dim light and saw her standing there. Chelsea. She hadn't gone inside.

Red hair flashed below me. Valerie slid out of my way and said, "Nice shiner. She must be special."

I tore my eyes from Chelsea and climbed into the backseat. "Don't even."

Chelsea had turned back. Why hadn't she gone inside the Franklin?

Valerie looked out her window. "Don't even what? You're the one who skipped town." She tilted her head my way. "Did you really think getting out would be so straightforward? Did you think Weyland wouldn't come find you before we left dock for good?"

I glanced at Valerie. Did she know about Chelsea's attacker? Or why my parents had sent him after her? She must. Of course she did. She'd always been the more loyal of us two.

Lieutenant Weyland claimed the driver's seat and pulled away from the curb. Was Chelsea still watching this? I wanted to look, to glance back into the alley, but I fought the urge. She was just as mysterious as the Lemurian attacker himself. How had that tiny girl sent her attacker flying?

Impossible things.

In my life, those impossible things only led to hurt and heartbreak.

I fixed my eyes on the seat in front of me and blocked out the rest of the world.

Chapter Two

Chelsea

Three Months Later

"Atlantis, City of Poseidon, the continent lost to us beneath the waves in the North Atlantic Gyre."

I dug the heel of my palm harder into my forehead. Concentrating on writing lyrics with this movie as a soundtrack made me want to punch the TV screen out. The narrator of this *ridiculous* movie had such a pompous air to his voice; he probably invented hot air balloons and powered them all with his brain. What Professor King thought picking this movie, I had no idea.

"It existed as an allegory in Plato's work—or did it?" the narrator continued.

I could hear everyone's thoughts echoing: *Who. Cares?*

We'd watched this movie for the sole purpose of holding a mindless session of class because Professor Miranda King had to grade final papers or something. With the semester—and my senior year—over in two weeks, she had to have a more logical reason, although I must have missed it somewhere between her stating how outrageous the notion of Atlantis was and her putting in the DVD.

Personally, I thought she should have ended class early instead. Some of us had theses to finish writing.

"Beyond the Straits of Gibraltar…"

Blah, blah, blah. I knew the story, had been obsessed with it as a child. I tried to tune the movie out and focus on my song lyrics.

"Evidence for Atlantis's existence is written in almost every civilization in ancient history. The Mayans, the Aztecs, the Egyptians."

And the Greeks. And the Romans. Did I need to go on?

"Most interesting is the assertion Lemuria may be Atlantis, or, in the very least, a sister-myth."

My eyes to lifted to the screen, and I cocked an eyebrow. *Lemuria. That's new.*

Professor King snorted a laugh from her desk. "This movie," she scoffed.

Then why make us watch it? I'd say it to her face if she wouldn't disown me, leaving me without a thesis advisor days before graduation.

The movie went on to describe Lemuria and, due to its "lost continent" status, its supposed connection to Atlantis. What the movie didn't say was where the heck Lemuria came from. I pulled my phone from my pocket to Google it for myself when Professor King stood and turned on the lights.

Guess I was more interested than I thought.

"All right, guys," she said. "Class is over. Get out of here. Jerry, turn the TV off, will you? I can't stand this movie."

I packed up my things, thanking all the classroom gods for Professor King's epiphany.

"Chelsea, can you stay behind for a moment?" Professor King asked.

I pursed my lips together. I had an hour and a half before I had to be at the Franklin for my band's show. But after falling behind on thesis work, I couldn't exactly walk away. Maybe she'd revoke my extension. Could she do that? *Shit.*

16

"Couldn't bring yourself to even touch the TV?" I joked. Maybe I could play this all off.

She chuckled and tapped a stack of papers onto her desk to straighten them up. "Funny, Chelsea. How's your thesis coming along?"

I swallowed hard. Guess not.

After having drama of the colossal scale interrupt my life three months ago—cheating boyfriend, skanky ex-best-friend, random mystery guy saving me in an alley before being hauled off by some dudes in a black SUV right before my eyes—I fell a bit behind. Okay, *a lot* behind.

"I should have a rough draft to you by Friday." I left the "hopefully" unsaid.

She nodded and picked up her papers and pen. "Great. And good job catching up after things got hectic. I look forward to reading it." She waved goodbye and strolled off to her next class.

"Well, that makes one of us," I mumbled. For the moment, at least, my extension remained intact. *Thank you, classroom gods.*

I exited the Social Sciences Building, the bright May sun warming my skin. I tried to bask in it, but dread regarding my impending deadline loomed above me like rain clouds. If my life hadn't gone to shit in a matter of hours three months ago, I'd have had my thesis done by now. But who was really at fault? Lexi for convincing my boyfriend to cheat on me, or me for letting it happen?

I shook my head and, with it, those negative thoughts. Two more weeks and none of it would matter anymore. I'd have no excuse to see their sorry asses on campus.

"Chelsea!"

A grin grew wide on my face. Logan, my best friend since diapers, barreled toward me.

He wrapped me in a bear hug then hung off to my side, an arm slung around my shoulders. "How's it going?"

"Good," I said. "Watched some bull movie on Atlantis in archaeology."

"Bet you enjoyed it, though."

I shrugged as we reached the Student Center, an old brick building smack dab in the center of campus. Logan held the door for me in a chivalrous act typically reserved for his less-than-sober moments.

"Let's get food and head out to the Franklin, okay?" I asked.

He flashed me a thumbs up. "I've got no plans. Need help setting up?"

God, yes. "*Please.* Battle of the Bands means reigning champ gets to prep the stage."

Logan grabbed a sandwich from Sammich Time's open-front cooler. "Oh, that sounds fair."

I shrugged and pulled one out for myself. "Our burden—for years to come," I said with a smirk. No one beat us at our home stage. No one.

<hr />

Fifteen minutes to go-time. My phone chirped despite terrible service that should have blocked messages from sliding through.

Logan: *Fucker is here with Lexi. Suggest you play something that rips into them hard.*

I groaned. If only. We played the best songs on battle nights, and nothing I wrote about those two ever sounded good. I threw my phone at the wall and let it sit there under my glare.

Wasn't it enough he had to cheat?

This whole hurting me in my venue thing had gotten old. Fast. *Screw this.*

Guitar still slung across my shoulders, I exited backstage through a side door and swam into the buzzing crowd. Audio Striker, our rivals, had the crowd jumping and fist-pumping. Their fans' enthusiasm played into my irritation, suffocating me in my own anxiety as I searched the masses for Lexi and Ray. I found them making out in a corner. Lexi had her hair up, her back-of-the-neck tattoo on rare display for all to see. Stupid 3D diamonds wrapped around each other, much like her tongue always seemed to be wrapped around his.

I tapped Ray on the shoulder. He spun, eyes widening the moment they met mine.

"Get out of here, now!" I shouted over the music.

Lexi, shorter than both Ray and I, stepped out from under him. I couldn't hear her over the music, but her lips, slathered in bright red lipstick, stuck out in the darkness like a freaking beacon to Hell. She mouthed something about the Franklin being a public place.

I rolled my eyes and pointed again to the exit sign on the next wall over. "My stage. My rules. Get out." While we didn't own the Franklin, my band, Phoenix and Lobster, played here almost every other week. We brought in tons of fans and revenue, paying the rent and then some on those nights.

Lexi's lips flapped like a bad monster movie dub, but the only words I caught over Audio Striker's shitty drum solo were, "*my* boyfriend." Call me crazy, but I didn't need to hear the rest, and I silently thanked Carlos for being so damned awful at drums that I couldn't.

Lights zipped around us. I lifted my hand and flashed Lexi the only gesture she deserved. Lexi slapped me across the face. White-hot heat and utter shock radiated outward from the point of contact. I stumbled backwards a few steps and bumped into a waitress carrying a full tray of drinks. What alcohol didn't coat the floor splashed onto me.

Did Lexi seriously just do that?

I fought every urge to rub my stinging cheek, to ring out my clothes, as I apologized to the waitress for Lexi's shit. The waitress glared at all three of us and retreated to the bar for refills.

My fists tightened, and I spun to hit Lexi, but the sight of her doubled over, laughing with Ray, halted me. My fingers rung the guitar strap across my chest, ripping it apart. My guitar swung low to my legs. I didn't move to rescue it. They laughed at me, *both* of them. Again.

19

Tears welled up and fogged my vision, but I swallowed down the hurt and tucked it away for another song, another day. I had a show to play. A competition to win. Getting thrown out now would botch the only thing I hadn't fucked up in my life. But not reacting would feel too much like running away, and I was tired of running.

Defend myself, or defend Phoenix and Lobster's title against Audio Striker?

"Screw you," I spat and picked up my guitar. Step by freaking step, I swallowed words like *coward* and *pushover* and forced myself into the bathroom. With no one else inside, I locked the door behind me and let out a throat-shredding scream.

Screw Lexi. Screw Ray.

I dropped my guitar on the grimy tiled floor and slammed my forehead against the door. Pain shot up my skull, retrieving memories I'd rather forget.

Three months ago, Trevor, this random guy, had swooped in and ran interference when some dude attacked me outside the Franklin. It'd been the same night I'd found Ray cheating on me. I'd never figured out who Trevor was or where he'd come from, and he'd never appeared in crowds since.

I could really use some of that miracle interception again tonight. This stunt, on top of the Battle of the Bands show, *and* a thesis draft to write? I banged my forehead again to clear my thoughts—or knock myself unconscious. I'd accept either right about now.

Music was my place of solace. I *craved* these nights on stage and the freedom that lifted me above my problems. But now, all I wanted was to leave. Not even the Franklin equaled safety anymore.

I slid down the door to the floor. Fuck this. *All* of it.

A sudden silence overtook the building, filled in by a roof-raising cheer that permeated the walls. Audio Striker just finished, *and* they played well. The floor vibrated with the crowd's footfalls.

My heart raced, a rhythmic pounding in my ears. I couldn't go on stage like this. How could I sing when I couldn't even catch my breath? It'd be forfeiting our crown.

Tears leaked out from behind my high-built wall. The exterior that'd held me together the last three months crumbled from the erosion of unshed tears. I wiped my nose. I needed to get the hell over this. But couldn't I go home and go to bed first? Start the day over?

Stop being pathetic.

I lifted my hand to the sink and pulled myself up. The world spun wildly.

Black spots danced around the edges of my vision. I threw my second hand to the sink to anchor myself against heavy seas of nausea. The floor turned into ocean waves, swimming up to greet me with equal parts kisses and razor sharp bites. My legs wobbled like Jell-O in summer as goose bumps galloped up my arms. The spots around my vision coiled together into a mask of darkness.

It swallowed all consciousness.

<hr>

My head was pounding and… cold? No, that wasn't right.

I opened my eyes and slapped a hand over them as white light assaulted me, triggering a headache instantly. I groaned and, finger by finger, eased my eyes into accepting the radiance.

A wall of grey and white met me—a ceiling with fluorescent bulbs. I pushed myself into a seated position and leaned against the closest wall. A chill ran down my spine at the sight of rows and rows of shelves stacked to the ceiling, like the back room at a chain store. *Exactly* like that.

The shelves held buckets of supplies. Bins of computer hard drives sat closest to me, but further down the aisle razors, deodorants, office supplies, and machine parts peeked out from plastic containers. Every bin had been placed with precision and marked with inventory barcodes. And it smelled clean. Almost sterile.

I shut my eyes against the onslaught, unable to comprehend

anything past the shivering in my bones. The chilliness here stood stark against the sweaty bodies and jumping crowd of the Franklin. Where the heat and humidity had overtaken me in Boston, my tank top now did nothing to warm me.

Did I fall asleep in the Archaeology Lab or something? Cold, clean air worked its way into my lungs, easy to breathe. No, this wasn't the Lab. Dust and rock particles leftover from experimental archaeology classes had littered the Lab's floor. Not a single speck of dirt touched this clean, white tile.

I pulled on a shelving unit, using it to steady myself as I stood. My legs shook, and each new object I saw quickened my breathing, heated my neck. I tried to slow my breaths to deep, life-giving pulls, but my body wouldn't oblige. What the hell even happened? Lexi had slapped me, then what? She'd hit me. I'd marched away. This wasn't the Franklin. The rest blurred together.

The Franklin. Holy shit. Did I miss the show?

My eyes darted around. I wasn't at the Franklin, but maybe I was close enough to get back and not miss the set.

Down the row from me, a steel door sunk into a wall. I rushed toward it with hard, thumping steps until a clipboard with signatures hanging on the back of the door came into view. It read: Supply Room 2L4D2, Inventory Check Chart. A logo for the U.S. Navy sat at the top of the paper.

My throat constricted as if I'd swallowed bubblegum, a sticky weight slinking down into my stomach. How had I gotten into a U.S. Navy supply room? Did the Navy even have a base in Boston?

The door swung open without warning, coming within inches of my face. I stumbled backward into a shelving unit. The room seemed to spin on its axis. Pens and clipboards flew from the shelves onto the floor.

A thirty-something, blond-haired man in a deep red uniform looked me over, eyes wide and mouth agape. His expression slipped into annoyance before settling on concern.

"Name and rank," he demanded in a clipped tone. "Who are you?"

I gulped.

Where the hell am I?

All around me, Navy officers argued my fate in controlled volumes. Their reasons for condemning or saving me sent my headache into overdrive, blurring together their arguments into an incomprehensible haze. Their stances blended in a whirlwind of "she's an intruder" and "no she's not." The officers threw around words like "treason" and "spy" in demanding tones. I processed it all in simple facts, uncomplicated words. Not. Is. Not. Is. All the while, I clung to my skin so it didn't crawl off me every time I thought of missing the Battle of the Bands show. Of how pissed my band-mates probably were.

An older man, middle-aged with wrinkles lining his eyes, had CAPTAIN MASON MARKS printed across the patch at his breast. He excused his Lieutenant, the man who'd found me in the supply closet and the only one who'd championed my cause, from the room.

A third officer shouted in a moment of failed self-control at the Captain. He had a large Military Police patch on one side of his broad shoulders. Every few seconds, the Military Police guy's frosty glare ripped through me, and his left hand, covered in veins protruding from beneath his skin, never lifted from the gun holstered at his hip. I gulped and straightened at the sight of his pistol. Yeah, I definitely infringed on something. But I wasn't a bad person, or a criminal. Would they really shoot me?

Of course they would. The military didn't fuck around. And I'd clearly done something horribly wrong. This was bad. So, so bad.

Another person entered the room, but the MP's shouts didn't stop. My eyes trailed a guy maybe a year or two younger than me as he approached the Captain. He almost swam in a pale yellow uniform two sizes too big, and a head of dark blond hair encroached on his face. He handed Captain Marks the CD he had stuck on the end of his finger like an awkward, shiny pinwheel. He turned, and I caught sight of familiar, piercing blue eyes, which twinkled with the slightest bit of recognition despite his otherwise-distant expression.

I froze. Trevor. On this military sub. *No freaking way.*

Something constricted my chest, but a bloom of hope rose amidst dark desperation. My last chance. My way out. How many times had I relived the night I was almost mugged by the guy with the weird tattoo? Almost every night, each spent trying to figure Trevor out. But I knew; he was a life preserver in a stormy sea.

I'd had the same feeling the moment I'd seen him standing there in the alley outside the Franklin three months ago, moments after finding Ray making out with Lexi. I'd met him right after I'd shoved my attacker clear across the alley. My first instinct had said Trevor was trouble, too, but all he'd wanted was to make sure I was okay. Me, a complete stranger.

Could he be my life preserver now?

His name rolled off my lips, and, dammit, my heart fluttered with it. "Trevor?"

Any amount of recognition I'd seen before was gone, replaced by a stern expression. My stomach tumbled to my knees. Did he not remember me? God, I must seem like a ridiculous girl grasping at air to save herself. I was nothing to him, but back in that alley without him, I may not have had the opening I'd needed to knock my attacker away.

He had to remember Boston.

"It's you, isn't it?" I said. "Don't you remember?"

Trevor's eyes lingered on me—*was that disbelief appearing?*—then he turned his attention to the Captain. I frowned, my shoulders slumping.

"The footage didn't tell me a how, just a when. I don't know how she got onboard," Trevor said. His eyes flicked to mine, a glint of worry in them, the same look that had been there when he'd found me outside the Franklin.

He *did* remember me. *Liar!*

"I *know* you." I tried to keep my voice from pleading, but the words came out somewhere between a squeak and a whine.

He'd seemed genuinely worried that night. Why then, of all times and places for him to absolutely need to recognize me, did he pretend he didn't? Maybe the alleyway lighting had been awful. Or maybe he really *didn't* remember.

A weight sunk me into the chair. My breathing slowed, hope evaporating with every exhale. We'd interacted for a span of five minutes. Of course he wouldn't remember.

Trevor's eyes jumped to the Captain's, his jaw taut like a child trying to cover up a mess by blaming it on their sibling. I watched the Captain's reaction with intense focus. Above all, his words could set me free. His face remained neutral, except for the slightest twitch of his lips.

Disappointment.

A spark of life ignited within me. The Captain knew I was telling the truth.

Chapter Three

Trevor

Not here. Not now, I begged Captain Marks, hoping the mental plea was loud enough. I couldn't protect Chelsea like this, and definitely not from Lieutenant Weyland's trigger-happy wrath. True, she deserved to be treated as an enemy intruder. She didn't have the clearance to be onboard a top-level classified Naval research station—the most advanced piece of submersible technology to pop out of Pearl Harbor. The law said to process her like a criminal, and Lieutenant Weyland was all too willing to oblige.

Except Chelsea hadn't appeared here on purpose. According to the Captain, she couldn't even remember how she got onboard. Only after reviewing the security tapes had I seen how it'd happened. Chelsea *teleported*. Honest-to-god teleported and got through the shield I'd built to make that very act not possible. How did she not know she had the ability? Why hadn't she teleported out of the alleyway? Moreover, why'd she teleport into the same supply closet I'd been in just three hours ago?

I held Captain Marks's stare, my brain buzzing. Dr. Helen Gordon had powers, too. Unexplained but accepted, sort of. She was on duty in the Science and Health Division, but grabbing her to talk to Chelsea or the Captain wouldn't be an issue. Helen, who could occasionally see the future, researched people with powers, like Chelsea and herself. She'd salivate at the chance to examine someone who could teleport, someone who's abilities could support her Atlantean theories.

It was kind of ridiculous how close Helen—and by extension, the Navy—was to figuring out the truth.

Regardless, Helen could sway the Captain into ignoring his Head of Security long enough to talk to Chelsea, if only Chelsea stopped digging herself a hole she couldn't get out of.

Chelsea glared at Lieutenant Weyland. "You look familiar, too."

His eyes skirted around her and called me out on my lie without admitting his own. Who wouldn't recognize this firecracker? He shifted in place, the fingers of his left hand still pressed against his gun holster. The action was enough to shut Chelsea up. Thank god.

"Are you both sure neither of you have ever met Ms. Danning?" Captain Marks waved her driver's license with one hand, the other still pressed palm-down against the Briefing Room's table.

I met Lieutenant Weyland's gaze, an eyebrow rising. I wasn't budging if he didn't.

"No," we said in unison.

"Are you freaking *kidding me*?" Chelsea stood, her face red and eyes glazing over.

The same ache which held me in place in Boston returned now. It almost made me come clean to Captain Marks. But now wasn't the time.

Chelsea huffed, arms crossing at her chest. "I know I can be imprisoned for this. I could—" She stopped, her head cocking to one side.

Why'd she stop?

Chelsea shut her eyes and scrunched up her face. I tensed. What was she doing?

Navy blue lights filled the room, flowing like a waterfall, each droplet over the other, until her form disappeared completely. Lieutenant Weyland pulled his gun. I spun around, searching for Chelsea, for any trace she'd been here at all. For proof I hadn't dreamt up the whole damn thing.

Chelsea disappeared. Gone from my life as fast as the first time we met. I rolled my head onto my shoulders. She'd slipped through my fingers yet *again*.

I sighed. "Guess it won't matter what you do with her now, huh, Weyland?"

He shot me a glare.

Dark blue lights rematerialized next to me until Chelsea appeared within the cascade. She did it. She teleported again.

The safety of Lieutenant Weyland's gun clicked off, a harrowing echo in the room. I side-stepped in front of Chelsea with one hand held out before me, the other on her arm.

"Don't, Lieutenant!"

He didn't react. He didn't move his finger off the trigger, either.

Captain Marks stepped toward me, his own hand held out as though approaching a wounded animal. I turned to find Chelsea's mouth open, lips pulled back. Her eyebrows rose to her hairline.

"Chelsea?" I asked.

Her jaw set and her eyes narrowed into small slits. Her hands slid up between us, shoving me away. "I knew it. I freaking *knew* it! You do remember!"

I met her eyes, wishing I hadn't. Her anger gutted me, stacking all my reasons for lying into a neat tower and whacking them over. "All right, yes. I do. Please, Chelsea, calm down."

"Holster your weapon, Lieutenant," Captain Marks barked before pointing to Chelsea. "Ms. Danning, I need you to take a seat."

The Captain was the type of person you could only read by their eyes. The rest of him remained the calm, in-control exterior that a military officer was supposed to have. But his eyes, so wrinkled in concern, gave him away. Judging by that alone, confidence surged within me that he wouldn't imprison Chelsea. I didn't think he wanted to. But until Lieutenant Weyland calmed the hell down, it looked like Captain Marks wasn't going to budge.

"No," Chelsea said, swiping the air. "Tell me what is *happening* to me, why *he's* here."

I had to get her to stop. What if she teleported again? What if she popped into the middle of the Pacific Ocean by accident or something?

She sighed, plopping into the chair. Her strong, defiant composure broke, cracking around her eyes, pulling her lips downward. "I have no idea what's happening to me." A tear broke free as she stuck her shaking hands between her knees.

I sank little by little into a chair beside her. "I know someone who can help. If you'll let her." My eyes lifted to the Captain's. "Captain, what about Dr. Gordon?" If Weyland wouldn't leave, Dr. Gordon was Chelsea's sole hope. Maybe she could nudge Captain Marks further into the "don't imprison Chelsea" zone.

Chelsea brushed away stray tears. "Why should I let you do anything?"

Fair question. Why should she? Instead of outright helping her, I'd lied. But she couldn't understand the reasons why. Hell, I didn't. So I settled on something else. "Because I'm still taking the saving thing too far."

She looked up at me with eyes like daggers. "You should've *said* something—"

"Ms. Danning," Captain Marks cut in.

Her mouth clamped shut, lips forming a hard line.

Captain Marks glanced at his Lieutenant. "I'd like to speak with Ms. Danning alone."

Chelsea stared me down, the room a deafening quiet. Her wild eyes burned with intensity. I tried to hold it, but her hazel irises smoldered and swam like a molten ocean sunrise. They seared me from the inside out. Not painfully, but thoroughly, into every crevice of my mind. Like she saw straight into my soul.

Lieutenant Weyland stepped forward, breaking the spell. "No way, sir."

Captain Marks leveled his eyes to meet with Lieutenant Weyland's, a warning.

The Lieutenant's lips sealed tight, then he nodded to me. "Let's go."

I gave Chelsea one last look. She trained her eyes anywhere but on me. Her lips quivered the tiniest bit, but she didn't speak.

God help me, I would make this up to her if it was the last thing I did.

◆

"Well shit, Trevor."

I tossed Valerie a glare and stalked past her into Engineering, two decks tucked near the bottom of SeaSatellite5. Whiteboards and chairs had been scattered between everyone's desks. A stack of reports, a computer with two monitors, and empty water bottles dominated my workspace.

"Why are you here?" I asked.

Valerie blocked the path to my desk, offering me a file folder. "The report on the hull's inner liquid, post-teleporting episode, as requested."

I eyed her. "Never requested it."

Valerie was part of the bio-engineering group, not mine. She only knew about the liquid because she'd sat in class next to me the moment I'd invented it. My shield. My ballast system design. I'd gotten this job because of them both. Valerie had happened to catch a ride in my tailwind, both of us products of a generation too focused on fairytales to risk the Navy finding evidence of the old maritime civilizations before they did.

I'd known Valerie for longer than I could remember, she being the daughter of a family friend. Both of our parents lived by the extreme version of our fantastical history, that our families descended from those who colonized Lemuria, a lost continent forever at war with the City of Atlantis. I'd grown up on the stories, thought it all nonsense until my tenth birthday. Ever since I'd seen my name scrawled in the language of the Lemurians, ever since they'd tested me for powers I didn't have, I'd believed.

Valerie, on the other hand, had welcomed stories of Atlantis and Lemuria seemingly since birth. She'd almost changed her major to history or archaeology to chase those dreams. Then her mother had convinced her the best way to be productive to the collective was to get onboard a SeaSatellite5 Navy vessel. Only these SeaSatellite ships traversed the seas with such speed at this depth. These vessels would find any remnants of the history our families believed in, if any evidenced existed to be found. And I didn't contend that point.

So when my parents had forced me through school after I'd designed Humming Bird, I'd accepted it. Until, at least, they'd revealed their plans to use my system to keep the Atlanteans out, to claim SeaSatellite5 and any other satellite ships as Lemurian pawns in their war, without the Navy's consent or knowing. They'd wanted my system, the very thing I'd thrown my entire being into, for war.

The Navy didn't even know what was happening. They'd employed us because they needed engineers like me and Valerie. Young, ingenious post-graduates willing to think outside the box. That's what had gotten my rotating ballast system off the ground. Who would think of making a ship that rotated orientation *around* a never-changing interior? No one. But the Navy had sure jumped on the idea real quick. You know, for "research vessel purposes." I still wasn't convinced there wasn't something more I'd never been told, but I doubted I'd ever find out for sure.

It's why I'd run. Like if I got far enough away, if the Navy no longer had the creator of the Humming Bird system, no one could use it—not the Navy for exploration, nor the Lemurians for war. To keep their ship afloat for long-term study, or to anchor the ship while they hauled Link Pieces from shipwrecks.

When my plan to run had backfired, I'd installed a shield to block *everyone* from teleporting onboard. The same shield Chelsea had bypassed an hour ago. I could only stay mad about it for so long, then I'd remember the night we first met, and my heart would leap around like an excited, confused animal.

"Yeah, well, I figured Teleportation Girl kept you busy." Valerie raised an eyebrow. "Did you tell Captain Marks the truth about her?"

I opened the file folder and glanced at the contents to give myself time to think. Until today, I'd never seen anyone teleport. With the exception of Dr. Gordon—where you couldn't even see her power anyway—I'd never seen someone use abilities, period. Where my parents had remained open about our history, they'd stopped sharing information about powers, Lemurian or Atlantean, when I was young. Probably because I'd never developed any. Thank *god*. Being a descendant of Lemuria I could handle (sort of). But having abilities to top it off?

"He's aware I've met her before, yeah," I said.

Valerie's hand appeared on top of the folder, drawing my eyes to her. "You don't think this is worth reporting?"

"You can't be serious."

"Have you ever known me to be anything but?"

I snapped the folder shut. "Those were fairytales. People don't teleport. People don't actually have abilities." Except apparently Chelsea. And Dr. Gordon.

"Dr. Gordon sees the future," Valerie argued, hands resting on her hips.

"Sometimes." With inaccuracy. I plopped into my desk chair.

She came to the other side of my desk and slapped both palms to the surface. "Teleportation Girl could be one of us."

I gave a slow shrug. "Maybe. Does it matter? If she's one of us, there's nothing to worry about."

Valerie leveled her chestnut eyes with mine. "It's a big deal—someone we didn't know about shows up on the ship we're assigned to?"

No one else had been assigned to any "ship." SeaSatellite5 was the only one. "I mean, it's whatever," I replied.

"It's not a freaking joke."

"I didn't say it was." But I didn't care, either. All I had to do was keep SeaSatellite5 out of my extremist family's hands and pacify their hell-bent determination to find enough Link Pieces to destroy to Atlantis forever. If I managed that, the rest didn't matter.

My endgame consisted of making video games for a living, or something like that. Anything but devoting my life to a war over time travel, something I didn't agree with doing, period. Time wasn't meant to be traveled or changed. By anyone, for any reason. That the Atlanteans did so because they wanted to modify history to their liking sucked, yeah. But the Lemurians didn't need to underhandedly employ the U.S. Navy and its most classified vessel to do their dirty work. It wasn't hard to find Link Pieces—artifacts and artwork made by men with the ability to be used for time travel. I didn't really understand how Link Pieces worked, only that they existed, and that Lemuria and Atlantis wanted control over all of them.

"*You* may find his orders funny," Valerie said, her teeth grinding together. "But ignoring them will get you killed. And believe it or not, I do like you, Trevor. Remember who the enemy is. 'Cause if she turns out to not be one of us, he'll find out, and no matter how into her you are, he'll end it."

"I won't tell if you won't."

But I knew she would, especially if Chelsea *did* turn out to be Atlantean. If Chelsea was, what would happen? My throat tightened around the thought. She'd be my enemy by birthright, and Valerie would turn her in to Thompson, our Lemurian boss. The guy who set us up on SeaSatellite5. The man Captain Marks didn't know we answered to, or that he even existed.

Valerie shook her head, confirming my thoughts. "I follow orders."

"Blindly."

Her hands balled into fists, and she stalked out of Engineering. I should have stopped her in case she planned to report Chelsea's appearance. But I didn't. For the moment, I wanted to believe this wasn't real. That everything I'd built my system for, every act I'd done to defy my parents and their stances on the war, hadn't been thwarted and challenged.

I tapped on my keyboard until the screen turned on, and I broke into the security camera feeds. Captain Marks and Chelsea sat in the Briefing Room. Her head rested between her hands, defeated. Captain Marks tried to keep his distance without appearing cold. He was freaked the hell out. That made two of us.

Please let her be Lemurian.

The thought struck like thunder snow, rare and unexpected. I'd never come across another Lemurian other than my family, Valerie, and Thompson. And there Chelsea sat, maybe one of us.

Maybe not.

I opened a new window on my second monitor and brought up the tape again, watching once more as she teleported into a supply room on the Science Decks. My breath hitched. Deep cobalt poured from an unseen source, depositing Chelsea on SeaSat5. Blue, not the red of Lemurian powers from the lore I'd read as a kid. But dammit, it was the most beautiful thing I'd ever seen.

A memory nagged at my brain, pulling me halfway in the right direction, but letting go before I could latch onto its meaning.

Think, Boncore.

Soldiers. On my tenth birthday, when my parents imparted most of what I knew about Lemuria to me, they'd warned me about abnormally powerful Atlanteans strong enough to match even the Lemurian soldiers who wielded fire as though they breathed it.

Strength.

I gulped, my brain struggling to wrap itself around a vague

memory from Boston. A kick so powerful it flung Chelsea's attacker clear across the alleyway.

This can't be real. This isn't happening.

Chelsea was absolutely not from Lemuria.

Valerie was right, but she didn't know about Chelsea's strength. I would have to keep that to myself. Because Valerie didn't know the very enemy we'd been warned about just waltzed aboard SeaSatellite5... and into my heart.

Chapter Four

Chelsea

What. The. Hell.

Teleport. The word rolled through my mind like a thunderstorm on a sunny day. Forming the syllables felt awkward enough: *Te-le-port*. Tele-freaking-port. Across the room to Trevor. Across the ocean to a military research station where the guy I met in an alley in Boston was employed.

I leaned my forehead against the cool metal table. I was screwed. The military planned to lock me in here forever—for experimentation and god knew what else—and I'd never graduate and practice archaeology. I'd never play on stage again. Both dreams, ripped from me by something unreal. I wouldn't have believed this happened if not for the cuffs digging into my wrists.

Unless I could figure out how this teleporting thing worked. Maybe if I could get farther than across the room to Trevor, I could escape.

I slammed my cuffed wrists onto the table for the tenth time, unable to calm down. Every time I got my mind off of being *handcuffed* for something I didn't mean to do, Trevor's face swam across my thoughts, reigniting searing-hot anger in my veins. He'd denied

36

knowing me at possibly the worst time to do so, then went back on it like he couldn't decide whose ass to save—mine or his own.

Really though, I couldn't blame him. He'd saved me in that alleyway, then got hauled into some black SUV. These Navy sailors had to have been his captors, which meant, somehow, the events were related. Mr. Trigger-Happy, the one who freaked the hell out when I teleported again, looked familiar, too.

I stood, hands cuffed in front of me, palms facing upward, and concentrated. All I saw was red. Trevor had lied. *Lied.* Lied like Ray had after he slept with Lexi. Lied like I didn't matter at all. Even if Trevor came out with the truth at the end—and thank god he did— that initial second-impression of him wouldn't leave my mind.

My heart submerged deep into my chest. Maybe I didn't matter. Maybe to him I was some stupid girl who shouldn't have left the Franklin alone. Maybe he was just some silly tourist who got lost and decided to help me on a whim.

My fists balled in front of me, painted fingernails digging into the skin of my palms. Maybe silly and stupid was all I'd ever be, thanks to Lexi. Thanks to this teleportation freak-show I'd become.

My hands shook. What if I could never play a show again because I'd accidentally *appear* somewhere else—in the crowd, next to our lead guitarist, or, god forbid, to Ray? What if I always teleported here, to Trevor?

"Everything okay?"

I startled, my hands up in defense. My heart raced. Didn't know why—not like I had shot of escaping from a military station I shouldn't even know existed. *Level One Secure Class Vessel,* the friendly Lieutenant who found me in the supply room had said. Lieutenant James, but he'd said to call him Dave.

Dave had to be about the only person on this sub convinced I shouldn't be jailed. Dave alone saw how terrified I was. Dave alone understood at all.

"Ms. Danning?"

A woman stood half in the doorway, half out, with eyebrows raised high. I probably looked ridiculous, frozen in the middle of the room, handcuffed and shaking.

"What?" I asked.

She stepped into the room and shut the door behind her without turning from me. She wore a white lab coat thrown over her pale yellow uniform—the same color Trevor wore—and had her light blonde hair pulled into a tight bun. She stood at my height and looked to be in her late twenties. She smiled gently—a doctor's smile, the one given before a life-threatening prognosis.

Who was she? For all I knew, what came of this conversation determined my fate. *Dammit.* If I didn't get out of here, I'd never graduate. Two weeks out from D-Day, and I'd ended up here, my thesis left to rot in student-hell forever.

"My name is Dr. Helen Gordon. I'm a scientist here on SeaSatellite5," she said.

"Hi." My pulse raced. Here was the person who'd be experimenting on me, no doubt.

Dr. Gordon gestured to the table, a haggard clunk of metal in an already steel-saturated cell. "Could we talk about what happened today?"

"Do I have a choice?"

Her eyebrows rose at my response. I sat down, ignoring the look of offense on her face. Dr. Gordon didn't appear hostile like Mr. Trigger-Happy or disbelieving like the Captain, despite his best attempts to hide the emotion. I shouldn't have mouthed off to her.

Dr. Gordon sat opposite me and folded her hands on the table's cool surface. "Captain Marks showed me the security tapes. Your ability is mesmerizing."

My eyes met hers. She'd been the first to say "ability" rather than "anomaly" or "weird thing." Why? A portion of my bottom lip fell into place behind my teeth. Two could play this game.

"If you want to call it that," I replied.

"I do," she said. "There are stories of others able to do the same thing, but I've never seen it firsthand. It's stunning."

I straightened. "You've heard of this before?"

What does she study that involved teleportation? Stupid question—urban myths about people with teleportation abilities have populated our world over the centuries, but they usually involved stories of Titans and gods and demons.

Something thick and sticky slunk down my throat. Was I a demon? I'd never paid attention in Sunday school—that was more my sister's thing—but… demons at least had the possibility of making sense.

"I'm not a demon, am I?"

Dr. Gordon chuckled. She actually *chuckled.* My chest rose and fell like a jackhammer, my lungs fighting for breath. I was a demon and damned to Hell. Well, at least I could accompany my thesis there. Maybe I'd give lectures to the other damned souls about Bigfoot and the pyramids being alien creations.

"No, you're not, Ms. Danning," Dr. Gordon said, leaning forward. She reached a hand across the table. "Are you okay?"

"Oh, thank god." The words flooded out of my mouth. A chuckle bubbled to the surface at the irony. "And call me Chelsea," I corrected her, ignoring her concern. I didn't need it. I needed a way off this damn *ship.* And besides, if she planned to condemn me to prison for something as personal as my "ability," the least she could do was call me by my first name.

"I'm Helen."

"Okay, *Helen.* If I'm not a demon, what am I?"

She sucked in a deep breath. Anyone not watching her as closely as I was wouldn't have noticed. She was ticked, hiding something— or wasn't planning on sharing all the details, given my current state of asshatery. Couldn't blame her.

"That is a more complicated question than the one you want an answer to," she said.

"Nope," I said. "Asking, 'What am I?' will definitely also provide an answer as to what happened."

Helen's demeanor didn't shift a single molecule. Her face remained calm; not quite blank, but not showing any more concern than interest or annoyance. They blended together in a thin mask of almost emotion. She took in slow, deep, near-imperceptible breaths.

Whatever I'd become, whatever had happened to me, must not be doom-worthy—it was classified. Mega freaking classified.

I took a deep breath, readying myself. If I wanted to get those answers she was withholding, maybe I'd have to divulge another secret of my own. "Look, I don't know what happened today, but I do know it's not the first time something... *odd* has happened to me."

The day the rumors about my break up with Ray first flew around boomeranged to the forefront of my thoughts. It'd been two days after the night I'd met Trevor at the Franklin three months ago. Then Lexi had managed to convince people Ray had broken up with me because, not only had I held out on him in the sex department, *I'd* cheated on *him* with someone. A whole slew of terrible things had been written on social media in the following days, and they'd brought my band into it. The whole thing was ridiculous from start to finish, so ridiculous that when Logan had come backstage mid-show a week later to give me a heads-up of what had happened, I'd gotten so angry that I'd snapped a mic stand in half.

And the tequila thing. I could also drink a bottle of tequila—or rum, or whiskey, I wasn't picky—by myself and come out barely buzzed on the other end. No matter how hard I tried or how much I spent on the good stuff, I never, not once, had gotten drunk.

Okay. So maybe that was odd, too.

"Oh?" Helen asked, drawing my thoughts back to the present.

Oh? That was the best she could offer? Crimson streaked across my vision. "Why bother sitting here surprised if you clearly know more than you're letting on?"

"Because I've never seen these abilities in anyone so young before. It's… strange."

My eyebrows scrunched. "Well I'm glad you think it's 'strange,' just like the rest of them."

She leaned forward in earnest. "I want to help you."

I glared into her unwavering stare. If she really wanted to help me, she should get me off this damn ship. "How?"

"Your abilities are genetic. Some fall down through family lines, but not all appear in every generation. Because I haven't heard of your parents, it's safe to say these abilities skipped a generation or two."

Confusion wormed its way through me, twisting my ability to focus into frustration on its way to my fists. I closed and opened them a few times. Why the hell did she need to be so cryptic?

"So…?" I asked.

Helen's lips pressed together then widened with a smile. "I don't mean to make you upset," she said. "I don't think you recognize how special you are."

I let my head roll onto my shoulders rather than speak, and breathed deeply. In. Out. Teleportation didn't equal "special" in my mind. Teleportation meant inconveniences, freakiness, popping into places I shouldn't be. *Not* special. That was reserved for something else. Some other power. Some other person.

"I want to learn from you," she said, which basically meant: *I want to study you.* The lingo wasn't new. We social scientists spoke the same way.

A startling seriousness darkened her eyes. Underneath it, though, rose a glimmer of fondness, of caring. "I have an ability, too, Chelsea, and I believe our abilities are connected in origin. I study this origin, to better understand it. I also want to help you learn to control the ability you have now. You deserve the chance to understand what's happening to you."

She was right. I did deserve that chance. But what did I want

41

more: to get off this tin can in one, un-cuffed piece, or to figure out what had happened today?

I brought my cuffed hands up to my forehead—or, I tried to. My wrists pressed against my eyes and nose with my fingers waving somewhere above my hairline. "How do you plan on helping me when the Captain wants me jailed?"

"Lieutenant Weyland wants you in the brig," she corrected. "He's doing his job, that's all. The Captain ultimately decides what happens to you, and he knows what I study and why."

I blew out a harsh exhale. What did my abilities being connected to hers have to do with the military? Flashes of black-ops soldiers danced across my imagination. How many things on this satellite station, research included, were classified, and how deep into all of it had I dove?

Everything, and damned deep.

Again, I found myself hoping all of this was a dream. Like, at any point, I'd wake up in South American Archaeology with the imprint of my pen and spiral notebook on my face, my professor babbling on about something I didn't care for because I took the class as an elective. I'd wake up, the confrontation with Lexi nothing but a dream, and Logan would point me out to the class.

"Damn, Chelsea," he'd shout. "Falling asleep *again*."

Our classmates would hoot and laugh, and the professor would chuckle, and I'd go beet red, and things would be normal again.

But a sinking feeling bloomed above my heart and trickled down my spine. "Normal" wasn't a luxury I'd get to enjoy anymore. I wasn't going to wake up. I wasn't going to pinch myself and suddenly be in the city, on stage, not seeing Trevor in any crowd. Because all of this started the night I saw him there. The night he chose to go to *my* city, to *my* show in *my* venue. He disrupted my life, and now here I was, disrupting his and everything else.

Chapter Five

Trevor

Absolutely not," she called from the bathroom.

Pacing outside Chelsea's holding room was all I could do to keep calm. I didn't know why she'd come here, but if she didn't take Helen's offer…

What if she did, but only because it was better than the alternative, and she ended up hating this place, hating me?

I stopped and leaned against a wall. She didn't even know me; how could she hate me? And, more importantly, why did I care?

Because I'd lied instead of immediately defend her. Because I was scared. Because she'd appeared out of nowhere and popped past the exact piece of technology responsible for my employment onboard this satellite station. Chelsea circumventing the shield meant my machine had failed, my shield was pointless, and I was back to square one. Add in Valerie's goading about our "orders," and everything grew into one large pile of crap.

And, not least of all, because some part of me still wrung itself at the sight of seeing her hurt and confused. In Boston, after her attacker had fled, and now, here, because of a power she didn't know she possessed. I wondered if the coincidence had struck her yet, how we'd gravitated toward each other three months ago, and how she now stood on the other side of this wall. Or how coincidental it was that Helen worked with Atlantean descendants. Or how great a chance that this was the vessel the Lemurians had their eyes on.

The door to Chelsea's holding room slid open, closing my thoughts with it. I saw the coincidences, yeah, but I had no idea what to make of them. Especially because she was Atlantean.

Helen strolled out of Chelsea's holding room, and I pressed off the wall to join her. "How'd it go?"

Helen sighed as the door slid shut behind her. "She's scared and frustrated, and she has every right to be."

My heart sank, a heavy weight falling into my gut. "So she's not going to take your offer?"

"No, I think she will. She's a scientist. Her curiosity will ultimately outweigh everything else."

"You hope." And so did I. Beyond figuring out how she got past my life's work, I couldn't knock the idea of getting a second chance with her, an idea soaked in stupidity given the last few hours. Everything about her called to me, even the way she'd looked at me from the stage three months ago only to turn away as if she'd never seen me at all. "So, what now?"

Helen adjusted her lab coat and brushed invisible dust off her uniform pants. "Now, I talk to the Captain and hope he'll hear me over Lieutenant Weyland." Helen frowned. "Chelsea needs help. I thought I'd found everyone who might exhibit abilities. I feel responsible for this, as if I've let her down for not finding her and her family sooner."

"It's not your fault," I assured her. "Sometimes people just fall through the cracks. You can help her now. Besides, I know Captain Marks will listen to you."

I didn't know where my confidence came from. It wasn't like Captain Marks was also interested in how Chelsea got through the anti-Lemurian shield—he didn't even know it existed in such a capacity, or how Chelsea teleporting onboard proved his ship was unprotected. Torpedo counter-measures were one thing. An all-out Lemurian attack was an unknown quantity. I knew so little about the Lemurians' supposed abilities, and the only person I trusted enough to ask was… unavailable at best. Nearly comatose at worst.

Helen tilted her head, questioning me without saying a single word.

I changed the subject. "Can I see her?"

Helen gave it a moment's thought, long enough that I thought for sure she'd say no. "She's still on edge."

"Can you blame her?"

Helen shook her head. "Be gentle. That's all I'm saying."

She had no idea just how careful I knew I had to be.

I knocked on the door to Chelsea's holding room. She didn't answer. I dug my keycard out of my chest pocket and slid it through the card reader to my left. Chelsea sat at table, arms resting across it. The second the door shut, her eyes caught mine, and her jaw locked.

My hands flew up in front of me like her glare had been a physical blow. "Look, I know—"

"I don't even want to hear it," she snapped, crashing her cuffs onto the table. The screeching clank of metal on metal echoed across the room.

"Chelsea—"

"You lied to a Navy Captain about knowing me." She lifted her hands like she wanted to point to herself, but she couldn't with the cuffs binding her wrists together. She cursed. "A single 'yeah, I know her' the second you'd ambled through the door could have saved me from this. Instead, my options are prison or lab rat. That MP thinks I'm a spy or something because you hesitated."

I swallowed my first response, something along the lines of "I barely know you!" and let air fill my cheeks before speaking. "I'm sorry, okay? Let me explain, please."

Chelsea scoffed. "Why are you here? You seemed pretty freaking anxious to get rid of me before."

"I was trying to diffuse the situation until Weyland left."

If she weren't cuffed right now, I bet she'd have crossed her arms. "Whatever. That was low, Trevor."

"I know. I'm sorry. Weyland was too focused on seeing you in the Brig. I can do more for you without him in the room."

She shook her head and looked away, but she couldn't hide her quivering lip.

"It's okay to be scared."

She shot me an incredulous stare. "I'm not scared."

I didn't know why I'd said it. She very clearly wasn't scared—she was pissed. "I'd be."

She rolled her eyes. "This isn't the first weird thing to happen to me, and, given the fact I live in Boston, it won't be the last."

Chelsea sounded confident, but her hands shook with every word. I wanted to reach out to her, to pull her hands into mine for some measure of relief. She wasn't okay, and I didn't know what to tell her to make it better. From where I stood, the version of the truth Helen told her was child's play. With Chelsea still frightened, telling her the real story wouldn't help at all. I didn't want to be the one to tell her about Atlantis, that it still existed somewhere in time, and that it made her my enemy. Like she'd believe me anyway.

I leaned in to sit and take her hands, but froze. The cameras. What good would come of Captain Marks or Lieutenant Weyland seeing me getting close and comfortable with their trespasser? None. I pulled back.

"Those military guys… they brought you here, didn't they?" she asked.

Couldn't deny that anymore. I nodded and sat across from her at the table. "I was late to head back once shore leave was over."

She scoffed and set her hands in her lap. "More like shore leave was over days before you showed up at the Franklin."

I snorted a laugh and shrugged. She was intuitive; I'd give her that. I'd made it four days before the SeaSat5 guys caught up with me. I didn't want to talk about my extended shore leave, but I'd play along if it distracted her. "Exactly."

Her eyes narrowed. "And they're the same officers who've locked me in here?"

"Yeah, why?"

"Why'd you run? If the Captain agreed to not throw *me* in jail, why'd they chase you?"

"Uh…" I sighed. "That's not exactly what happened. I disagreed with some stuff and decided to try and get out of it. Didn't work. It's not the military, really—it's complicated." I crossed my arms at my chest. "Very complicated."

"No elaboration?" she asked, eyebrows raised.

"Like I said, complicated." That was the best I could offer without breaking military or ancestral rules.

"Well, then what do you think happened to me?" She looked away to study a wall. "I mean, what Dr. Gordon said about powers was weird, and she didn't seem willing to clarify, either."

Helen didn't share yet because her research was classified, and I couldn't explain its nature to Chelsea. Helen thought people with powers—like her and Chelsea—were direct descendants of Atlantean refugees, a fact much closer to the truth than Helen may ever learn. The knowledge would've made them *both* my mortal enemies a few thousand years ago. Lemurians against the Atlanteans, both lost civilizations so mythological that most of the world didn't even know what their names meant. I wasn't sure where Helen got her information, but I'd be lying if I'd said her research wasn't part of the reason Val and I got placed here. The Lemurians were as scared as they were intrigued by Helen's progress in mapping Atlantean powers throughout many generations.

I gave Chelsea an honest shrug. "You teleporting was cool." Not necessarily a lie. If you took out what I knew about people with powers—that their ancestry traced back to Atlantis and Lemuria—being able to teleport around the world seemed like a fun power to me.

"Yeah, cool. Because I love waking up on secret military operations. It's my favorite pastime, actually." She huffed, floating some of her wildly cut bangs.

"Good to know," I joked, hoping she caught the sarcasm there.

"Right, then."

Something in her clipped, scripted responses worried me. Urged me to get her mind on something else. "So, what do you do for fun? When you're not popping onto classified military property, I mean." I smiled to let her know it was a joke.

She rolled her eyes. "I'm on campus twenty-four-seven. When I'm not there, I'm in band practice or at the Franklin."

"Yeah, your band. It had a weird name, right?"

The corners of her lips perked up, and her eyes smiled. Damn. Her smile stole my breath. It whooshed out of me, and I couldn't breathe for fear of never seeing that smile again. But as long as she was smiling, I didn't care. Take my breath.

"Phoenix and Lobster," she said. "Yeah, it's weird, but it does have meaning. Sort of."

"Well, explain it to me then, because I'm still confused." Confused but grinning.

She shook her head a little. "It's ridiculous."

"I could have told you that." It was a weird name for a band, but coming from someone who listened to music as often as this Xbox fan enjoyed a PlayStation, it didn't mean much.

She didn't reply to that, but at least she smiled. My plan worked.

"Come on, it can't be worse than the name," I prodded.

"Thanks," she said slowly. "The name was inspired by a story my sister and I wrote for a class we had together in high school."

Oh, this would be good. "Please, tell it." I leaned back in my chair and would have put my feet up, too, if we weren't on camera right now.

Chelsea fought a grin. "The gist of it is: a lobster was gazing at the sky from under the surface of the ocean. One day, he saw a beautiful phoenix fly overhead. She kept coming back, interested in the oceanic world the lobster lived in. But she knew if she landed her firebird body on the surface of the water, she may risk warming it up—thereby hurting the lobster."

Phoenixes didn't exist, and lobsters couldn't think in-depth. I scratched the back of my neck. "All right, this *is* weird."

"I told you! Anyway, the phoenix visited every day, growing more and more curious. She found herself in love with the lobster. The lobster couldn't understand why they couldn't be together, until, one day, she flew too close. The water heated up to an almost unbearable level, and the lobster retreated further into the ocean. Then he knew"—she looked at me—"the one thing he found most beautiful could kill him up close."

Silence echoed in the wake of her story. I didn't know what to say, so I held her gaze for as long as possible and tried to ignore the way her spicy perfume filled the air. Somewhere in those hazel eyes, the sadness of her story echoed something broken. Was it her situation? What happened between us months ago? Or could it be something else?

That same ache for action I'd had in the alley returned. I wanted to punch whoever caused that sadness, to make sure they couldn't do it ever again.

"That's depressing," I said instead.

Chelsea shrugged, but the sadness remained. "We wrote it for this fantasy class. We had to write a cautionary tale."

"Which you then named your band off of."

She held up a finger. "They did. Not me. I went along with it because I joined the band a few months later."

I sat back. I didn't believe her. The grinning manner in which she told the name's origin story spoke volumes—she'd had more say than she claimed. "Of course," I said.

"Oh, come on. Like you don't have something weird in your own life."

I did have plenty of weird going on. I just didn't parade it around.

She leaned back in her seat and tried to cross her arms. She winced, probably from the metal digging into her wrists.

I scooted closer and reached an arm across the table. She straightened, lifting a brow.

"Give me your hands," I said.

"Why?"

I spun to look at the camera behind me. The red light blinked in response, reminding me someone on the other end observed us. "Because I don't think you'll hurt me, and you're clearly uncomfortable. I can help you."

She considered the cuffs and offered me her hands. "Yeah, maybe they're a bit tight."

If someone viewing the security camera feed cared, they'd already be in here, so I took her hands in mine and pulled them to the center of the table. They were soft and warm, the purple of her nails stark against her creamy skin and the metal slab. A small, grey box rested on the cuff band in between her wrists. I flipped open the cover and withdrew a pen from my pocket, using the uncapped end to type in combinations until one worked. Valerie had figured out the override codes months ago. Said it would be "helpful for the future" if we knew them. *Score one for you, Valerie.*

The cuffs beeped and popped open. Chelsea withdrew her hands and rubbed her wrists. My own hands felt cold and empty with hers gone.

Her eyes found mine. "Thanks. Hope you won't get in trouble."

"I won't." My radio beeped. Or maybe that was a total lie. I fished it out of my pants pocket and held it to my face. "Yeah?"

"Could you escort Chelsea to the Dr. Gordon's office? She'd like to speak with her," came the Captain's voice on the other end.

"Uh, yes, sir."

The radio clicked off.

Chelsea didn't need a military escort? Either Dr. Gordon had convinced Captain Marks of Chelsea's innocence, or Lieutenant Weyland wasn't on duty. The latter must have been the case, or he'd have been down here the second I'd taken Chelsea's hands in mine.

I stood from the table and gestured for the door. "We should go see what Helen wants."

Chelsea nodded. "Hopefully not to imprison me."

Chapter Six

Chelsea

Trevor led me through a labyrinth on our way to the Science Lab, where Dr. Gordon's office apparently was. Every corridor and grated floor blurred together save for the color-coded markings labeling each intersection. This maze of colors and halls made learning the human skeletal system look like painting with watercolors in kindergarten. It didn't help that we were in a time zone far off Eastern Time. I'd ticked off the hours as they passed. What felt like midnight to me was late afternoon for them. Maybe we're in the Pacific somewhere?

Captain Marks and Dr. Gordon greeted us at the Science Lab, a large room with mobile half-walls littering the floor, breaking up the space into smaller work zones. The white walls and steel floor matched the rest of the station. Bland, boring, but intimidating in the severe, cold colors.

Lieutenant Trigger-Happy lurked off in a corner of the main area, watching every step I took. His eyes zeroed in on my wrists, which hung free at my sides. "Trevor?"

Trevor stopped short of a table in the center of the room. "Yes?"

The Lieutenant gestured at my wrists. "Why are her cuffs off?"

Trevor didn't falter or glance my way. "Because they hurt her."

Captain Marks cleared his throat—a warning. The Lieutenant's narrowed dark brown eyes met mine with a threat, like he thought I'd try to escape now with all the freedom a lack of cuffs afforded. *Where would I run to?*

Dr. Gordon ushered me into her office and shut the door behind us, leaving the men outside. "Have a seat. I'd like to talk to you about working with me here on SeaSat5."

I sat. Apprehension spread like New England fog across my bones, slowly but with purpose, condensing tighter with every inch. It started with a clenching of muscles in my neck and jaw, sliding downward into my arms and fingers.

"So by asking me to 'work' with you," I started, "I'm assuming you've looked into those other cases of teleportation."

Dr. Gordon gave a small nod. "They're rare, and some don't involve the waterfall-like light show."

So I'd received the crap end of that stick. Lovely.

"What other abilities are there?" I asked. She'd said she had one, and I might have two. So, what about everyone else who had these strange powers?

"So far, we've recorded teleportation, super strength, future-sight, telekinesis, and control over elements, amongst others. Sometimes, although extremely rare, two abilities show up at once."

I shook my head. "Abilities like those have been recorded since the beginning of time, but they're usually tied to mythology, like the Titans or gods—or to people in the loony bin."

If I didn't have powers, I probably wouldn't believe her.

Dr. Gordon nodded grimly and fiddled with her hands. "Of course. I'm not discounting history and mythology; I'm merely interested in modern day cases, the ones directly affecting people in positions such ours."

I.e., those of us lucky enough to accidentally trespass on super-secret military property. At least I wasn't alone.

"So what's the overall story? Do you think all of the instances of strange abilities are connected?" I asked.

She inclined her head. "Yes, and no. I hypothesize the connection is based in genetics. I'm not entirely sure how, since the gene seems to be passed through family lines, but these groups can go generations without seeing it. I do, however, strongly believe the powers to be traced to Atlantean refugees."

I sucked in air through my mouth so fast it drew spit into my lungs. I coughed to clear it. "*Atlantis?* Are you serious?"

Dr. Gordon regarded me with hard eyes. Of course she was freaking serious.

Well, no wonder why they'd trusted me so quickly. They must have looked up my school records and saw my thesis, too. My archaeology professors would shit chickens if they knew what was going on right now. An archaeologist in military hands studying Atlantis? What a joke.

I had to be dreaming. Any minute now, Logan would wake me up. Back to South African Archaeology, I'd go. *Please, please, please.*

I stood. "Look, I'm pretty sure none of this is real, so I'm going to go walk out and—"

"Sit, Chelsea."

I shook my head, restlessness and panic urging me to pace the room. "You're trying to tell me Atlantis is real—or was—and, well, no, I'm not sorry. I don't believe you, and I think you're nuts."

Dr. Gordon's lips pressed into a hard line. She paused for several long, agonizing moments before speaking again. "You study myths, do you not?"

"Yes, which is especially why I think your hypothesis is heavy on the side of crazy." My bite hurt even me, but, dammit, could she hear what she was saying? Atlantis? Seriously?

"We don't have evidence for Atlantis, no. But consider for a moment why humans never let the thought of other-worldly abilities go. Or why every society has a flood myth."

"Maybe because things flood all the time?" I snapped.

"Chelsea."

I leveled my gaze with hers. She hadn't appeared to be crazy when we first met. But I hadn't pinned Trevor for a liar, either. "What?"

"I followed all the records we have to the beginning. I've had countless experts weigh in. They all trace to Greece and a war hard-fought but from which no evidence was left—save the stories and abilities passed down for generations. How else do you plan to explain what you and I can do, along with everyone like us?"

I took slow breaths to steady myself. She had some good points, and I doubted the Navy would've hired a complete lunatic. She either *did* have damn good proof to support her claims, or she was working on something even better, and the Navy humored this side research.

I sighed and retook my seat, but left my guard up. How far would I go to stay out of prison?

Helen relaxed into her seat and resumed her questions. "Have you had teleporting episodes before you appeared on SeaSat5 earlier today?"

"No. I don't even know what happened the first time." How many times did I have to explain that to people?

She leaned forward. "The first episodes of my abilities occurred in instances of intense anger or fear. Did you have a similar experience?"

Images of Lexi and her open palm flying at me smashed through my vision. My fists tightened, nails digging in hard. I wanted to play one show, *one* damn set, without having to deal with them. I shouldn't have looked at my phone. Bless Logan for the warning, but that text started it all. He couldn't have known what I'd do. Tears stung my eyes. I hated Lexi for what she did, for how she *continued* to tear me down. And I hated myself even more for letting it happen. In the moment she slapped me, I feared it'd never end.

I swallowed down memories of that night. One tear escaped despite my efforts. Then another. I wiped them away in quick, frantic movements. "Yeah. Anger. Some fear. Then black. I don't remember teleporting anywhere."

"Did you have any association to SeaSat5 before today?" Hesitation hitched her voice, as if she, too, worried over the answer. "I find it strange you teleported here, out of everywhere else in the world."

Only one response existed. "I met Trevor a couple months ago. Kind of. But I wouldn't call what we had a connection. I barely know him." And yet, here I stood, with no other correlation to offer as explanation.

"Interesting."

"Is Trevor in trouble for lying about it?"

Helen shook her head. "I'm sure Lieutenant Weyland will have words for him, but Captain Marks understood."

This Captain Marks seemed quick to understand a whole lot of things, his crew's immature decisions included. "Why is the Captain so eager to let me on board? I haven't done anything to prove I'm trustworthy… or worthy of anything, period."

"Because he knows of the work I do. And, to be quite frank, at twenty-one, you're the youngest person to discover their ability, which is something I'd like to look into."

I frowned. Under normal circumstances, I wouldn't enjoy being made akin to a necessary research subject. However, her honesty after the last year of lies and drama was welcome, respectable. Maybe she could help me after all. But first, I needed to know how much. "What's your ability, if I can ask?"

"I can see future events, how they may end up. Although it doesn't happen as much anymore," she answered without hesitation.

"Could be interesting." *Or dangerous.* She didn't say one way or another.

"And twenty-one is young for abilities manifesting?" I asked.

She nodded. "Mine appeared at twenty-five. The second youngest was twenty-four. I don't know why they manifest so late in life, and that's part of the reason I'd love to work with you. But there's more."

She leaned forward and placed her forearms onto her desk, linking her fingers together. "Like I said before, you deserve to know what's happening to you and how to control it. Captain Marks has also proposed you join the Science Staff as an archaeology intern. Believe it or not, we don't have an archaeologist on board. We need one, and you would need something to do during the hours I'm not available."

I tilted my head, eyes narrowed. They didn't have an archaeologist? That seemed awfully stupid for a ship scouring the ocean floor. Shipwrecks could be anywhere. And where shipwrecks lurked, artifacts rested. "Why don't you have an archaeologist?"

"Our primary research focus is the ocean itself, not any archaeological sites, wrecks, or artifacts we may find."

I shrugged. "Fair enough. So, we work together on figuring out my teleportation thing, and I play unqualified archaeologist in my spare time?" It seemed too easy, too unreal, that someone wanted to hire me straight out of college. My powers were worth that much?

Helen's eyebrows rose in scolding. "It'll be hard work, Chelsea."

A long moment passed while I extricated my foot out of my mouth. "Well—I mean—I'm sorry. I know, and I'm willing to do it." Maybe. Who knew what kind of work this would entail? And to be a lab-rat on top of it?

With nothing lined up for after graduation, an internship, especially one that paid, sounded fantastic. Grad school wasn't an option, given my GRE score. Until I retook them and reapplied to my dream school, my plan consisted of continued customer service employment at the local record and comic book store. Totally classy. While too classified to flat-out state, "Naval Archaeology Intern" seemed like a great addition to my resume.

I rubbed my face. Was I really going to sign up to be a lab-rat in exchange for the prospect of future employment? God, this sucked. But what other choice did I have?

To save my ass from imprisonment, I asked, "Where do I sign up?"

Chapter Seven

Trevor

After leaving Chelsea with Helen, I spent hours investigating how Chelsea got through Humming Bird, my ballast system turned secret shield. Humming Bird was meant as a doodle, a drawing I had made in class alongside lecture notes my freshman year of college. Then my parents had found it, got excited, and pushed me through school early to make the system a reality. To mold me into the perfect spy for their organization.

The thought of the lengths Lemuria would go to end Atlantis made me ashamed to call my parents my own. They had started the extremist campaign I'd been unwillingly roped into, the one aimed at obtaining as many Link Pieces as possible to travel through time to Atlantis. War over control of time travel was stupid. And risky. Anyone willing to mess with time, willing to go to war over the ability to travel it, deserved what they got.

The data from the diagnostics readouts from earlier reminded me why I built Humming Bird the way I did. With added electromagnetic wave capabilities, it should have been enough to screw with the brain's normal makeup and keep any powers from working. But Chelsea had jumped past it like the shield didn't even exist. Her powers resonated on a different frequency, but calibrating Humming Bird again sounded like something I didn't want to do right now.

My stomach growled as I reached the last line of the data. My clock read 7:32 p.m. I dragged myself out of my computer chair, saved the diagnostic results, and logged off. I slipped into a shower for a few minutes to rinse away the confusion. Mom had always said the Lemurians had had the powers, not the Atlanteans. At least, not until the end.

Captain Marks had decided to hold Chelsea in the Briefing Room for the time being, and I hopped on the elevator to see if she wanted dinner. The Lift ride to the Briefing Room dragged on forever. Every lurch in the Lift reverberated throughout my body, judging my intentions. I tried to ignore the machine's fifth degree.

Did I want a shot with Chelsea? We barely knew each other. I'd tackled her attacker and gotten my face smashed in. He'd run off, then we'd walked away, and that was it. I hadn't really done anything to help her, but she'd convinced herself I had. Already, I'd failed to live up to that guy I'd been in the alley. Would she even be interested in me if she knew how non-hero-like I was? And could I risk starting something with her, knowing she was Atlantean—someone my own parents wouldn't hesitate to destroy?

The doors slid open on Level 2. I came to a stop outside the Briefing Room door. Maybe meeting her months ago wasn't random, and maybe that's why I couldn't let it go now. Something tugged on my brain, like I had the answer buried deep inside somewhere, but nothing burrowed forward.

I gave up and looked through the porthole window on the door. Chelsea wasn't inside. No one was. My surge of courage dissipated in an instant.

I trailed back to the Lift, determined to find out who'd escorted her. Dave, probably. He'd found her in the storage closet. But if

Valerie had gotten to Chelsea before me and filled her head with thoughts of Lemuria, I didn't know what I'd do.

I jabbed the Dining Decks button on the Lift's control panel. It shouted a long, high-pitched beep at me before complying.

"Yeah, whatever."

Every piece of machinery on this station was fighting me today.

The Dining Decks contained two floors connected by stairs, with food lines on each. They weren't segregated for military and civilian, though birds of a feather and whatever. I always ate on the main deck, oftentimes alone.

Chelsea sat across from Dave with a near-empty tray of food. Seeing her was like hearing a slow song accelerate. It squeezed my lungs then released them at the sight of her. I grabbed a dish of mystery meat and mashed potatoes and approached their table. "Hey."

They both looked up. Dave gestured for a chair. "Evening, sunshine. Finally decide to join the land of the waking?"

I ignored him and turned to Chelsea. "I meant to come by earlier to take you to dinner." Translated: *I could have come by, but my computer work was more important*. I couldn't keep eye contact with her, knowing the truth.

She either didn't notice or chose not to call me on it. "It's fine. I worked on my thesis until Dave came. What I could do from memory, anyway."

"I barely dragged her away from the computer." Dave pointed the end of his fork at me. "It's like you and your work, I swear."

"Workaholic?" Chelsea asked.

"More like it seems to pile up no matter what I do," I replied. Which was truer now than ever before. I foresaw many nights at the Humming Bird console in Engineering. "Besides," I said to Dave, "You've got at least a novel's worth of a to-do list written on your hand. It's the most professional I've ever seen you."

He looked down at the words with a smirk. "Whatever. Speaking of your work, maybe she'll listen to you. Chelsea doesn't trust submarines."

I gave her a sidelong glance, rewarded by a flush of her cheeks. Maybe I had a shot after all. "Why not?"

"It's just not natural, okay?" She folded her arms across her chest. "I don't like flying, either. Humans are meant for solid ground."

I swallowed a laugh. If I'd never been on a submarine before either, I supposed I'd be just as nervous. "The station's completely safe. It's not going to sink."

"Yeah, whatever. I'm more worried about teleporting across the globe again, anyway, *Dave*." She pinned him with a look caught between a glare and a smile.

He grinned and raised his hands. "Just wanted to get it out there, that's all."

I couldn't hold it in anymore, and Dave laughed along with me. Chelsea's arms dropped. She smiled, small and guarded.

"For the record, Helen thinks the powers are event-based," I pulled out of my ass. Chelsea clearly needed some kind of reassurance, and, although I couldn't guarantee she wouldn't teleport again, Helen always said her powers had first appeared in a combination of something bad happening and emotional strain. "As long as you don't go through the same emotional stress, you should be okay."

Chelsea sat up straighter, one eyebrow rising a centimeter in time with her upper lip. "Well, that'll be easy since Lexi isn't here," she mumbled.

A cough came from Dave's direction, and he gathered his things. "I have to get to Engineering. If you need anything, Chelsea, have Trevor let me know." He stood and placed a hand on her shoulder. "Everything's going to be okay."

She nodded, but her heavy sigh told a different story.

Dave left on purpose. He didn't do girl drama. He was into some Navigation and Analytics (or NANA) worker here a few months ago, but she'd played way too many mind-games for someone who worked in NANA. I hadn't blamed him for ending it. Dave was a nice guy, and, at thirty-seven, he deserved to find someone who wasn't incapable of holding down a relationship. Not that being a sailor helped that any.

Chelsea seethed in silence beside me.

I took a bite of mystery meat before approaching the topic. "So, what happened with this Lexi?"

She didn't say anything.

"I mean, it's not any of my business or anything. I—"

"She's a bitch, all right? Stuff happened right before that guy attacked me behind the Franklin. Cheating boyfriend *and* a mugger."

"Oh. Sorry." I shouldn't have asked.

She waved me off. "It's fine. I keep trying to get over it, but she makes it impossible."

"How so?" Though I suppose the answer was related to what brought Chelsea here to begin with.

Her cheeks reddened again. "Let's just say Lexi knows how to make a spectacle of us—and not in a good way."

Air filled my cheeks. I blew it out slowly. "I wish I'd been there to stop it, like last time." I startled. *Really, Trevor?* Our eyes met, hers wide and questioning. Foot in mouth again, I raised a hand. "I didn't—"

She shed a small smile. "Thanks."

I smiled back. I did wish I'd been there. Even on the night at the Franklin, I'd wondered what might have happened differently if I'd gotten outside sooner than I did... or if I'd arrived later. I shuddered at thoughts of the latter. No one would hurt her ever again. Not on my watch.

A flash of red hair and a pale yellow uniform reset the tension as quickly as losing a boss fight on the last level of a new game. Valerie stood behind Chelsea, coffee in hand, with a grin that gave the Cheshire cat from Alice in Wonderland a run for its money. The arrogance—a promise to ruin my day, I was sure—hitched my breath. Chelsea's eyes shrank, and her eyebrows furrowed at my sharp inhale. She followed my gaze to Valerie.

"Can I help you?" I asked Valerie, my tone cold.

She shrugged, circling the table until she sat in the seat Dave had vacated. "I came to keep Chelsea company. Chief Tanner said your pet bird is on the fritz again, so here I am." She sipped her coffee, smiling around the edge of the cup before extending a hand to Chelsea. "I'm Valerie. Bio engineering."

Chelsea offered Valerie a tight smile along with her hand, her eyes skeptical. Valerie wouldn't win Chelsea over right away. I breathed easier, knowing our secrets might stay hidden for that much longer.

"Hi," Chelsea said, clipped.

"So, archaeology, yeah?" Valerie asked. "I almost studied that in college, but bio engineering took up a lot of my time. Maybe you can teach me a thing or two."

Chelsea leaned back in her chair, unenthused and uninterested. "Sure. I'm not big on bio engineering, though. I won't have questions to swap."

Valerie waved her hand. "I'm sure there's something we could exchange."

I choked on my soda at Valerie's thinly veiled intentions. She thought Chelsea lied about not knowing her ancestry, and that she had war secrets to share. The carbonated liquid jumped pipes, drowning my lungs instead of filling my stomach. They both watched me, amusement wrinkling their eyes, and even Chelsea didn't seem concerned.

My eyes met Valerie's, daring her to continue her train of thought, as I beat my chest. She kept grinning. She wouldn't tell Chelsea everything, would she? Or corner her? Threaten her?

I gulped and counted the ways I could get in trouble for not assisting Chief Tanner, for not leaving for Engineering this very moment. Answer: too many. *Dammit.*

Chapter Eight

Chelsea

I'd like to think I'm not one to jump to conclusions, but the thought made me a liar. All I knew for sure was Valerie made Trevor uncomfortable, which sent my hands into a jittery frenzy. Aside from Dave, the only other person I trusted on this stupid satellite station was Trevor. Dave hadn't sent me directly to the Brig, and Trevor had come clean about lying and undone my cuffs. So, anyone who made my champions uneasy didn't sit well with me, either.

Our shoes clanged against the metal grating as we walked the corridors of SeaSat5. Valerie reminded me of all the girls on orientation day my first week of college. Nice and friendly, all wanting to establish some sort of pecking order on campus. Her questions seemed innocent—*how are you doing; crazy stuff that's happening, huh?*—but the winding way she steered me around the station left me wondering about SeaSatellite5 itself and their mission directive. How many people worked here? How many "interns" did this place employ? Why all the interns in the first place for something supposedly super top secret?

Nothing on this research station made sense. Doctors who studied people with powers. Kid geniuses and recent graduates working internships out of their league. Civilians employed on a military base. What had I gotten myself into?

"The ship is designed in Levels," Valerie said. She pressed her hands behind her like a soldier, left hand clasping the right, but her hair cascaded in a fiery mane right down to her shoulders.

"There's five of them," she continued, "although, you'll spend most of your time on levels three and four, Science and Residency. You'll actually be rooming with me—I found out before I came to get you."

"We're roomies?" I asked. No one had told me. Though I supposed no one had to.

Valerie nodded. "I have the open space and volunteered. Better than ending up in a triple, and you'll be only a deck away from Trevor."

"I guess." I'd never had a dorm room in college. Never lived anywhere but home, either. I wasn't sure I could handle a roommate. "What about the rest of the decks?"

"There's a dozen or so single-quarters for the senior officers, senior civilian staff, and those of us who happened to luck into it. Some of the work Trevor and I do is high up, like his Humming Bird system."

"So he doesn't have a pet bird?" That he owned a bird underwater made little sense, but they had all talked like the bird existed. Did that mean Trevor had a single room? My stomach fluttered, and my face warmed. Who said he even thought that way about me?

"No," Valerie said. "That's what we call the ballast system responsible for SeaSatellite5 changing between a fast-moving sub and an anchored stationary research outpost for long-term missions. The ship's basically a mobile science station, hence the term 'satellite.'"

"So, if the ship can remain stationary, with parts above the surface, then how is SeaSat5 a top secret station?" I asked.

"Good question." She stopped walking and clapped her hands

together, a bright smirk on her lips. "We have a cloak. Pretty sci-fi, right?"

Well, they had every solution ready to go, didn't they? "Yeah, sure." Sci-fi, indeed. And, quite unfortunately, military. Cloaks meant no transparency. Even if for the right reasons, non-transparent projects made me cringe.

"You don't look as excited as most newbies," Valerie said, bumping her shoulder into mine.

I swallowed down my first retort: *It's been my experience that if you can't say what you're doing, then you shouldn't be doing it at all.* They probably had their reasons, so whatever. But I had to know.

"The secrecy just makes me question what's going on here," I said. "I mean, you've got a scientist on board happily conducting human research on people like me, who don't come around often enough to warrant her working here at all." I was sure Dr. Gordon had other research interests, and that's how she'd become employed. Dr. Gordon's research wasn't what I questioned. I hoped Valerie read between the lines, the ones suggesting the military's condoning of Dr. Gordon's research wasn't entirely ethical.

Valerie started walking again, so I followed.

"That's not your real question," she said.

"No."

"Dr. Gordon has a wide variety of interests, mostly sea creatures. But her side project, my guess, is her true passion: understanding her abilities and those of people like you. As for the question you're not asking, no, the military isn't trying to weaponize them."

I would. Black-ops with the power to teleport in and out of hazardous missions? It was a no-brainer.

"Then why all the secrecy?" I asked.

She stopped again, eyeing me like an impatient parent. Her glance curled my fists out of habit, out of experience dealing with Lexi.

"SeaSatellite5 is a multi-million-dollar endeavor," she said. "The station consists of technology not yet known—at least publically—

to most of the world. Take Trevor's rotational ballast system, for example, or his resulting shield capable of thwarting torpedo strikes like nothing else the Navy has on tap. This station is a bypr—" Valerie shook her head. "This station is part of a concerted effort to look for viable oceanic energy, residency, and research alternatives to many of the U.S.'s land-based programs. Should we be fully equipped for war? No. But what do you expect when scientists pair up with the military to exploit their funding?"

I froze mid-step, unable to agree. "Hide the boat, cover up the expenditures to build it… in return for what? The U.S. sharing research?" So backhanded when the work they did here was so innovative.

Her eyebrows popped up. "Try not to dig so deep into something that's only politics. We're here, and we're doing research. Enjoy the internship while you can."

I set my eyes on some distant point down the steel-coated corridor. "I will."

We continued in silence to the end of hallway and turned right, following a sign pointing to stairs. Painted lines adorned some of the walls and continued around corners. A string of numbers and letters embellished a sign at the start of every new hallway. How anyone never got lost, I didn't understand.

"So, powers, huh?" Valerie asked out of the blue. "Cool."

I forced myself to breathe before responding. This misplaced frustration needed to go away. "Not really. I keep thinking I'm going to do it again and teleport somewhere else I shouldn't be." The word still tasted weird on my tongue. Foreign. *Wrong.*

"Have you always been able to teleport?" Valerie, however, had no issue with the word. What did she say her internship here was in, bio engineering?

"No. Today's the first time it's happened."

"Interesting."

I rolled my eyes as we climbed a flight of stairs. "I wish people would stop using that word. It's not interesting or cool."

"Then what do you call it?"

"Inconvenient." Mortifying. The proverbial straw on an already bad day. *Why does she even care?*

Valerie remained quiet until we stopped outside a set of doors inlaid on a wall, halfway down the corridor. She spun to me and smiled. "Here's your quarters for tonight." She pointed to a sign— GUEST QUARTERS A. "You can move into our shared room when you return for the start of your internship. I'm sure Trevor or Dr. Gordon will come by later to check on you, but I can go ahead and show you around."

At this point, I almost wanted no one to come. If Valerie left soon, it'd be my first time alone since accepting Dr. Gordon's ridiculous job offer. I needed time to think, to regroup. To figure out how the hell I'd ever play a show with Phoenix and Lobster again without dematerializing mid-chorus. Assuming, of course, they still wanted me to front their band after ditching the Battle of the Bands show.

Valerie dug into her pockets, pulled out a white, plastic keycard, and swiped it through a reader to the right of GUEST QUARTERS A's door. The light on the reader blinked from yellow to green, then the door slid open. A grey-walled room greeted me, with lead-colored flooring and basic furniture. A splash of navy blue colored the pillows on the bed, off-setting all the grey.

So simple. So… dorm room.

"I know, it's nothing fancy," Valerie said. "Bathroom's through that side door, and there are uniforms in the dresser. They took a guess on the size. If you need something else, let me know. I think that's it."

I nodded despite my whirring thoughts about the job, Valerie, Trevor, and the station itself. "Thank you for showing me around. I think I actually want to rest now." And figure out what happened to my life over the past twelve hours.

Valerie nodded. "Long day?"

"You have no idea. It's also like two in the morning for me."

"Time zones, right. I'll leave you, then." She took a few steps toward the door and then turned around. "Look, I get a feeling we got off on the wrong foot."

Gee, I wonder why? "I didn't mean to push the cloak stuff," I offered.

She tapped her open palm on the doorframe. "You looked uncomfortable on the Dining Decks earlier."

I lifted my hands in surrender. "Seriously, this has been the most confusing day of my life. Let's call it even and start over, okay?" I tried to smile, to make the peace seem genuine when really I just wanted to be left alone.

Valerie returned the smile and stuck out her hand. "I'm Valerie McAllister."

"Chelsea Danning."

"Welcome to the SeaSat5 crew, Chelsea. We might not get to work together a lot, but know you can find a friend in me. There are a lot of interns here, older than us and fresh out of masters programs, so you won't be as out of place as you believe you are, even as an undergrad."

Because adding a flock of interns to a military research station totally made this entire situation less weird. And friends? I wasn't so sure that'd happen. I got the feeling Valerie and I were extremely different. And then there was the whole making Trevor nervous thing.

"Good to know," I said finally.

"Have a good night, Chelsea."

"You too."

As soon as she left, I plopped onto the full-sized bed. The softness of the blankets lulled me into relaxation, soaking up all the tension in my bones. The ceiling held my interest for a long time, a blank slate for my mind-made pros and cons chart. Sarah, my sister, gave me this technique for when a decision seemed too muddled to easily choose one way or another. Usually, it gave me an answer: archaeology, not anthropology; the deep blue guitar the same shade as the water off Castle Island, not the less expensive purple guitar.

Today, Sarah's method failed me.

On the pros side: This internship meant something to do, an internship to add to my resume, and an explanation of whatever the hell happened earlier today.

On the cons side: I'd be away from the band all summer, I'd be studied like a test rat, and, honestly, being underwater and stuck in a tin can made me all sorts of claustrophobic.

The lists evened each other out.

I closed my eyes and wrapped myself in a cocoon of blankets. A good night's sleep would make everything easier. Maybe in the morning teleportation would make more sense, and the rest would fall into place.

Maybe I'd wake to find all of this nothing but a dream.

Chapter Nine

Trevor

Chelsea couldn't leave today as planned, and though that messed up her plans, it brightened my day. It meant more time spent with her before she left. Stormy seas and skies kept SeaSatellite5's helicopter grounded, and would for at least another twenty-four hours.

I showered early to wash away the dark bags under my eyes and then watched my alarm clock until its red numbers announced 7:30 a.m. I wouldn't make the same mistake twice and miss bringing Chelsea to breakfast. I wanted to make sure she knew of the change of plans, and I hadn't talked to her since she went off with Valerie last night.

Anxiety washed over me, heated my neck. I didn't have a plan for if Valerie had told her about Atlantis and Lemuria, the truth about the war and our people. I didn't *want* to have to plan for that.

The Lift travelled slowly to spite me. Like the diagnostics I ran on Humming Bird and the shield system yesterday, one by one the ship's systems ridiculed me for wanting Chelsea. For wishing like a child for Chelsea's powers to be a fluke. For hoping nothing else happened to escalate the situation on SeaSatellite5 into something war-worthy.

As if to reinforce the mocking I deserved, the Lift stopped on the last floor of the Dining Decks. Valerie stood in the doors' wake.

"Do you make it a habit of stalking me?" I said.

She lifted the coffee and muffin in her hands, not a smirk in sight. "It's called breakfast."

I scrubbed my face and moved aside. "Just get in already."

"Jeez. Bad morning?" Valerie stepped inside and hit the Science Deck 3 button.

"Long morning." Long *two* mornings.

"It's past eight." She sighed. "Didn't sleep, did you?"

The Lift's doors shut, and we started our ascent.

"If the engineering interns would stop messing with the Bird, I'd be fine," I said, passing off the blame. My irregular sleep schedule had always been my fault. I had tried to change it after joining SeaSatellite5, but college habits die hard—even harder when you're doing the work of eight others.

My interns thought an engineering degree meant they could operate the world. Humming Bird's day-to-day issues, on top of yesterday's events, had proved them wrong. I had scheduled a meeting for 10:00 a.m. to address it before I learned of Chelsea's schedule change. Now she'd be stuck here another day, without real work to do and without many people she knew.

Valerie reached over and hit the stop button on the elevator.

"Hey!" I shouted. I reached out to start us moving again, but she stepped in front of me, sacrificing some of her coffee to the ground.

"We need to talk," she said.

"Can we do this some other time?"

Her eyes set firm on mine. "No. She's *Atlantean*. This is a problem."

My right fist curled, and I chewed on all of my first responses to keep them from spilling out. I wasn't an idiot. I understood what Chelsea's presence meant. But she barely had control over her power and didn't seem to even understand what having that power meant. I.e., *not a threat.*

"Oh, let me guess," she said. "You don't think so."

"No, I don't."

She scoffed and rolled her eyes. "No, of course not." Her glare tore through me, like we were kids and I didn't understand something she'd perfected. "You're an idiot, and she jeopardizes the mission."

"You're crazy—"

"Dr. Gordon thinks Chelsea's Atlantean, and her powers don't match what we know of the Lemurians' abilities. That puts us at odds and your romantic fantasies at a full standstill."

My tongue found a home squished between my molars. What did it matter if Chelsea had an Atlantean heritage if she didn't know what it meant? I'd been born Lemurian and didn't fight in the war. Didn't even have powers. What amount of threat did I pose? None. Nothing.

Breathe, Boncore. "You have no idea what you're talking about," I said.

"Oh, come on. You meet randomly in Boston then she shows up here? Don't you understand—" She stopped, forced a breath into her lungs, and fixated her eyes on mine. "It's a fluke, but it's not the coincidence you want it to be, either. And don't you dare forget for one second what her kind did to Abby."

My chest constricted around my lungs, rendering them useless. "You have no proof of that."

Fire lit in her eyes, burning the amber into molten lava. Her grip tightened around her coffee cup. "She's in a fucking *ward*, Trevor! What more proof do you need?"

I stepped forward and nudged Valerie out of the way so I could jab the STOP button again to restart our ascent. "Leave Abby's situation out of this. Chelsea's just a girl. A confused, scared girl who didn't know she had powers until yesterday. If she can't control her powers, they're not useful. And before you say it—she's not faking it. We don't need to do anything about her, and we're not going to. Let's continue the mission."

"Thompson will have your head if you're wrong and he finds out you kept this from him."

"Then you're going down with me because you're not saying anything, either."

"We're making the wrong move, Trevor." Her eyes widened, and her mouth tugged down into a frown. *Almost* beseeching me. Except pleading wasn't something Valerie did.

"If anything else happens, if any other powers show up on anyone onboard this station, I'm following orders," Valerie said.

That was the closest I'd get to an agreement, and I knew it. I also knew nothing would happen. Or, at least, I hoped. "Fine."

The Lift halted and beeped. The doors opened.

"Have a good day, Valerie," I said before ambling out of the Lift.

"You too," she said. "One last thing."

Not good. I turned to find a wicked grin on her face.

"If I can't report her, I'll have to watch her closely." She flashed me a mischievous expression and winked before flipping her hair over her shoulder. Couldn't deny Valerie was gorgeous in a breath-taking way. Her round, brown eyes sucked you into her world, and her personality, when not annoying, kept you there.

"Hope you won't mind," she said, smirking one last time as the Lift doors shut.

My brain conjured up images of Valerie questioning Chelsea about ancient history and archaeology late into the night, things Valerie wanted to study but couldn't. What if Chelsea was into painting, like Valerie? Or the same movies? Or music?

Valerie planned to befriend her. Valerie and Chelsea, friends? *Shit.*

My heartbeat still thundered in my chest when the Lift dropped me off on Level 2, home to the quarters of Captain Marks and any guests. An angry Valerie—or a Valerie with a challenge—wasn't easily dealt with. Our freshman year of college—the only year we'd shared in school because of my accelerated plan—our Advanced General Physics professor had told her she'd never pass the course with five other classes and a full set of extracurriculars. He'd said no one had ever passed his class with so much on their plate. Valerie had not only passed, but ended up correcting him on his creative license tangents from our textbook *every* single lecture.

I should have run the day Valerie joined SeaSat5, not the first day I had an opening. Running with a reason would have gotten me farther.

I knocked on Chelsea's door, forcing myself to cease worrying about what would happen once she boarded SeaSat5 for good. About what a friendship between Valerie and Chelsea might look like. About how it could twist my judgment regarding working here to appease my family. I'd only returned to keep SeaSat5 safe from those crazies in case they weren't bluffing. In case they really wanted the station for war.

My palms and forehead started to sweat in the time it took Chelsea to answer. What if she wasn't awake? What if I woke her up? *This was a bad idea.* Damn Valerie for setting me on edge.

My feet followed the unspoken command to leave.

No. Grow a freaking pair and stay.

The privacy screen on the window slid up, and Chelsea's face appeared. Her eyebrows furrowed, confused, then she smiled and opened the door. "Hey."

Her smile grew into a grin, and she combed a hand through her hair, a slight blush rising in her cheeks. I didn't see why she'd be worried—she looked gorgeous. Her short blonde hair curved around her face, highlighting her wild hazel eyes and full pink lips. What would it feel like to kiss them?

My breath hitched. Where the hell had *that* come from?

Rubbing the back of my neck, I cleared my throat. *Idiot.* "Morning. I didn't mean to catch you sleeping."

"Me? No." She shook her head. "I've been up for hours. Didn't sleep well."

Dammit. If only I'd known. "Seems to be the norm around here, lately."

She frowned. "You didn't sleep?"

"Usually don't." I shifted my weight and swallowed. "I didn't want to be the bearer of bad news, but… Captain Marks wanted me to tell you that your disembarkation was put off for twenty-four hours."

Her eyes widened and filled with despair. Her voice rose an octave. "A whole day? Why?"

The sadness and panic in her expression gutted me. Why couldn't Valerie have told her? Or Dave?

"The weather's too bad for takeoff," I said. "And we're too far out for a shuttle."

"Shit," she said, rubbing her eyes. "Only a day?"

"Yeah, why?" I didn't understand what had her so anxious besides wanting to get home. And it definitely seemed like there was more to it than that.

"Finals are next week, and I have a *ton* of work left to do." She paused, wringing her hands together. "And a draft of my thesis is due in two days."

My body soaked up her anxiety and made it my own. "I can set you up with a computer. You can't retrieve files, but if you want to continue more from memory, I can make that happen. It's only twenty-four hours." Maybe more. But maybe less, too. Weather never cooperated. But I'd do whatever necessary, within my power, to help her out.

She looked to me with eyes that said if I could make this happen, I'd be her hero. "Really?"

"Absolutely." I'd do just about anything to make her happy and comfortable right now. The Last thing she needed was to accidentally teleport again. And if she failed out of school because we couldn't fly a helicopter out of the Pacific, I'd never let it go. "Give me some time later this morning, and I'll work it out for you."

She hugged me like one might a new friend. The casual touch lit my skin on fire, and I fought everything within me wanting to hold her close for longer.

"Thank you. Seriously," she said. "You're a lifesaver."

A swell of accomplishment flourished in my chest. I tried not to let it go to my head. Or the other one. "No problem. Are you up for breakfast?"

"Yeah. Let me clean this up real fast," she said, pointing inside the room.

I strode inside and found a notebook with its guts ripped out over the bed covers, pens littered on top. My eyes widened. "If you wanted to bomb the station, maybe I shouldn't have vouched for you."

She spun, her eyes darting to mine like I was serious.

"Joke," I said and pointed to the gutted notebook. "What happened?"

Chelsea piled the papers into a neat stack and set the heap inside the notebook's remains. "Dave got me paper and pens so I could write music after I wouldn't stop drumming the table in the Briefing Room. Something about not wanting to see me fail at drums or something." She shrugged, a smile tugging at her lips. "When the songs come, I have to write them down. My brain won't shut off. Even under impending imprisonment of the U.S. Navy."

"Imprisonment?" Captain Marks hired her, not signed her prison papers.

She pointed to the ceiling as if the gesture answered everything. "That's how I'm choosing to think about the fact I'll be trapped inside a tin can, half a mile under the surface of the ocean, for at least six months."

It shouldn't have, but her words struck a painful chord. Yeah, sometimes I couldn't protect people, and the structural safety of this station was my job. But lying about a stupid ancient war to Abby—and now to Chelsea, too— was, in every way possible, absolutely different than failing to do my job as an engineer on SeaSatellite5. The former I couldn't do anything about. The latter I refused to do anything but excel *at*. The station was structurally secure. I didn't intend for that to change.

"You're one hundred percent safe. I promise," I said.

She shrugged then placed the notebook on the top of the dresser paralleling the door. "Yeah, well, one man's treasure… or whatever."

"Chelsea."

"Hm?"

I tried not to smirk. "SeaSat5's not going to sink. It's my job to make sure it doesn't." Claustrophobia I understood, but, with Chelsea onboard, I'd definitely make sure Humming Bird didn't go belly up.

"You?" A disbelieving smile formed on her lips. "'Cause you're an engineering intern or something, right?"

"I'm not an intern." I wasn't allowed to say anything before, but she'd find out eventually.

Her eyes narrowed. Did she think I lied? I mean, after denying I knew her, I suppose I understood why she would. But she had to know I'd do anything to keep her safe.

I opened my mouth to convince her, but the lines around her eyes softened, and she grinned. "I figured. Just wanted to hear it from you."

"Excuse me?" My heart pumped a little harder. How much did Valerie tell her on their short walk last night?

"Valerie said the work you two do is high up. Although, she swears she's in bio engineering, so I don't understand how you're involved, but"—she held up a finger—"you've been informal with the officers. That suggests you're not as far down on the food chain as an intern."

Well then. Leave it to the social scientist to study workplace culture. "I'm a full engineer. I built the ballast system."

"Valerie told me that, too."

I forced a sharp breath. "Did she?" At this rate, Chelsea would know all about my true position on SeaSatellite5 by the end of her first week. Hell, even Captain Marks would know, and then the fireworks would really fly. Treason. Espionage. So many charges, all applicable.

Chelsea nodded and paused, eyebrows scrunching together around her thoughts. "You two aren't—I mean, you guys don't seem to get along well, but Valerie made it seem like you two were... friends. Which is fine. I..."

Chelsea used "friends" instead of "dating." Was she jealous? My pulse locked into flank speed, fast and uncontrollable. Could she be interested in me, too?

Chelsea watched me, waiting for an answer.

Swallowing, I shook my head. "Val's one of a kind." A very special, annoying kind. "We've only ever been friends. Our parents knew each other, and we graduated from the same schools."

"Schools plural?" Chelsea shook her head. "How'd you both land a position on a classified Navy vessel at nineteen, anyway?"

"Valerie's twenty-one." The need to clarify was childish, but our age difference had been a point of contention between Valerie and me for years. Specifically, that I had accomplished more in nineteen years than she had in twenty-one. I personally didn't care—I never wanted this, anyway—but Valerie's jealous, competitive switch flipped every time someone brought it up.

"So, how'd you end up the engineer and she the intern?" Chelsea asked.

I snorted. "Would you believe a doodle from my freshman year of college is to blame?"

Chelsea's eyes flicked to mine, jaw dropping. "You're not serious."

A bubbling rose in my chest. I couldn't help but laugh. "I am."

She threw her hands up in the air. "I give up."

"On what?" I asked, still trying to reign in my laughter at her exasperation.

"I work my ass off studying for years, and what finally lands me a paying internship? Witchcraft anomaly." Her eyes met mine, light and no longer chiding. "You *doodle* and land a career."

I shrugged. "Some of us luck out." And the rest of us are thrown into rigorous studies by our parents.

"*And* you play it off like it's nothing." She grabbed one of the pens and shoved it in her pocket. "You're a piece of work, Mr. Boncore."

Chelsea moved for the door. Her arm brushed mine as she passed, leaving the hair on my arm standing on end where her warm skin touched mine. My chest tightened, the need to kiss her returning like we were magnets, opposite and gravitating toward each other.

"I'm starving. Let's go get breakfast," she said.

"Me too," I resigned with drooping shoulders. *Next time.*

Chelsea's gaze followed the numbers and colored lines on the walls. "I'm going to get lost each and every single day on this job."

I chuckled and pointed to the markings. "Blue always denotes the way to the stairs. Yellow, the science areas. Red, command and security areas. And when you get your keycard, it'll be loaded with electronic signatures. If it doesn't open a door, you shouldn't be in there. It's easy, though. The station's basically a square."

"Yeah." She waved a hand in front of her. "All I got out of that is: uniform colors equal accessible areas."

I glanced around the halls and spotted one of the engineering team's diagnostics stations. "Come see." I signed on, calling up a schematic of the station. "See? A square." SeaSatellite5 itself wasn't a square, obviously, but its innards were. A box of decks inside levels, stairways connecting the decks, with the Lift running up the center.

"Okay," she said. "Then what happens when the station flips or whatever?"

"Dave didn't explain?"

Chelsea shook her head. "He said it 'flips.' When he first found me, he said something about being on a 'sometimes sub, sometimes station.'" She laughed. "Poor guy was too flustered at finding a random girl in a storage room to speak properly."

"Probably." *Sounds like Dave.* I replaced my fingers on the keyboard and pulled up a schematic showing the whole station. "SeaSat5 is comprised of the shield, the outer hull, and the inner square with the actual body of the ship. Between the square body and the outer hull, there are ballasts and a layer of classified material that work together with my system, Humming Bird, to flip the station when we blow or fill them."

"Sounds complicated."

"It is."

She paused, a finger pressed against her lips like I wanted my own lips to be. I watched her finger, unable to tear my eyes away.

"So, if this station is SeaSatellite5, are there four more of these research ships sailing around out there, cloaked and everything?" Chelsea asked.

Valerie even told her about the cloak? *Dammit, Valerie.*

"No," I replied. "The others were failed attempts to build a certain class of mobile research vessels. SeaSat5 was the first to succeed, and, subsequently, the only one to be outfitted with Humming Bird."

"Interesting."

I raised an eyebrow. "I tell you all that, and 'interesting' is the best you can do?" Most people zoned out at this point, so I didn't blame her. But I wanted more from her.

She pointed at me, her purple painted nail inches from my chest. "You just regurgitated years' worth of engineering work to me, an archaeology student. So yeah, that's the best I can do right now."

I smirked. "Yeah, whatever. What do you do when you're not mulling over bones and pottery?"

She scoffed, a hand flying to her chest in mock offense. "I have the band." She said it like there was a whole list of things but then changed her mind. *Cute.* It showed her priorities, which made me question whether I really wanted to ask the next question on my mind. If Phoenix and Lobster was her only priority, did that mean there wasn't room for more?

"No special guy to hang out with?" I asked.

She leveled her eyes with mine. "Seriously?"

Crap. I raised my hands in my defense—and stupidity. "Hey, had to try." *No, you didn't.* My face warmed, and my stomach sank to my feet. Any shot I had with her just left the station. Gone. Never to return. *God, you're such an idiot.*

Chelsea's face flushed, hot and unmistakable. The fire dispersed some of the darkness my stupidity left behind.

"Yeah, well, it was charming," she said.

My eyes darted to hers. *Did she just call me charming?*

She continued before my mind leapt off, lost inside that thought. "And to answer your question, no, I don't."

Bullshit. "No way." Chelsea was gorgeous and talented and absolutely brilliant.

Her cheeks grew brighter. I loved that blush, craved it as a kind of twisted reminder of the night we met. Her face, a lighthouse guiding me to sanity, flushed from cold and adrenaline. It was the night my life changed course. Without meeting her at the Franklin, we wouldn't be here and I wouldn't be questioning everything I'd accepted all my life. I wouldn't have this beautiful, amazing girl in front of me, who left me grasping to stay ahead of her—so I wouldn't lose her again. I didn't want to lose her again.

Chelsea shrugged. "The last guy wasn't exactly impressive, so I've been laying off the scene ever since."

Not exactly a rejection. I'd take it. "Shame."

She rolled her eyes, but she smiled.

Nice save, Boncore.

"What do *you* do for fun when you're not playing Tinker Toys with a military research station?" she teased.

Ouch. "If you're unimpressed with the Tinker Toys, you're going to laugh at my answer, so I'll pass."

"Oh, come on. The name of my band is Phoenix and Lobster. It can't be more embarrassing than that."

My hobby wasn't embarrassing, just uncool. So when I did get the small chance to talk to girls, I usually left it out. But something about Chelsea had me wanting to spill everything about myself. My past, my hobbies, even my feelings. All of it. Except for the obvious.

"I make video games," I started. "Not your flash animation stuff, but immersive games. Simulators. Hazard of engineering school with a computer science interest, I guess."

She grinned, leaning in. She brushed hair behind her ear. "Not gonna lie, that's pretty awesome."

Doubt bloomed in my chest, a reminder this is where I lost most girls. "You don't have to lie. I believe the term is 'deal breaker.'" A geeky, loser one.

"Most guys are creeped out by the sometimes literal skeletons in my closet from bio-anthropology classes, but you found it cool." She watched my face for a reaction.

I smiled. I hadn't seen one of the said skeletons yet, but I'd probably find it cool, yeah. Creepy but cool. The exact opposite of Chelsea herself. She was beautiful, wild, *interesting*. So unlike the girls I'd met in college. I hadn't noticed it in Boston because the rocker girl persona she put on overtook the rest. But here, on SeaSat5, the difference stood in spotlight. Chelsea carried herself with sarcasm and confidence, but an academic air laced it all and meshed with my own intellectual side. My desire to learn more, about everything.

"Touché," I said.

I wanted to get to know *her* more. For the rest of her internship. For a good long while.

Chapter Ten

Chelsea

Helen retrieved me from my guest room sometime after breakfast. We weaved through decks and stairs until we came to a stop outside a lab in the science area. Helen ran her keycard through the reader and pushed open the door.

"This is our office," Helen said, flipping light switches. An empty desk sat opposite hers. My desk, I guess?

"The real treasure is behind door number two," she continued, gliding across the room to a door on the far side. She punched in a code on yet another lock. "Only we, Commander Jackson—our Communications Officer—and the Captain have access to this room, to preserve artifacts when we have them."

She pushed open the door to reveal a second twenty-by-ten-foot room, lined with shelves like the supply room I'd appeared in hours ago. Except these were empty.

"We dropped off everything we had before you arrived," she said. "Hopefully we'll find more for you soon."

I sure hope so. My fingers itched for archaeology work again.

Hopefully we'd find *something*. With any luck, it'd be more exciting than a Massachusetts dig site."

"What are we doing today?" I asked.

Helen sat at her desk and straightened out a notebook. "First, I'd like to get some more background on you, if that's okay?"

I didn't sit. "Background?" Didn't she have enough already? No powers until the Franklin, minus things I didn't tell her. Things I hadn't told *anyone* and didn't intend to. The mic stand incident wasn't a fond memory. That thing had cost half my paycheck to replace.

"Well, you say you've only recently developed powers, yes?" She didn't wait for me to respond. "And you didn't know you might one day have them, which means, as we've established, abilities have skipped a generation or two in your bloodline."

"I guess." So what? Was it possible my parents had them and never told me? No. We had a good relationship. If they knew, if they had powers, too, Mom and Dad would have said something. They would have warned me about what might happen.

"What about your sister?" Helen asked.

My eyes narrowed, fists clenching of their own accord. Too many years of being an over-protective older sister, here we go. "How'd you know I have a sister?"

"We did a background check, remember?" Helen said, eyes flitting down to my hands.

I glanced at them, too. "Duh. Sorry. I..." *Be honest with her. She's trying to help you.* "The thought of her getting caught up in all of this makes me want to punch something." Just because my life got uprooted by powers and some supposed connection to Atlantis didn't mean Sarah's should, too. Even if she had powers. Which she doesn't. "What do you want to know?"

"Has she exhibited abilities at all?" Helen asked, pen at the note-taking ready.

"No," I said, shaking my head. "Not once. You said I'm the

youngest you've heard of, anyway. Sarah's younger than me, so she probably wouldn't yet."

Except I'd shown signs of something that night at the Franklin with the mic stand three months ago, the one I'd bent in half. Solid steel had crumbled in my hands like putty. I'd been angry, *so* freaking angry that night. Logan had to come to calm me down after I'd read those nasty social media posts. Everyone had written shit about what had happened with Lexi, bringing my band into it. Bringing Sarah into it. I'd never been as mad as I had been that night, not before and never since. I'd also never been able to explain how that steel bent to my will. Ever. This had happened two days after I'd met Trevor and a week before my twenty-first birthday. If the freak of nature strength exhibited that night had been a power and not a fluke, that'd make me twenty-years-old with powers, almost twenty-one. Sarah wasn't even twenty yet.

"No, I suppose not," Helen said.

I wanted to tell her about the mic stand incident, but I didn't think she'd even believe me. Who would? I was five-four with no real muscle to speak of, and that steel was at least three inches thick. An obese mic stand because we couldn't afford a nice-looking one.

Then there was the whole alcohol thing…

"Howdy everyone."

I glanced at the door. Dave stood half in the room.

"Hey," I said.

"What can I help you with, Mr. James?" Helen asked.

He pointed at me. "Making sure Chelsea here got to your office okay."

"She picked me up," I said. "I doubt Mr. Trigger-Happy would be okay with me wandering on my own."

"That's *Lieutenant* Trigger-Happy to you," Dave said with a smile and wag of his finger.

I rolled my eyes. "Whatever. Point is, I'm here."

"Good." Dave gave me a nod. "Mission complete. Back to Bridge Duty it is, then."

"Didn't know you'd been assigned as my designated babysitter."

He shrugged. "Me either. Captain's orders. Probably thought you've had enough of Trevor for one day."

My face warmed, betraying any argument I could give. I didn't think I'd ever get enough of Trevor. "Well—"

"Joking," Dave said. He smacked his hand on the doorframe. "I'm off, then. Call me if you need anything, Chelsea. Dr. Gordon."

"Actually"—Helen stood from her desk—"might I borrow you for a moment longer?"

Dave brushed up his sleeve and checked his watch. "I've got twenty minutes to make it upstairs. Why not?"

"Good." Helen crossed her arms at her chest and regarded me with narrowed, thinking eyes, and a pensive furrow in her brow. "I have a hunch."

"A hunch?" I echoed. How did our non-conversation about my sister's non-existent powers spark a hunch? "Why do I not like the sound of that?"

"Before you, I worked with another young woman. We've since parted ways, but she had an interesting blend of abilities."

Blend? God, could Helen read minds as well as see the future?

"Why'd she leave SeaSatellite5?" I asked.

"She's never seen the station," Helen said. "We worked together a few years ago. I was her mentor before SeaSatellite5 was built. She accepted a position in Ireland to be closer to her family. We keep in touch from time to time, but I haven't talked to her since SeaSat5 launched."

"And what was this blend of abilities she had?"

Helen shook her head. "It doesn't matter right now, especially if my hunch is only a hunch." She pointed over my shoulder to my desk. "Dave, will you please join us?"

Dave thrust his hands into his uniform pockets and swayed on his feet. "Not that I don't trust you, Dr. Gordon, but why?"

Helen flashed him the sweetest doctor smile I'd ever seen. "I'm not much of a match for Chelsea when it comes to arm wrestling, which I would like you to do."

"Wait a second," I said, stepping toward her. "First off, I resent that you think I can't take Dave because I'm a girl." Dave's face flushed. He clearly thought Helen was in the right. *Pfft.* "Second, what the hell is arm wrestling this guy going to prove?"

"Uh," Dave said. "Don't I have a say in this?"

I side-eyed him. "No." I sized him up. Adult male. Built. Navy officer. He'd been the first friendly face on board, my only real friend besides Trevor and, possibly, Dr. Gordon. And no one in this room knew about the mic stand incident, the accident that might prove I could not only beat Dave, but that I might break his arm in doing so.

"You seem like the type of guy who'd let me win to not hurt my feelings, Dave," I continued. "No offense."

He cocked his head to the side. "Thank… you? I think?"

I placed my hands on my hips. "I just don't see what it's supposed to do."

Helen inclined her head. "Humor me, Chelsea?" Her eyes pleaded with mine, and I found it hard to not want to humor such a good-natured person.

"Fine," I said. "But I want it on record I think this is a stupid, probably embarrassing idea."

"Hey," Dave said, a scoff in his voice.

Oh, he could be offended all he wanted. "I meant for me," I said for his benefit. After all, if what happened that night with three-inch steel wasn't a fluke, he'd need the cushion for his ego.

Helen tapped the table. "Thank you. Now, ready-up, you two."

I resisted the urge to roll my eyes, choosing to purse my lips instead. Dave's eyes met mine, and I shrugged. "Might as well get it over with, Dave. Go easy on me, will you? I need this hand to play guitar."

"I won't hurt you," he said. And I believed him.

We placed our elbows on the table, and he refused to lock hands with me for too many moments. Finally, he gripped my hand like one might a guitar or a cello, loose but with purpose. He wouldn't risk losing, despite the fact he'd obviously win, but he didn't want to hurt me, either. In that case, I'd give him all I had. What did I have to lose?

I wiggled my hips and settled into an anchoring stance. Dave didn't even bother. He just stood there, everything about him loose as a goose. His hand was cold, clammy. I suppressed a laugh. What in the world did he have to be nervous about?

"Ready?" I asked him.

"Oh hell," he said, finally falling into a solid stance. No turning back now. "Sure."

"Three," I said, initiating the countdown.

Our eyes locked, but I didn't give away my plan.

"Two," he replied.

On the, "One," I abused his loose grip and really dug into his hand. I didn't give him a single second of downtime, and threw everything I had into it.

Then his wrist snapped.

Chapter Eleven

Trevor

I sat at my station on the Bridge, face inches from the computer screen while I awaited the latest round of results. Humming Bird wasn't broken, per say, but Chelsea shouldn't have gotten through. Therefore, her arrival presented two possibilities: my system was never correctly calibrated to block teleportation abilities in the first place (plausible, though unlikely), or Chelsea's Atlantean abilities vibrated at a different frequency than the Lemurians'. If they did, I'd have to find a common frequency to block incoming traffic.

My head fell between my hands, my forehead resting on the desk. I couldn't test either of my hypotheses without Chelsea knowing how to use her powers and me getting one of my mother's employees—someone with powers—on loan. In other words, it'd be impossible.

The system beeped, demanding the entering of a code to continue. I sighed and pecked the string of letters and numbers with a single finger.

Powers didn't matter. My system was fallible, and that was not okay.

Someone paced beside my station and rested a hand on top of the monitor. Captain Marks's Executive Officer.

"How are the ballast diagnostics going, Mr. Boncore?" he asked.

The Commander was a middle-aged sailor, still tanned from shore leave. The contrast between his bright blond hair and tanned skin startled me into sitting up straighter, like I wasn't a civilian and actually had to pay attention.

"Almost done," I said.

It'd take another five minutes for the ballast portion of Humming Bird's diagnostics to finish, but I needed my time on the Bridge for the hidden shield side. I hated working in secret like this, betraying Captain Marks. He was a stand-up guy who didn't need people like me on board, whose indecision made the military an unwilling bit of collateral damage. I could see that conversation—*yes, Captain, there's a shield to block my teleporting parents and their Lemurian friends from wrecking the station if we find artifacts*—and wanted to save myself the embarrassment.

Another beep signaled the "progress complete" window on my screen. I scrolled through the data without finding anything indicating if either hypothesis was truer than the other. Yes, Humming Bird still functioned as the shield system always had. No, the readings didn't discern Chelsea's vibration frequency.

My eyes slid shut, and I slammed down the escape key with my thumb. Screw this stupid shield. "It's done," I called to the Commander and took off my headset.

The problem was, if I was wrong, SeaSat5—one of the few vessels able to travel the seas unnoticed at this speed—was a massive target. One that could not be taken. Any of those supposed time travel tools the Atlanteans once had—the Link Pieces—laid somewhere on the ocean floor, below a depth at which most vessels could travel. The Lemurians needed this ship. And it's not like exposing a time travel war to the government so they could take military action to protect it would help. They'd want to study the

Link Pieces, or weaponize them. And I'd been trying to prevent the latter all along.

No. This was my secret to keep for as long as I could. My duty was to keep this station safe and out of the hands of anyone wanting to use it, or the time traveling capabilities of Link Pieces, for war.

I left the Bridge for the Dining Decks. Lunch could last long enough to grab food and set Chelsea up with a computer. Right now, she was with Helen, but not for much longer. I pushed open the Dining Hall's doors too roughly. Curious glances vaulted my way. I ignored them and poured coffee into the largest cup I could find and then looked for a place to sit.

Michael, an engineering intern under my watch, sat by himself against a wall midway down the deck. He'd finished graduate school last year and had worked on the station since SeaSatellite5 first launched. His father came from a long line of Naval officers, so in combination with his 4.0 GPA and three co-ops, Michael had a free ticket to SeaSat5.

"Hey," I said.

He nodded his greeting and moved paperwork to make space. His eyebrows rose at the size of my coffee. "Rough day?"

"Six hours on the Bridge. Maybe more later."

He cringed. "For fun?"

"The Commander needed me to update the Bird." Half-truths were, evidently, how I got by.

"As if the system wasn't already beyond most of us."

I shrugged off the compliment. SeaSat5 itself was such an advancement for science and technology, my little system barely compared.

"Hey, you finish *Mega Rush 2*, yet?" Michael asked.

I thought everyone knew I'd finished making the game weeks ago. *Mega Rush 2*, a game I'd been working on since holiday leave in December, was a beat-the-world-clock type of game. You grabbed a 3D work headset (courtesy of Engineering) and logged into the game. The players raced against the world clock to complete their objectives and achieve the "winning goal" before I, the overlord, ended their runs. The game utilized an open-world set up, with free range for roaming and a virtually endless "map," and I controlled a lot of things from the outside. With rules of course.

"Yeah. Want to grab who's free and try it out?" I glanced down at my watch. I had an hour of break time to kill. I could set them up with the game and still have time to find a computer for Chelsea while they waded through the first half.

"Do I?" Michael's eyes brightened as he stood and began packing up his paperwork. "About damn time. I'll meet you in the Lounge in ten." He practically ran out the door.

I shoveled my lunch into my mouth and followed him.

◆

We gathered inside the Civilian Lounge, in front of the biggest recreational TV SeaSat5 had to offer. Those in attendance for *Mega Rush 2*'s unveiling consisted of Michael, some Bridge staff, a handful of other engineering interns, and myself. I hooked up my computer, and all the 3D headsets we could round up on short notice, and booted up the game on my screen. From here, I would monitor the progress of each player from a screen they couldn't see, and wreak havoc on everyone. I smirked a little, imagining the shouts and curses that'd be flying in a few minutes.

I called up the game's main title sequence onto the TV, some borrowed 8-bit theme playing in the background. Maybe now, with Chelsea joining the crew, I could get some original music for the game.

Anxiety crawled up my spine, sending chills shooting down the opposite way. Both the best and worst came out of Chelsea boarding SeaSatellite5 for good. I'd get to know her, get to (maybe) be *more* with her, but dammit if having an Atlantean onboard didn't complicate everything. Valerie still wanted to turn her in, and it'd taken some serious convincing to persuade her to hold off for now. Chelsea simply wasn't a threat—except to me.

I'd be lying if I said the thought of her being so close for so long didn't screw with my head. I wanted her. I craved the way she kept me on my toes, foot in mouth. But she was Atlantean. My enemy. And if it came down to it, the war—my family—wouldn't care how I felt. They'd simply destroy her—and me, in the process.

Clearing my throat—and my mind—I sat up straight to get everyone's attention. "I finally present to you *Mega Rush 2: The Race.*"

They all looked at me like I picked the corniest name possible, and maybe I had, but "The Race" fit too well.

"Each player will start in a different corner of the modern-day world," I instructed. "You'll each have an object. Together, those pieces fit together to make a device—the *only* device—which can deactivate an unknown weapon of mass destruction. Where said device is, and how you'll get there to disarm the weapon, is part of the mystery—a puzzle which can be solved from clues given to you upon completing quests. You'll each have a restriction on travel, so creativity is the name of the game."

The look of sheer terror on their faces said I'd finally hit the mark on a good game. They'd be addicted immediately, and I might finally win.

"There's a max of seven players on this one. Sorry guys. One for each continent." Meaning one unlucky fool would start on Antarctica. "But you'll have a collective in-game time of about four months."

"Which means what? One month outside the game?" Lieutenant Commander Christa Jackson, SeaSat5's Communications Officer, asked.

I nodded. "Thereabouts."

Freddy Olivarez, the Ensign heading up Navigations and Analytics, scoffed. "Why don't you make the game a bit more impossible?"

I grinned. "I wasn't done. I still control the game from the outside, but with rules. Mostly weather in this case. A plane can't take off in a snow storm."

Michael and Freddy threw up their hands in disgust, waving Engineering's 3D headsets precariously in the air. My heart leapt over itself. That's one-thousand-dollar equipment!

"I did throw in one handicap," I said, trying to placate them.

"Yeah?" Michael asked.

"You respawn if you die." The statement drew a few sighs of relief, even from the interns who wouldn't be playing. But I wasn't finished yet. "At your point of origin."

Exasperated, Michael leaned back in his seat. "This'll be fun," he said, his voice laced with sarcasm.

I shrugged. "Well, you did ask me to make the game harder. Who's ready to start?"

"You mean who's ready to kick some ass," Freddy said. "'Cause bring it the hell on, Boncore."

"You sure you're going to win?" I asked him.

"We beat the crap out of you last time," Christa said. "Anything's possible."

"If you're so sure…" I said and started up the game. The players locked into their starting locations, and the world clock began its countdown.

Michael got out of his spawn area before the thirty-minute mark. I sat poised to send a small tornado his way, waiting for thunderstorms to brew, when something in the corner of my eye caught my attention. Some*one* who wasn't there before.

Chelsea stood in the opposite corner of the room, a bright blush creeping up her cheeks to wide, terrified, watery eyes.

I jumped up and threw my computer onto the couch cushion beside me. I dashed across the room and checked her over, eyes darting from her head to the rest of her body. "Chelsea, what's wrong?"

She shook all over, and her eyes darted around the room. Her expression slipped from terror to humiliation in an instant, a brilliant red blooming across her cheeks.

"What happened?" I asked again, my hands on her shoulders,

trying to ground her as much as myself. The terror on her face took me straight back to the alleyway in Boston. To wanting to pummel whoever did this to her, my own well-being be damned.

She brushed me off. "I—I need to go."

I grabbed her arm before she could leave. The wildness in her eyes froze me in place like a challenge. I forced words out to meet it. "Hey, it's me. What's going on?"

She nodded quickly, an irritated expression twisting her face. "I know. You're the problem."

I dropped my hand, letting her go. "What?" *What the hell did I do?* "I was going to get you your computer in an hour when you finished with Dr. Gordon."

She was shaking her head again. "That's not it. I just need to go."

"When'd your girl get here?" Michael asked from the couch, insensitive as ever.

Really man?

Chelsea's face flamed to fire-engine-red. I tapped her shoulder and pointed to the door. Chelsea wasn't my girl—at least not yet. And maybe not ever after today.

"I'll be back, guys." I reached for Chelsea's hand. "Come on." I led her into the hallway before letting go, afraid she'd run away rather than talk to me.

She slid down the wall to the metal grating on the floor. Face in her knees, she said, "I am *so* sorry."

I took a seat next to her, grateful for every moment she let me in. "For what?"

Her reply was muffled by clothing and tears. "I have no idea."

"Hey," I said again, touching her back. What could I say to convince her I was worth talking to?

She regarded me with sharp eyes. "I don't know why this keeps happening, or why I always show up near you, or why—but you don't need to babysit me now, I—"

"Chelsea."

She slammed her mouth closed.

I stared at her, my airways pinched off. What did I say? How could I help? I didn't even know what was wrong.

"What?" she asked.

I inclined my head. "What happened? Is everything okay?"

"No, everything's not 'okay.' Helen had me do this *stupid* experiment, and it went wrong, and I panicked and freaking teleported to you again. I'm a freak." She said it matter-of-factly, like nothing I said would change her mind.

Unfortunately for her, I didn't agree. "No, you're not. What you can do is cool." Teleportation definitely fell in the realm of useful, as far as powers went.

She shot me an incredulous look. "You think me being a freak is *cool?*"

How would I get her to understand? "Look, you appeared in a waterfall of navy blue lights in the Lounge. It was the most beautiful thing I've ever seen." After seeing her onstage at the Franklin three months ago, anyway.

Her face scrunched up, still not believing me. "Beautiful?"

I grinned. How could she not see it? "Is that so hard to believe?"

Chelsea opened her mouth to speak, but then she sighed, her shoulders relaxing. "Yes."

I sucked in a breath of relief. I couldn't begin to understand what discovering something so incredible and scary about yourself was like. But Chelsea had to see she's nothing short of amazing.

"Thank you," she said after a beat of silence.

"You're welcome. Do you want to talk about it?"

She shook her head. "It's fine. I have to get back upstairs. Dave and I were arm wrestling, then I… got freaked out."

"Freaked out?" And—*that* was Helen's experiment?

She banged her head against the wall. "I took out a middle-aged military guy at arm wrestling like his arm was made of Jell-O. Don't you see what's wrong with me?"

Couldn't she see I had the same issues? No. I didn't tell her, and no one except Valerie knew how much I wanted a normal life. No war, no protecting the military from becoming an unknowing pawn.

"I'm sure Dave's going to be okay," I said.

"Well, yeah. Still." Chelsea stood up. "I'm pretty sure he's terrified of me now. I should go apologize. Helen's going to wonder where I got to, anyway." She brushed some invisible dust off her uniform bottoms and then placed her hands on her hips.

I rose to my feet. "I'm sure she knows you're around the station somewhere. She's probably not worried."

Half the reason he's hurt is because he probably underestimated Chelsea. He wouldn't blame it on her, and neither would Helen.

Chelsea exhaled and rubbed her neck. "I did this after locking myself in a bathroom stall." She glanced away, a frown threatening to manifest on her lips.

I reached into my pocket and pulled out my radio. "I'll call Helen, don't worry."

Her hand shot to mine. "No, please don't. She'll analyze the whole thing, and I so don't want to talk about it anymore."

"Analyze?"

She hesitated, covering up the pause by letting go of my hand and making a show out of putting hers into her pocket. She bit her lip.

"Chelsea?"

She stayed silent for so long, I thought she wasn't going to tell me. An ache burrowed in my chest. Couldn't she see I just wanted to help her? To be there for her?

She finally answered, "Helen thinks you and I are connected, or, in the very least, I feel connected *enough* to you—because of what happened in Boston—that my abilities draw me to you. Because of... things."

Chelsea's words had spilled out so fast, I struggled to take them in. Connected? Boston? What was I supposed to think, other than Helen's definitely crazy?

But Helen wasn't. I cared for Chelsea in a way I hadn't cared for anyone else before, so it wasn't Helen's hypothesis that scared me. It was that Helen might be right. That we *were* connected, despite me being Lemurian and her this powerful Atlantean. And if that were true, if all this took place on SeaSatellite5, the vessel with every potential to become a pawn if we found Link Pieces, what did that mean for the war? What would my parents do when they found out I'd fallen completely for an Atlantean? Kill her?

My jaw clenched. I'd sooner die than let that happen. Chelsea had become everything to me in a matter of weeks, a connection that ran deeper than either of us wanted to admit. When I looked at her, I saw life and freedom and hope. A promise that maybe, one day, normalcy was something we could both achieve. And that was that.

But she also deserved the truth, no matter what might become of it.

"Trevor?" she prodded.

I raised my hands. "Hey, I like you and all, but we don't know each other that well. 'Connected' is a bit too strong of a word... no offense or anything."

Coward.

She threw her hands up, exasperated. "That's exactly what I told her. We met, we have fun together, you're great, but—hello—it's essentially been two days. Her hypothesis is a load of bull."

I agreed despite a nagging in my gut. It grew into more of an ache, a yearning, the longer I considered it. "Let me call Helen for you."

"I got it," she said, grabbing the radio from me. "Dinner tonight? We can talk more then."

"Yeah." Well, at least she still wanted to see me despite all that.

She turned and paced a few feet down the hall. Watching her walk away from me suddenly felt like a bad idea. Like something I should stop at all costs. What if she walked away forever?

Chapter Twelve

Chelsea

I'm *fine*, Helen," I told her. *Chill out already.*

"Okay," Helen said, but her voice was tight. She must still be worried. "Where are you? I can get you or have Valerie come by."

"I'm outside the Lounge, but I think I can make it back." Obviously a total lie, but the last thing I wanted right now was to be babysat by anybody. While Trevor was right, maybe I wasn't this super weirdo with powers, I needed time to process this on my own.

"Are you sure?" Helen asked.

I nodded, though she couldn't see it. "Yes. Just give me a few minutes."

"I can do that," Helen said. "But you should know, Dave won't be here when you get back."

My heart sunk into my stomach. "Why not?" I'd hurt him. That was the only explanation. But I *knew* I'd hurt him because as soon as I slammed his arm down, something cracked. So I'd run and didn't stop until I hit the bathroom.

"He's got a very badly sprained wrist," Helen said. "I've sent him to get it looked at."

"Shit." Guilt formed a rotting pit in my stomach. I hadn't meant to hurt him. I hadn't wanted to arm wrestle him period. But Helen had pushed us and now... now Dave was hurt, and that had been my fault.

"Chelsea?" Helen asked after I'd been silent for too long.

"I'll meet you in your office," I said and hung up.

I walked. And kept walking. Up some stairs, down the Lift. Lost. I didn't stop moving until my calves hurt, which took a while. I bounced and jumped on stage all the freaking time. So, it turns out, I could handle stairs pretty well. Who knew? Maybe that's *another* super power of mine. Chelsea, Climber of the Stairs.

Screw this. Screw all *of this.* I stopped and slapped a pipe-laden wall, forcing all my anger into a single blow. I froze as pain and stinging bloomed across my palm, but nothing happened. *Stupid, Chelsea. Fucking stupid.* If the arm wrestling mishap was any indication, I could of put my hand right through the metal. Could have put a hole straight into the freaking ship for all I knew.

I forced myself to take my first deep breath in two hours. I'd sprained Dave's wrist badly, but I hadn't known it would happen. Except I did. I did because the entire time I'd sat with Helen, I'd thought about what happened at the Franklin and hadn't said anything. And now I couldn't imagine telling her, couldn't imagine being *here* anymore because what the hell could these people do for me? Try to smooth out my edges with kind words and attempt training me and my powers like an old dog in obedience school for the first time? No. I'd go to the Captain, rescind my contract, and leave. For good. I'd figure it out on my own where no one else could get hurt. My super strength... it wasn't normal, and it'd already put one man in a doctor's care.

"Calm down," I told myself.

My eyes wandered the walls and I tried orientating myself. A sign on one wall read REACTOR/LS with an arrow to the right, and another had the words ENGINEERING and an arrow pointing to stairs. I wracked my brain for a memory of the schematic Trevor showed me. Great. I was several decks away from the science area, even farther from my guest quarters. Fucking hell.

"Can I help you?" someone asked from behind me.

Lieutenant Trigger-Happy scrutinized me like I was sneaking around on purpose. I wasn't supposed to wander alone, but that rule had broken the second I'd teleported out of the bathroom to Trevor.

I sighed and resigned to needing help, even if it came from him. "I need to get back to the science decks. I'm lost."

"How'd you end up down here?" he asked, arms crossing at his chest like he wouldn't believe a word I said, even if it were the truth.

"My work with Helen went badly. I freaked and teleported again, which I'm sure you're ecstatic to hear."

Lieutenant Weyland sucked in a shallow breath and pointed toward the Lift at the end of the corridor. "You're on the wrong Level. I'll walk you there."

"Thank you."

I tried to be pleasant, but I knew he didn't like me. He waited for me to start moving then stalked behind me like a prison guard. He stepped in front of me to press the CALL button on the Lift then ushered me inside when the Lift arrived and selected the Level I was supposed to be on. The doors closed, and we were off.

"Next time, do me a favor and use that radio of yours to call for help if you're lost?" he asked.

"Sure."

The Lift doors opened at the correct floor.

"This is the main science deck," Lieutenant Weyland said as we stepped out. "Dr. Gordon will likely be in her office, two doors down on your right." He pointed down the hallway.

"Thank you," I said again, turning to stroll away.

He cleared his throat, stopping me. "We got off on the wrong foot when you teleported here."

I eyed him. "You think?"

Lieutenant Weyland shook his head, an unfitting smile forming. "The second Captain Marks signed you on as a member of this crew, I should have let the grudge go. But you broke through some of the most secure protocols known to this military."

And thwarted his role as Security Officer in the process.

"Uh... yeah. Sorry. The whole teleporting thing was unintentional, I assure you." Anyone who still thought I purposely teleported onto military property to see a guy I met once was, at this point, definitely insane.

"I don't want you to think I'm the bad guy."

To be honest, I didn't. He had done his job, something I couldn't—and wouldn't—fault him for. What I *hadn't* liked was him almost shooting me despite the Captain not finding me a threat.

"I'm the Head of Security," Lieutenant Weyland said. "I can't have misunderstandings with the crew. That's all."

That was the closest thing to an apology as I was liable to get, so I accepted it in full. "None here. You were doing your job. Thank you for escorting me to the Science Decks."

Lieutenant Weyland nodded. "Good day, Ms. Danning."

I flashed him a smile and pushed open the doors to Helen's office. She wasn't alone inside.

"Oh, thank *god*," Valerie said. She jumped out of a chair and tackle-hugged me. "We were worried!"

"Worried?" I asked, extricating myself from her lanky arms. "We're half a mile under the ocean. Where would I have gone?"

Valerie made a weird motion with her hands, like she was doing a magic trick and lacked the special effects to make a rabbit appear. "You can teleport."

"Not on command."

"Exactly why we worried," Helen said. "What happened after our call?"

"It's been longer than a few minutes," Valerie added. Her eyes rounded around genuine concern, and I felt bad. Kind of.

"I needed to walk around, clear my head. I figured it was okay." Total lie. I knew it wasn't fine for me to waltz around a classified military station unattended.

Valerie reached out and held my arm. "Helen told me about Dave. Are you okay?"

"Not really. Does Trevor know I disappeared for two hours?"

"No," Helen said, shaking her head. "Given all that transpired, I figured it best not to tell him."

"Thank you," I said.

Helen leveled me with a look. "I think we've discovered a second ability of yours."

"Second?"

She nodded. "My other associate exhibited super strength, as well. She's the only other person I've seen with Atlantean lineage that has two powers, though we hadn't had time to explore this one very much."

Great. Two powers. One to get me lost in the middle of nowhere, and the other to sprain men's arms. Where was this power three months ago in the Franklin's back alley?

A lump solidified in my throat. It *had* been there. I had flung that dude into a wall.

"Why don't we go grab some lunch or coffee or something," Valerie suggested. "Get you out of the lab and away from this for a bit."

My stomach growled. I hadn't eaten since breakfast, and maybe all those stairs *had* gotten to me. "Yeah, that sounds good."

Helen locked her hands together in front of her, like she had more to say but wasn't sure she wanted to. I didn't give her a chance.

"I'll see you after, okay?" I asked.

Helen nodded. "Before you leave today, if you can, so we can talk about this. Otherwise I'll see you when you return."

I nodded. "Sounds good."

Valerie and I coasted through the food line on the Dining Decks and retreated to her quarters. Or, I supposed, my quarters, too, if I came back. We sat at a small table to eat, music from a radio playing in the background.

"I know it's not quite your speed," Valerie said, referring to the country pouring out of the speakers. "But it's all I brought with me."

"Guessing you don't get good signal down here, either," I said.

"I wish. Sometimes I throw on a music streaming service. I could do that, if you want."

I shook my head. "Country's fine." She didn't have to cater to me because I'm her guest. And, country or not, the music soothed my ears, which had gone too long without tunes. If music could be called a drug, I'd be its number one addict. A few hours without music made me stir crazy. But until the country music had graced my ears, I hadn't even noticed how long it'd actually been, with all the madness going on.

My fingers contorted around the strange chords, itching for my real guitar instead of one made of air. My heartbeat relaxed, along with my mind, and, in a matter of seconds, I'd made up my mind.

"In fact, you can keep playing what you want," I said. "I don't think I'm coming back."

Valerie's eyes met mine, and I swore a flash of relief flashed across her golden brown irises.

Quickly, she snapped her gaze elsewhere, blinking away whatever thought had passed through her mind. "What? Why? Yesterday you were all for it."

"No, I wasn't."

She put her sandwich down and leveled her stare. Her dark eyes pinned me to the chair like a predator asking its prey to stay longer before being devoured.

"Because you don't agree with the 'cloak and dagger' business?" she asked. "Everyone has issues with that at some point. You think the bio engineering work I do isn't subject to questioning because of how we conduct research, under a cloak and a mile of ocean?"

"That's not what I—" I hadn't meant to offend her, and that's not what I didn't want to stay. "Yeah, that stuff weirds me out, but I get why SeaSatellite5 is classified."

"Then what's the problem? You have an once-in-a-lifetime, career-launching opportunity. You're one of the few, probably *only*, undergraduates to be given a position on board, and you're in the very place you need to be to understand your teleportation power. Helen's the only person on the planet capable of helping you with that."

"She said there was another—"

Valerie flicked her hand, karate-chopping the air, to cut me off. "She's studied her ancestral roots to Atlantis practically her entire life. If you want to understand your own ties to the city, you need her. And from what I know about the archaeology field, you need this job to make it." She paused, letting her words sink in. "So, Chelsea, what's the problem?"

Blunt much? What if it wasn't about my career? "I'm a freak." But even to me, the excuse was getting old. I didn't want to talk about the real reason.

Valerie's eyes narrowed. "We all have problems. I wanted to leave when I first boarded, too, because Trevor has the job *I* should have." She swallowed hard, her hand clenching around her drink. "But luck sided with him; he got the honors, had the idea, and look where he is."

Trevor mentioned Valerie's jealous streak. But how much of it was her fault? Trevor did seem pretty damn lucky, that his doodle freshman year turned into a high profile, albeit classified, career.

"My problem is exactly what happened today," I amended, skirting around the real issue.

"Teleporting?"

"No. I put Dave in the freaking Infirmary." My cheeks warmed at the memory. I shook my head. "Yeah, I need this job. And I want it. But not if people are going to get hurt because I'm here and can't control how hard I hit or touch something, or, I don't know, hug somebody."

"And?"

"And what?"

Her lip quirked, not in a laughing sort of way, but like she was egging me on. "Felt like there was an 'and' coming."

So much had been shoved into that unspoken 'and' that I didn't want to touch the subject with a ten-foot pole. But Valerie didn't back down.

"And," I said, my hands shaking, "Maybe, for once in my life, I just want normal. Because nothing's been normal for years. Not since college. Now, I teleport all over, to a guy who's probably faking his ability to handle it all, and the only job I can find after graduation is as a research assistant on a *classified Navy vessel*. Where did normal go?"

I sucked in deep breath. It didn't calm my shaking hands, only added weight onto my already heavy chest. "All I wanted to do after college was archaeology during the day and play shows at night. Somehow get the band a record deal."

"Then what?" Valerie asked, leaning in.

"That's it," I said. "There's no long-term plan, because any long-term plans *I* make fail. So, normal for me was *that plan*, and that's all I wanted."

"Life doesn't always agree with your plans. And rarely does 'normal' stay the status quo. I would know." She sighed heavily, her shoulders slumping. "I can't tell you what to do, and, clearly, anyone who tries is fighting the hardest upward battle known to mankind."

My face scrunched up. Should I be offended by that? "Thanks?"

A smile edged her lips. "My point is: take the risk. Seize this opportunity while it's here, because, despite everything else—and I *know* there's a lot of everything else—SeaSatellite5 is a fascinating place to be. You'll be able to gain lab experience, and if we come across any shipwrecks or anything, you'll be the first one to see them. Board them, if we can. And you're in the very best place in the world to learn how to control your abilities. Helen's the best there is. Will it be challenging? Hell yeah."

Her hand curled into a fist on the table. "I think you'd be stupid to turn this down, or to run because things aren't working out. The more you work with Helen and practice teleporting, the better you'll get at it. And if it's Trevor you're worried about..." She stuck her tongue in her cheek, mulling over her next words carefully. "He's a good guy, and he's not scared away that easily when there's something he wants at the other end."

My face flushed hotter. Was I that something he wanted? I hoped so. I hadn't really noticed it until earlier this morning. I'd been attracted to him since I saw him at the crowd at the Franklin. And the sight of him in the alleyway, tackling the mugger, had taken my breath away. That a complete stranger would put themselves in harm's way for me—I hadn't expected it to happen in Boston. Or anywhere.

How stupid I'd been, thinking my feelings for Trevor burned gradually. The magnetism was a sledgehammer, a wrecking ball that slammed into me at the Franklin, with aftershocks that struck every time our eyes met. The feelings weren't gradual, weren't grown. They had burst into a slow motion chorus that shattered a quiet song, bringing the rest of the music to life. And maybe, just maybe, Helen's theory wasn't bat-shit crazy after all. Maybe Trevor and I were connected on some level, deeply. And maybe, possibly, I liked it.

Would I forever be afraid of hurting someone else? Yes. But maybe teleporting to the one guy who made me feel safe wasn't such a bad thing. Like Valerie said, life didn't let us choose whether or not to be normal. And maybe that was okay. Maybe I'd been running for so long that chaos *was* my new normal. But could chaos be sustainable? Could I hold onto that forever?

"Good to know," I managed to squeak out. I hoped she couldn't read my thoughts on my face. If Valerie could, she didn't say anything about it.

She grinned and said, "Besides, trust me. He's used dealing with interesting women. He grew up with me, after all." She winked.

I relaxed into my chair and met Valerie's eyes. She didn't look away or say anything, only waited.

"Maybe you're right," I said.

"I've been known to occasionally be correct, yes," she replied with a smirk.

I couldn't help but laugh. "Thanks for talking me down. I know we didn't exactly get off on the right foot." Which killed me to admit. "You, uh, kind of reminded me of someone I don't get along with."

She shrugged it off. "It's fine. I egged you on about the cloak stuff. And maybe I knew someone once who didn't have anyone to talk her down."

"What do you mean?"

"A family friend. Some crazy stuff happened to her, too. She had amazing gifts. Things got rough, and no one was there for her."

"I didn't know," I said, frowning. "I'm sorry. I hope she's okay." I almost regretted asking.

Valerie nodded and stretched her arms out before her. "She's okay now, but I regret not being there. So I'm glad we talked, Chelsea."

"Me too." I didn't know what else to say. Heart-to-hearts weren't my thing. Thankfully, Valerie seemed to end the conversation. But there was one thing I wondered about. "So, uh, back home, I'm used to partying my nights away."

Valerie's eyes lifted to mine, questioning. "Yeah?"

"What do you all do for fun around here?"

She grinned, stood, and turned on her tablet. "Oh, wait until you see this."

Chapter Thirteen

Trevor

L ate. That was the name of the game lately. Stuck in work with systems flying off the hook with issues, I'd missed the whole day. Now I was late for dinner, or at least dinner eaten at a normal time.

I glanced at my watch and climbed the last staircase to Valerie's cabin. Soon to be shared with Chelsea. Frustration had me rubbing my eyes with vigor. I'd eavesdropped on that bit of information while in Engineering all afternoon; one of the other interns complained Valerie no longer had solo quarters and how inconvenient that'd be for them. Supposedly, Valerie invited Chelsea there to start rearranging the room.

Now it was half past seven. Chelsea had to be waiting for me, right? *No, idiot. She didn't.*

The door to Valerie and Chelsea's cabin stood ajar. Laughter emanated from within. I pushed open the door with two fingers and knocked on the exposed frame. Two heads turned, their laughter stopping. Awkward.

"Hey," I said.

"Hey," Valerie replied.

Chelsea gave a wave, smiling from ear to ear. They huddled on the floor around Valerie's tablet, watching *Mega Rush 2*. Looked like Michael was still leading the pack.

"I didn't mean to interrupt," I said. "I was looking for Chelsea."

"Well, you found me." Chelsea smiled and pointed to the tablet. "You made this game?"

How'd they even patch into it from here? Easy answer: Valerie. Of course.

"Yeah," I answered.

Amusement and awe danced in her eyes. "This is the coolest game I have ever seen. Ever. And I worked in an arcade for years."

She worked in an arcade? *Closet gamer*. Hell if that wasn't a turn on. And she liked *my* game, something I'd poured everything into creating. Warmth flooded my chest. The reaction caught me so suddenly, so unexpectedly, I had no response. *She liked my game.*

"Looks like you screwed them over this time, Trevor," Valerie said, halting my thoughts. "Michael talked about nothing else when we saw him at lunch, and it's the first day. What the hell did you do to them?"

I shrugged. "I made the game harder, like they wanted. They should be careful what they wish for next time."

Valerie chuckled. "Yeah. Definitely. I'm almost glad I'm not playing this time around."

Funny, so was I. She'd destroyed the competition in the first version of the game.

Chelsea stood. "I'm starving. Did you already eat?"

Relief flushed my system. She'd waited. "No. Want to go?"

"Absolutely."

She turned to Valerie, who rolled her eyes. "Oh, just go."

Chelsea spun to the door and linked her arm through mine. "To dinner, then!"

The dinner line, even this late, slowed to a dead stop with people getting off mid-shifts. We stepped in behind other science staff and grabbed trays, an apology gnawing its way out of me. "I'm sorry I'm late."

Her eyes echoed a hint of disappointment. "It's cool. Valerie picked me up from Helen's lab. We've been watching the game ever since."

The line hit the salad bar first. I passed, but Chelsea fixed herself a mish-mash of items.

"Interns," I mumbled. "There was a major hiccup in Engineering." In fact, these hiccups had *kept* happening ever since Chelsea had arrived.

"And you've been there ever since I teleported earlier?"

I nodded. "Unfortunately."

She smiled at me over her shoulder. The light caught her hazel eyes and washed them with green. They stunned me, hitching my breath and making eye contact hard to keep.

"Well, you're here now," she said.

"That I am."

Her face flushed, and she abruptly turned forward. We approached the main course. Unfortunately, the meat looked like charred zombie flesh.

We both grabbed portions and scouted a two-seater booth off to the side. The second we sat, all the weight and stress of today scurried outside the Dining Decks in a flash. I was here, with her. Like I'd promised. I didn't enjoy breaking promises.

"So, how was your day?" I asked then pressed my lips together. *Really, Boncore?*

"Good. I mean, I basically got babysat the whole time, so nothing went wrong. Valerie showed me around some more. Hopefully I won't get lost when I come back."

"I doubt you'll get lost." Though I'd heard about her run-in with Lieutenant Weyland.

"I'm glad you have faith in me," she said.

"If I survived Boston, you'll survive SeaSat5. Much smaller. No crazies. No drunks."

She made a *tsk* sound. "Shame."

"Ha, ha."

She grinned, eyes flitting up from her plate. When they met mine, she froze. Moments passed while a smile sprouted across my face. Everything about her still held wild beauty despite her monotone uniform. Her nails were painted a bright color, her ears pierced by three small studs on each side. Valerie must not have told her the whole dress code. But it didn't matter. Chelsea wasn't like anyone else on board.

The edges of her mouth twitched, sliding down the smallest bit. She glanced at her plate and took another bite of dinner, breaking the spell.

I frowned. "What's wrong?"

She shook her head a little. "Nothing. Really. We, uh—"

"Got stuck there for a second?"

Her face flushed, and she lifted her glass to her lips. "Yeah."

I shifted in my seat and grabbed my drink. I hadn't meant to make her uncomfortable. "Do you start work with Helen when you come back?"

"Yeah," she said, pushing food around her plate with a fork. "Not sure how that's going to go, after today. Especially the lab stuff."

"Chelsea, you're going to be fine." Where was the confident singer from the rock band?

"I know." But her voice was quiet. Eventually she looked up to me and sighed. "It's different for you. Engineering is legit. People take you seriously. I went to school to dig up old civilizations, dead people, and their stuff. Despite what I told my parents all four of those years, and despite what my professors always told me, I never once thought I'd get a legitimate job doing this. Ever. If anything, I figured I'd end up teaching intro courses amidst band practices and shows at regional venues. Now I'm here."

If only she knew how similar our situations were. We both had plans, ideals demolished by this stupid Atlantean-Lemurian war. In that moment, I wanted to tell her about it. I *should* tell her about it.

But the more she stressed about powers and being here, the less appealing telling her got.

"I get it, Chelsea. You're scared of screwing it up."

"More than anyone can understand." She shifted in her seat. "It's like, I know I'm here ninety-percent because of my accompanying powers. The archaeology intern bit is as much a cover story as an excuse. And you know what? Fine. Whatever. Fair game on the Navy's part. But it's still a job I shouldn't have landed. If this ends poorly, it's the end of the line for me. And, given my abilities, I'm thinking there's a whole score of ways this can go south."

I reached my hand out to hers. Her skin was warm and soft, except around her fingertips, which were calloused from guitar strings.

"It's going to be okay," I said. "Tell Helen about all of this before you leave, or when you come back. She can make sure you do as much intern work as research on your abilities, so you're contributing more than you think you're going to."

She nodded. "That'd be great. And my weird heart-to-heart with Valerie helped, too."

Uh, what? "I'm sorry. Did you say heart-to-heart and Valerie in the same sentence?" Valerie didn't have caring feelings, none that weren't anger-based.

"Yeah. She basically grabbed me from Helen's office and convinced me to stay because she felt bad for not doing it for a friend years ago, or something."

My breath caught in my throat. Chelsea thought of leaving? My mind skipped over the thought as soon as it came. The last half of her sentence was more important. "Abby."

Her lips fell, eyes dropping. Silence. "Bad topic?"

I wanted to say yes and leave it be, but I couldn't keep Abby's story from Chelsea forever. It struck me then how much I didn't want to. I'd kept it to myself for too long, and, now, the sadness of it bubbled in my throat. Telling Chelsea felt like the only course of action I could take to release the pressure of it, even for a little while.

There was no saving Abby. Not now.

"Kind of," I replied, finally.

Chelsea's fingers tightened around mine. "It's okay. We don't have to talk about it."

"It's fine. Just still raw." It'd always feel that way; I was sure of it.

"Who was she?" Chelsea asked, her voice low, giving me an option to back out if I wanted.

"Abby's my cousin. She, uh…" Had issues with the same reality I've been dealing with. Only she hadn't had the truth. "She had a mental breakdown. It's bad. She's in a facility now. Happy, so I'm told. Blissfully unaware."

Or, we hoped she was. I hadn't known it then—and hadn't accepted it until I witnessed Chelsea fight off her attacker in Boston—but Abby had found out about the Lemurian-Atlantean war in the worst way possible.

Where Valerie and I had grown up knowing about the conflict, the truth, Abby hadn't. Her parents had kept it from her because she'd suffered several bouts of childhood illness. They'd decided she couldn't handle it on top of everything, so they'd lied to her. Asked *me* to lie to her. And I did. To protect her. By the time I was old enough to understand my mistake, it was too late.

Throughout her freshmen year of college, Abby had written home about strange experiences, all of the *impossible things* she couldn't explain. Then, one day, my mother had gotten a call from my aunt. Abby had been admitted to the hospital with a broken leg and arm from a car accident. She'd been driving to campus from work when someone had run straight out in front of her car. She'd tried to stop but, in doing so, Abby's car had scrambled with the car behind her. Abby had said she'd watched the jogger waltz away from the scene, unharmed, before help got there. My aunt had pleaded with my parents to let them tell Abby the truth, but my mother had said they'd waited too long.

Abby's accident had been the first of many major episodes. Our parents had kept quiet after each one, and every time I'd tried to talk to her, they'd stopped me. They'd thought of her as a liability, so, instead, they'd let her spiral into insanity, with nothing but memories of impossible things no one had been there to protect her from. If I'd graduated faster, been smarter, I might have been in school with her. I might have saved her. If I'd had the capacity to understand the war and everything involved with it at a younger age, if I'd had the courage to defy my parents, I could have decided not to lie.

Valerie's hypothesis as to what had really happened, what had fueled her initial dislike of Chelsea, didn't make the situation any easier to think about. Valerie thought Atlanteans had stolen Abby away and interrogated her about things she couldn't possibly have known. I still didn't know what I believed.

"I'm so sorry, Trevor." Chelsea squeezed my hand, snapping me back to reality.

I nodded, dread pulling me down into a guilty ocean I knew so well. "It happened a while ago."

"Doesn't make it hurt any less."

"No."

This was depressing. More depressing than today should have turned out. I sucked in a deep breath, lifting myself a sail to lead me out of the ocean. "Anyways, now that I've killed the mood."

Chelsea shook her head and pulled our hands an inch towards her. "No way. You didn't."

I smiled. "Okay. I hate to ask, but when do you leave?" Being locked in Engineering all afternoon, I hadn't heard anything, and, while it wasn't exactly the best follow-up question, I wanted to know how much longer I had her for.

"Tonight," she said flatly. Like she hated it. I did, too.

"Are you still worried about finals?" I asked. It was the only thing I could think of that'd upset her about leaving. I'd rather she not go, period. I just started getting to know her, and I didn't want to think about what two weeks apart would do to that.

"Kind of," she admitted, her eyes finding mine. "And teleporting while gone. And that going home will make it all *real*, you know? What if I teleport in front of somebody, or break something a normal person wouldn't crack? Then they'll know about all of this, and I... don't know what I'd do about that yet."

Was she really that embarrassed by all of this? Did that mean she was embarrassed of me?

"I doubt anything will happen." I hoped.

She played with her fork, twirling it around. "I know. I just don't want to deal with it on top of everything else."

"Then go home," I said, despite my brain and heart wanting the exact opposite. "Finish school, tie up loose ends and get that stuff over with. Then come here and deal with this, whatever worries you about it. You didn't teleport or exhibit super strength for the first twenty-one years of your life. What are the odds you'll do it again in the next two weeks?"

The corner of her mouth quirked up in a smile, and she threaded her fingers between mine. "You're right. I... I wish you could come with me. Just in case."

Because she wanted me to go, or because she always teleported to me? I didn't want to know. If I had a choice, I'd live in the world where she wanted me for me, not as an anchor point.

"It's only two weeks," I said.

"That's a long time," she replied.

It felt like forever. "I'll be here. We can message each other in the meantime. And I'll be there when you board again."

Her eyes lit up. "You will?"

I nodded. "Yes. I'll even try to make it to port, but, if not, I'll wait for you in Shuttle Dock."

"Awesome. Thanks."

Truth was, I'd wait for her anywhere, anytime.

Chapter Fourteen

Chelsea

To my surprise, two weeks at home was enough. Logan had schooled me for disappearing. My thesis had gone shaky, but I'd passed, so that's all that mattered. I hadn't run into Lexi, so yay there. But, dammit, the whole time I was home, I'd just wanted to get back to SeaSat5, to Trevor. Text messaging hadn't been enough, and damn the time difference and all the all-nighters I'd pulled that had made us unable to call each other. Throughout the first day I'd had this ache, a sense of restlessness in my chest and arms, an anticipation of returning to SeaSatellite5. I hadn't expected to, but I'd missed it. Or, more accurately, I'd missed Trevor. The guy who'd come out of nowhere and enraptured me from the very first second.

I arrived at port exactly two weeks after I left SeaSat5 by helicopter, not a minute late.

SeaSatellite5 was nowhere at all.

My heart flapped in my chest. Had they forgotten about me? Had I missed the shuttle back?

Something in the distance caught my attention, a figure walking up the boardwalk. Dr. Helen Gordon. *The cloak.* Duh. Valerie had talked about it. I'd been stupid to forget. They'd cloaked SeaSat5 somewhere out in the distance. They'd had to have in order to keep it hidden.

I exhaled in relief, both at the knowledge I was about to be back onboard and because I was *so* looking forward to someone who wasn't a sailor. The guy who drove me here hadn't talked the entire four-hour trip to port. Awkward. As. Hell.

Helen wore civilian clothes, tan pants, a light blue blouse, and a wide doctor's smile. "I see you got here all right."

"Long ride, but I got some music writing in."

"I'm glad to hear that." She looked down the length of the boardwalk to a set of docked boats. "We'll board the shuttle through a drop-door in the hull of that boat there. It'll take us out far enough to board SeaSat5. We're looking at least a two-hour ride."

Great.

We made our way down the dock. I climbed into the twenty-foot boat with the name *Seafarer* inscribed on the side. An officer waved at us from across the deck to board and descend into the cabin below, where a door in the floor greeted us. Not a door—a lighted hatch with a ladder down the middle.

Claustrophobia squeezed my lungs. *Shit.* "You want me to climb through that?"

"It's how we board shuttles we don't want the public to see," Helen said.

If the boat was only twenty-feet long, how small was the shuttle beneath it? It had to be tiny if they hoped to disguise it at all.

I gulped and stared at the hatch.

"Chelsea?" Helen asked.

"Not a fan of tight spaces," I mumbled. SeaSatellite5 already gave me anxiety, and it was practically an office building compared to this thing. Huge. Open-ish. Safe. A shuttle? Not so much.

Teleporting I could handle, but not *this*? I punched down my fear, a fire lighting courage in my bones. I could do this. I could get on that shuttle, get to the station, and figure my powers out. Work an internship. Shit, maybe even have some fun doing it. All I had to do was get through that hatch.

I swallowed hard and stuck my foot on the first rung of the ladder. *Here goes nothing.* I scaled the hatch, watching each rung that passed. When only five rungs separated me from the floor, I let go of the ladder and dropped of my own accord. Anything to get me out of the tube faster.

The shuttle fit only a pilot, co-pilot, Helen, and me. The co-pilot stowed my bags above Helen's bench. I took a seat in the rear compartment, opposite her, and looked for windows. One was in the wall of the forward compartment, but I couldn't see out of it.

I leaned my head against a headrest and pulled in as much air as I could. I'd waited for this since leaving two weeks ago. In between stressing over my thesis and graduation, I'd dreamed about coming back here. For Trevor and for a chance to understand what happened to me. But now that I was here, all I wanted was a window to gaze at my home for the next six months or the dock I'd come from. Anything to give me a reference point, a closure to an old chapter and the launching point for a new one.

Minutes dragged into an hour. Helen pulled out her tablet and worked. I stood and collected the smaller of my two duffle bags, retrieving a notebook and pens from inside. My hands ached to write lyrics, but I instead ended up doodling Pac Man running from ghosts on his way to gobble fruit. Not much time passed before my thoughts drifted to Trevor. When hearts appeared on the page alongside Mr. Pac Man, I quit and put the pen down. This wasn't the time or the place. But Trevor hadn't been at port, which meant he'd be waiting for me in Shuttle Dock. My heart skipped at the thought of seeing him. Anticipation flooded my veins, making my feet and hands restless. How much longer until we got to SeaSatellite5?

The shuttle swayed as we docked with the station an hour later and disembarked into Shuttle Dock. The co-pilot emerged with my bags, saying he'd take them to my quarters.

I searched Shuttle Dock for Trevor, my heart in my throat. He'd *said* he'd be here. My stomach somersaulted over and over itself with every empty corner searched, every crewman that wasn't him. Trevor wasn't here. He didn't show. My lips tugged into a frown. *Figures.*

Someone called my name from the other side of the room, the voice high and disappointingly feminine. I turned to find Valerie where Trevor had promised he'd be. I sighed. Not sure why I'd thought he'd actually be here. Guys rarely did what they said they would. Trevor wasn't any different.

I squashed down the part of me wanting to pout, if only to keep Valerie from reading every thought I had.

Valerie smiled and waved me over. "Glad you got here okay. How was the ride?"

"Uneventful. Wrote some lyrics." A whole five lines. Pac Man had more fun than I did.

She nodded, eyes bright and happy. "This is going to be so fun! I rearranged the room the best I could. I'll take you there now so you can unpack."

Since my bags went on ahead of me, I had no choice but to once again follow Valerie through the maze that was SeaSat5. At some point in the labyrinth, we boarded the Lift and tucked ourselves in the back, out of everyone's way. My shoulder bumped someone's files, and I fumbled to keep them from falling to the floor. *Good going, Danning.*

I picked them up and handed them over. "Sorry. I'm a klutz."

"It's okay," a woman said. She wore a warm, genuine smile, and was probably only a few years older than me.

"Hey Julie," Valerie said, smiling. "How's it going?"

Julie gave her a small wave. "Good. New blood?"

Valerie nodded. "Julie, meet Chelsea, our new archaeologist. Chelsea, this is Julie. She's a chemist who works with Dr. Gordon."

Julie tapped her files back into order and extended a hand.

I shook it with a smile. "Nice to meet you."

"You too. If you're working with Helen, we'll probably see each other a lot. Holler if you need anything."

The Lift crawled to a stop, and a bell dinged.

"Well, this is me," Julie said.

"Want to come with us?" Valerie asked.

Julie thumbed out the door. "I was on my way to lunch. Can I meet you after?"

"Yeah," I said. "I'm sure this is going to take a while, anyway." I really wanted to unpack. So, it was awesome she declined, at least for now. One needed friends to survive in a new place, and I'd be stupid to admit this wasn't a mostly new environment. Not that I'd been grand at the whole friend thing lately.

"Sounds good," Julie said, stepping toward the door. "Later, then."

"She's cool," Valerie said as Julie left. "She'll show you the ropes on your first day in the lab."

"Hope so." Science labs were not my thing.

We rode the Lift for a little longer before finally getting off. Valerie led me to her—our—room. She had her stuff placed neatly on her side of some invisible line. The room looked like it belonged in a 90's sitcom about roomies or siblings; picture frames lined her walls, a throw rug on the floor, nothing passing an invisible line down the middle.

"I figured you could unpack and then we could get rid of the line in the sand, so to speak," she said.

"Right." My bags and guitar waited for me on my bed. I caressed the guitar case. Would I be able to play with Valerie around?

Valerie stepped in beside a dresser and touched each drawer in succession. "Uniforms. The bottom drawers are for your personal items. If you end up needing something else, let me know." She turned a half-step and faced a door on her side of the room. "You can change in the bathroom if you want."

"Mind if I unpack first?" As much as the prospect of a moment alone called to me like chocolate after a no-sweets Lent season, I needed something I could control to fight all the new things coming at me. Unpacking would do that.

"Go for it." She kicked back on her bed and took off her shoes. "I've got some reports to read. I'm off duty until Captain Marks is free to speak with you."

I unzipped my duffle bags. My clothes went into the bottom drawers of my dresser, and I stacked some books on my desk. I sat on my bed, guitar across my lap and read through lyrics in my notebook. The few I wrote before diving into Pac Man doodles were obviously about Trevor; my face warmed reading them. Something twitched in my chest, anxiety laced with a feeling I couldn't identify. Longing?

"Hey, Valerie?" I asked.

She lifted her head. "Yeah?"

"Um…" There was no way to ask this without sounding annoying, but I needed to know. "Trevor said he'd be there to get me today. I'm not saying I'm not grateful for you—"

She tossed her hand. "No worries. He's busy. Something went haywire in Engineering."

"Haywire?" That seemed to happen an awful lot. Maybe he really just didn't want to make good on his promise, two weeks being enough to kill whatever we had going, and didn't want to say it to my face.

"That's all I caught of the story," Valerie said. "I'm sure he'll be free after you talk to Captain Marks. Trevor is excited to see you."

Was he now? I looked at my notebook. Maybe being upset was stupid after all. I shoved the journal aside and pulled out a uniform from my dresser. "Any special rules I need to know for dress codes?"

"Uniform while working, appropriate civilian clothes while not. But they basically would like to see everyone in a uniform whenever possible."

Which might not have been bad if mine wasn't pale yellow. I suppressed a cringe and made my way into the bathroom. The jumpsuit sort of fit. I was shorter than the intended victim, so the fabric hung loose in weird places. Whatever. It worked.

Valerie waited for me on the other side of the door. "Off to the Captain's Quarters, if you're ready."

"This look presentable?"

"Well, you look better in the uniform than Trevor does, so there's something." She winked then nodded at the door, leaving me more confused than ever.

The Captain's quarters were larger than I expected. A desk and two chairs claimed the main area. Two doors led off the main room, and I assumed they led to a bedroom and bathroom. A half-empty bookshelf lined one wall, home to two dozen books of varying genres. The floor was plain tile or plastic, save for a circular, navy blue rug beneath a desk and chairs. The same light grey walls that lined the rest of the station dulled the room here, too. It settled my nerves, only because the paint was depressing. Maybe I wouldn't have to worry about writing only love songs after all.

Captain Marks sat behind his desk but stood when Valerie and I entered. He smiled and extended a hand. I shook it.

"Welcome aboard," he said.

"Thanks for having me," I replied.

He nodded at Valerie, and I watched her go. Would she wait for me?

The Captain gestured to a chair facing his desk. "Please, have a seat." When I did, he continued, "I know Dr. Gordon is excited to have you here."

"Yeah, we're already making progress."

"Excellent." He rested his arms on the top of his desk, fingers interlocked. "You'll begin working with her immediately. We don't have much in the way of archaeological work for you to do at the moment. We sent out the artifacts from the last find we came upon prior to your appearance two weeks ago."

Appearance. Interesting word choice. "That's okay."

"Until we have more, Dr. Gordon will have tasks for you in addition to working with her regarding your abilities. Before I release you for your first day, I'd like to give you this." He opened the top drawer of his desk and pulled out a white plastic card. "This keycard is programmed to open the doors you'll need. If they don't, you are not supposed to be in there."

I nodded and accepted the card. "Understood."

He stood and stepped away from his desk. "One last thing: I want to introduce you to our Communications Officer. You'll be working with her, too."

"Sounds good."

Captain Marks led me out of his quarters and up a level to the Bridge. He swiped his card at the reader and the blast doors opened. The Bridge itself stood fifty feet wide, longer in length. Most stations rested at ground level, but one in each section sat higher than the rest. Each workspace had two monitors with data moving too fast to read. Officers moved around the space in fluid motion, like a practiced dance.

Three huge screens in the center of the far wall mesmerized me. One held a view of what, I presumed, was in front of us in the ocean. The other two showed status updates and a diagram of the station, which currently resided in a horizontal orientation. A platform with a chair and a console took up the middle of the area. Probably the command post, if movies counted as a reference point.

A tall, sun-tanned man stood there. He looked like he'd come off three months of tropical shore leave after applying a chain store's entire supply of tanning oil. "Captain on the Bridge," he announced.

Fifteen people stood to attention. Captain Marks set them at ease.

"This way," Captain Marks said. I followed him to a station near the front. "Lieutenant Commander," the Captain addressed a tall woman with long blonde hair pulled back into a tight bun beneath a blue headset.

She stood. "Captain."

"This is our new archaeology intern, Chelsea Danning. Chelsea, Lieutenant Commander Christa Jackson, my Communications Officer."

"Pleasure to meet you," the Lieutenant Commander said. "I can't wait to work together. We haven't had a real archaeologist aboard before. It's made things interesting when we come across wrecks."

I shook her hand. "I could see why." Having to fly someone in every time probably got tiring.

"Captain, could I speak with you for a moment?" the man standing on the command platform asked. His uniform bore a name patch reading CMDR DEVINS.

Captain Marks nodded at him. "I'll leave you two to get acquainted. Could you escort Ms. Danning to Dr. Gordon's office afterwards, Lieutenant Commander?"

"Aye, Captain."

"Thank you. Enjoy your first day, Ms. Danning."

After he left, the Lieutenant Commander said pulled a second chair over and told me to sit. "What's your area of expertise?"

"I do folklore, though I have done field school. It's a weird combination."

She shrugged. "So are the languages in my repertoire, but hey. Weird is cool."

What languages did she know that she classified as weird? "Which do you know?"

She ticked them off on her fingers as if it helped her remember how many she actually knew. "Spanish, French, Russian, Latin, Mandarin, and some Greek. Sometimes cuneiform for fun. I'm working on a few others."

"Cuneiform. For fun," I echoed. I'd *kill* to know cuneiform. "Maybe you could teach me some while I'm here?"

She tapped a finger against her lips. "Yeah, we could make that work."

A grin spread wide across my face. "Awesome. Thank you Lieut—"

"Nope. If we're working together, call me Christa. No ranks, all right?"

I nodded. I'd call her whatever she wanted if she taught me cuneiform. "Then no 'Ms. Danning.'"

Christa held out her hand. "Deal."

My grin grew wider. *Cuneiform, here I come.* Maybe this internship wouldn't be so bad after all.

Christa's smile grew into a grin, and her eyes focused in on something over my shoulder. "Hey, Trevor."

My toes curled, and my face flushed. *Trevor.* I turned and, sure enough, there he stood.

"Hi," he said back to her, but his eyes were on me. The sight of him was as warm water on a cold winter morning, refreshing and necessary to every fiber of my being. I drank in his presence like Christa wasn't there at all.

His eyes never left mine, but his fingers twitched, like he wanted to reach out and take my hand or touch me, but couldn't because of where we were. "Sorry I wasn't there this morning," he said instead.

"It's okay," I told him. And it was. Because he was here now, and that was all that mattered.

"Trevor," Christa said, "Captain Marks wanted me to escort Chelsea from the Bridge, but I can't leave just yet. Would you mind?"

Was that a wink she flashed him? I fought the laugh that wanted to bubble over. Was our attraction to each other that obvious?

"Of course," he said, waving toward the door.

"Thanks again," I said to Christa before Trevor and I wandered off the Bridge.

Chapter Fifteen

Trevor

I t'd been a week since Chelsea had been back—and I'd never smiled so much in my life, even despite the Engineering hiccup that'd made me unable to meet her when she'd docked. As I was, somehow, the beacon to which Chelsea teleported, Helen had incorporated me into Chelsea's daily practice. I didn't ask about the other pieces of Helen's methods because I knew a lot of Chelsea's control came from dealing with personal things that I didn't want to invade on, but however Helen had instructed Chelsea to focus on teleporting, it was working. In the last week since she'd boarded, Chelsea had made incredible headway with her ability.

I bounded down the inner staircases of the science decks, winded but still moving. Chelsea's countdown sounded over the radio. "Five, four, three."

"Need a bit longer. Not stopping in a hallway," I returned.

I swore I heard the smile in her voice when she said, "Four, four and a half, three, three and a half…"

Launching off the staircase with a snort of amusement, I slipped down the corridor and into Helen's office. I sat in Helen's chair. She roosted in the security office (to Lieutenant Weyland's *amusement* I'm sure) so she could watch Chelsea's progress. My chest heaved, trying to catch enough oxygen to breathe properly.

I depressed the TALK button on my radio. "Ready when you are."

"Olly olly oxen free, then," Chelsea returned.

It took a few moments, but, sure enough, a magnificent cascade of lights like shimmering blue stars filled the room. It looked like a lighted waterfall, tumbling down out of nowhere. Chelsea materialized in front of the desk, hands on her hips and grinning from ear to ear.

"Yes!" she said, fist-bumping the air. "Two for two, baby!"

Seeing her confident and happy again made my chest swell with emotion—pride for her, for what she was becoming: a powerful Atlantean.

"Good job," I said, smiling. I didn't mind getting to see her all day, or the smile on her face when she succeeded. Those brief moments had become the best part of every day for the last week. "Should we go again?"

She nodded. "Absolutely. I'm on a freaking roll, for once. We're not stopping now."

I couldn't stop grinning. I ran a hand through my hair and glanced at my watch. "Well, you've got me for another hour or so. You call the shots."

"Scoot," she said, brushing me away. "Go find another hiding spot, then. You don't mind staying a bit longer?"

"Absolutely not. You're getting really good at this."

She grinned, chin up. "Thanks. I don't even have to get mad anymore. I just... go. Poof. Right in front of you."

Please let that never change.

"All right. I'll make it harder this time." Maybe I'd disappear to somewhere she's never been before. Somewhere like a supply closet on an engineering deck, tucked away in a corner.

"Sounds good. How long do you need?"

"I'll radio you when I get there. Did you catch that, Dr. Gordon?"

"Yes," Helen said. "Good work so far today, you two."

"See, even she's impressed," I said to Chelsea. "Okay. Give me... at least ten minutes, maybe more."

"Jeeze, where are you going?" she asked, eyebrows furrowed. "A shuttle outside the station?"

"No, but that's a good idea. I'm going somewhere that requires the Lift to behave," I said, walking out the door. "Ten minutes at least. I'll radio you when I'm ready."

I ducked down the corridor and jumped on the Lift. Ten people had boarded before me, all headed up instead of down. *Dammit.* I waited out their rides until the Lift finally descended toward Engineering. I radioed Chelsea the moment my feet hit the deck. "Gonna need a few more minutes."

"Lift didn't behave?" she asked.

"Never does." At least Valerie hadn't interfered this time.

Scurrying down the hall, I dodged my staff, lest they get the idea I was available for questions or concerns. *Not right now, guys.* At the end of the main corridor, off into an alcove, was a rarely used supply closet barely big enough for the computers it stored. I slipped inside and leaned back against a wall, lungs gasping.

"Okay. Come get me," I radioed.

"Anytime," she said, and my heart nearly leapt from my chest.

Not a second later, her lights brightened the room, and, for the first time since being in here, I sensed the tightness of the space in the darkness. My shoulders bumped shelves, my feet kicked computer parts, and if Chelsea didn't land correctly, she'd materialize within one herself. *This was a bad idea.*

"Chelsea," I said into the radio, but I was too late. The waterfall crested, a body underneath. Chelsea's body. Not in a wall, but inches from my own. With her lights gone, I couldn't see her because I'd forgotten to turn the lights on first. But I *felt* her presence, like electricity zipped between us, outlining her body for me, keeping us bound together. Her breath warmed my neck and smelled like peppermint.

"Hey," she said. "Oh, damn. Why's it dark? Trevor?"

"I'm here," I said, reaching out for her. I meant to grab her arm but brushed against her breasts by accident. My face shot up with warmth, surprising since all other blood surged south in a mighty roar. "Shit, sorry."

She laughed and ran her hands up my arms until her palms rested on my chest. "It's fine. Where's the light?"

I explored the wall behind me with my free hand until I flipped the switch. Light gushed through the room. I slammed my eyes shut. "Crap."

"Damn," Chelsea said. "Okay. Maybe dark was better."

"We'll adjust," I said. I didn't want the lights out again, or to touch something else by accident.

Oh, who the fuck was I kidding? I'd give anything to touch more of her, to *see* more of her.

"If you say so," she said.

We stood there, our eyes shut and adjusting for long moments. I held up my radio and told Helen the good news. Three for three today.

"Good work," Helen echoed again.

I dropped the radio into my pocket and peeled open my eyes. Chelsea's face was inches away from mine, her lips twisted in a smile and her cheeks flushed.

"You're getting good at teleporting," I said. My heartbeat raced. I swallowed, my mouth drying. She was so close; I needed to feel her lips on mine.

"Thanks," she said, chin tipped up. "It's because of you, though."

"Me?"

She finally opened her eyes, the green flecks in her irises arresting my breath. Gold encircled the edges, something I hadn't ever been close enough to appreciate before. God, I could get lost in her gaze for eternity.

"Yeah, you," she said. "I don't know how to describe it, but you're like a lighthouse on the coast. I can *feel* you, your presence, from everywhere on the ship if I concentrate. It's... weird."

"Weird," I echoed. "Well, at least it's not a bad thing."

Sweat beaded on the back of my neck, and the slight touch of her chest against mine sent tingles down my legs. Only Chelsea's hands separated us now. My pulse thundered in my ears, made sounds feel like they had to wade through cotton balls to get to my brain. Her fingers played with the chest pocket of my uniform. Goosebumps road up my arms at her touch.

"No, I didn't mean it like that. It's not at all bad. It's just weird. Like, I can't feel Helen, despite the fact we're supposedly both descended from Atlanteans. But you"—she tapped my chest once—"you're different."

Was it because I was Lemurian? Or because of that connection she and I supposedly shared? The words, "Well, I hope I feel good," tumbled from my mouth.

Are you fucking kidding me?

A snort emitted from Chelsea's nose, but she kept her face straight—for like a brief moment, before the corners of her mouth twisted up, and she laughed deep and loud. It was, hands down, the best sound I'd ever heard.

"God, I love you," she said. "Hilarious, and you don't even know it. Or mean it."

She gave me a compliment in there somewhere, but my idiot brain repeated its idiot actions and focused in on one word, and one word only. *Love.*

She cocked her head to the side with narrowed eyes, lips quirking. She stumbled back on her words. "I mean, not like *love*, love, just like... love." She punched my chest lightly. "Like, 'oh you, love you and your craziness.'"

She paused and looked up at me, her eyes searching mine. For what, I wasn't sure, but the light caught them just right, and, in a single second, I was mesmerized. Possibly for life. She'd never stop being this beautiful, and I never wanted her to stop being this close. Warmth bounced between us, piggybacking on the goose bumps I got every time she touched me.

I shoved my hands in my pockets, afraid of what I might do— not because I didn't want to kiss her, touch her back. But because I wasn't sure what signals just got the hell mixed up.

"Trevor?"

"Hmm?"

She snapped her fingers in front of my face. "You there?"

"Yeah."

She licked her lips. "Don't be mad."

"Mad?" How could I possibly be mad? "I'm not. You, uh, you caught me off guard. Like you always seem to do."

Her eyebrows rose playfully, her free hand moving to her hip. She still had one hand fisted in my shirt from the thwack she'd given me while retrieving her foot from her mouth. "Good thing?"

I scrunched my forehead, pretending to really give it a good, long thought. Her mouth opened, offended by my debate. *Good. Give me the upper hand for once.*

"I guess so," I said, finally.

"You *guess* so?" she asked, biting her lip.

My eyes zeroed in on the action, like she was freaking daring me to kiss her rather than jump on it herself. Seriously? Dare it was, then.

"I mean, normal is pretty boring," I said. "So is predictability."

I leaned in closer to her, running the back of my knuckles lightly up her arm. Her breath came in quick puffs as my fingers trailed over her shoulder to her chin. I cupped her warm cheek and lowered my head toward hers, my pulse punching in my chest. This was it. The moment that'd change everything.

"I kind of like how you're always three steps ahead of me." I leaned in closer still, hovering just above her lips and said, "Not many can claim that title."

Her fist tightened around my shirt and her eyes met mine. "Challenge accepted."

She closed the gap between us. Her mouth on mine felt like the first breath after a deep dive. It lit a fire inside of me, released a pressure on my lungs I didn't know existed. That freedom burning feeling I'd had the first time I saw her at the Franklin rushed me, washed me over with warmth and life. I cupped the back of her neck, adjusting the angle of the kiss. She slid her arms around me, pressing me to her, holding me there like she was afraid to let go.

So was I. I didn't want to leave this moment. Time hung around us as her tongue caressed mine and she pressed her fingers into my back. She gripped the front of my shirt and walked me back against a shelf. Items tumbled to the ground but neither of us moved to pick them up.

My radio blared to life. I jumped as the screech echoed off the walls.

"Boncore, pick the hell up already." Dave's voice. I hadn't even noticed it went off the first time.

"You've gotta be kidding me," I breathed. *Asshole.*

Chelsea snorted. A laugh exploded from her lips. I laughed right along with her.

"Seriously, Trevor. Pick up," Dave said again.

I depressed the TALK button, reaching behind me for the door handle. "Yeah. I'm here."

"Engineering. Now."

Chelsea rolled her eyes as we stepped out of the supply closet with drooped shoulders.

"Yeah," I said. "Literally here. Give me a minute." I shut off the radio and reached for her arm. "Sorry about that."

She shrugged, smiling. "It's okay. Go save Engineering."

I felt like that's all I ever did.

Chapter Sixteen

Chelsea

One month later.

My radio sprang to life, interrupting my amazing guitar riff. I tutted at the radio. It was hard enough writing new music while I was here, forget being constantly interrupted. The radio chirped again, demanding I answer.

"Danning," I said, finally.

"This is Captain Marks," he said on the other end, a slight hitch of *something* audible in his words. "We've found something I want you to look at. Could you please come to the Bridge?"

"Of course."

What'd they find? I set the radio aside and placed my sapphire blue guitar on its stand. I tugged on the top half of my uniform and zipped it up. Butterflies dashed laps in my stomach as I departed the Lift on the Bridge's Level. If what they'd found was something they wanted *me* to see, the find had to be big.

The Bridge doors opened. The Commander stood on the other side, his hands pressed behind his back. "Welcome back to the Bridge, Chelsea."

I flashed him a grin and joined Captain Marks in the center of the Bridge. I hadn't been up here since I met Christa. The Captain greeted me with a nod, then addressed an officer typing furiously at a station toward the front of the Bridge. "Ensign Olivarez, could you please put the structure on-screen for Ms. Danning?"

"Aye sir," Ensign Olivarez said. The name wasn't familiar, but I hadn't met many of the senior staff.

"What is it?" I asked the Captain.

My eyes caught Trevor at his station and Lieutenant Weyland standing guard in a corner. Trevor smiled and waved, launching my heart into somersaults, churning the butterflies with giddy, erratic thoughts.

"I hoped to get your impression first so it's an unbiased view. We're currently in the Sargasso Sea, much to Helm's dismay," Captain Marks said, looking over to his helmsmen. "Even with a SeaSatellite's design, it isn't very safe for us to be here, but this find is large."

"Why?" I asked.

"The Sargasso Sea is full of seaweed. It blocks up the engines and can hold us down for too long," Ensign Olivarez explained as he placed the external camera's view onto the center of the three main screens.

The reason they'd wanted an unbiased opinion became immediately apparent. Unfortunately, I didn't think I could give it to them. The structure, or, rather, the remnants of one, stood out even in the clutches of seaweed. Writing covered the roof, like a banner or a sign, but I couldn't make it out, much less translate it. I didn't know what I was looking at or why they thought I, a recent graduate, would. But the name 'Sargasso Sea' did ring a bell, nagging and high-pitched.

"Huh," I said.

The building was Greek, judging by the architecture. That's all I could surmise, and, because of that, it being here didn't make sense. Our depth and location in the mid-Atlantic didn't correlate to Greece in any way.

"What are your thoughts?" Captain Marks asked.

"Honestly? I don't know what to think. It looks Classical." Even though that didn't make sense. Then the bell regarding the Sargasso Sea chimed again, spilling its secrets. *Oh, hell no.* I turned away from the screen and met the Captain's gaze. "What you're thinking, it's not right."

"That's why we wanted an unbiased opinion," he said with a little nod, either to patronize me or suggest I'd be stupid not to accept his hypothesis.

Too bad I didn't care.

"That's not possible. You wanted me here because you know I've done research on Atlantis." But that didn't make this structure Atlantean. This *was not* Atlantis. Denial bloomed in my chest and hands, wringing them until it budded refusal. "No."

"Plato's story places the city here, or closer to North America," Ensign Olivarez cut in.

I pivoted my feet and faced him. His brown eyes glinted with surety. He wanted so desperately to be right. *Tough luck.*

"If it even existed, which it didn't," I said. There's no way in hell Atlantis was real. It's supposed to be a story, nothing more. But Helen's research...

"Then what are we looking at?" Captain Marks asked.

My eyes darted to the screen. What did they want me to tell them? "We're looking at a building that shouldn't be here." It was the only conclusion to make.

Ensign Olivarez chimed in, saying, "Readings suggest the building has air in it, probably thanks to the way it fell into the ocean. If we bring oxygen tanks until we can confirm the air is safe to breathe, we could take a quick look inside, Captain."

If only we could x-ray it to make sure an expedition like that would be worth it. "Who's to say the structure's even pressurized?" I asked.

Ensign Olivarez shrugged. "I can't explain it, but everything here says the main chamber is, in fact, pressurized. Air tight."

Captain Marks's fist rose to his mouth as he thought it over. He turned to me. "Do you think you could get a better idea of what we found if we sent a party over?"

Well, hell, I didn't know. This was so far above me. But I was hired to do exactly this, so how could I say no? And if he wanted to send people over, he must not think it was dangerous. In which case, I *so* wanted in. "Yes. But I want to go."

"We'll send over a party first to make sure it's safe. Weyland, you'll lead it. Take Lieutenant Commander Jackson, Ensign Olivarez, and a contingent with you. Secure the area and make sure it's actually as pressurized as the Ensign believes."

As Captain Marks spoke, officers stood and replacements took their seats. Everyone moved with a fluidity I hadn't seen before. I had to keep moving an inch or two around in a tiny circle to stay out of their way.

Captain Marks regarded me. "If it's safe, Dr. Gordon will go with you. Go meet with her, and she'll go over our landing procedures. Trevor, you go, too."

Trevor stood from his station with a nod and removed his headset. "Come on," he said, slipping his hand into mine. "Let's go."

◆

Dr. Gordon outfitted me with a wetsuit and a headset radio like the Bridge officers wore. We followed a science contingent to Shuttle Dock. I couldn't keep still on the Lift ride over. I held onto a handhold instead of sitting, bouncing on the balls of my feet and throwing my shoulders into a tiny dance as a tune hummed its way passed my lips. This wasn't Atlantis, *couldn't* be Atlantis, but it was cool. More importantly, this find was everything I'd ever dreamed of doing—and it was nice to get away from practicing teleportation, for a change.

There was always the possibility we wouldn't find a single thing—like with any archaeological site—but the prospect of it being a complete failure didn't remove the thrill. Surprisingly, I missed being in the field almost as much as I missed playing on stage.

"You look like you're going to explode with excitement," Trevor said, grinning.

I beamed at him. My heart fluttered as his grin reached his eyes. His blue irises danced like ocean waves in sunlight. After too long for my antsy brain to handle, we paired up to leave the shuttle, mocked up in wetsuits and scuba gear.

Trevor came up beside me. "Have you been diving before?"

"A long time ago as a kid in a ten-foot-deep swimming pool."

He exhaled a quick breath and smiled. "Right, so no."

He went over the basics and tugged at my suit straps so the oxygen tank fit tighter—a good thing, as him being this close swept all the air out of my lungs. My arms prickled with goose bumps as his fingers brushed my neck.

"You don't want your tank to go anywhere," he said.

I didn't want *him* to go anywhere. "Thanks."

He smiled, his fingers lingering. "Anytime."

My eyes fell to his lips, and I wet my own. Damn these people being around. I could sneak just one kiss, right?

Officers ushered us into the small dive pool before I could make a move, and we swam into the structure. I pulled myself out of the water, once we entered the room with the largest air pocket, and set the vest and tank aside. Not until I took off my goggles and pulled them down around my neck did I see the sheer splendor of the area. My breath caught in my throat, and my heart fluttered with butterflies of a whole new kind. I was so worried we wouldn't find anything; I hadn't given a single thought to the exact opposite.

Trevor nudged my arm with his elbow, smiling. Only he could make a wet scuba suit look this hot. It hugged his fit form, snug around his muscles. "You might want to shut your mouth sometime soon."

Mouth closed, I stood up and got a better view.

I'd been wrong about the Greek-style architecture, but what I was looking at, I had no idea. Graceful, wide arches stood with detailed, decorated columns marked with script—the weirdest mix of ancient art styles I'd ever seen. My eyes danced over the artwork strewn along the walls, a colorful, confusing mixture of frescos, reliefs, and paintings from a myriad of different eras. I had no other choice but to believe them all real and oddly familiar.

The muscles in my fingers tensed like they did when a surge of inspiration lit up my body. It shone a light into my mind that marked the way home. It urged me to move, to act, to grab a hold of this feeling and use it *now*.

But nothing lessened the puzzle of this place. The only other time in history I could think of something on this level happening was the Library of Alexandria—but those were books, not art. I mean, books lined the walls here too, but the sheer amount of sculptures, statues, and other art pieces and artifacts vastly outnumbered them. And the smell—musty, humid, but somehow also clean.

This wasn't possible. This was not possible at all. Moreover, a wave of nostalgia punched me in the gut, like when you walk into your childhood home you don't remember having lived in, but know, from your parents, that you did. You walk in and, instantly, you just *know*.

I'd clearly never been here before, but something—some part of me—sure made it felt like I had.

The Captain started to say something along the lines of, "So what do you think?" for quite possibly the eighth time in the last hour. I stopped listening as my eyes found the one oddity in the room that stood out amongst the others.

"Chelsea?" Captain Marks asked.

The rectangular chunk of black, reflective rock resting ten feet away seized my attention, demanding every stare and breath. The light in the room bounced off the relief in shimmering echoes, like a mirage on a road in the summer. Like waves reflecting sunlight.

The relief depicted a set of malnourished Egyptian figures with elongated heads and frumpy bellies, and with the wrong Egyptian god as the center of attention. It was the most distinctive thing in the room, especially to this archaeologist who loved Ancient Egyptian history.

I unzipped my wetsuit, shrugged off the sleeves, and demanded gloves from the closest science personnel. Someone handed me a pair, and I ambled over to the artwork. I lifted the relief carving off the mantle it rested on and inspected it, still unconvinced this wasn't a dream.

"One of these things is not like the others," I sang. To the Egyptian art piece in my hands I said, "You shouldn't be here."

Trevor came up beside me and peered at the object.

Captain Marks asked the question first. "What is it?"

"An Amarna period Ancient Egyptian relief," I whispered, not wanting to disturb the piece's submerged slumber. "Captain, I don't know what we've found, but in the interest of preserving this site until we do, I'd suggest we keep this a secret."

"Meaning what exactly?"

"Don't report this." I ran a gloved finger over the glazed ridges. It seared warmth into my hands in a good way—wild, pure, and warm. A magnetic force glued my hands to the piece.

"Why?" Captain Marks asked.

"Because we've stumbled across something that shouldn't exist," I told him, holding up the Amarna period piece in my hands. I displayed the artifact for all to see and met the Captain's eyes. "This clearly isn't a hoax, and there are easily hundreds of priceless ancient artifacts in here. That alone is worth protecting. But this"—I moved the Amarna piece for emphasis—"this shouldn't be here. When Akhenaten died, the Egyptians erased what they could of his effects on Ancient Egyptian history because of all the things he'd done. Amarna, the city he'd founded, was abandoned, his statues destroyed. Obviously some of it survived since we know about it, but this…"

I looked down at the relief. "Everything, to my knowledge, that we have from this period is… not this pretty, for lack of a better word. Nothing we have is this well taken care of or created in such a rich stone. If this piece sat here throughout the Amarna period, it would've been destroyed. And even if the Egyptians hadn't destroyed it, this wouldn't have been displayed on a mantle like a prize."

"What's the bottom line?" he asked.

"I don't have one. At least not yet." Like I'd said before, the sheer number of artifacts here demanded we lock the site down. Preserve and protect it. Beyond that… I didn't know. "Look, Captain, if we were closer to the Mediterranean and in the right area, I'd say this was a section of the Library of Alexandria. But even that wouldn't make sense. And, we're in the middle of the Atlantic, inside the Sargasso Sea, way too far away from Egypt to—"

Captain Marks is right.

The thought stole my breath and thundered through every bone in my body. A lead weight fell onto my shoulders. It rooted my words in my throat, unable to be spoken.

I looked around at all of the artifacts and books, and then again at the Amarna period piece, debating whether I should tell the Captain what I thought. Discoveries like this had a habit of changing the course of history. Like when archaeologists finally discovered the ruins of the city of Troy and discovered perhaps the story presented by Homer in his *Iliad* might have actually been true.

If my suspicions were correct, this find would do way more than change history.

It would rewrite it.

I swallowed hard, unable to make up my mind. To tell the Captain this room belonged to a long dead, assumed fictional city, would result in him either thinking I'm completely batshit crazy or, far worse, wanting to tell the world. But if you told the whole world Atlantis honest-to-god existed and ruins remained intact today, it'd open a large can of worms far beyond what the United States Navy could handle.

Still, I couldn't lie to the man who hired me instead of throwing me into the Brig. The Captain bet on me to be able to do something like this, to take a find and figure it out. I owed him. Even if it meant dumping Atlantis on his plate.

"Captain, I think this is something worth keeping quiet about for now," I reiterated, hoping he'd catch the implication so I wouldn't have to say *Atlantis* out loud. If this was related to Atlantis, the amount of wraps this would have to be kept under would surpass the sad attempt at keeping Area 51 on the down-low. Alien hunters had nothing on treasure hunters, that'd been proven time and time again.

The Captain shot me a meaningful look. "Is this what we thought?"

I nodded. "Maybe. We'll have to catalogue everything to be sure." I left out how the task would take longer than my internship would last for. In fact, this was way above me. "Captain, I think you need to bring someone else in. This isn't the kind of find you want to leave to an intern with a BA in Archaeology." When he hired me, he banked on shipwrecks or random amphorae, not possibly Atlantis.

Captain Marks nodded slowly. "My thoughts exactly. I'll have to speak with Admiral Dennett." His breath hitched, strained, against his words. He turned to the pool where we'd entered, a barely visible tremor wracking his hands.

He was panicking? In his position, with the possibility of hordes of treasure hunters bearing down on our position if this got out, I'd freak out, too.

Though, really, I already was.

Chapter Seventeen

Trevor

I knew exactly what SeaSat5 found. The recognition was instantaneous. A building in the middle of the Sargasso Sea— what else could these ruins be?

Then they called in Chelsea, like she had the answers. Like she was an *expert* on Atlantis. The Captain knew, though. The realization in his eyes, the indecision over what to do mixing with his own pride for finding the city, swirled together like a violent, jade gyre.

It wasn't Atlantis, but it was Atlantean.

It wasn't a city. It was an outpost, a lab, an archive.

It wasn't a museum, but a laboratory of all the things my parents told me bedtime stories about.

My chest constricted like I stood in a vice grip as I watched Chelsea pick up the Egyptian relief. Was it Link Piece? Assuming Helen's guesses about Chelsea were correct, I'd bet my head it was. A tiny old time travelling device just sitting there in Chelsea's hands, her none the wiser.

Shit. Did Valerie know about this? How long until she did?

Her words rung in my ears. *If any other powers show up on this ship.* Valerie didn't count Chelsea's strength. She'd definitely count this, not as a power but as a development toward war.

Chelsea continued making her deductions, and the others gawked at the artifacts, all oblivious to my anxiety. I turned away. If I told Thompson, he'd show up here in mere hours and cause hell to get the Pieces. But if I didn't…

I pulled in a deep, shaky breath. We'd finally become a pawn in their war.

"Trevor?" Chelsea called.

I turned to her with a fake grin fixed to my face. They didn't even know the weight of what they'd found, so giddy about something so dire. Would Chelsea forgive me if she knew?

"You're probably right," I said.

A half-smile slide across her face like when she was excited beyond words. She blushed when she noticed me looking. Then her smile sank.

"What's wrong?" I asked.

She frowned at the artifact in her hands as if told a bad joke. "I can't decide if I'm excited or terrified. If we don't protect this…" she trailed off, leaving the words unsaid.

The statement was truer than she knew. "We will," I assured her. We had to. *I* had to. "I need to go to the station."

Her frown deepened. "What for?"

"I want to get some notepads." A swift lie. It ripped my guts apart, but I needed time to think. To decide how this all might play out.

Her eyes lit up. "Good idea. Can you bring me a camera, too?" She cocked her head like she didn't want to burden me with the task, but I couldn't see her leaving this place anytime soon. Kid in a candy store? The analogy was a severe understatement. Chelsea looked at everything with such an innocent wonder; it made me unable to believe she was Atlantean at all.

An Atlantean would know what she'd found.

An Atlantean would find the biggest, most secure vault in the world and lock it all up.

I brought Chelsea the camera and then paced around my room for an hour. Thompson would be here within days, maybe less. And when he got here, he'd take the artifacts, he'd take SeaSat5, and he'd take Chelsea. Use her. Keep her. She'd be lost to me and there was nothing I could do about it except not say anything first. And I wouldn't. My lips were sealed tighter than my never-opened James Bond Golden Eye N64 game. I wouldn't tell anyone. So, the only way Thompson would find out was from Valerie, and she absolutely would spill every last bean.

Someone pounded loud and unyielding on my door. "Open the hell up!"

Valerie. I banged my forehead against a wall. Maybe she didn't know I was here.

"Now, Trevor," she growled.

She barged through the moment I loosened the lock and strode to the far wall before turning around and slamming her hands onto her hips. "Why didn't you tell me?"

"You know why, and it's not like Chelsea even knows what she's found. We can handle this; we can keep it safe. The find will still be in Lemurian hands, and the Atlanteans will never get it."

She clamped her mouth shut, looked away, and breathed in deeply. "An Atlantean *already* has the artifacts, Trevor. I'm not screwing around anymore. I'm following orders."

"Val—"

She held up a finger to stop me. "Don't even. We should have ended this before today. That *site* your girlfriend is freaking out over is filled with artifacts. It's a veritable tool shed."

So Valerie thought Link Pieces littered the place. The way Chelsea looked at them all, maybe they did. "Not today. Please don't report the find today."

"Why the hell not?" she snapped, venom lacing every syllable.

Because this was Chelsea's dream? Because she didn't even know the power she held in her hands? "We have no reason to believe any of those artifacts are what Thompson's and my mother's crew are after."

"We also have no reason to think the contrary." She charged toward me. "Listen, Trevor. This is why we got assigned to SeaSatellite5. To covertly observe and report if anything was found. If even *one* of those stupid artifacts is a Link Piece, it's over. The remaining Atlanteans will be here in days, and they'll take Dr. Gordon and your girlfriend, too."

My stomach somersaulted over itself, shrinking and spinning. "I'll up the shield. Increase power output." But Chelsea would be taken either way. The Atlanteans needed her. The Lemurians want her kind killed.

Valerie shook her head. "The shield didn't keep Chelsea out. Sure as hell won't keep Thompson out, either. The shield never could."

My eyes met hers. She *had* known all along. But had she never once called me out on my shield modifications until Chelsea arrived. Why?

"He won't come," I said.

"You're in the absolute worst type of denial, Trevor. Get the hell over it."

I ran my hands through my hair. I'd give anything for a moment alone to think. "Not today. Give me a day or two. Let me at least figure out a way to keep Chelsea from getting caught up in this, then you can do what you want."

Valerie swallowed her conviction so hard, her throat convulsed. Her fists clenched at her hips. "Fine." Detestation punctuated the word. "You have two days, because we've been good friends for so long. But, I swear to god, Trevor, if this goes south, our friendship won't mean shit. I will *not* fail them."

She stormed past me, knocking her shoulder against mine, and stomped out of my quarters.

I was so screwed.

I gave myself my own form of quarters confinement, not moving from where Valerie fled past me until my stomach rumbled. I hadn't eaten in over nine hours. Or moved in four.

I shook out my shoulders and headed out for the Dining Decks, praying not to run into anyone. I couldn't hide the way my chest constricted around every rib, or how my palms grew slicker by the second. If the Captain found out what Valerie and I actually got assigned here for, assuming they believed all the Lemuria crap, we'd be thrown off in seconds. SeaSat5 wouldn't be protected and then there'd be no barrier between the artifacts and Thompson. Between Thompson and Chelsea.

I traveled to the Lift and through a food line on the Dining Decks in solitude, for which I was grateful. Most of the guys were at the outpost or on Bridge duty. With any luck, Valerie got involved in one of those things, too. Was Chelsea still over there?

After a few moments of deliberation, I gulped down a heaping plate of pasta and a soda, then rode the Lift to Chelsea's quarters. I padded along to her door and looked through the opening at the top. She sat at her desk, Valerie nowhere in sight. All anxiety washed away in an instant.

Chelsea. Maybe she'd help me clear my head, help me figure out a way to keep her safe without me telling her anything.

I knocked on the door. She didn't move. She hunched over her desk, reading, so I tried the door handle. It was unlocked. I grinned and snuck up behind her.

Mouth pressed against her ear, I whispered, "Whatcha reading?"

Chelsea jumped a foot into the air. She spun her chair and swatted at me. "That was mean!"

I raised my hands in defense. "I knocked."

She huffed. "You scared the crap out of me."

"Yeah, yeah," I said, bending down to kiss her soft lips. The scent of her vanilla shampoo lingered in the air around us. She must have gotten back earlier than I thought. My thumb traced a lazy circle on her cheek. Was every part of her this soft? "What's the book about?"

She turned her head into my palm. Her warm breath on my hand made me feel alive, like I could hold onto her forever if she let me. "It's one of the texts from the outpost. I can't understand it, but it's still fun to look at."

I shook my head. "You archaeologists."

Her eyebrows rose. "And what do you do for fun again?"

My jaw slid open and then closed. "Touché."

"What brought you here? Not that I'm not happy to see you." Chelsea stood, and we moved to her bed.

I lay back and pulled her to me so her head rested on my chest. "Just checking in."

"Uh-huh."

"You don't believe me?"

A wicked smile encompassed her face. "I don't believe you came here without ulterior motives."

I shrugged. "You were excited earlier, so I backed off to let you have your glory. I haven't seen you since."

"So, you missed me?"

"Of course." She nestled closer to me. She was so small, lying there in my arms. "How's it going over at the outpost?"

She blew out a breath that shifted her bangs. "It's a lot. Captain Marks called in for a military archaeologist. Someone they can trust."

I lifted a hand and twirled a lock of her hair around my fingers. Her hand rested on my abdomen. I let go of her hair and intertwined my fingers with hers.

"Hopefully they'll find someone soon," I said. Otherwise the forty-eight hours Valerie had given me to get Chelsea to safety would be up, and who knew what would happen next. There's no way Chelsea would leave without a replacement archaeologist being here first.

She nodded. "I hope so. Guess we'll see, won't we?"

A chill ran through me as she untangled our fingers and leaned over me. Her lips began a slow dance with mine, turning slowly into something wild and fierce. I tangled my fingers in her hair, trying to hold her there for as long as possible.

The memory of our fleeting encounter in Boston grasped at my mind like a vice grip. How different would things have been if I'd managed to stay hidden from Lieutenant Weyland and the rest of the soldiers a little longer? If I'd accepted her invitation inside the Franklin, or met her before she exited into the alley?

Ah, hell, who was I kidding? Chelsea still would've teleported to me. The only way I could've made absolutely sure she'd never gotten wrapped up in this stupid war is if I'd never met her.

I squeezed my eyes closed. Gently, I pulled away, blinking hard at the burning in my eyes. I tucked a loose strand of hair behind her ear as my heart lodged in my throat. "I actually need to get back to Engineering. I just wanted to stop by to see how you were doing."

I must've been doing a great job keeping my emotions hidden because Chelsea smiled. Her grin lit up her face in ways that left me feeling as if a battering ram had slammed into my gut.

"Never better. I can't believe I almost didn't want to take this gig. Seriously, being here with you, finding this site... it's the best I've felt in a long time," she replied.

My ribs felt like they were breaking, I placed a long kiss on her forehead, then stood from the bed. "Check in with you later?"

Chelsea nodded. "Sounds like a plan."

Forcing a smile, I left her room and casually walked to the Lift, in case she was watching. But the moment the Lift's doors closed, my happiness, my hope to keep Chelsea safe and outside of this war, shattered.

The only way to protect Chelsea was to convince her to teleport off SeaSatellite5, forget about me, and never come back.

Chapter Eighteen

Chelsea

Christa picked me up at 6:30 a.m. sharp. I hiked my pack over a shoulder and followed her onto the Lift.

"We have a helper for today," she said, arms filled with folders and binders. "Two, actually."

"Who?"

"Trevor and Lieutenant James, but let's enjoy company without the boys while we can." She inclined her head. "How are things going with Dr. Gordon?"

Guess Dave's wrist had been getting better fast if he was coming out to help.

"Good," I answered honestly, smiling. "I figured out a new way to control my teleportation." Connections mattered more than intense emotions, like the connection to my quarters, to Trevor, or to Helen's office. I still had to figure out how to establish connections outside of constantly visiting a location, but it was still progress.

"I'm glad," Christa said.

The Lift stopped, and we picked up a few lab techs on the science decks and continued downward.

"I can't even imagine having that ability. Seems equal parts frustrating and convenient," Christa said.

I nodded. "Yeah. I'm hoping I'll get good enough at it, though, that I can drop back to Boston for band practice whenever I feel like it."

"See, convenient. Also, I was thinking"—she tugged a file folder out of her stack—"that we could start those cuneiform lessons."

Excitement bubbled in my throat, and I fought not to squeal like a thirteen-year-old girl. I flashed her a grin. "Seriously?"

Christa laughed and handed me the file. "Yes. I've seen it at the outpost, and I already promised I'd teach you, anyway. Figured you can help until Captain Marks gets a military archaeologist here."

"You mean a real archaeologist," I said dryly. I skimmed the paper containing an alphabet and other basics. *Cuneiform basics.*

"You're a real archaeologist, Chelsea."

"Okay, yeah, but I mean an experienced one. You know, with a PhD and publications and decades of field research."

"This will launch you in that direction."

I looked at her. "Atlantis? Yeah. Let me hand in evidence for a fabled lost city as my application for grad school. That'll go over *real* well."

She shrugged, smiling. "Just trying to help."

The Lift *dinged* its arrival, and the doors opened to Shuttle Dock. Trevor and Dave stood in the middle, ready to leave. Dave still had a cast, heavy and blue, around his wrist, but he wore a smile so I assumed he was okay. Aside from the four of us, only one other officer remained to operate the doors and docking clamps.

Trevor had two coffees in hand and offered me one.

"Thanks," I said, smiling at him.

"Anytime." He brushed his lips quickly over mine. "Ready to head over?"

"Oh, yeah."

We donned our gear and ambled to the outpost. This place, so filled with ancient artifacts and trinkets from all over the ancient world, places I'd only ever dreamed of being able to go, captivated me. It stole my breath every time I set foot on the marble floors. Every fresco, every relief, all the artworks and amphorae; it was hard to believe this place was actually real. But the saltwater outside the walls vibrated in my bones, like it was a part of me as much as a cocoon for this building. It ripped away any doubt.

This outpost was real. Maybe it wasn't even an outpost. It looked more like a library or museum or… anything but a settled garrison.

"I'll start on the west side of the room today," Christa said. "Maybe we can explore farther if Ensign Olivarez gives us the okay."

"He's still imaging the extent of the building?" Trevor asked.

"Yes," answered Christa. "Turns out it's a lot more expansive than we thought, but we can't be sure how structurally sound everything is."

"This room is protected for some reason," I told Trevor. We still hadn't discovered how the original builders had waterproofed and pressurized the room given their probable technology level at the time it was built.

"Interesting," Trevor mumbled.

He studied the walls and some of the artifacts for long moments. He'd acted weird yesterday after we'd found the structure, almost scared instead of excited. I didn't expect everyone to fangirl like I did over archaeological finds of the century, but his reaction had felt out of place. I'd shaken it off and focused on the work ahead of me, but the worry circled back.

I stepped in beside him as he paced toward the east side of the room and slipped my hand in his. "You okay?"

His eyes met mine. Dark bags hung below them. "Yeah. Just tired."

"You could have slept in."

He shook his head. "No. This find is huge, and until archaeological back-up arrives, you and Christa need whatever help you can get."

"We have a whole science team," Dave called from the far side of the room. "It's kind of their job."

"To work with sea fungus and biologics, not artifacts," Trevor said.

"It's whatever," I said. "We'll be okay as long as no one breaks anything." Would I have preferred other archaeologists do the work? Yeah. But these scientists could handle it.

I approached a wardrobe in the corner. It had caught my eye late last night, sometime after Trevor left for SeaSatelite5, but I hadn't gotten the chance to check it out. It was made out of a dark wood, sanded cleanly, and finished with some weird dye. Markings I didn't recognize covered its face. So, not Greek, hieroglyphics, or cuneiform. Not that I could read any of them, anyway. No, its clearly struck lines and curves held unmistakable age, like the book I'd become attached to and had snuck over to SeaSatellite5. It had called to me, begging me to pick it up and take care of it.

My fingers brushed the metal knobs of the wardrobe, and I tugged, lightly at first, then harder. The doors didn't budge. "Hmph," I muttered. "Why won't you open?"

"Here, let me try," Trevor said, taking my spot.

I wanted to say if *my* strength couldn't get it open, his surely wouldn't, but I didn't have time. He heaved hard, once, and the doors gave like nothing had held them shut the whole time. Something tumbled out with the swing of the doors, landing on Trevor and dragging him to the marble floor in a wave of bodies.

He stared at it for long moments before reacting. Trevor's eyes grew wide and he paled to the shade of paper. "Shit, what the fuck? Get it off. Get it *off*." But his hands wouldn't cooperate with the command.

I stood, frozen, stuck between wanting to laugh at the scene and wanting to rid him of the remains.

"Holy fuck," Dave exclaimed, rushing over with Christa in tow.

"Careful," I said, finally bending down to help Trevor. I slid the remains off his chest and gently placed them on the floor. "Don't break anything."

"Don't *break* anything?" Trevor breathed. "Are you *kidding* me?"

I slapped a hand over my mouth to keep myself from laughing.

"Not everyone likes this crap," he said, eyes wandering again to the remains.

I followed, taking in the sight of skin dried tight around an adult body. Dark hair remained intact, but the lips had shriveled away, teeth fully barred. Dark eye sockets sat pitted where eyes used to be. Its—*her*, I decided, looking at the dress she'd been entombed in—arms weren't bound in front like Egyptian mummies but fell around the body, which had given the earlier impression of hugging Trevor. She had been an adult when she died. But without time and someone more qualified to deal with remains, I couldn't determine anything else.

Trevor paled more, if possible, before his face took on a sickly green color.

"Trevor?" I asked him.

"Oh god." He rushed for a trashcan left here overnight and hurled his breakfast inside. Possibly dinner last night too, because it kept coming until he did nothing but dry heave.

I rubbed his back. The first time I'd seen remains up close, I'd been pretty nauseated, too.

He brushed me away. "Go do your thing. God that's disguising."

"That's mummification. Not *Egyptian* mummification, but what happens when—"

"Dry space over time, I got it." His face flushed green, and he heaved again.

"Shit," Dave interrupted us. "Chelsea, look at that."

"What the hell?" Christa chimed in.

I spun to see what enthralled them so much—and couldn't breathe. In my rush to glance over the woman's remains and help Trevor, I'd missed the inside of the wardrobe completely. A reflective surface covered the inside. Tubes like those on life-support machines hung down from the ceiling, but a quick glance above revealed the tubes didn't run through the wardrobe's top. "What in the world?"

I stepped in beside Dave and Christa, and ran my fingers along the inside. It was smooth like plastic but heavy like metal.

Restraints for arms, legs, and a torso had been soldered against the back wall. If the woman had been hooked into them, she wouldn't have fallen.

A crack caught my eye at the bottom of the chamber. I knelt down and ran a finger along it. Sure enough, it ran deep. I plucked a flashlight from my uniform pocket and flashed it over the crack. Marble showed through from the bottom. It was the floor beneath the wardrobe.

"I have no idea what this is," I stammered. Actually, I had a million ideas, all based on sci-fi movies and books and things that shouldn't exist in real life.

"Any ideas I have involve aliens," Dave offered.

Christa nodded beside me, her eyes running the length of the wardrobe. "Oh yeah. That's all I got, too."

I glanced over my shoulder at Trevor. "You should take a look. You and Dave are the only people here who might figure it out."

Trevor hobbled over, a hand pressed to his stomach. "Is it that strange—" He froze five feet from us, his hand falling from his stomach to his side. "Ho-ly shit."

"Awful lot of that being said today," I pointed out.

"What do you think?" asked Christa.

Trevor pointed to the wardrobe. "I think I agree with Dave. All I got is aliens." But the way his eyes wouldn't quite drift from the innards of the wardrobe made me question that. He definitely had an idea. He just wouldn't voice it. I frowned. Why?

"We should tell the Captain," Dave said. "Pronto. Mummified remains and a sci-fi wardrobe is too much to wait."

I nodded. "Absolutely. I'll go back now."

"We all should," Trevor said.

"No. Someone's got to stay here with the remains," I said.

Dave clapped my shoulder. "Think it's all you, Chelsea. No one else has the stomach for it." He winked at Trevor, who flipped him the bird in return.

"I'll stay, then." To Christa I said, "Bring back a science team. Tell them we need a bag, a stretcher, and a way to preserve the remains."

She nodded and waved Dave and Trevor to the entrance pool. "Will do. Come on, boys."

Trevor groaned. "Sorry, Chelsea."

"For what?" I asked. "Not holding your stomach?"

He nodded.

"I don't do remains either, Trevor. That's why I'm in archaeology, not bio-anthropology. Mummies are different, I guess." My eyes wandered to the remains. Yeah, it was pretty gross. But nothing oozed or pulsed or anything. It was basically a skeleton. "Just go. It's cool."

He shed a small smile, but it ended on a wince. "Have fun or something."

I snorted. "Get out of here."

They went, leaving me alone with Mrs. Mummy.

Chapter Nineteen

Trevor

Absolutely disgusting, that's what that mummy was. And to discover some advanced tech had housed that *thing* for thousands of years on top of it? Nothing in this outpost-museum-whatever made any sense. Until I remembered it belonged to the Atlanteans, who had to advance technologically to battle the Lemurians for control of time travel. *Then* it all started to make sense.

Dave wasn't far off in his 'aliens' deduction. I guessed the woman had tried to preserve herself in a life stasis chamber or something, a machine that'd keep her alive. But why she felt the need to use it, and why Atlantis had them in the first place, I had no idea.

My stomach calmed after a stint in the Infirmary, where the on-duty doctor sent me on my way with some anti-nausea pills. I took some and hurried for Chelsea's office to see if she'd ever returned from the outpost. She sat at her desk, typing away at her keyboard. I knocked on the door frame.

She looked up and smiled easy. "Hey. Feeling better?"

My breath hitched. Would I ever get over her smile? God, I

hoped not.

I nodded. "Yeah, thanks."

She leveled me with her stunning hazel eyes. "Most people can't handle bones. Mummified remains? Yeah, it's okay to puke."

"I know."

Chelsea finished her email and swiveled the desk chair my way. "The military archaeologist is flying in tomorrow morning. I can't wait to show him the remains."

I tried to look enthused. "I'm sure he'll love it." Although, I couldn't fathom why.

She smiled and reached a hand to mine. I took it and interlocked our fingers. Having her hand in mine felt like home, like becoming whole. I ran my thumb in circles over the knuckle on her thumb.

"I kind of want to go over one last time before he gets here," she said. "You know. One last adventure on my own in this."

"We were all there this morning," I said. Which was stupid because it didn't matter to her. She'd live over there if Captain Marks let her.

"Go with me?" She flashed me wide, hazel eyes. How could I say no?

"Right now?"

She bit her lip. "Yeah? Is that okay?"

I glanced at the clock. 5:36 p.m. Too early to say it was too late. But she was so eager, so enjoying living her dream. Honestly, being over there creeped me out. Not because of the mummy or the weird tech in the wardrobe, but because the more time I spent within the outpost's walls, the more foreboding the place felt. Like the walls would cave in on only me, drowning me and my Lemurian heritage, reminding me how desperately I needed to find the courage to convince Chelsea to leave SeaSatellite5 for her own safety.

Instead, I went with, "Sure, why not. Want to grab dinner and eat it there?"

Coward.

Her face contorted mischievously. "Think you can stomach eating dinner near the wardrobe?"

"Hilarious." I stood. "Yeah. I'll pick us up some boxes and meet you down there?"

She stood on her tiptoes and wrapped her arms around my neck, her breath warm on my face. "Sounds like a plan."

I pressed a hand to the small of her back and kissed her. She fell into it, a quick kiss diving deeper, becoming more ferocious as her fingers slid into my hair. The taste of her was intoxicating; her touch lifted weights off my chest, sent my stomach fluttering. I held her to me, not wanting to ever let go. How had she come to mean so much in so little time? Why could I not let her go, even if it meant she'd be safe?

Her kiss was my air, her body my earth. Grounding me. Keeping me sane and level while lighting a fire inside me; I had no idea it could blaze so bright and wild. It's like her entire being gave me more purpose in life than I'd felt in all my nineteen years. I pulled her closer, tighter, soaking up her strength and fire and love of life while she still offered it to me.

She pulled back, breathless, and it nearly killed me. Like someone had dumped water on the only fire keeping me warm.

"If we keep this up, we won't make it," she said.

I rested my forehead on hers, my cheeks aching from a forced smile. "Then why don't we pick it up over there?"

Chelsea grinned and relaxed away from me. "Okay. I'll grab my pack and meet you in Shuttle Dock in five."

"See you there."

I watched her go. The find made her happy and—despite what it might mean for me and the war we're all wrapped in—I'd do anything to keep her in this moment. She'd uncovered evidence of Atlantis, something people had tried to prove for centuries. Something she certainly never intended to discover. It was a career-defining find. But it was also a death sentence, the first shot in a war between our ancestors—ancestors she didn't even know I had.

I had to tell her the truth.

I was running out of time.

We ate dinner on a tarp that covered the marble floor, underneath lights left by the science team in an unexplored section of the chamber. Chelsea had wanted to see what else was in this area, but we'd gotten sidetracked by dinner and talking.

"This is the coolest thing to ever happen to me," Chelsea said. "Even if it might end my career before it starts."

"Why would it end your career?"

She waved at the magnificence of the artifact cache around us. "Even if people took it seriously, this find will rewrite history. People don't like to do that. And, besides, no one's going to believe all these artifacts came from one spot. No one's going to accept it all as evidence of Plato's lost city. Assuming our guess is correct to begin with."

"I think it is." I *knew* we sat on Atlantean territory. But I couldn't tell her why without explaining Lemuria and the war, and, though I knew I had to at some point, the fact this night was going (pretty much) perfectly made me not want to open *that* can of time traveling worms just now. "For what it's worth."

"Well," she said, leaning in closer to me, "If you had any sort of background in archaeology or history, I'd believe you."

"Wow. So glad my master's in engineering means *so* little."

She laughed. "I didn't say that." Chills ran down my spine as her lips brushed my ear. "Just means you know how to work things." Her finger trailed a line up my arm. "Fix them. *Play* them."

Her words sent a tidal wave of chills down my spine straight to my dick. I cupped her cheek and drew her lips to mine. She responded instantly, deepening the kiss as her fingers ran through my hair. I wrapped an arm around her and drew her close. Her tongue caressed mine, and I savored her taste, her presence, as if it were the only thing keeping me alive. How had she become everything so quickly? So *suddenly*?

I pulled back and searched her eyes for any semblance of what I felt being reciprocated. And I saw it. God, I saw it. It was like her soul peaked through, reached right out and tugged on mine, drawing me in, holding me there.

I held her face, losing myself and seeing clarity in her eyes all at the same time. So what if she were Atlantean? So what if her parents knew? She wasn't my enemy. This wasn't 2,000 BC. This was here and now, and all that mattered was this girl in my arms. I didn't need more encouragement than that. Fuck this war and everything it stood for. Let Valerie tell Thompson Link Pieces were on board. God help me, I'd make him see reason when it came to Chelsea. She wasn't a threat, and I was never, ever letting her go.

She rolled her hips and nipped my lip. It hauled me back into the moment. Blood surged south like a thunderstorm with every thrust, lightning striking everywhere her hands explored and massaged. I rolled us over and hovered over her, drinking in the need in her golden ocean eyes. It pulled me under until I could barely breathe. Who needed to breathe? I needed her, all of her. She alone was my life preserver *and* the water tugging me down. As long as I held on tight, as long as I never let her go, I'd surface in time to inhale. In time to be drawn back under. I didn't need to worry at all as long as she was with me.

I kissed down her neck, across her collarbone to the bare skin above her tank top, before returning to the soft spot on her neck. She moaned, holding the back of my neck with one hand. I rocked against her and shot out a hand to steady myself.

Only, I didn't land on the floor, but on a round, hard object that tumbled under my weight. I fell with it, rolling to not land on Chelsea, and the floor gave out underneath me—just a few inches, dipping me down. Like a pressure plate. Like all those damned Indiana Jones movies.

I snapped into action, fully expecting a shower of poison darts, and tumbled on top of Chelsea just in case. My body tensed, ready for the hit. But nothing happened.

"Whoa," she said. "What was that for?"

I pointed to the indent in the floor. "Pressure plate."

A rumbling sounded near our heads. We both looked up through dust clouds at the shaking walls. A portion of the wall behind us receded until the only thing left was a doorway that wasn't there before.

"*More* secrets?" I asked.

"It's a thousand-year-old building. Should we check it out?"

My Indiana Jones loving heart said no, because secret passageways usually led to death—and because I *really* wanted to resume what we'd been doing—but Chelsea was already wiggling out from under me. She reached into her pack and withdrew two flashlights and a pair of gloves for each of us. I turned mine on and shone the beam through the doorway. The light bounced off walls and dust, then reflected against something shiny. A whole *lot* of something shiny.

"Oh my god," Chelsea exclaimed. She pushed past me into the room. "Trevor, grab one of those lamps."

I didn't want to, mostly because I wasn't sure what we'd found. I grabbed a lamp and placed it right inside the new room. The light revealed shelves of relics like our Artifact Room on SeaSatellite5. My eyes scurried to count them all. Five. Ten. Twenty shelves, stocked *full* of busts, small statues, pottery, paintings, and things I didn't recognize.

Chelsea looked at each in turn, her fingers brushing some longer than others. Were those the Link Pieces Valerie and my family were so concerned about? Had we found an entire *room* of Link Piece time travel tools? My heart thudded in my chest so forcefully, I thought it'd explode out of its confines, but it continued to beat like a bass drum.

Chelsea finally stopped and turned to me, a hand running through her hair. "Trevor."

"I know."

"This is amazing."

"I know." No, it was terrifying. All these tools, all these *weapons* Thompson and my mother would go to war over.

"What if this whole structure is filled with artifacts? Every single room on every floor. Every wing. Every *thing*."

It'd be my worst nightmare, that's what. I wouldn't doubt that Atlanteans hoarded Link Pieces in this place. If they were fighting a long-time war, if Atlantis really wanted sole control of time travel, they'd absolutely stockpile them.

Except this building wasn't just a museum or lab. It absolutely *was* an outpost, a platform for war, and I'd inadvertently handed it over to an Atlantean. To Chelsea. To the military.

I just reignited a war.

Chapter Twenty

Chelsea

I swiped my keycard at the console outside the Bridge and entered. For two days, I'd had the outpost-lab to myself, and today I'd have to hand it off. Was it possible to be excited and sad at the same time? Because that's how I felt: excited to share but overprotective of the find. Sad to see it be explored by someone else. Someone outside the crew of SeaSatellite5.

Ensign Olivarez sat ready for me at his station, views of the outpost onscreen.

I stood beside him. "Hey. What's it looking like, Ensign?"

"Freddy," he reminded me again. "If you insist I call you by your first name, call me by mine."

I flashed him a smirk and checked out his name patch. "Okay, *Alfredo*." He gave me a *come on* look, and I shrugged. "Fine, Freddy, what's it looking like today?"

Freddy shifted screens and pointed to a part of the complex I hadn't seen before. "We found a fourth floor, also flooded. I didn't expect to find a lot from a bird's eye view, and the auto-DSVs aren't finding anything, either. Everything else will have to be discovered hands-on."

Figured. I sighed. "Sounds good to me."

Freddy shifted screens to NANA readings. "It'll also have to sound good to the Captain, or you aren't going to explore anything, period."

"I know." I stepped away from Freddy's station. "The military archaeologist is flying in today, anyway."

"When?" he asked, eyes on his station.

I didn't know for sure. Didn't even know their name. "I'd assume not long after we flip."

"So, about thirty minutes from now."

I checked my watch. Just enough time to catch breakfast. My stomach grumbled an agreement.

Freddy laughed, apparently having heard it. "Better get some food, then don your briefing look. Rumor says you're the one giving it."

Public speaking, my favorite thing. "Great."

<hr/>

Exactly forty-two minutes later, SeaSatellite5 flipped to accommodate a helicopter landing to drop off the military archaeologist. I sat in the Briefing Room and stared at the Amarna piece, waiting. The door clicked open to Captain Marks and another man. He shut the door behind him and greeted me.

I stood and shook hands with the military archaeologist. "Hi, I'm Chelsea."

"Doctor Connor Hill." Dr. Hill was in his early thirties, with dark charcoal hair and a strange favoritism of his left foot. He stood there, off-center, his right foot stretched out before him.

"A civilian?" I asked.

Dr. Hill gave me a small smile. "I work for the military, but I'm not one of their flyboys."

I smiled. To be honest, I was afraid of what a strictly military archaeologist would mean. There weren't many, and of those who bore actual ranks, their duties weren't exactly condoned by the rest of the archaeological academic body.

"Thank you for coming," I said.

"Rumor has it you think you've found something Atlantean." He paused before adding, "and a mummy."

We all took our seats at the table, and I pushed the Amarna piece to Dr. Hill.

"This is what gave it away for me, but yes, Atlantean. The complex is made up of a small number of rooms and a few floors, so it's not the whole city. But the amount of artifacts, art work, and texts in there is far too overwhelming for me to handle alone. It's incredible, as are the remains. I'm not good with that stuff, though, so I can't tell you much about her."

"I'll have my archaeological team work on that immediately." Dr. Hill looked at the Amarna piece for a few more moments and then up at me. "*This* is incredible."

I smiled at him. "Wait until you see the rest."

"When can we go over?" he asked, eagerness lacing his words and expression. I couldn't blame him. Atlantis. It still didn't feel real half the time.

"If you go now, you'll have to stay there until we flip the ship, or we can wait an hour and all go together," Captain Marks said.

I looked at Dr. Hill, who stared at the piece, mesmerized. "We can go over now, and I can babysit Dr. Hill," I told the Captain. "If it's okay with you, sir."

"I'll send Lieutenant James with you," he said. "I would send the Lieutenant Commander, but I need her at Communications for a bit longer."

"Should I take Dr. Hill to get suited up?"

"Yes. I'll have Lieutenant James meet you downstairs."

He stood from the table, and the rest of us followed. I led Dr. Hill down to Shuttle Dock and got him set up in a wetsuit before donning my own. On the ride over, we discussed how unqualified I was for this, and if he had the connections to get me qualified when this was complete. I then recounted the mummy story for him. And the secret room.

When we got to the complex—Dave in tow—Dr. Hill couldn't keep his jaw from falling open. He looked like I must have: giddy with excitement but focused with intrigue, like he couldn't believe this was real. Then he pulled himself together with a deep breath, and headed straight for the books.

"Most of them are in a language our Communications Officer can't read," I said, trailing after him. "We think it's related to Greek, but she can't figure out how."

Hill nodded. He picked up a book and, after a few moments, said, "I've seen this language before, but it's rare."

He can read it? Or does he just recognize it? And just how rare was *rare?*

"What is it?" I asked him.

"I suppose it'd be the written language of the Atlanteans, if you found the texts here," Dr. Hill said with a shrug, like his words held no weight at all. But they did. *The written language of Atlantis.* So. Freaking. Cool. *Ohmigod.*

"Cool," Dave said, flipping through the pages of his own book. He had it balanced on his good hand, using his knee for support. Seeing the cast still on him made a guilty pit form in my stomach.

I wandered over to a table we set up and snagged the journal that'd captivated me since the other day. "This is written in the same language. Think you can read it?"

"Maybe," he said, eyeing the journal. He took it from me and scanned a few of the handwritten pages. Some had a string of letters near the top or bottom of the pages, written in a different style from the rest of the words. "Huh."

"Huh, what?" Dave asked before I did. *Huh* wasn't a good enough response.

Dr. Hill held up a finger, remaining silent a moment longer. I turned from him, busying myself with surveying our findings. Art. Texts. Thousands of years of history slept here in a watery slumber. I didn't want to disturb any of them, but the prospect of what we'd learn was too tempting to leave the artifacts alone. When I was sure it'd been at least five minutes since he last spoke, I asked Dr. Hill again what the journal said.

His eyebrows furrowed together. "It's an interesting story about a couple who escaped Atlantis with a small child."

"Escaped?"

Dr. Hill nodded.

"Why would you want to escape a supposedly amazing city?"

"Why do people want to escape paradise, you mean? Plenty of reasons. I can work on a translation, if you'd like." He didn't look up from the text once.

All righty, then.

We went over what I'd already done and what we still needed to do. During the third or fourth hour, after Dave left due to boredom, I moved to the wardrobe, intent on showing Dr. Hill how we'd found the mummy. But I stopped short, my eyes zeroing in on a drip of water. Then another, and another. I walked underneath the drip and inspected it. The hole widened, water slicking my face in a steady stream. "Uh, Dr. Hill?"

"Yes?" His face didn't leave the book in his hands.

The crack widened again.

"We've got a leak. I need something to plug it with," I said.

Dr. Hill looked up to where the water now flowed in a steady stream above my head, soaking my clothes and the floor beneath us. I grabbed a stool and stood on it, throwing my hands up, trying to plug the leak.

The water rushed out past my hands in torrents.

"Help!" Panic sparked a flush of adrenaline. *The artifacts. This can't happen!*

Dr. Hill ran to where I stood helplessly staring at the water. The pressure around the hole broke, and it expanded, allowing waves of water in. I was thrown off my stool and landed hard on the ground, wind knocked out of me. This was the find of the century, and it would be drowned like its parent city. I couldn't let that happen. I couldn't.

No! The word echoed through me to the very core of my being. The torrent slipped into focus, like a super high-def camera had sprung to life inside my mind. I stood up through the torrents of water with my palm held toward the hole, focusing on nothing but the flow of the water and wanting it—no, *needing* it to go the opposite way, out toward the ocean.

Something snapped taut inside me and laser-focused my vision. The water flowed backwards, following some invisible push from my hands.

Then I blacked out.

◆

They ran, feet plunking against the puddle-ridden road. The man gripped his wife's arm tight, her other arm pressing her toddler flush against her chest. The baby didn't make a sound, despite the rain pouring down on all three of them.

The family took refuge in a building with walls and staircases spiraling to a high ceiling, every surface laden with artifacts and paintings. The toddler stared at them, unaware of her parents' frantic movements.

A flash. A crashing sound. A blue light.

Then nothing, nothing.

◆

My eyes fluttered open, head pounding. I lifted a hand to cradle the aching, but an IV line greeted me instead. I cringed. *Gross.*

"I see someone's finally awake."

Trevor sat in a chair next to my bed. He closed the book in his hands and scooted the chair closer with a smile that shone like sunshine. It cut through my grogginess.

"You okay?" he asked.

I looked down to my hands and stared. "I had a weird dream. How long have I been out?"

He glanced at his book for a moment. "Not as long as you think. Only about an hour or so. Dr. Gordon thought you'd be out for longer. She said you're fine but wants to know what happened."

I let my head fall against the pillow. Memories of me pushing water out through the hole into the ocean bombarded my brain. "I developed another freak show."

His eyebrows furrowed. "Excuse me?"

I lifted my hand as if holding a ball. "A power. I developed another power. Most people just have one, right? Maybe two. Now I have a third?"

Trevor shrugged and relaxed into his seat, but his breath caught loud enough for me to hear. Why?

"Do you remember what happened?" he asked. "Dr. Hill said the room flooded, but you plugged the leak somehow."

"Yeah, with my bare hands. I think I forced the water out into the ocean." But then how did they plug the leak? "What happened after I passed out?"

"They sealed the hole for good. Don't worry about it. How are *you* feeling?" He grabbed my hand and held it between both of his, a warm cocoon for my cold, trembling hands.

I wanted to respond with my normal *peachy* but mulled it over. Other than some aches, I seemed to be all right. "I've got growing pains."

He smiled at me then stood and kissed my forehead. "Helen will check on you soon. I'll let her know you're awake."

He retreated. Helen appeared not long after. She checked me over and, finding nothing amiss, rambled on about my newfound affinity with water. She asked a lot of questions about what happened and made me try to control water again. But of course the ability didn't work a second time, and it appeared learning to control this ability would take as many sessions with Helen as controlling my teleportation had.

"The weird thing is," she said, "to the best of my memory, I've never heard of someone housing more than two abilities within themselves. Most of the time, it's just one. Rarely, two. That you have three is remarkable."

"Can you control water?" I asked her. "Maybe you have two, too."

She only shook her head in response and flitted away to grab her clipboard.

My thoughts swirled to the story about the couple who escaped Atlantis. Why would they want to run away? Why did they bring their child? Clearly they'd run from something, and that I could understand. But to run *from* Atlantis... their reason must have been a good one. Maybe they'd run because they'd had multiple powers, too. Maybe it was against their rules to have more than one. Perhaps having more than one was a genetic mutation that had occurred over the years and wasn't common at the time Atlantis fell. It sounded ridiculous, especially coming from me. But it sure as hell explained my three powers.

But the dream I'd had while passed out wouldn't leave me. I'd been there with them. Running. Escaping. Their adrenaline had become mine, catching in my throat every time a memory of the dream seared across my vision. I shook my head to clear the apparitions.

When Helen came to discharge me, I relayed the extent of my hypotheses to her.

"Atlanteans had powers," she repeated. "We know that. Do you think this couple or their child had multiples like you?"

I nodded. "I don't know how. It was like... I could feel it. If having multiple powers wasn't something they could control, and was therefore illegal, they could have been trying to escape some form of punishment, or losing their child."

"Even if having multiple abilities was illegal, what were they supposed to do about genetics?"

I resisted the urge to point out the obvious examples in our own history. "Look, my hypothesis could make sense. Think about all those stories of Atlantean survivors founding civilizations elsewhere. How many of those could have been people escaping, instead?"

Helen shrugged, mulling it over. "I think it's plausible."

Plausible. Completely reassuring. Something told me Helen didn't know as much about Atlantis and the associated folklore as I did.

There was a soft knock on the door, and Dr. Hill poked his head in. "Glad you're awake."

"And feeling better," I said. "Sorry for the scare back there." I couldn't imagine what he thought of me now. Unqualified *and* uncoordinated, with funky abilities to plug ocean leaks to boot.

He shook his head. "No scare. I'm glad to see you're okay."

"She should be able to continue to work with you later this afternoon." Helen glanced at me. "If you're feeling up to it."

"Oh, I definitely am."

Nothing would keep me from the outpost. Not crazy powers, and definitely not vivid Atlantean dreams.

Chapter Twenty-One

Trevor

My radio beeped, the only sound I registered in the darkness of sleep. I rolled over and almost onto someone. Chelsea lay on her back, her face in a book from the outpost.

"Did you sleep at all?" I asked her.

After she'd been released from the Infirmary and had rejoined Dr. Hill in the outpost, we'd spent most of the night tangled up together on my bed, looking at stuff from the find. I must have dozed off sometime after midnight.

"Uh-uhn."

Uh-uhn had become her typical, distant response ever since she'd started cataloguing the find. If you gave her time to examine anything, digging her out was impossible.

My radio beeped again. "What time is it?"

"Six. It's been going off for a while now."

I climbed over her and off the bed. "Why didn't you wake me up?"

She shrugged.

Okay. Enough distant responses.

I moved over her until she had to drop the book to the ground. I leaned in, watching her expression turn from annoyance to happiness right before our lips met. She smiled against my mouth. There was my Chelsea. Beautiful and alive, not hyper-focused and distant.

"Good morning," I whispered against her ear.

"Morning, yourself," she murmured.

She pulled me in, slamming her mouth against mine. Every hair on my body stood on end, like her lips were an electric rod against my soul. Her hands ran along my back as she rolled her hips against mine. Blonde hair slipped onto her face. I brushed it back and let my fingers glide along her temple, down her neck, and over her torso. Her hands trailed leisurely down my chest and between us, brushing against me, massaging me through my uniform. I throbbed beneath her touch. My hands passed over her breasts, kneading in slow circles. The same moment she fumbled with my uniform's zipper, my radio blared.

We both jumped.

"Bridge to Mr. Boncore. Bridge to Mr. Boncore."

Chelsea's face flushed, and she nudged me. Breath ragged, she said, "It's probably because you didn't answer."

I let out a long sigh and slouched over. "You could have woken me up." Whatever they called me for, it had better be good if it had to interrupt this.

I drew away from her, strode over to my desk, and flicked the switch on my radio. "Boncore."

Christa Jackson's voice flooded through the other end. "You've had a call trying to come in for the past three hours."

Her informality said everything I needed to know. "I'm happy I slept through it, then."

"We have a contractual obligation to place your parents' calls—"

"Straight to me, I know, I know," I said, readying my computer to take the call. The only reason the contract was in place was because I'd been a minor when the Navy hired me. *Need to change that arrangement.* I pulled up the phone-dialing program and plugged a headset into the jacks on the side of my CPU. "Put them through."

"You don't want to talk to your parents?" Chelsea asked.

I winked at her, hoping it hid the real reasons for my anxiety. "Not while my girlfriend's in my bed."

The lie worked. Chelsea smiled and grabbed the book off the floor to keep reading. "Hurry back."

I hadn't wanted to leave the bed in the first place.

Christa connected the line to my parents, and my headset clicked in acknowledgement. A man's voice came over the speaker, sinking a knife into my gut. "Trevor."

Not my father. "Thompson."

Thompson's voice slithered through my headset. "Is there something you'd like to tell me about?"

"It has been a long time!" I said, forcing a smile despite knowing he couldn't see it. Maybe it'd help play this off so Chelsea wouldn't be suspicious. "How are you?"

"Who's in the room with you?" he snarled.

"No, I haven't talked to Dad in a while. I'm having fun here, though." I leaned back in the chair, bracing myself for whatever hell he'd prepared.

He huffed. "We know about the outpost. Whatever game you're playing, it ends now."

I rubbed my mouth and chin with my knuckles to stop myself from getting smug at being able to piss him off from so far away.

"What outpost?" My eyes shot to Chelsea. Had I said that out loud? Her face was still in the book, lost to the world. Like tunnel vision but worse.

"The one you failed to inform us about," Thompson accused. "JoAnne isn't happy Valerie said something and not you."

JoAnne, my mother, probably didn't care. The feeling was mutual.

"I have no idea what you're talking about," I said.

"Stop playing the fool!" His retort roared through the headset. I pulled them away from my ears. "If Valerie wasn't there, this whole mission would have failed."

Dammit, Valerie. "Good for her."

"Trevor—"

"Yeah, yeah, I know."

He grunted, and anger seized his voice into something animalistic. "Help Valerie take the artifacts, or the other operative will. Then you'll find yourself in a very nasty position."

He ended the call.

I sat there staring at the screen. *Another* operative? They'd placed someone here besides Valerie and me? I wracked my brain for the crew list, zipping through it. No. None of these people were tied to Thompson. Not without me knowing. Not without Valerie saying something. And even if Thompson spoke the truth, the third agent had to have gotten here recently, sometime between when I returned from Boston and now.

I glanced at Chelsea. She was the only person onboard who fit that description. A petite blonde with *Atlantean* teleporting abilities working for Thompson and his crew? I chortled. I got played by Thompson. "Jerk."

Chelsea glared up at me from her book. "Excuse me?"

Jesus. "No, not you!" I strode to the bed and placed my hands on either cheek. "Never you."

She put the book down and reached an arm behind my neck. "Good."

She caught my lips with her own in an agonizingly slow motion, a harsh punishment for an insult not slung her way. Chelsea may be torturing me now, but she couldn't be working for them. I would know. I knew I'd know.

Maybe it was a good thing I hadn't said anything to her about my parentage, after all.

✦

I flipped the Atlantean outpost upside down. Building models from the bottom up was easier on my tablet, especially with the software I used. This wasn't anywhere near as fun as building videogames, but Chelsea would love the rendering, even if I'd built the model for the Admiral and not specifically her.

I added a few more pieces to the model before flipping it back. My eyes stung from looking at the screen for hours while I waited for Chelsea to finish her work at the outpost for the day. I glanced up at the Dining Deck's clock for confirmation. Three hours. Three hours filled with recreating the outpost in a 3D environment for the Admiral's benefit. What did he want with the model, anyway? To share it with the entire brass?

"Mr. Boncore?"

Dr. Hill stood on the other side of the table. He wore a warm smile and an armful of books. "Can I bother you for a brief moment?"

What did an archaeologist need me for? Unless he meant the rendering. "You're not interrupting me, although the model isn't done yet."

Dr. Hill set his books on the table and pulled out a chair. "There's something else I'd like to talk to you about. May I?"

"Sure."

He sat and scooted forward, one leg stretched out before him. "I know you and Chelsea are close."

My eyebrows rose. *That was blunt.* "What's that got to do with anything?"

"You're aware of her abilities, are you not?"

My heart dropped straight through my chest to the floor. What? When the *hell* had he learned about those? Chelsea had said he believed the leak on the outpost was a freak accident.

I leaned across the table so he wouldn't mishear me. "Who told you?"

Dr. Hill held up a finger. "Chelsea saved my life at the outpost. Water poured in through a leak in the roof. I lied about what I saw."

So what? Not to mention, *Why aren't you scared?* I would be in his place, if I'd seen powers for the first time.

"I'm aware of your connections and lineage, Mr. Boncore."

My blood ran cold.

"I also know you're aware of what your satellite station has found. If you intend to hand over all of these artifacts to your employers, I have been given permission by mine to stop you at all costs."

I fought to keep my expression deadpanned while the rest of me wound up into a tight coil of anxiety and defensiveness. Who was this guy, thinking he could come here and sling threats around?

"I don't know what you're talking about," I said. Maybe if I denied it, he'd go away. But part of me wanted to know what he knew.

Dr. Hill leveled me with a look. "Chelsea speaks highly of you, so I don't want to assume you're allied with her enemy."

"What enemy?" The coil unwound an inch, lacing my voice with anger. "Chelsea's just some girl from Boston."

He glanced around the room and, satisfied no one sat within earshot, leaned in. "And you're a boy from Tennessee, whose ancestors came from Lemuria. I know why you're here, Mr. Boncore."

"Then don't you think that if turning SeaSat5 in was my plan, I'd have done so days ago?" My fists clenched. I didn't like how he knew so much about me, or that he thought he could make assumptions as to my course of action.

"I don't support what they do, or fight for," I continued. "So, if you'll excuse me…" I stood, eyes focused on the door.

Dr. Hill grabbed my arm and held fast. "The Lemurians will come for her. You know that, right?"

My heartbeat raced. "I know they'll try, but once they see she's not a danger—"

Dr. Hill narrowed his gaze. "You don't know?"

I fought the urge to roll my eyes. Screw this stupid game. "Know what?"

"She's a genetically modified Atlantean super soldier. Chelsea is a danger to them, and they *will* take her."

He'd said it matter-of-factly, like I should know what that meant. I didn't. The stories my parents had told me included soldiers, but never genetics or "super" anything. Helen had, though. She'd based her entire hypothesis around genetics.

A deep breath swept my lungs as puzzle pieces fit together before my eyes. *Chelsea...*

"She has multiple powers," he explained. "The people I work for study the Link Pieces and individuals like her whose ancestors escaped testing labs on Atlantis. They tried to modify humans to win the war."

"Clearly their plan didn't work." Lemuria won with flying colors.

Hill shook his head, and I sat down at the table, now too intrigued to leave. How'd he know all this? And why had he chosen me to tell it all to?

"No, it didn't, but the traits have been passed down through the generations," he explained.

"Why are you telling me all of this?"

Hill looked down to his stack of books before speaking. "Chelsea—and the artifacts—would be safer if she left with me."

My stomach dropped to my knees. Hadn't this been what I'd wanted? A way for her to escape, to keep her safe? But hadn't I also decided to hell with the Lemurians' war, to try to convince Thompson that Chelsea wasn't a threat?

My fists tightened as another thought hit: this guy had to be allied with Atlantis. Maybe Chelsea *would* be safer with him, with her own kind. Assuming he was actually Atlantean.

Was I actually considering this?

"So, you want me to talk to the Captain?" I asked.

"And have to explain to him everything you already know? No."

"He kind of controls the boat and all hands on it." What did he expect me to do about it? Did Dr. Hill know about Valerie, too?

"What *you* don't understand is that no one on this tank, besides you and me, knows the first thing about the Atlantean-Lemurian war.

Without telling Chelsea or the Captain, you're not going to get her to leave."

"But you can."

Guess he didn't know about Valerie. So Valerie was safe, and he thought me the only intermediary between Thompson and Dr. Hill's employers. Meanwhile, Valerie thought me a traitor, and Chelsea counted me as what I hoped was an amazing boyfriend.

God, I missed college. Homework. Advising meetings. Working on my thesis project. Making videogames. Not these lies and secrets and pretenses.

I shook my head. "No. I won't get involved in this. SeaSat5 is the safest place on the planet for her right now. Our prototype shield blocks the Lemurians from getting onboard." Or at least I hoped it would.

"If they boarded via teleportation," Dr. Hill countered.

My eyes narrowed. "How do you know about Humming Bird?" So much for secrets.

He cocked his eyebrow the slightest bit. "Let's just say Lemuria isn't the only entity with a watch on SeaSatellite5."

So SeaSatellite5 had an Atlantean mole on board, too? My fingers itched with ideas for a major Humming Bird update. *This has to stop.* "Look, Lemuria hasn't caught wind of the find or they'd be here already."

Except they *had* caught wind of the find, which greatly increased the probability they'd come to SeaSat5, especially after Thompson's call. So why was I rejecting his help?

"It's only been a few days," said Dr. Hill.

"Long enough. I thank you for your concern, Dr. Hill, but I can keep this under control."

I'd do everything in my power to keep Lemuria away from Chelsea. Captain Marks would protect every one of his crewmembers, and Helen could help Chelsea understand, even perfect, her abilities without testing them for god knows what purpose. And she'd do it all without becoming a pawn, a warrior, for Atlantis.

My fists clenched and unclenched on the tabletop. Dr. Hill had made all the wrong impressions.

He reached into the top chest pocket of his fatigues and pulled out a pen, then slid a tiny notebook out from his stack of books, ripping off a piece of paper. He wrote as he spoke. "If anything happens—and I mean *anything*—after I leave here, you give me a call, all right? Especially if she develops another power. It's important."

He held out the paper, and I took it from him. He'd written down a phone number with a sequence of extensions.

"Ask for TAO and then me," Dr. Hill said.

"TAO?"

"My employers."

My eyes narrowed. "I thought you worked for the military."

Dr. Hill stood from the table and grabbed his books. "I do."

He left without another word.

I dropped the 3D modeling program and pulled up a military database I had access to, thanks to my work with Humming Bird. TAO didn't show up anywhere. To my knowledge, SeaSat5 was the most classified project in the military's entire repertoire, followed closely by Humming Bird.

This TAO beat it out, and yet… if they studied Link Pieces, Thompson and my mother should have known about it. Why hadn't they told me?

Chapter Twenty-Two

Chelsea

I looked up from the mess of papers on my desk to my clock. Its numbers screamed 12:03 a.m. in bright red colors. The Atlantean journal had enthralled me for hours. *Shit*. I'd missed dinner and seeing Trevor because of it. But he hadn't come to find me, either.

I frowned. Why? It wasn't like I'd meant to fall into a research hole. The more I looked at the artifacts, the less I slept or was able to maintain focus on anything besides the art pieces and texts. Some of them glimmered a blue hue in the right light, but once you looked closely, the twinkling went away. Like you couldn't look at it head-on and expect the shimmering to still be there, a mirage on a hot summer's day.

I also still couldn't read the journal's entries. Dr. Hill had said some parts drifted from Atlantean into Ancient Greek, making the text hard for him to read and translate. Sometimes when I read it, the words shifted into English, and I understood every page. But as soon as I'd noticed the shift—which wasn't always right away—the words reverted into scribbled Atlantean and Greek. I swore it had happened, but because the words had never stayed, I attributed it to lack of sleep and decided to still not tell Helen.

I gave the journal one last glance-over before looking to the clock again. 12:15 a.m. Helen had wanted to meet early to work on my new ability to control water. With a groan, I stood from my desk and locked the journal safely within its bottom drawer, wrapped up in a swath of fabric from the site. Too tired to try teleporting to my quarters—or risk showing up in Trevor's—I traversed the Science Decks en route to my quarters.

Laughter permeated the hallway near the Lift. My ears strained to identify who the out of place noise belonged to. Light shone from beneath a door to a small lab and out of a small window near the top. I peered inside. Freddy and Trevor sat next to one another, pretending not to look at each other's cards despite obvious signs to the contrary. Across the table from them, Julie sat in Michael's lap, shielding her cards from view. Dave appeared to have recently folded, and Helen drew her winnings to herself.

I pulled myself from the door, feeling left out. A black pit rotted my stomach. Why hadn't Trevor invited me? Was he mad I'd missed dinner because of the outpost? Tendrils sprung from the pit of my stomach. I'd lost track of time, not intentionally ditched him.

I shoved down the feeling. *I'm just tired.*

The door opened on my loneliness. Trevor grinned at me. "Want to join?"

My thumbnail looked mighty interesting right then. I picked at the skin around it. "I don't know. Looks like you guys are far into the game."

He held out his hand. "Oh, come on."

I shook my head, arms crossing at my chest. "You didn't tell me you had plans." *Stupid. Why'd you have to bring it up?*

He shrugged. "You looked tired. You've been at the outpost basically since we found it. I figured you wanted alone time or sleep."

Fair enough. And considerate. Still, I didn't want to intrude if they were so far into the game.

His eyes widened, eager. "Please?"

Assuming they hadn't wanted me there now felt idiotic. I'd feel like a fool if I went in there now, but dammit if I didn't want to spend time with Trevor.

"Okay. Do you have coffee?" I asked.

He grinned from ear to ear. "Absolutely."

I lazily pointed past him, resigned. "Then let's go."

He planted a quick kiss on my forehead and held open the door.

Julie fist-pumped the air the moment I joined the room. "Yes, another girl! I'll win the solo quarters for sure."

Supposedly, somewhere on Res Deck 4, there was a winnable solo quarters, so those with roommates could live a month or two without them. I guess this was how the room was won, which left me to wonder exactly how legitimate the whole thing was.

"Is that what you're playing for?" I asked. A bunch of the guys nodded. Looking to Julie, I said, "Guess I can't leave you hanging."

Dave dealt me a hand. His fingerless gloves and hockey shirt were both marked with a Boston Bruins hockey logo. Guess his wrist had been feeling better. At least the cast was finally off.

"Good team choice," I said. I wasn't much of a sports fan, but I supported my city to the grave.

He winked at me. "Coincidence, I assure you."

They played some weird SeaSat5 version of poker I couldn't follow. I tried my best to keep up, but only became an easy opponent for the rest to beat. Within two rounds, Julie won the solo quarters for three months. She winked at Michael, a hot blush creeping up her cheeks as he squeezed her thigh, and I understood why she'd wanted the room so badly. I smiled at my cards, not trying to ruin their moment.

Trevor didn't seem to pick up on it. Had he never considered how lucky he was to have solo quarters? Did he ever think about the benefits at all? It wasn't always about the peace and quiet of not having a roommate.

I studied his profile. He either had a hell of a poker face, or he really was that oblivious. The light in the room caught the stubble growing along his jaw and cheeks. It gave him a sense of ruggedness he hadn't had before, making him look like a man instead of the genius guy I'd met. He'd been a *man* all along, but for whatever reason, now, in light of a poker game and Julie's victory, I noticed it for the first time.

My breathing grew shallow as my eyes locked onto Michael's hand as it trailed up Julie's thigh, just low enough to remain decent. My mind skipped to thoughts of Trevor's hands on my skin, the way he whispered in my ear, the feel of his breath on my neck and chest. My stomach tightened, heat pooled somewhere lower. I wanted him. Bad.

He raised an eyebrow. I'd been made. "What's so fascinating about my face?"

Julie giggled and said, "Gee, I wonder."

Was I that obvious? "2 a.m. shadow looks good on you, that's all," I said, smiling.

He grinned and took my hand in his, rubbing his thumb on the inside of my palm. His light touches tickled. It felt so good, so intimate, in spite of how small the motion really was. It was like his thumb encircling my palm held me together, and I'd fall apart if he stopped.

Everyone but Trevor and I left for bed. Coffee had been a terrible idea. Caffeine whiplash stirred with thoughts of Trevor while we wandered to the room I still, technically, shared with Valerie—though, I hadn't seen her in days—me a jittery, giggle-filled mess the entire way.

I glanced at him when we came to a stop outside my door and rolled my eyes. "Why'd you let me have coffee?"

"Because I know better than to tell you no," he murmured as he leaned in and kissed me.

Something caught his eye in the window on the door. He drew away and glanced through. Valerie stood, brushing out her hair. Her tablet sat perched on her dresser while she read.

"Maybe you shouldn't go in there in your… current state," he said.

I followed his eyes. "You mean my caffeine high?" Not a great idea with Valerie on edge lately. "Guess it's to the Lounge for me. Too bad you can't make me a game profile. I'd probably beat The Race in one sitting right now."

"Probably," he agreed. He grabbed my hand and spun me toward the Lift, setting off another round of high-on-life giggles. I loved the way he always made me laugh, like all my troubles left the second he entered the room.

"Where are we going?" I asked him.

He didn't answer until the Lift doors shut, then he jerked me to him and looked deep into my eyes. Need danced a duet with longing, and the lights from the Lift pirouetted in his ocean-blue irises, like sunlight on the tops of waves. Seeing the ocean reflected there felt like the outpost did: like home and safety. I snaked an arm around his neck and crashed his lips to mine.

He didn't respond at first—shocked, probably—but then his lips moved with abandon. The butterflies in my stomach evolved into fireflies, lit with a low buzz. Swarming. Igniting. He pulled me in closer, tighter, and nuzzled his nose and lips on my neck. His scruff tickled the sensitive skin there. Goosebumps road up my arms with every kiss, every nip. I moaned softly, unable to keep the reaction to myself.

"What was that about 2 a.m. shadow?" he asked, smile pressed against my skin.

I chuckled a heady laugh. "Trying to dig my way out of being caught."

"You know," he said between kisses, "Julie's not the only one with solo quarters."

I moaned and reached above us for one of the handholds. Warmth bloomed in my chest, misting lower and lower the longer our embrace went on. He smelled like Irish Spring soap and clean air. I pulled his face to mine and kissed him again, like I needed his touch to breathe. To be whole. I needed *him* in order to be whole, and he knew it.

The Lift *dinged* and we broke apart for the walk to his quarters, but only enough to be decent if we ran into anyone. We made short work of the distance between the Lift and his door, and as soon as his door shut, I slammed down the privacy screen.

His fingers fell to my uniform, ripping the zipper down with a confidence I didn't know he had. Every touch lit my skin on fire so that every layer of clothing was too much, too heavy, too constricting. Like I'd spontaneously combust if I didn't cool down. I yanked off his uniform top, leaving only the t-shirt beneath. He tangled his hands in my hair, and we kissed again.

My fingers skipped down between us as his tongue grazed mine, exploring, tasting. He was already hard, and he grunted as I massaged him through his pants, rocking his hips into my hand. He ambled backwards to his bed, tugging me with him like if we waited any longer he'd lose all control. I straddled him, my knees dipping into the mattress, as his lips fell to my neck. His nose trailed a methodical path, paving the way for his lips and teeth as he kissed and nipped his way from my collarbone to my neck.

I gasped as goose bumps sprouted in his wake. His fingers slipped beneath my top, inching up my stomach and chest, thumbs swirling in tiny circles. His touch, reverent and adventurous, drew a chill down my spine. *Fuck.* No one had ever touched me like this, as if they were in awe of my body, of everything that I was. I swallowed the insecurity and lifted my shirt above my head, sure it'd catch on fire from my skin if he didn't remove it himself. Trevor hooked his thumbs beneath my bra-straps, brushing them aside and pushing down the cups. His eyes raked over my chest, studying every part of me. I'd never felt more vulnerable, so open and naked, like his eyes saw past skin to my very mind and soul.

He lifted his eyes to mine. "You are amazing."

I smiled, but I couldn't keep self-doubt away. Did he like what he saw? Had he slept with someone more attractive in his past? Stupid thoughts. Stupid, stupid thoughts. Every move he made, every look he gave, held nothing but love and admiration.

He kissed me again, strong hands cupping my face, chasing away all doubts. His mouth found my neck, leaving kisses on every available centimeter of skin. He whispered in my ear, "You're beautiful, more than I thought possible."

And fuck, no one had ever said that to me before. No one had made me feel like *this* before. I drew his lips to mine, enjoying that every part of me snapped to attention where he touched. Alive. Electrified. Trevor simply brought me to life, had from the beginning, in every single way. He'd become everything, a lifeline, my first love, in a matter of weeks. And here in this moment, I entrusted him with that power forever.

His excitement rose between my thighs. Heat pooled where he rocked against me, hard and purposeful. I ground down onto him, biting my lip in a smile at the groan it elicited from him. I brushed my fingers along his cheek, trying to get across in gestures what I couldn't in words, the desire and love I had for him. I slid my fingers under his shirt, lifted it from his body, and replaced my arms behind his head. I toyed with the small, barely-there curls at the base of his neck as he nipped the skin beneath my collarbone. One side to the other, then lower. An ache grew where his excitement met mine and in an instant, this wasn't enough.

Skin. I needed more skin, nothing between us. A physical connection to match the one we'd already made, the one strong enough to bring me across the world to him. I pulled him to me, foreheads pressed together, and reveled in the closeness of us. Our breathing ragged. Fingertips restless and wandering. But I'd lost the upper hand I craved.

I pushed his shoulders until he lay down flat on the bed beneath me, and I relieved him of the rest of his uniform—and mine. We became a whirlwind, a gyre of frantic, lust-filled motion and passion, filled with sensations and emotions I'd never imagined possible. Constantly moving, always exploring. Teasing. Touching. Fulfilling.

I fell asleep on Trevor's chest, listening to our racing heartbeats fall into peaceful sync.

Chapter Twenty-Three

Trevor

Waking up with Chelsea in my arms, her breath warm against my bare chest, was the best feeling I could ever remember having. I wrapped her in my arms, aching to never leave this moment.

She looked so different asleep. Her wild flare disappeared, leaving calm, almost angelic features. The difference struck me hard, and I pulled her closer, emotion constricting my throat. Dr. Hill would take her away, make her some kind of soldier, and never, ever would I lose her to Thompson and my parents. But I'd still lose her to them, to TAO. She'd be gone.

Right here, right now, this was the Chelsea I wanted to be with. The wild side, the quiet side. Powers there but not used for anything other than teleporting to me. I could no more now envision her the soldier from my parents' stories than I could weeks ago when Valerie insisted Chelsea were Atlantean. Chelsea may be a firecracker when awake or on stage, but she was no soldier.

And I love her. The thought startled me, but it wasn't a surprise. I was destined to love her from the night we first met. She was my freedom from myself, this war. My hope. My happiness. She was my everything. And no matter what happened next, I'd fight for it. For this. For us.

She stirred beneath me, her eyes fluttering open. My breath caught. Yes, I definitely loved her. The thought made me grin like an idiot, and, for the first time in a long time, my mind flew, all responsibilities and anxieties gone. Last night had sure helped with that, too.

"Morning," I whispered, sliding hair out of her face with a finger.

Her eyes flitted up to mine, and she smiled. "Hey."

A comfortable silence enveloped us. For once, no radio interrupted.

"Last night was fantastic," she said.

"Yeah," I replied. The control she gave me, that power I'd given her, twisted my lips into a grin. I wasn't sure what I'd expected—I'd been nervous as hell—but I was glad it had happened.

Chelsea lifted up to kiss me. Then her eyes bugged out.

I tensed. "What? What's wrong?"

She pointed to my alarm clock. "It's already eight!"

Shrugging, I said, "Oops." I didn't have anywhere to be for another hour.

"Yeah." She climbed out of bed, laughing as she pulled a sheet around her. "*Oops.*"

We showered and ran to the Dining Decks for a quick breakfast. Dr. Hill waited there for Chelsea, a pen in one hand and coffee in the other.

"Good morning, Dr. Hill," Chelsea said.

He looked up and waved. "Good morning, indeed. About ready to head over? My team from the Army will arrive in a few days."

Chelsea frowned. "Why so long?"

She wanted to get cracking on the find, on the things she couldn't help with, but Dr. Hill had probably told his team to hold off while he assessed the situation. Part of me wondered if they waited because he wanted to see if my family would act first. Maybe they would, maybe they wouldn't. Chelsea shouldn't have to wait either way.

"I wanted them to pick up some texts for translating before

coming here," Dr. Hill said. "Besides, anything with the military takes a lot of time and red tape."

Chelsea frowned and sat at the table. "Guess that makes sense."

"Don't worry," Dr. Hill said. His eyes leveled with mine. "The find isn't going anywhere. It hasn't for thousands of years."

Yeah, buddy. We both hope nothing happens to it. But today, outside the warm, cozy world Chelsea and I had created last night, anxiety resumed its clawing.

Dr. Hill stood. "Shall we, then?"

"Morning, campers!" All three of us turned to watch Dave's mock salute. "Christa can't leave her post today. So, you've got me instead." He crossed his arms at his chest.

"Glorious," Chelsea said dryly. "What do you even know about archaeology and linguistics?"

"Absolutely nothing," Dave admitted. "But I can pilot a shuttle, and I've been there with you before. That's once again good enough for the Captain."

"Of course it is," I said. "Have fun."

Chelsea's eyes met mine, and she gave me the warmest smile I'd ever seen. Her hand sought mine. I gave hers a squeeze, as much for my own benefit as hers.

"Lunch?" she asked.

I nodded. "Yeah, I'll see you then."

They left, and I headed toward Engineering to prep for bridge duty, my stomach churning like never before.

◆

For once, nothing was amiss in Engineering. In fact, it wasn't until I'd wandered up to the Bridge Deck an hour later that I noticed something was off. The air buzzed with electricity, raising the hair on my arms. It hummed, felt alive. Maybe Humming Bird had decided to work correctly for a change. Or maybe an intern had broken my system *again*.

As I slid my keycard through the scanner outside the Bridge, a low rumbling reverberated in the air. Deep vibrations pulsed around me and inside my bones. I hesitated. *What's going on?* Three big *booms* resounded from the deck above me. I ducked down, cowering against the wall as a fourth and fifth *boom* sounded, rattling the floor and walls.

"What the—"

The Bridge doors *swung* open, like someone reversed their hinges, then kicked them down. Smoke from broken gaskets consumed the area. I stumbled away from the open doors, blindly backtracking to the Lift, out of harm's way. Someone tugged on my shirt, yanking me into the hallway. Smoke seized my lungs. Another man stood in front of me, hand held out. *Gun.* He's got a gun. A shiny, deadly gun.

"Long time, Mr. Boncore."

Thompson.

Panic flooded my body, tensing my muscles for fight or flight. I fought against his hold. *How'd they get in?*

Explosions. The electricity in the air. They caused Humming Bird to malfunction. They got *in* thanks to the shield malfunctioning.

Thompson, my old boss and my mother's right-hand-man, glimpsed the realization in my eyes. "Don't worry; it's still working. Sort of." He chortled and barked orders to his men to overtake the rest of the crew before returning his attention to me. "You'll be coming this way." He gestured towards the Bridge. Shouts and screamed echoed out the door, followed by gunshots.

A cough wracked my lungs as his crewman shoved me forward, parading me into the command center of SeaSat5. I struggled and kicked and shoved, but this dude's arms didn't budge. His feet never lost a millimeter of purchase. He was strong. Super strong. Like Thompson. Like Chelsea.

How many of these assholes have powers?

Bigger things to worry about.

The Bridge had been wrecked. A station or two sparked and

flamed. Some of the Bridge staff huddle in a corner, pressing uniform pieces onto the injured, providing pressure to wounds. Blood spatter marked the floor, some stations, and the command platform in the center. *The Commander.* He was among the wounded in the corner, but rather than taking care of himself, both his hands occupied rags for others' injuries. Freddy and Christa sat toward the back, with three of Thompson's men guarding them all.

My eyes swung up to a hole ripped into the ceiling. Above us stood the domed off room where SeaSat5's helicopter sat on its pad. They came in through the heli-dome. *Shit.*

"Let them go," I told Thompson. "This isn't—"

"Should have thought about the crew before you kept your mouth shut, boy." He set his gun on a nearby console then gestured to me with an open palm. "Go ahead. Make any necessary adjustments to keep this rig running until we hit port."

My heart stopped. "Which port?"

His smile gleamed of something evil. "Home."

The Security Office door off the Bridge burst open. Captain Marks charged in, gun pointed. Resignation shown in his eyes even as he shouted at Thompson. He was outnumbered. His ship had been taken over. His crew was out of commission. Now, he himself was caught. Struggle seized the Captain's face, jaw muscles taut, eyes flicking about.

No. He couldn't give up that easily.

With my guard distracted by Captain Marks, I stood up quick and reached for the gun holstered on his belt. I slipped it out of the holster and fumbled with the weapon.

"Hey!" Thompson shouted.

Ignoring him, I flicked off the safety. A gunshot rang out across the Bridge, and Captain Marks yelled. A bullet whizzed past my ear, damn close to my face, and sunk into the wall behind me.

"I won't miss next time, Trevor," Thompson said. "Put it down."

I locked eyes with the Lemurian brute. His jaw was locked, head cocked to the side, waiting to see what I would do. My lungs scrambled to bring in enough air to fuel the fire inside. If I didn't make a stand now, Chelsea was as good as dead. The whole crew was. All Thompson wanted was the artifacts and the station to get them back home. He didn't *need* the crew if he had half a dozen men of his own.

But I'd never shot a gun in my life, and dammit if I missed the shot, he'd shoot me dead. No question about it.

He doesn't need you.

Besides, I wasn't any good to Chelsea or the crew dead. And as one of the very few people onboard who knew exactly what we'd found ourselves in, getting killed was immeasurably stupid.

No matter what I did, Chelsea would still be in danger.

I swallowed my pride and any control I had over the situation as I unfurled my fingers. The gun tumbled to the ground. The metallic echo as it landed rang throughout the Bridge.

Thompson nodded to my guard, who slugged me in the gut.

I bent over as a gasp slammed its way into my lungs. I barely remained on my feet. *Son of a bitch.*

"Now you, Captain," Thompson said.

Captain Marks charged forward again. Thompson's men were quicker. But instead of fighting them, the Captain set his gun on the floor of the Bridge. He'd surrendered, too.

I held my breath while Thompson's men slapped cuffs on him. The Captain's eyes settled on me, asking without words why I wasn't also restrained, deducing I was somehow involved in all of this. My chest constricted. I should've let Dr. Hill take Chelsea and just given Thompson the damn Link Pieces days ago.

"We go way back," Thompson supplied in the silence. "Don't we, Mr. Boncore?"

I marched to my station, arm wrapped around my middle, refusing to make eye contact with Thompson. There'd be plenty of time for that, and, right now, checking the damage they'd inflicted on Humming Bird and the outer hull was more important.

Captain Marks grunted against the restraints. "What do you want?"

Thompson paced away from Captain Marks, following me to my station. "Your satellite station."

"Why?"

"I need it. Don't I, Mr. Boncore?" Thompson scratched at his ratty red beard.

"It's Trevor, you idiot. Mr. Boncore is my father," I snapped as I called up the diagnostics program. The good news: they hadn't severely crippled the station. Life support was still running, but they'd nicked one of the generators on the way in.

"You damaged life support," I said. "The hull can be patched by extending the prototype shield. As for the rest..." They'd cut through the decks, destroying wires, and they needed the crew to run the Bridge. I couldn't do it alone.

"How long until you have everything repaired?" Thompson questioned.

"Are you kidding me?" I pointed to the ceiling. "You blasted your way in. What do you think?"

He picked up his gun—completely for show. If he wanted to kill me, he would have done so two minutes ago. "Watch yourself, Trevor."

"Like you'd shoot me. My mother would have your head." The threat sounded nice, but she'd pick her ex-lover over me any day after I'd betrayed them by keeping the outpost a secret.

"JoAnne wants the ship." He leaned in close and whispered, "I don't think she cares who's still alive on it." He tapped the barrel of his gun on the side of a console. "Run a biologics check and pull up a schematic onto one of those main screens. I want to make sure we've got everyone."

My stomach sank. Everyone would be caught. How long would it take them to find Chelsea at the outpost?

I melded the two screens onto one, so he could map where the crew was. Deck by deck, they corralled the crew like sheep.

Thompson wandered off, waving to one of his men. "Take the Captain and put him with the others."

I blew out a deep breath. If Chelsea stayed at the outpost, unnoticed and unaware of the situation, maybe we had a shot. As long as I knew she was safe from Thompson's guys, I could think. But Thompson came here *for* the outpost. Chelsea was *not* safe.

I glanced around the Bridge. Could I make a run for it? Could I get down to Shuttle Dock before they caught me? Some mad part of me thought so, egging me on. I waited until Thompson was on the other side of the Bridge and then I sprinted out of my station.

Bright red and orange lights blinded me ten feet from the blast doors. I stopped short and threw my arms over my eyes, lowering them only after the lights dimmed.

Valerie stood in front of me with her hands on her hips and a smirk on her face. "Did you really think you'd get away?"

Holy. Shit. "D-did you—?"

"Teleport?" Her smirk shifted into a grin, lifting up the corners of her mouth. "I've been able to teleport since the day I was born. Did you really think they'd send two incapable people to watch the station?"

My chest constricted. My breathing came fast, uneven. Valerie had powers. Valerie was one of *them*. One of the extremists I'd set out to protect SeaSat5 from. One of those who'd fought the war, so they could destroy Atlantis. And they just took the station, a cache of Link Pieces sitting not a quarter mile away. A trail that could lead them to the very city they wanted to extinguish.

Valerie wasn't just on Thompson's side.

Valerie was one of them.

Chapter Twenty-Four

Chelsea

Here's another," I mumbled, marking the size, color, and length of the text in my lap in my notebook. More Atlantean texts. More things I couldn't read. More things to pile on Dr. Hill's plate, if he could figure out how to translate them. If not, we'd never be able to read any of this, never mind get around to cataloguing the rest of the artifacts.

"Add the text to my pile on the station," Dr. Hill said.

"I shouldn't have to. Can't we take some time to figure out a cipher or something? Isn't that how you translate languages you don't understand?"

He chuckled. "Kind of. I'll have my team work on it once they get here."

I huffed, blowing hair out of my face. "Your team better be miracle workers. Don't know how else they'll get all this done."

"We'll likely have to take some with us."

That bit me the wrong way. SeaSat5 couldn't anchor here forever, but we had enough room to store the artifacts on this floor. Why did Dr. Hill need to take them?

To work on them. Duh. And yet…

Some invisible force tugged on my heart, yanking it in different directions. Could I leave Trevor once my internship was up? I'd never thought about what would happen until now. Once we found the outpost, I'd assumed we'd be here for months. But would we? Would Captain Marks keep me on staff? I wasn't qualified to stay onboard SeaSat5 when everyone my age had master's degrees or higher—and years of genius research under their belts.

I frowned. Grad school would take two years. Two whole years away from Trevor. Two weeks ago, I could have maybe been okay with leaving if I knew I would return afterwards. But now?

I hadn't grown up a genius like the rest of them. What made me think I could date one without jumping hurdles?

"I actually wanted to talk with you about that," Dr. Hill said.

Wiping the frown from my face for now, I looked to him. "About what?"

He shut the text in his hands and shifted on his step stool. "When our contract here is done, I wanted to ask if you'd like to join me to continue the work elsewhere. We obviously can't publicize the find with articles, but I think it'd be a great experience for you."

"I…"

Water in the main pool rippled until a head broke the surface. A thin frame pulled itself out of the water. The red mane unfurling from underneath could only belong to Valerie. She pulled down her scuba mask.

"Morning," she said, wiping her face with a nearby towel. "Dave, Captain Marks said to let you know you'll be relieved around lunchtime. Christa will be over by then."

Dave turned and rubbed his stomach. "Thank god. A man could starve with the way these two work."

I rolled my eyes and resumed taking notes.

Valerie joined me, looking over my shoulder. The hairs on the back of my neck stood up. A chill rode down my spine. Why did

Valerie suddenly care about what we were finding in here?

"What are you looking at?" she asked.

"Another Atlantean text."

She chuckled. "Still can't believe we found this place. Ancient history lover's Disneyland, don't you agree?"

Nodding, I said, "Absolutely."

Something grew warm next to me, turning into a full-on blazing fireball ten feet away. Heat enveloped the space, instantly drying out the air.

Fire! There's a fire!

I stood but was shoved down from behind without care, my ass smacking hard on the stool. Fingers gripped my shoulder and held me in place. My hands curled into fists, ready to fight, but anyone able to hold me down couldn't possibly be someone small enough for me to knock out. A body builder. A wrestler. I turned my head, a snarl building on my face.

And froze.

Valerie smirked down at me, her eyebrows lifted as if to say, *Well, what now, sunshine?*

Across the way, a guy pulled Dr. Hill up and slugged him across the face.

"Watch it, Georgie," Valerie said to him. "Thompson said no more casualties on the first day."

Georgie sneered and threw Dr. Hill to the ground. Dr. Hill wiped his bleeding nose and reached for something behind him.

Gun! Dr. Hill carried a gun?

Georgie shot out his foot, kicking once to knock the object away from both of them. He kicked a second time, attacking Dr. Hill's ribs.

"What the hell!" Dave bellowed from his corner.

Valerie's head snapped up. Dave had his own attacker in a chokehold.

Valerie's distraction provided me the opening to lift up an inch, hook my foot under a leg of the stool, and fling it up at her legs. She stumbled, giving me the chance to retreat and pull water from a puddle in the corner. She giggled and swiped her hand at me, a trail of freaking *fire* snapping to the water, evaporating my only weapon. Steam rose from where the water had once been.

What the flying hell *is going on?*

Lights like a thousand fireflies lit up behind Dave. A man materialized from within and smacked Dave's head with the butt of a gun. My stomach leapt as he fell to the floor, unconscious.

I withdrew until my back hit a bookshelf. A rattled urn shattered on the floor at my feet.

"Well, look what you went and did," Valerie said, making a *tsk-tsk* sound.

The last man to appear, a dude at least a foot and a half taller than me, joined Valerie. "Boss wants to see you, little girl," he growled at me.

"Fuck you." I was no one's little girl. I searched out the area again, calling to water the way Helen had me practice. None came.

"You're untrained," Valerie said. "And I think Georgie's idiotic entrance dried the place out. Nothing you can do, girlie."

Why did Valerie attack me? Why did Dr. Hill carry a gun? What the *hell* was up with the fireballs and red lights?

Teleportation. Mine were blue. Theirs were red. Valerie's were red.

Valerie had powers?

My eyes flicked from her to tubby, to Georgie, then to Dr. Hill. He looked up at me with pleading eyes, though what he was begging for, I had no idea.

"Stop trying to get out of this," Valerie said, stalking toward me.

I stood my ground. "Who are you, really?"

"Same as Trevor, just a bit more advanced and a hell of a lot more loyal." Valerie stopped three feet from me, grinning from ear to ear. "My employers need these artifacts. We're going to spend the next twenty-four hours collecting them for storage on the station. Then we're going to take the station away from here. You"—she tapped the space between my collar bones—"you're going to cooperate. None of this powers crap."

I grabbed Valerie's finger and twisted it away from me. Something snapped, and I winced. I hadn't meant to break her finger, to hurt someone again, but the curse flying from her mouth was satisfying.

She shoved me hard against the bookshelf. "I told you not to try that shit!" Valerie's fist connected with my jaw with incredible force.

I yelped as the back of my head smacked the shelf behind me. Tears blurred my vision. When she drew her fist back, I tasted blood.

"Valerie," tubby warned.

She took a deep breath to calm down and waved him off. "Yeah, yeah, I know. Bitch broke my finger."

"Knew there was a reason I didn't like you," I hissed. But what I'd thought was jealousy turned out to be something more.

Was Trevor involved, too? She certainly made it seem so.

No. No way in hell. Trevor wasn't violent. Or evil. But if Valerie had hidden so well, who else was hiding?

My eyes skittered to Dr. Hill. They'd beaten him up, but he knew how to read Atlantean. And Helen studied people with powers, for god's sake. Was there anyone left I could trust?

Tubby and Georgie manhandled Dave and Dr. Hill into standing (though submissive) positions. Valerie's other guy, the one who Dave had knocked unconscious, stirred.

Valerie reached out and slapped her hand onto my shoulder. Heat radiated from her fingertips. *She's gonna burn me! Shit!*

"Ready to go?" she purred.

I threw my head back but didn't connect. "Fuck you."

"Yeah, yeah. Love you, too, girlie. Let's get the hell out of here."

I swung at her. She caught my fist and crushed it with her own. I couldn't help but cry out.

"Why do you keep fighting this?" she scolded.

Foreign red lights encompassed us before I could spit blood in her face.

Chapter Twenty-Five

Trevor

My teeth gnashed together as I fought the intense desire to punch Thompson. It'd get the crew nowhere and me knocked out. And since I was the one crewmember who knew exactly how screwed we were, I figured I better do everything possible to stay alive and conscious.

They'd screwed up Humming Bird bad. The system emitted the strangest electro-magnetic field I'd ever seen. Not good. And that was just the start of our problems.

The fiery light of Lemurian teleportation filled the center of the Bridge. The moment Thompson's crew teleported in from the outpost, Chelsea's eyes were squeezed shut, her body relaxing like she was trying to teleport. Except she didn't. She hadn't moved an inch. Valerie chuckled and scolded her for trying to use her powers.

My thoughts swam back to weeks ago, to the question about how Atlantean and Lemurian powers interacted with my shield. The answer I was looking for? Atlantean and Lemurian powers *did*, in fact, vibrate at different frequencies. Whatever they'd done to Humming Bird had stopped Chelsea's powers but hadn't inhibited the Lemurians'. Damn.

"Let her go," I demanded as I stood. If Valerie fucking hurt Chelsea, I'd kill her.

Freddy, the only senior staff left on the Bridge, managed maybe three strides before one of Thompson's men stopped him.

Thompson gestured over his shoulder. "Who? This girl?"

"I'm fucking serious, Thompson," I growled.

"Yes, I believe you are. Unfortunately for you, she's the enemy."

"You're the enemy, you asshole," Chelsea shouted, wriggling in Valerie's grasp.

Valerie laughed and tucked her mouth near Chelsea's ear. "Told you Trevor lied."

Chelsea's eyes snapped to mine, narrowing to slits the second they connected. Too many emotions mixed there for me to hold her gaze for long. I drew my eyes away, looking instead at the others. One of Thompson's men slumped an unconscious Dave into a station chair. Georgie, a distant twice-removed relative, seized Dr. Hill, but it didn't look like he wanted to escape. His free hand hung near his ribs, and his nose was jagged and bleeding.

I glanced at Chelsea. I hadn't registered her bleeding lip when she glowered at me. "What happened?"

Valerie shrugged. "She wouldn't cooperate."

I shot a glare at Valerie. "Bitch."

Her eyes widened. "Trevor, the language."

"That's enough," Thompson shouted. "Get the TAO scum down to the Brig. Valerie, take the soldier and watch her. Our focus is on holding the station until we get to port."

"Yeah, good luck," I said. "Even if you can keep the crew corralled for now, you'll never be able to hold us. We out number you ten to one."

"It's called abilities, you idiot," Valerie said.

Didn't matter. Sixty percent of the staff carried a weapon or had one nearby. If they hadn't stripped them of firearms and locked them far away from the weapons closets, I gave Thompson twelve hours max before someone got loose.

I groaned inwardly. Maybe not. They'd taken the Bridge in seconds, their powers would overrule guns, and I doubted Captain Marks would let his crew risk civilians getting caught in the crossfire.

Dr. Hill struggled as they hauled him off to the Brig, shouting, "They'll figure it out!" the entire way. Figure what out?

"Didn't know you mingled with those guys," Thompson said, shaking his head.

Play dumb. "Who?"

"TAO."

So everyone knew about them but me. "I didn't know."

"Right. A whole lot of that going on here, wouldn't you say?" Thompson asked of no one in particular.

"What the hell do you want?" Chelsea asked.

Valerie shoved her toward a station. Chelsea couldn't catch herself, but to her credit, she spun fast, fists up.

"Didn't we decide struggling wasn't worth it?" Valerie asked her.

Chelsea stilled but didn't lower her guard.

"Ah, yes." Thompson paced toward her. My body tensed, but I didn't move to intercept. Thompson leered at Chelsea. "I need you safe and in one piece for later."

Chelsea snarled and charged a step despite the shaking in her hands.

Valerie stepped in and pulled Chelsea's arms behind her. "I'll watch her."

"See that you do," Thompson said. "Finally got one alive."

Alive? What the hell?

"Come on, girlie, off to our room," Valerie said.

"Call me girlie again, and I'll—"

"What? Splash me to death?" Valerie tugged Chelsea up off the station. "Get over yourself, you stupid Atlantean bitch. I hope they let me at you."

"One piece," Thompson reminded Valerie. His warning didn't

matter. Valerie hated Atlanteans, thought they'd tortured Abby, left Abby as nothing more than a catatonic shell of the colorful person she used to be. Nothing in the world would keep Valerie from acting on that hatred now. Nothing Thompson could offer, anyway.

"Keep your hands off her, Valerie," I warned. "Don't do it."

Valerie rolled her eyes at me and laughed. She and Chelsea disappeared in a wave of orange and red. My mouth ran dry. She'd hurt her, and there was nothing I could do.

Thompson marched to my station and stooped over it. "How are we doing with the shield repairs?"

"It's covering the hole you burst your way through," I snapped.

He smacked the side of the station, causing me to jump. "Good. Keep it that way. And Ensign?" He directed a pointed look at Freddy. "Intervene again, and I'll shoot you."

Freddy's jaw clenched, but he sank into his station without protest. There was too much at stake to blindly fight back.

"Now," Thompson said, "Let's get to work."

He barked orders at his crew, half of them tasked with holding SeaSat5's crew on the main dining deck and the Bridge. He assigned the rest to collect artifacts from the outpost and bring them to the science decks. "I want to shove off within a few hours. Work fast," he said.

"What will you do with us then?" I asked.

Thompson holstered his weapon and scratched his ratty beard. "Not sure yet. Right now I want to dispose of you all, but let's see what changes, eh?"

Let's see how long it takes the crew to kill you, eh?

"But don't worry," he said, leaning in. "Your girlfriend will live, regardless of what happens to you. *She's* actually valuable."

"Screw you."

"You know, JoAnne was ready to take you back, even after you ran."

"I don't care what my mother wants." I returned to SeaSat5 out of a naïve obligation to protect the crew from these crazies, an obligation that had been cemented only when Chelsea showed up. I'd hoped my presence alone would deter Thompson from coming here, even if we'd found something. But my plan had failed, I hadn't been able to protect them, and everything had gone horrifically wrong. Everything. Chelsea had even looked at me like I was one of them, and, from her viewpoint, I couldn't blame her.

What the hell had Valerie said to her? More importantly, would Chelsea give me the chance to explain if we got out of this alive?

Gunshots reverberated in the corridor outside the open blast doors. Caught between wanting to duck and make a run for it, I stood, scared shit straight out of my mind. Every one of Thompson's guys drew their guns, but he held his hand up, a fireball growing. The second a small group of soldiers with guns, led by Lieutenant Weyland, appeared in the doorway, Thompson launched his fireball. They ducked but didn't rise again. Thompson's guys teleported behind them and tackled Weyland and his MPs to the ground.

"Ah, yes. Chief Security Officer. The last of the crew I had to find." He chuckled, deep and dark. "Thanks for making it so easy."

My stomach churned, and I vomited on the floor.

Chapter Twenty-Six

Chelsea

Fucking bitch had a mean right hook. And, unlike me, she clearly hadn't cared about hurting people.

I couldn't think straight. I was Atlantean. They weren't. But I couldn't figure out what they were, and I refused to look at Valerie. No matter how I examined it, terrorists taking a high tech station made sense. Terrorist taking a high tech research station for ancient artifacts did not. Besides, these guys had organized themselves too well to be treasure hunters, not to mention their powers.

I wracked my brain for ideas on who these people could belong to, given me being Atlantean, but stopped when my imagination soared to thoughts of the Minoans and El Dorado. Their powers were different, but that's all I'd figured out.

Then there was Dr. Hill, someone these guys were… not afraid of, but not a fan of, either. Which had me rethinking his job offer, stupid as the thought might be. At this point, I had no idea what I'd be joining, only that "Tao" was a shitty name for an organization. I mean, really. Tao? Tao Te Ching or something? But you know what they say about the enemy of your enemy. Maybe Dr. Hill wasn't so bad after all.

Too early to tell.

These guys knew Trevor. They knew Valerie. Which meant Trevor and Valerie's lives somehow intertwined with each other and all of this beyond what I knew, and that betrayal cut deeper than everything else. I frowned and rubbed my eyes to hide thoughts of them together, super spies for organizations filled with crazy, pyrokinetic people.

Valerie sighed loudly, breaking the silence that surrounded us. "Breakups suck. I know."

"Oh, fuck off," I said through my palms.

"I'd love to, but I'm kinda stuck with you for now. Believe me, I'm not thrilled about it, either."

Yeah, whatever.

I raised my palm above the cup of water on my nightstand and reached for my power. For that connection to water I'd thought was engrained in my spirit. But none came. Nothing happened aside from Valerie laughing.

"I told you they adjusted Humming Bird so your powers won't work," she said.

"You told me a lot of things." So had Trevor. He also apparently hadn't told me nearly as much as he knew, at the times I'd needed to hear it all most.

"Which one are you wondering about now?" She moved to the edge of her bed, looking honest-to-god ready to answer anything I threw her way. I wanted to ask her everything, but would she tell me the truth?

"Who are you and Trevor, really?" I asked.

"People," she said with a small shrug. "Same as you. Except, he doesn't have powers. He's the odd one out, not you." Her words didn't ease the pain, nor did her explanation.

"Then why?"

"Why what in particular?"

I wrung my hands rather than flip her off. "All of it."

She smiled, digging the knife in deeper. "I can't give you that. You're not ready. But I will tell you this: you and Trevor meeting that night was some damn act of fate."

My eyes narrowed. "What do you mean?" How'd she even know what happened that night? I'd never told her, and she wasn't there. Was she?

"Trevor was in Boston because he ran from the military," Valerie said.

I shook my head. "Because his family pressured him…"

Dots exploded across my mindscape, connecting themselves only long enough to fly off again. He and Valerie were long-time friends, *family* friends, and he'd been running from the military. From this, whatever this was. Had he known all along that people wanted to take SeaSatellite5, wanted to take the artifacts?

"Mhm," Valerie said. "They wanted him here, with me, like we were supposed to be. To keep the station in line. And safe."

I chortled. None of this made sense. "'Cause it's the picture of safe right now."

"With you on it, absolutely not."

My eyes snapped to hers. "What do I have to do with it?" *I* wasn't the one helping hijackers capture crewmembers and steal artifacts.

"You're *Atlantean*, Chelsea. Our enemy." Her eyes flashed red-hot anger. "Trevor shouldn't have talked to you that night. He should have let you get mugged."

If Valerie knew what had happened that night, did that mean Trevor knew my attacker?

That's why he'd jumped into the fray in the first place.

Oh, my god. That's why my attacker *ran* rather than turn on Trevor.

God, Helen must be in bed with them, too. She and Trevor had known what I was, and they'd used her whole Atlantean hypothesis to keep me out of the Brig when Lieutenant Weyland had every right to put me there. They'd wanted to keep me onboard, a research pet, when I should have ended up in jail or back on campus. To lure me in, keep an eye on me so I'd come to feel safe aboard this damn prison. I'd fallen so hard for their stupid games. *So* freaking hard.

I laughed. Trust the archaeologist dreamer to be swayed by Atlantean dreams.

I threw my head against the wall, still laughing at my stupidity. Believing the scientist who wanted to "help" me. Falling in love with the boy who only saw me as a target to be acquired. As long as I kept banging my head, or as long as Valerie pushed me to the edge of rage-filled insanity, I could keep from getting scared about it all. I could stay angry. Anger was sustainable.

My shaking hands fooled no one. I was already scared.

"Don't hit your head too hard," Valerie said. "We need your pretty little brain intact."

"Please go away," I whined, not quite begging, but close. I just wanted to be alone.

"No can do."

Rather than throw anything at her, I lay down, stewing quietly in my anger. I had to escape. It'd take me maybe five seconds to grab my guitar and hit her with it. Could I take her down long enough to get through the door? She wasn't bigger than me, but she was stronger. Stronger than normal humans. I hadn't been ready for her earlier, which was the only reason she'd won then. Now, though, the fight might be even.

"I'm wondering what even possessed you to go outside that bar alone," Valerie said after long, drawn out moments of silence.

I ignored her, still planning.

"I mean, I get it," she continued. "The Franklin is your band's main venue, so you thought it was safe. But it's still downtown Boston. It's seedy. Young girls like us shouldn't be out there alone."

Young girls like us shouldn't be walking freak shows either, but here we were.

"Long story," I mumbled.

"I don't think so," Valerie said. "Girl comes along, sweeps your boyfriend off his feet. I get it. I'd be ready to run, too, if I caught them." She paused and pressed a finger to her lips. "She must have been some brave bitch, that's all I'll say. Stealing from someone like you."

Valerie gave me too much credit. My arms and legs ached for movement, for a fight or flight that wouldn't happen. I couldn't run and hide or face this head on. It was too big, the threats too real. All I could do was buy time. Without powers, I was nothing, just a girl. Even my strength didn't match theirs.

"Can I ask you one thing, Chelsea?" Valerie asked.

My eyes wandered to her form, lithe and confident. "What?"

Valerie regarded me for long moments, peering deep into my eyes, her head tilted, searching for something she couldn't find. Her eyes narrowed, confused. "Do you honestly know nothing?"

I raised my hands in front of me. "I don't know what you *mean.*"

She pointed in the vague direction of the outpost. "About any of it. The source of your abilities. Your heritage. What's resting a quarter mile away. You don't know?"

I didn't know what I knew anymore. "I didn't have powers until recently. Helen thinks they're Atlantean. Helen thinks me having three is weird. And while we think we've found an Atlantean outpost, we don't know for sure. That's all I know, Valerie. I swear."

"Well then," Valerie said, disbelief masking her eyes. She slapped her thighs and stood up. "You're officially the most ignorant, yet dangerous, person on this station." She strode to the door, hands glowing red and orange.

What the hell?

Valerie pressed her palms against the hinges and the center turnstile of the door, melting the steel into something unmovable.

"You can try getting out, but I doubt it'll open. They need me upstairs to sidestep whatever your lover-boy is doing." She pinned me with a glare. "Stay put, girlie. Don't make me hit you again. You have a pretty face. Oh, and"—she thrust her finger in my direction—

"you better hope I never find proof of what your kind did to Abby. Because if I turn out to be right about that, I'm taking it out on you."

With a flash of fire, she was gone.

Abby? Trevor's cousin? What did her situation have to do with Atlantis?

Chapter Twenty-Seven

Trevor

Six hours. Somehow, they'd managed to hold the station for six anxiety-ridden hours. At least another sixteen remained until we hit port.

Freddy was the only Bridge staff they'd brought up to help me, but everything—patience, hope—wore thin. There hadn't been any more casualties so far. Didn't mean there wouldn't be any. The crew also hadn't made a move to retake the station yet, which played a part in that statistic. But what if they *did* make a takeover attempt? Why hadn't they? I could understand civilians not wanting to risk it, especially if the military staff told them not to. There had to be protocols somewhere, although Thompson's crew and their abilities cancelled out any planning. But still. Someone had to do *something*, and I was out of ideas.

Pain stung my chest. Valerie had Chelsea, and now that the pretense of friendship had been shattered, what would keep Valerie from hurting her? Chelsea couldn't defend against an angry Valerie. Not before, with powers, and definitely not now that hers were gone and Valerie's were revealed.

I ran my hands through my hair. *Think, Boncore. Think.*

Dr. Hill. He was the unknown factor. Whatever TAO meant and whatever they did, he'd known about the war and the Link Pieces. He'd known about Chelsea. Maybe he'd know what to do now.

I looked up. Thompson stood over Freddy's shoulder while he worked on his own to stabilize the destroyed systems. Georgie sulked a few feet away. If I could distract him for long enough, could I make it to Dr. Hill?

My fingers slid over the keyboard in front of me, dancing six steps ahead of my mind. I closed the windows, plan in place, and glanced at Georgie. "I need to go to the bathroom."

"Hold it," he snarled.

"You know that's not healthy, right? It's been over six hours."

He sneered my way, arms crossed above his beer-belly. "Tough shit. I ain't stupid. I let you go, you run. Then I gotta chase you, and I don't feel like running."

I shrugged. "So shoot me. I'm not stupid, either. I just gotta piss."

"Take him," Thompson said over his shoulder. "His whining is as irritating now as it was when he was eight."

Georgie drew his gun and waved it my way. "All right. Let's go."

He escorted me off the Bridge, his biker swagger and the gun in his hand the only thing keeping my senses on edge. Getting slugged by him and his tree-trunk arms would hurt. A lot. But he was stupid. He followed Thompson's commands like a trusting, loyal dog. He didn't even notice when the lights overhead dimmed to emergency floodlights. Just kept on walking. Not good. He was too focused on me and not on the distraction I'd planned.

Halfway to the restrooms on this level, the lights shut off for a split second that seemed to last forever.

Wait, I told myself. *Not yet.*

Sparks burst out of every bulb and fixture like handfuls of sparklers on the Fourth of July.

"What the hell!" Georgie shouted.

I spun and shoved a shoulder into his chest, knocking him away.

My eyes darted around, looking for a weapon, anything I could use to defend myself long enough to get Georgie out of the picture.

The locker!

I sprinted back the way we came, fumbling with my keycard. It slid out of my shaking fingers to the floor.

"Shit," I said, bending down. It took several tries to pry it from the floor, my fingers not cooperating. I rushed the reader at the weapons locker door and slid the card through. Nothing happened. I flipped the keycard over and over in my hands. No, no, no. I turned it upside down and slid it through the right way. Still nothing.

"Screw this."

I tore off the shielding and entered my authorization code directly into the keypad beneath.

Beep beep. Red light.

I tried my code again.

Beep beep. Red light.

"What the hell!" I yelled, slamming my hand against the reader. They'd locked me out of everything. *Valerie* had locked me out.

Georgie barreled down the hall, gun waving around in the air like a madman. "Stupid brat! Get back here!"

I was done for. Dead.

A bright red object hanging on the wall caught my attention. I flung myself away from Georgie and crashed into the fire extinguisher. I yanked the extinguisher off the wall, raised the canister above my head, and charged him.

Georgie must not have expected a direct attack. His head clanged against the extinguisher, and he slid unconscious to the floor. I stood there, frozen despite the adrenaline, the sense of satisfaction coursing through me.

Footsteps echoed down the hall from the Bridge. *Keep moving, Boncore.* The Brig sat one floor down. I had to get there—quick. But how?

Thompson's voice soared through the corridor. "What the hell's going on out here?"

I was running out of time.

Left. Right. My eyes searched every inch of the corridor. No more weapons. Nothing an extinguisher could do against guns from far away. I had *nothing*.

I backed up against the wall, heart threatening to jump right out of my chest, followed by my lungs. *Think, think, think.*

My fingers brushed metal along the wall. *Vent!*

I spun and tried prying the vent cover from the wall. It didn't budge. I grabbed the canister and hammered it against the vent, denting the frame and popping screws loose. The vent cover clattered to the ground, and I peered inside. It'd be a tight fit, but they wouldn't be able to follow. For the first time, I was actually thankful I was no more than skin and bones.

I dove into the vent head first and army-crawled my way through the first fifteen feet.

"Trevor!" Thompson yelled through the hole. "Get the hell back here!"

Keep going. Don't respond.

"I'll vent out the oxygen!"

No, he won't. He won't kill you.

He absolutely would.

I crawled faster.

It got easier when the venting opened up at an intersection. The expanding metal walls gave me brain-space to think about the station's blueprints. A nearby service staircase linked a small security office off the Bridge to the Brig.

I charged onwards through the vent, kicking open the entrance to the service staircase with aching shoulders. No one was there. I slipped down the ten-foot drop, onto the staircase. At least they hadn't guessed where I'd gone, yet.

Down the stairs and around the corner I jogged. I went through the same motions with the Brig's lock as I did the weapons locker. But instead of denying me entry, this door beeped once and glowed green. I pushed open the door. The sight inside shocked me frozen.

Dr. Hill rested limp in a chair, his face battered and bloodied. His shirt had been torn. Nasty, angry red burns trailed down one arm and all along his chest. His matted hair shielded his eyes. I couldn't tell if he was awake. Or alive. He'd been tortured pretty badly. By who? Thompson?

My blood ran cold. Had Valerie done this?

I shut the door behind me and rushed to his side. "Dr. Hill? Dr. Hill, are you with me?" I shook his leg, the only unmarred part of his body.

He groaned and shifted in his chair.

Relief lifted my lungs. *Thank god.* "It's me, Trevor. I escaped to see you."

He gave me a look that said I'd have been smarter to get to Shuttle Dock and make a run for it.

"Are your people coming?" I asked him. His archaeology team had been on their way. What would they do when they found the station had moved?

"Didn't…. no time… to call," he wheezed and pressed a hand against his chest. He coughed, blood spewing from his mouth.

Shit. I didn't know how to help him, or even if I could.

"How do I contact them?" I asked. "Why can't Thompson take the artifacts and go? Didn't they have a sub of their own to get them here?"

Answer: There were too many artifacts. Still, why the whole damn station?

"Gave you the number," he whispered.

The card. Dammit. "It's in my quarters. No way I'm getting there." I'd been lucky enough to get here relatively undeterred.

Dr. Hill's eyes shut, and he listed off a string of numbers. I burned them into memory, repeating each one after he said it, and again when the string restarted.

"This is… our war…" he sputtered.

"Yeah, I know. My parents started it."

He shook his head and winced. "TAO—"

"Are a bunch of idiots with their heads stuck up where the sun don't shine," came Valerie's arrogant, shrill voice.

My stomach churned.

She stood in the doorway. "Kind of like the Brig of SeaSatellite5, if you ask me."

"This isn't how it was supposed to go," I said, standing. "Think about this, Valerie."

She stepped into the room, her hand raised above her, a fireball growing in her palm. "It's *exactly* how things were supposed to go, Trevor. Except you're supposed to be standing here with me, not beside the enemy."

The fireball danced in her palm, no bigger than a grape. She lifted her hand to her mouth and blew the fireball off like a kid might a dead dandelion head. The fireball hurried from her hand and raced past me at lightning speed to Dr. Hill's chest. A new scar on his body. Dr. Hill grunted but didn't shout.

"Valerie, stop!" I searched her eyes for reason, for anything resembling understanding or the Valerie I used to know. Her loyalty, her defining feature, remained intact—just for all the wrong individuals. There wasn't a way to reason with Valerie. Except maybe with her own life.

"He'll destroy the station," I said. "You know that, right? It won't matter what you do here, who you torture to make yourself feel useful to him. He'll destroy the station first, then you."

"Not with everyone still on it," she argued. "Trust me, Trevor."

"He will. He doesn't care. If he can't find a way to get all of the artifacts off, he'll sink us all before you and his other lackeys can do anything to stop him. How do you expect anyone to find the station when they don't know where we are, or when the cloak's up? Or do you not care at all about what happens to me, to your friends?"

Valerie faltered for a single moment, a second so minute, I almost missed it. Her diamond-strength confidence had been obliterated by two simple questions.

"Our only mission is the artifacts. The station is safe," she said. "Unlike you."

She charged me, yanking me roughly into a standing position. Her strength scared me into not reacting. This power, hidden for so long. And the fire. The torture. What other surprises did Valerie have? Who was the real Valerie?

She tugged me to the door, stopping to glance at Dr. Hill. "Toodles, Doctor. Stay alive, will you? We're not done." So cavalier. Did this cold, uncaring Valerie torture Chelsea, too?

My fist flew toward Valerie before I could think better of it. She deflected my punch without effort and slammed her elbow into my gut, pinning me to the wall.

"I meant what I said before," she hissed. "We're friends, Trevor. Despite you being on the wrong side of this, I don't want to see you killed. That I do mean for real." She leveled me with a look. "Don't make me regret it."

Chapter Twenty-Eight

Chelsea

Valerie left thirty minutes ago. The disaster the room had become in the meantime evidenced my escape attempts, despite my lack of progress in doing so. My guitar case rested mangled on the bed, an unfortunate piece of collateral damage. For some reason, I'd thought I could punch through Valerie's melted metal doors with my supposedly abnormal strength. I couldn't. I'd wrapped my fists in impromptu bandages to stop my knuckles from bleeding, not pausing to weep over the loss of my favorite cardigan to the cause.

Next up, the towel rack from the bathroom. I ripped it off the wall, lifted the privacy screen on the door, and slammed the metal pole through the glass. It echoed like a high-pitched clap of thunder, and glass scattered everywhere.

Carefully stepping over it, I peered outside. No one. For someone they deemed important, they sure didn't seem too keen on watching me. Or maybe Valerie assumed I'd never get out. Well, Valerie didn't know the first damn thing about me, and that bitch would *pay*.

I reached through the hole, searching for the keycard reader.

There had to be some sort of alarm button. I knew they didn't kill the entire crew because doing so didn't seem smart on their part. Then again, I hadn't seen anyone other than Trevor and Freddy since returning from the outpost. Maybe they *did* kill everyone.

Bastard. Trevor took the No. 2 spot on my ever-growing "punch in the face" list. I thought I'd grown out of such childish ways of thinking. Guess not. Suddenly, dealing with job-hunting and skirting Lexi's boyfriend-stealing attempts didn't seem so annoying anymore.

This wasn't working. All my fingers brushed was wall. I retreated back into the room. "What next?"

Desk. Both of our desks were the right height. I grabbed mine, wanting to vomit at the sight of Valerie's. If I could move my desk across the room, maybe I could gain enough height to reach the card reader. I glanced up at the ceiling. *Or climb up through the vent.*

Something on Valerie's desk pinged, heralding the stupidity of the vent idea. The beep rang throughout the quiet room before her tablet screen flared to life.

What the hell?

I crossed the few paces to her tablet and leaned in closer. An icon at the bottom danced and shook every few seconds. *Mega Rush 2.* Someone was legitimately playing the game right now? In the middle of a freaking hijacking?

Curiosity propelled me into Valerie's desk chair before frustration could convince me otherwise. I needed to know who was this bored in the midst of guns and fireballs. I clicked the icon to bring up the game. Valerie wasn't a player this time around, but she must have been in Trevor's first version because she had a user profile and inbox set up.

1 New Message bounced on the main menu screen.

Two taps of the mouse had her in-game inbox front and center. It was a message from Emma Rose, Chief Engineer I, according to her signature. Frilly-ass name if you asked me. I opened it.

Chelsea,

The following are instructions to reconnect the Communications Buoy and contact Admiral Eliot Dennett. No one knows about our situation or are likely to find out. Be quick. I can't keep them occupied for long.

Emma

Trap. Absolutely a trap. Valerie's tablet *happened* to get a message for a game Trevor made while I'm stuck in here alone? Absolute. Freaking. Trap.

I backed away from her desk. Clearly no one outside the station knew about our situation. But there had to be check-ins, and if we missed them, help would come. Dr. Hill's archaeology team was already on their way anyway, and, if they were as involved as he was, they'd know what to do.

Who'd sent me the message, Valerie or Trevor? Could I trust one over the other at this point? My heart said yes while my brain scolded my heart for allowing myself to fall for Trevor in the first place.

Was Emma Rose even a real person?

Valerie had loaded a staff directory onto my tablet on my first day. I pulled my tablet out of the drawer next to my bed and opened up the directory. Sure enough, Emma Rose was an Engineer listed as working under Trevor and Dave. Maybe someone knew I had some autonomy. Maybe they knew I'd get a chance.

I sat in Valerie's desk chair and opened the attachment from Emma. Her instructions weren't complicated. According to Emma, Valerie's tablet had already been hooked into the communications system. Emma had designed a way to hack into the system, get to the Bridge's controls of the communications buoy, and reconnect it to outside transmissions. Emma said she was holding the door open for all of this to happen for as long as she could from another location, one directly hooked into the buoy. I followed Emma's directions, and when the buoy connected, I called what appeared to be Admiral Dennett's personal line.

"Sir," I said before a video screen popped up and the webcam light turned on. "Admiral?"

His screen flashed and an older man in military dress uniform appeared. "Who is this? How did you get this number?"

"An engineer gave it to me," I said. "I'm an intern on SeaSatellite5. My name is Chelsea Danning."

His brow furrowed. He didn't believe me and likely wouldn't. Who would help SeaSatellite5 if he didn't? "The archaeologist we brought on?"

I nodded. "Yes, sir."

"An engineer had this number?"

"Yes. Chief Engineer Emma Rose. Sir, the station's been hijacked. They've had us for almost..." I checked my watch. "Eight hours now. I guess no one had time to get the word out."

His eyebrows disappeared into his receding hairline. "Excuse me?"

"SeaSat5 was hijacked. Sir, I'm not sure how much time I have."

"By who?"

I shook my head. "I have no idea. But they're like me, they have powers." I hoped someone had filled him in on me having powers, or he was liable to think me crazy and never send help.

He leaned off-screen and dialed another phone. "Stay on the line."

I tapped my fingers against the desk while he called someone. I gritted my teeth together, my fingers' drum solo speeding up. Valerie could teleport in at any second, fiery show and all. "Sir."

He stopped for a moment and looked into the camera. "Can you stay on the line and give me more information?"

"I don't have time, and I don't know what's going on. I've been locked in my quarters for most of it."

"We'll send help. Can you keep us updated using this channel?"

Emma hadn't made it seem like she could keep the line open for a while. "I don't think so."

The Admiral's lips pursed together and he stilled for long moments. "Stay safe and hidden. Help is on the way. Do you know the status of Captain Marks or the Commander?"

"No, sir."

Admiral Dennett grimaced. "Thank you for taking a huge risk in contacting me. A rescue team is being organized right now. What is your current location?"

I wanted to smack my head against the desk for being so unhelpful. "I don't know. They flipped the station hours ago, after collecting artifacts from the outpost. We've been moving ever since. They keep saying something about going to home port, but I don't know who they are or where that is. They want the artifacts." *And me.*

"I'll have our people here ping your location. We'll—"

The call disconnected with a vacuum of black enveloping the screen.

I wacked the keyboard. "No!"

Bright lights filled the room. Someone's hand clamped down hard on my shoulder, their fingers digging into my skin. "Stupid bitch." Spittle sprayed my face.

We teleported to the Bridge where I was met with the angry lead hijacker. Trevor stood some distance behind him, restrained by one of the other goons, his arms pinned behind him.

"No! Don't do it, Thompson!" he shouted.

Thompson waved Trevor off. "I need her alive, you know that." He approached me, reeking of cigarette buds and grime. "I want to know why you called someone on the outside."

"Did what?" *Dammit, Chelsea.* Sarcasm was not okay right now.

He lifted an eyebrow. "Who did you contact and how?"

I risked a glance at Trevor. His face contained a mixture of desperation and confusion. It really must have been Engineer Emma Rose. Could he see that's how she'd contacted me? Did he know she helped me?

"Even I'm not entirely sure," I said. Honesty seemed like a decent idea.

Thompson's eyes snapped to Trevor. "Only someone who works on the Bridge or in Engineering could reconnect the buoy. You're the common denominator, and yet the signal originated from her quarters. Explain."

Trevor's eyes met mine, pleading. I didn't have answers for him. I wasn't sure I had anything for him anymore. For whatever reason, he deemed me worthy of lying to, which made him little better than Ray in my eyes. Everyone had lied to me. But Trevor lied about *this*, and his lies had endangered everyone on board as a result.

"She doesn't know how," Trevor pleaded. "She didn't do this."

"Bullshit," I said before thinking better of it. "And you don't get to speak for me."

Again Trevor's blue eyes pleaded with mine, begging me to be quiet. *Hell no.*

"If you didn't, who did?" Thompson asked.

"Valerie, obviously," Trevor spat. "She doesn't trust you, either." He turned his head at his captor. "Let me go. I'm not going anywhere."

My head spun with all the accusations. Trevor had thought Valerie was to blame, and the message *did* go to her computer. But Emma knew I'd be in the room, and I didn't have a Mega Rush 2 profile. Besides, Valerie hated both Trevor and me, and if Emma knew that, then the whole station did.

"I freaking did it, okay? Okay." I forced my eyes to level with Thompson's. "I used a Chief Engineer's profile to hack into the system from a computer in my quarters, reconnect the damn buoy, and make a call to the outside."

Thompson's fingers wrapped around his gun, reminding me of Lieutenant Weyland's exact posture the day I'd first teleported onto SeaSat5. Was Weyland also amongst the trail of liars Trevor had left in his wake?

"To who?" Thompson asked.

Did it matter if he knew? The senior military staff would call the Admiral first if the Captain were compromised. "Admiral Dennett. He can't rescue us if he doesn't know what's going on."

Trevor shrugged out of his captor's grasp long enough to pace toward me. "You did what?"

Thompson shot out an arm and tossed Trevor to his captor.

"Behave. I don't care what JoAnne wants. Remember that, kid."

My fists closed and opened, torn between letting Trevor take the threat and defending him.

A shrill alarm blared to life, the lights on the Bridge dimming to a red hue. My captor's grip on me tightened the moment it happened.

Thompson cocked his gun. "What the hell is that?" he shouted.

"Let me look," Trevor said, already trying to inch his way to a station.

My heart sunk as Thompson pointed his gun at Trevor. Liar or not, he didn't deserve to die.

"Don't!" I screamed. "Leave him alone!" I kicked and wriggled, trying to get free.

My captor's grip loosened as he grabbed a gun from his holster and brandished the weapon close to my face. My heartbeat thudded in my ears, coldness freezing me in place. My fingernails dug into his arm.

Thompson waved his gun from Trevor to a Bridge workstation. "Look." He nodded at Trevor's captor, who let him go.

Trevor leaned over the station and tapped the keys. The alarm silenced but a scowl marred his face. "What in the hell?"

"What is it?" Thompson demanded.

Trevor collapsed into the chair. "I need Ensign Olivarez. Now. I can't do this on my own."

Thompson shifted, gun pointed at me. I slammed my eyelids shut. *This is it. This is the end. Teleport. Teleport. Teleport already.* What good were these powers if they didn't work when I needed them most? I thought of Sarah. Of home. Of the Franklin. Of anything but right here and now, where a liar's words had held my fate too many times over.

"Someone's disabled the shield," Trevor spoke quickly. "Water's rushing the top level. I'm doing what I can to minimize damage, but I can't do that *and* restore the damn shield so it stops." He looked up at Thompson. "You either need to get some Bridge staff up here, or reverse what you did to Humming Bird and let Chelsea plug the leak. And for god's sake, control your men."

My eyelids slid open at my name. "I'm not helping them."

Trevor's eyes bore into mine, pleading, hoping. "We'll all die if you don't."

"*You're* helping them," I insisted. "You're doing whatever they ask."

"To keep everyone alive." He rose from his chair. "Please, Chelsea."

"Don't bother trying to suss it out, solider," Thompson said. He pointed at one of his lackeys. "Get the Ensign and Lieutenant Commander ASAP. That's all you're getting, Trevor." Thompson turned to me. "Trouble or not, I'm taking you with us. Even if it's to the grave."

Trevor's eyes narrowed into a glare. "And if they can't get the breach under control?"

"Better hope your girlfriend changes her mind," Thompson growled. "I'm not letting this station sink with those artifacts on board."

I let out a stream of profanities all to the effect of: hell no.

Chapter Twenty-Nine

Trevor

Five minutes. That was all it'd taken to convince Thompson that more hands on the Bridge wasn't going to fix the problem. The station took on water no matter what we did, and the hull breach alarm's shrill call squawked every time someone shut it off.

They held Chelsea in a corner. She refused to make eye contact with me whenever I tried. I deserved it. I didn't know what Valerie told her, but she clearly knew enough to know I'd lied. Now Chelsea hated me, and she may be the sole person able to plug the leak long enough to get the shield over the breach and temporarily patch it. But they'd have to fix Humming Bird to do it—and convince Chelsea to cooperate.

"You have to fix what you did to Humming Bird," I pleaded with Thompson. "Just guard her. She's not going anywhere."

"Stop talking about me like I'm not here," Chelsea snapped as she tried to wriggle free.

"Enough," Thompson barked. He stared me down. "I need this ship."

"Then repair Humming Bird, and let Chelsea fix it."

"I said I wouldn't help," she insisted.

My fingers wrung around each other, frustration rising above the anxiety inside me. "You don't have a choice."

"The hell I don't," Chelsea said.

Thompson's eyes shut for a moment. Valerie appeared beside him in a fierce shower of burning flames. Were they telepathic?

"Undo what you did," he said to Valerie. "We need the soldier's abilities to patch the hull."

"You're nuts, right?" Valerie asked, stalking up to an Engineering station.

"She's not going to do anything," I repeated.

Chelsea huffed from her corner.

For god's sake, Chelsea. She could hate me all she wanted, but only after the station was safe.

Valerie chuckled. "Like she could. She'd just teleport to you, and I don't think she wants that right now." She tapped commands into the system, and it beeped. "Reversed." To Chelsea, she said, "Fix the hull. I'll find you if you try to escape."

My heart sank.

"*You* compromised Humming Bird?" I asked. After all these years, Valerie destroyed my system? I swallowed hard and beat the station in front of me. My knuckles split and bled. My once best friend, now competitor, crippled my life's work. Disabled the system as easily as jail-breaking a phone.

Valerie's eyes slid to mine with a gaze somewhere between pride and remorse. "It's a good system. The only downfall is it's easily meddled with."

My breathing hit a fever pitch. Too many secrets, too many hidden agendas. SeaSatellite5 was being ripped away from me. Chelsea was already gone. And now Humming Bird, the only thing I had left.

Thompson stalked to Chelsea and ripped her off the floor. "Come on." Chelsea grunted against his hold.

Valerie's hand shot out to my arm. Next thing I knew, we all stood on an overhang over SeaSatellite5's helicopter, underneath the broken section of hull. Water rushed inside in torrents. The only thing keeping the station pressurized were the remaining portions of the shield, but those were quickly fading. Water spat on our faces, drenching our clothes.

"Plug it," Thompson ordered Chelsea, finger thrust at the leak.

"No," she said.

"Chelsea," I pleaded. "Come on."

"No—fuck you," she spat. "I can't believe *you* of all people did this to me."

Her words were a kick to the balls. I never intended for any of this to happen. Protecting her was all I ever wanted. "It's not what you—"

"On the contrary, it's exactly what she thinks," Valerie said. "You lied. You hid secrets about yourself, your role here, and all the things you knew about her from the beginning. Things *she* didn't know and needed to. I'd be pissed, too."

"We don't have time for this," Thompson declared. Two more of his lackeys appeared beside us, Captain Marks and Lieutenant Weyland in their grasp.

"No!" Chelsea shouted, lunging for them.

I stood frozen in place. A sinking feeling in my chest said this was about to go belly up. All of it.

Thompson gripped her by the arm and pointed to the leak. "Fix it, or they die. You all will."

Deliberation sparked in her eyes. She was calculating something. Maybe how long it'd take her to teleport out of here? Her hands shook, fingers curling and uncurling.

"I can't," she said, voice shaking. "It's too much water. I don't have control."

"Then you'd better learn some," Thompson said as he shoved her toward the edge. "Now."

My lungs left the building. Gone. I couldn't breathe. An invisible hand constricted my throat. This was it. This is how it'd all end.

Chelsea shook her head. "No."

Thompson nodded, and the guy holding Weyland pushed him to the edge to the overhang. The only thing keeping Weyland on the platform were his feet and the guy's arm. Captain Marks's eyes widened, but he stayed silent. Why didn't he act? Why didn't he move to stop this?

Because he couldn't. No one could, except Chelsea. And she didn't *want* to.

"Chelsea, you don't understand," I pleaded, my words tripping over each other. What would make her understand? This wasn't about *her* and what *she* wanted to do. It was about the whole damn crew. The entire station. "The more water that rushes in, the bigger the hole will get. Eventually the shield won't be able to compensate, and it'll collapse. We *will* die when that happens, Chelsea. The station will implode."

"So, flip it upright," she said, eyes darting between everyone in the room, down to the drop below us, landing last on the leak.

"Flipping the station won't help. I know you can do it, Chelsea," I said. "Just concentrate." We were too deep to be waterlogged. If she couldn't—or wouldn't—fix this, this would be the end.

"With them on a precipice? Yeah, right," she said, hands jutting toward Captain Marks and Weyland. "Take them away from the edge, then I'll try."

"Trying is not an option." Thompson waved to the man holding Captain Marks.

Thompson's lackey shoved the Captain onto the edge next to Weyland.

"Don't!" I shouted at Thompson. "Chelsea, you can do this."

She shook her head. "I am terrified of heights and nothing works right when I'm scared. Trying is the best you're gonna freaking get."

Thompson's chest rose and fell in a heavy motion. He nodded at his men, and they pulled Captain Marks away from the edge. "You've saved your Captain. Plug the leak to save his Lieutenant."

Chelsea's eyes met Weyland's for a long moment before Weyland nodded.

"Fine," she spat. Chelsea approached the edge and held her hands up. "I don't even know how to do this."

I wanted to say *chill out first*, but knew it wouldn't help her.

She lifted her hands and, slowly, the water obeyed some unseen command. Across a span of pregnant minutes, the water stopped rushing in, and what was inside returned back out into the sea in a raging torrent. She did it. She honest-to-god moved waves of water like all the stories of Atlantis I'd been told about as a kid. Like she was the maker of waves, or Poseidon himself. She was Atlantean, powerful, beautiful, and in total control. Her display took my breath away.

"Now," I told Thompson. "Have Olivarez try now."

He spoke into his radio. Above us, a glow announced the shield's recovery. Chelsea let go, the leak plugged.

"Good job," I told her. Except she wasn't looking at me. Or anyone.

Her head pointed to the ground below us, then she lifted her arms in a quick motion. In the blink of an eye water soared at Thompson's head in the shape of a sword. He raised a hand and blasted fire, vaporizing the water. Chelsea's eyes widened, and she stumbled backwards, away from the flame. She slid on the slick ground, slipped, and tumbled over the edge. I lunged for her, but Thompson tugged me back. Chelsea fell, shrieking as she plunged downward through three stories of empty space.

My heart dropped alongside her.

That scream… God that scream. Chelsea. *My* Chelsea. Scared of heights, plummeting three stories, down, down, down.

I thrashed and beat Thompson. Got an elbow into his side. A heel into his shin. I thrust my head back at his nose. It connected and he cursed.

"Let me go!" I screamed. *No. No, no, no.* Fuck. "Chelsea!"

It was stupid. The drop was too far. Her screams had stopped, but I heard no sound of impact. God, why was I listening for one? A wave of chills and extreme heat overtook me all at once.

"Dammit!" Captain Marks shouted. "You bastard."

Both he and Weyland struggled with their guards, but neither found purchase. Georgie struck Weyland across the face. Captain Marks took the butt of a gun to his head.

Thompson threw me into the wall, my body connecting hard. I slid to the ground. I pushed myself up and wiped my face free of water and tears. It didn't help. One or both constantly rushed my cheeks and lips.

"Chelsea," I said her name, quieter this time. She'd have responded if she were still alive. But she wasn't. She was gone.

Dead.

Lost.

I drew a ragged breath past my lips and wiped my face with my arm. My body shook, tremors from quick, uneven breaths, from the echoing of Chelsea's scream, from losing her.

I shivered. Cold. Impossibly cold from the only fire in my life being snuffed out in a single, shrieking moment.

I stared into nothingness, the empty space she occupied moments ago.

Blue lights began to fill that space and, dammit, my heart skipped straight to the hope that maybe, just maybe, the impossible had happened. Maybe she'd survived. Maybe she'd teleported to me, just how she'd always had.

I hated that hope. Hope had never done me any good.

Then a waterfall cascaded in front of me. I sucked in a deep, long breath as Chelsea materialized from within the torrent. She'd teleported out of the drop. She survived. She was *alive*. Happiness surged through my veins.

"Chelsea," I said, reaching out to touch her, to convince myself she wasn't a mirage.

She spun around, eyes wild, and struck Thompson. His head snapped back, but he recovered quickly. Chelsea swept up a kick to his stomach. He flew backwards into the wall beside me.

"Valerie!" Thompson bellowed.

Chelsea waved her hand over a lingering puddle. No water followed her command. Valerie had disabled her powers once more, leaving her helpless. She charged, but one of Thompson's lackeys tackled her to the ground.

"Chelsea," I croaked. I hiccupped past tears. She was alive.

She didn't respond.

"Nice try," Thompson said, grasping his middle with one hand. He wiped blood from his nose and mouth with the other. "Nice try."

I hadn't seen Chelsea since they'd dragged her away, tears in her eyes. And every minute, every second, that had passed since was another nail hammered into my heart. But Thompson didn't slip up again until hour eighteen, when he strolled over to Christa and diverted his attention from me.

I glanced across the Bridge at Freddy. Despite the look of concentration on his face, his fingers were casually placed on the side of his head. Three of them, just sitting there, gently tapping his headset.

I reached up nonchalantly and flipped mine to channel three. "Am I that obvious?"

He removed his hand from the side of his head and placed his fingers under his nose to cover the headset's mic. "You kiddin' me? I've been waiting for hours."

I closed my eyes and tried not to think about it. "I need you. I'll buy you a drink if my plan works."

"Hell, I'll buy *you* one after we get off this tank." He shifted in his seat like he was ready to jailbreak himself, no matter the cost.

A chuckle broke through me, despite all the other negative feelings. "Deal. Can you do something for me?"

"Say the word."

I hesitated. What I wanted to ask of him wasn't fair. "Be a distraction. I'm going to send a transmission for reinforcements."

His eyes flitted to mine. "Didn't Chelsea call the Admiral?"

"The Admiral can't help us. I need to call someone else."

Freddy tilted his head, thinking, and raised one bushy eyebrow. "Well, this oughta be fun."

He took off his headset and jumped up from his station. He made a mad dash toward Thompson but stopped short and jumped, yanking down a pipe from above. Smoke sprayed into Thompson's face. Freddy punched his jaw, then his gut. Christa, who'd been sitting at the secondary communications station, stood and made her way toward them for back up. One of Thompson's guys pointed a gun at her. She froze.

I took my opportunity and hopped onto the primary communications station, dialing the number Dr. Hill gave me. It patched me through some awkward dial-up noises to a military base. A click sounded. The call had gone through.

"I need to talk to whoever's in charge of TAO right now."

The female voice on the other end tutted. "You've reached a wrong number. This is a U.S. Army—"

"I'm a member of SeaSatellite5. Dr. Hill can't contact you right now. We need—"

Someone dragged me from the console and threw me to the ground. My shoulder slammed into the metal grating. Thompson's creep stood over me, foot poised for a kick in the ribs.

"That was stupid," he said and shot the console with his gun. Electrical sparks sputtered everywhere with the tiny explosion.

"Did you seriously do that?" I thrust my hand at the console. "You shot Communications!"

He kicked me in the ribs. I curled my body and coughed blood. Every sharp inhale stung. He holstered his gun then lifted me by the sides of my shirt, turning me to face Thompson.

"Trevor!" Christa yelped, backing off from the fight. She stepped back onto the communications platform.

"You're quickly becoming more trouble than you're worth," said Thompson. He had Freddy in cuffs.

Freddy sported a new gash above his eyebrow and a bloody lip. His eyes asked if I'd done what I needed to.

I nodded at him. *Yes.*

The secondary communications station chirped to life before they removed us from the Bridge. I glanced up at Thompson to see if he'd answer. Was TAO calling back?

Thompson strode over and keyed in some commands. "Accept the transmission, Lieutenant Commander."

"Do it yourself!" she snapped.

"Do it, Christa," I said.

She looked at me.

It's important. Please.

She nodded like she knew my thoughts and stepped into Thompson's space. After a few seconds, her eyebrows bunched together.

"What is it?" Thompson asked.

Her eyes drifted to mine. "I'm not sure."

Thompson all but shoved her out of the way and glared down at the screen. His eyes snapped to mine. "What did you do?"

"Ask for help," I answered.

He pointed at the screen. "It's Atlantean!"

"Is it?" Why would TAO send a message in Atlantean? I held onto the thought as he got in my face, spittle flying into my eyes.

Thompson's face reddened to a deep purple. "Are you working for TAO?"

Not a word spilled from my lips.

He pointed to the console once more. "The message. What do they know?"

"I can't read Atlantean."

He stepped away from me and scanned the message again. The more he read, the closer his hand got to the gun at his hip. I swallowed hard. He flicked his pistol out of his holster and clicked off the safety, pointing the barrel at me. "I knew you weren't right for this job. You're a double-agent, aren't you?"

Thompson stepped toward me, but spoke to his lackeys instead. "Get more engineers up here. I need this ship in top shape." He glared at me. "Humming Bird included. We're going to see what your machine is capable of, Trevor. And this time, you better be willing to risk your life for it."

Thompson stormed off the Bridge, barking orders as he went.

Of all the engineers Thompson could have brought up, I was thankful it was Michael that Thompson's guys had dragged onto the Bridge. He knew how Humming Bird worked, and I knew I could trust him. Thompson sat him at a station and told him to work.

Michael's eyes drifted to mine, a silent question swimming within them. I shook my head. We couldn't speak. Not now.

Christa still held her station. Weyland had taken position at Freddy's NANA station, for a reason I didn't catch, in the time it took Thompson to find another engineer. But Christa, Weyland, Michael, and I were not enough. I understood why Thompson wanted the station— Chelsea and the artifacts—but running the ship ragged wasn't the way to do it. Every problem we solved, every repair we made to fix something Thompson's ungraceful takeover caused, a new issue took its place.

Without warning, Weyland crouched next to me. "How many are onboard?"

My gaze darted around the room. Thompson and his crew had disappeared.

"Ten including Valerie," I said. "But don't plan a takeover attempt."

His brow furrowed. "I have to."

"Don't. I can't explain everything—we don't have time. This situation is unstable."

"There are one-hundred-and-one innocent crew members onboard, Trevor. Most of them civilians. I have to do *something.*"

How could I explain this without having to tell him everything? "Weyland, these people are like Chelsea—but the enemy. They may have *abilities* we can't account for."

The information didn't seem to faze him. "So what? We sit and wait? That's not going to happen." A pause. "And how do you know?"

"Because I've seen them. Trust me, just this once. Help is coming."

His eyes grew hard. "You get three more hours, then I act."

I was surprised he'd given me that much. Maybe something would change his mind in the meantime. I had to believe something would, or their takeover attempt would turn into a bloodbath. TAO had contacted us. They had to be coming. And if Dr. Hill knew about the Lemurian-Atlantean war, his people would be armed to handle this situation... right? Did they have their own soldiers like Chelsea?

"Deal." I couldn't ask for more.

"Hey!" Thompson shouted, striding back through the door. Weyland and I both turned, thinking we were caught, but Thompson's focus wasn't on us.

Michael had changed places and was fiddling with the command station where Captain Marks usually stood. I hadn't even seen him move. He had half the command station broken apart, digging around inside, wires askew. In a matter of thirty seconds, he'd nearly taken apart the whole thing. Why? For what?

Thompson and one of the guards in the hallway both charged Michael. The guard's shoulder dug into Michael's chest, but Michael held his ground. He held two stripped ends of wire together, forcing them to spark. Why?

"Get off of him!" Weyland shouted, joining the fray.

Freddy jumped in as well. I stood there, frozen, as Thompson and his guard made short work of the men. Freddy and Weyland both took blows to their faces, chests, and sides before being thrown off the command station's platform like sacks of feathers.

Thompson drew Michael up and slugged him across the face. Michael grinned. I narrowed my eyes, scanning the command station. What did he do?

Michael laughed and spat blood in Thompson's face. "Good fucking luck stopping it."

An alarm from the lead weapons station behind me blared, and what Michael had done snapped into focus. No way. No *fucking* way he knew how to—

"Torpedo 1, prepping," the station's automatic firing process sang.

Thompson jerked the hand holding Michael by his throat. "What did you do?" he spat in Michael's face.

Michael only smirked.

Thompson's nostrils flared, his face a deep shade of red. He tightened his grip around Michael's throat, his knuckles whitening. "Speak!"

"Torpedo 1, firing," the station announced. "Torpedo 1, away."

"What's the target?" Thompson demanded of Michael, but Michael couldn't form words with Thompson's hand at his throat. Not that he even would.

"Target destroyed," Weapons Station One sang. "Torpedo 2, prepping."

"Sir," Thompson's guard said. Somewhere in the course of the altercation he'd manned the lower NANA station. "Sir, he destroyed our sub."

"What?" Thompson reeled on Michael, who was quickly fading.

Holy shit. Michael had destroyed Thompson's only way out of here if this went south. Somehow, he'd known the override codes. Weapons weren't meant to be fired from the command station without Captain Marks's or the Commander's override. There shouldn't be a need for that to happen except in emergencies. Michael had somehow gotten around it.

Weapons Station One chirped. "Torpedo 2, firing at full blast. Torpedo 2, away."

"Where's that one going?" Thompson demanded, shaking Michael as he screamed in his face. "Where!"

Full blast? Destroying their sub made sense. But what did he—

"The air," the guard said. "He fired it straight up into the air. It's a fucking *flare*."

"Hell," Thompson snarled. His hand moved from Michael's throat to the front of Michael's shirt. Thompson yanked him off the command platform and toward the blast doors.

"This ends now," Thompson practically growled. "These people need to learn a lesson."

Michael coughed and struggled. I bounded down from my station and tried to block their way. I had no plan, but I couldn't stand by and watch my friend die.

Thompson drew his gun and pointed it at me. "Back off right now, Trevor, or you're dead too."

"You won't," I said, taking another step in their direction.

Thompson's finger closed on the trigger, and I slammed my eyes shut. *This is it.*

The loud crack of a gunshot echoed in my ears.

I held my breath, waiting for the pain to strike through me at any moment.

It never came.

Christa cried out. I opened my eyes and spun to her. She was hunched over her station, clasping her arm and gritting her teeth. Blood flooded out through her fingers.

"Christa!"

She locked eyes with me to let me know she'd be okay, but *dammit* the guilt struck anyway.

"Next one's between your eyes," Thompson warned. "I'm done."

I locked eyes with Michael, and he shook his head, eyes pleading with me to stand down.

"But—" I said.

Michael cut me off with a look that shredded me to the core. He knew he'd been marked for death, knew there was no way out, and he didn't want me to risk my life, too.

He'd sent up a flare the Navy could track, and that had been worth the risk.

Thompson trained his gun on me until the blast doors closed, separating me from my friend as he was yanked to his death.

Chapter Thirty

Chelsea

In my mind, I was at home, playing videogames with Logan. I kicked his ass for once instead of the other way around—my main indication I was dreaming. I held onto it like a lifeline until the vision shifted into something else, into the dream I'd had after I'd plugged the leak at the outpost.

I ran through the streets of Atlantis, through the rain beside the same family, jogging next to the mother. I tried to sooth the toddler with songs and words. She wouldn't stop crying. She screamed and screamed, and soon I awoke shouting.

Someone's fingers dug into my shoulder, shaking me. "Shut the hell up." Georgie.

I startled and clamped my mouth shut, gathering myself. Fear seared my veins and clenched my fists. Why wouldn't the toddler stop *crying*?

"Get up." Thompson's voice, rough and deep, came from behind me. It differed so starkly from the toddler's that I jumped.

He jerked me off my bed to stand beside him. The sudden change from dream-state to waking left my brain sloshing through too many thoughts.

"Get the hell off me." I pulled my arm from his grasp.

Thompson slapped cuffs onto my wrists. Georgie snickered.

"You're coming with me," Thompson demanded.

Panic shot through all my remaining grogginess, a strike of lightning in the middle of a stormy night. I couldn't fight him, and leaving him in full control sent all my mental alarm bells to red alert. He tugged and dragged me along like I weighed nothing at all. My wrists ached where the cuffs dug into my skin.

He and Georgie led me into the Artifact Room. Valerie leaned against the counter, arms across her chest, looking bored. She smirked when her eyes met mine.

Thompson let me go and stomped off toward the shelves of artifacts. He reached for an Egyptian canopic jar and held it out. I cringed. He wouldn't break it. Would he?

"Tell me what these are," he said.

"Artifacts." *Drop it. I dare you.*

He tutted. "Specifically. This is quite the collection of pieces—texts and art from all over the globe, from different time periods."

"You know exactly where we found them. SeaSat5's been researching artifacts and shipwrecks for months." Why did he care so damn much? I tugged my arms apart, trying to break the cuffs. The metal only dug in harder.

"But you're only now on-tap as an archaeologist," Thompson said.

I shrugged, betraying the anxiety throwing a dance party in my gut. "Coincidental. They used to outsource, but they needed an in-house intern."

He came so close his putrid breath suffocated me. "I am not as stupid as you think," he said. "Are these Atlantean?"

I jerked back, sucking in fresh air. "Why? Fancy yourself a treasure hunter?"

I shouldn't have asked.

Thompson looked over my shoulder to Georgie and said, "Bring him in."

Valerie continued smirking, watching the scene play out as Georgie left and returned with Michael. Georgie shut the door behind them then cuffed Michael's hands at his back. Dark circles haloed Michael's drawn eyes, and blood seeped out of his mouth. What had they done to him?

I lunged at Georgie with bound arms, but Thompson tugged on my uniform. Michael's eyes met my mine, his expression telling me to stop, that fighting wasn't worth it. I didn't care. He didn't deserve this any more than I did.

I spun on Thompson, hands still cuffed behind me, and broke his grip on my uniform. "Leave him alone."

"Tell me if these are Link Pieces!" Thompson snarled.

I hadn't the faintest idea what a Link Piece was. "They're artifacts. What more do you want?"

"He wants the truth, girlie," Valerie supplied. "You wouldn't tell me, so now you have to tell him."

"Fuck you," I spat. What the hell were these crazies talking about?

"Enough!" Thompson threw the canopic jar onto the ground. It shattered to pieces and dust.

"Bastard!" I shrieked.

Thompson struck me, whipping my face to the side. Valerie laughed. Thompson reached into his pocket and pulled out a leather case. He opened it, revealing a needle and vial.

Nerves bundled in my gut. "What is that?"

Thompson filled the needle in a slow pull. Was it poison? "Tell me the truth."

"They're *artifacts*," I exasperated. "They're from all different places. Everywhere. That's it. I don't understand what you want from me."

I cowered away, panic pulsing through every inch of my being. Sweat beaded at my brow and neck. This was the end for me. I'd never thought about death before, or what my death would look like. But now that death stood before me, I couldn't focus on anything else.

Thompson strode straight past me to where his lackey held Michael. He bared Michael's throat. "Tell me the truth, or I'll kill him."

"I already told you the answer!" Did he want to know if the artifacts were Atlantean, or something more?

"Don't tell him anything, Chelsea," Michael said. "They'll destroy it all. It's not worth it."

I knew that. *But they'll destroy you, too.* I worried for him, not some cache of artifacts. Why did Thompson have to do this? Why did they all think I knew things I didn't?

Thompson positioned the needle above Michael's carotid artery. "This is your last chance."

He wouldn't do it, would he? Casualties would complicate things. Someone like him wouldn't care. But Valerie should. Even if she worked for them, she didn't strike me as a murderer. I considered her, but she stood there passive, like she and Michael had never even met before.

"You're gonna stand there let them kill him?" I asked her, my eyes stinging with tears. Why was all of this happening? Why couldn't this just *end*?

Valerie shrugged, not the slightest twitch in her face revealing her true thoughts. "Not my problem or my fault. This one's all on you, Chelsea. All you have to do is tell us the truth."

"Don't," Michael said. "They can't know."

Know? Did Michael know, too? Oh god, was Michael as involved in all of this as Trevor and Valerie? My eyes narrowed. No. The whites of his eyes, the fear wrinkling his face—he didn't know anything.

My eyes snapped to Thompson's. "Who are you to come onto this station, take over, demand answers, and kill interns? What could you possibly stand to gain from all of this? I *do not* know what you want me to tell you. Are they Atlantean artifacts? Yes, they are! But I'm pretty sure you already knew that, so let him go."

"Wrong answer."

Before my lips could even form a response, Thompson jammed the needle into Michael's throat. I dove for Michael, but Valerie wrapped a fist around my hair and jerked back, hard. I yelped and cursed. Valerie swung me around so she stood as an extra, traitorous barrier. She tried to hide it, but sorrow sped across her dark eyes. For a split second, the old Valerie showed through.

Michael convulsed in his guard's hold even as the guard placed Michael's body on the floor.

"I'm sorry. I'm so sorry," I said again and again, begging him to live. I thrashed in Valerie's hold, but she didn't let up.

Michael's body stopped twitching as he took his last ragged breath.

I stared at Michael's lifeless body, a young bright life snuffed out in seconds. I vomited on Thompson's shoes as tears spilled from my eyes. Thompson swore and shoved me into a metal folding chair. He pulled up his own and stared, his gun lazily pointed in my direction.

I couldn't keep my eyes from Michael's body. I *did nothing* to stop him from dying. I alone was to blame—because I had something Valerie and Thompson wanted, but I had no idea what that something was.

Anger flooded a well inside me, and I shook, readying to burst like a geyser. I ripped my wrists sideways, pulling and pulling until the metal shattered and my hands came free.

Thompson jerked upright and pointed his gun between my eyes. "Now, now, soldier. Don't go getting all heroic on me."

"Screw you," I spat.

He shook his head, his gun still trained on me. "I can't believe you're one of them."

I had no words for him. I barely knew what being "one of them" meant.

He waved the gun up and down a few inches. "Look at you. So small. So fragile. Yet impossibly strong."

My jaw set hard.

"You let your friend be killed, you know that? You could have saved him—were supposed to save him. I didn't want to murder him."

I looked away.

Thompson leaned forward, his face inches from mine. "I'm your *enemy*."

"Well, no shit," I spat.

He struck me across the face with his gun. I swung at his jaw, but he grabbed my wrist and wrenched it as he stood, tugging me along with him.

"I don't understand," he said. "Why make it so you super soldiers can pass down the genetic enhancements if it makes you lesser models?"

My face ached. I wanted to rub it, to sooth it, but didn't want to give Thompson the satisfaction. *Super soldier? Genetics? What the hell is he talking about?*

His eyes narrowed. "The fact you don't know also makes me question things. Are you lying about that?"

"No."

He stepped closer to me. "Are you sure?"

"Oh, absolutely. I knew the whole time I'm some Atlantean *freak show* and that, hey, I have friggin' *magical powers*. Presto chango!" I waved my hands in front of my face. "No, I have no idea what you're fucking talking about."

He slammed me against the shelving unit. The metal connected with my back, jarring my spine.

"Fuck off," I whined through the sharp pain. That fucking *hurt*. "I didn't know, and I'm still not interested."

Thompson pressed his body against mine and breathed in deeply. My skin crawled where his fingers brushed my face. I turned my head away from the touch, wanting to vomit.

"Now you're getting it right," he said.

Fight, Danning, my mind sung, urging me toward freedom. I dug my fingers into his shoulders and brought my knee up between his legs as hard as I could. He yelped and his grip on me loosened. I wriggled out of his arms and rushed the door, yanking on the handle.

I pounded on the cool metal. "Help! Somebody help me!"

The damn thing wouldn't budge. I didn't even know you could lock this door from the outside. How the hell would you be able to get out? Maybe they'd melted this door, too. Thompson trudged toward me. I yanked on the door handle for all I was worth. I was strong. This thing should have fucking *budged*. But nothing. Nothing.

Thompson grabbed me by the shoulders and ripped me off the door. I fell to the floor and slid along the tile, pain bursting over my side and shoulders like a supernova. He stood above me with an arm outstretched, palm glowing with fire.

An instinctual need to douse the flames at all costs flooded my system, taking over my actions. I stood, ran to the sink a few feet away, threw on the water, and held out my hand. It wasn't until the heat from Thompson's fire scorched the air around me that I remembered my active abilities didn't work anymore. He aimed a fireball my way and fired. I ducked, narrowly missing it.

My reflexes had never been this fast. Ever. I was not the sporty type. I moved fastest on stage, plucking away at guitar strings. Logan had taught me how to throw a punch years ago, but these ducks and swings were so very different those. Whatever switch had been flipped by Thompson igniting his hand in flames wasn't one of my own.

My vision narrowed, intensely focusing on Thompson and his fireballs. Like I was another person, someone who could do this, could fight.

Thompson and I traded blow after blow until he managed to reach out and clench onto the front of my uniform and lift me off the ground. He grinned from ear to ear. "There you are, soldier."

My hands wrapped around his arm, trying to pry myself from his grip. I'd almost convinced myself his super strength was due to his size. Now, I wasn't so sure. If normal Atlanteans had only one power, but more than one made an Atlantean like me, what did that mean for their enemies? Was that what a super solider was, someone with more than one power?

Thompson nodded off to the side, some kind of signal, and Valerie and Georgie teleported to me. Each of them took hold of one of my arms. They extricated me from Thompson and dragged me a few feet away.

"Valerie, let me go," I said through gritted teeth. I fought against them with all I had.

"After what your kind did to Abby?" she growled. "Not a fucking chance, girlie. This is payback."

"That wasn't me. I didn't do whatever happened to her. Please, Valerie."

Her hand reeled back and slapped me across the face. The sound of it echoed off the walls. Thompson took a calculated step toward me, coming into the creepy range. I wished I hadn't worn my reaction so loudly the first time.

"Ever wonder why no one knows what Lemuria is?" Thompson asked. "Why they think Lemuria and Atlantis are one in the same, or that it doesn't exist at all?"

I clamped my mouth shut. No one thought Lemuria was real because the evidence supporting the lost continent was so lame that fire-breathing dragons looked more legit.

"No answer?" Thompson lifted his still-lit hand to my eye level.

I watched the flames jump into the air, mesmerized. What did Lemuria have to do with all of this?

"Lemuria was better at hiding," he said. "No one who found Lemuria from the outside ever returned home alive. Want to know why?"

"Let me guess, the Lemurians killed them?" I asked.

He chuckled. "They sent them spiraling through time."

I tried not to let my curiosity sound too eager when I asked, "Spiraling through time?"

Thompson's gestured to the room at large and chuckled. "You really don't know, do you?" He paced toward a shelving unit full of artifacts. "Some of these ancient items are tools, keys to a lock that opens pathways through time."

I snorted and then let out a full-belly laugh. This guy was cracked. They all were! Atlantis and Lemuria? Time travel and powers? What kind of whack situation had I fallen into? Maybe I'd wake up in my bed, or a white padded room, wrapped up in my own arms.

Thompson picked up two of the artifacts. One shimmered, weird mirage-like waves dancing over it.

"This is one, isn't it?" Thompson asked, lifting the ceramic bowl an inch before setting it down on a counter. "I'll need the artifact later. Thank you for pointing it out."

What the *hell* was going on?

Thompson snapped his fingers. Valerie and Georgie tightened their grip on my arms.

"The problem was you Atlanteans kept finding our homeland, so Lemuria had to keep moving," Thompson said. "My ancestors left our old home-time, but the Atlanteans kept searching, amazed and terrified of what Lemurian power could do. But Atlanteans didn't always have the right tools, and they certainly never had the Waterstar map. The Atlanteans didn't even know the map existed until they made super soldiers like you."

"You need me for a freaking *map*?" I hissed. "Are you fucking kidding me?"

Thompson sneered. "It's more complicated than that, but, essentially, yes. Super soldiers had access to the map while the rest of the Atlanteans did not. It's imprinted on their minds. My ancestors' natural-given power is why the Atlanteans resorted to genetic engineering in the first place, to give their people enough power to fight us. The ability to see the map was an added bonus." He jabbed a finger into my sternum. "The Atlanteans had to make your *kind* to battle *our* natural abilities. To travel through time, chasing us, because you Atlanteans are never satisfied."

"Are?" Like they still existed in present day?

Thompson unzipped the top of my uniform, and Valerie moved the straps of my black tank top and bra down my arm with shaky fingers. I tried to meet her eyes but couldn't. She'd made a point to look directly over my shoulder at the wall. Thompson folded his fire-hand so the flames took on the form of a pencil—the most ridiculous and terrifying writing instrument I'd ever seen.

"When Atlantean super soldiers or other citizens breached their security measures and got onto their land, they let them go. Want to know why?" he said.

"Why ask if you're going to tell me anyway?" *Not good.* Berating him and being snarky would get me nowhere. Not when he brandished his powers right in front of me. Not when every impulse told me to run. My instincts wanted me gone from this room, away from this guy who could control fire. They wanted me away. So far away.

My entire body shook with fear and despair. Tears stung my eyes. Michael was dead, and I'd soon follow him—both of our murders *my* fault.

My heartbeat thundered in my ears. The pull of my teleportation power was there, waiting for me on the other side of this wall. But I couldn't reach it. We stood too far away from each other, with too many obstacles in between. Thompson. Valerie. Their powers. My lack thereof.

The very moment Thompson inched toward my skin with the fire pencil, I screamed for the first time since this hijacking started. I screamed so loud the entire station probably heard me as fire seared through my flesh and muscle, blazing a path across my skin. I never imagined being burned with fire could hurt this bad. It couldn't hurt this bad. Not normally. No way.

The smell of burning flesh made the piercing pain unbearable. I screamed until my throat shredded and my knees gave out. Thompson slipped up on his drawing, the pencil digging a jagged, unintended line.

How could Valerie stand there? How could she let this happen, to Michael, to me? Even if she hated me, even if she hated Atlanteans for what happened to Abby, how could she do *this*?

"The Lemurians let the Atlanteans go because they needed to send the rest of Atlantis a message," Thompson said.

I couldn't keep my eyes open anymore. No sound came out of my mouth. My body clenched up, taking the pain and sending it everywhere all at once. Trying to mitigate. Attempting to stay out of the blackness. I couldn't decide what hurt the most anymore. Heat registered in my mind, immense heat burning through the core of everything I was. Skin and bone. Atlantean. Super solider. Human. Just human.

"That message was this brand," he said. "A seal to keep you under control."

The intense burning stopped, leaving an aching heat coursing through every inch of me. Valerie and Georgie hauled me up, holding me in a vice grip even though I couldn't move right now if I tried.

Thompson put his lips next to my ear. "This station is ours. My employers require the artifacts be delivered to them, so we can bridge the time-gap to Atlantis and eradicate your kind. It'd be best if you don't fight this."

"So, kill me," I mumbled through a groan. "Kill me so this ends."

"We need you alive. That seal should keep you in check until we arrive in port."

The gap between me and my teleportation power grew further apart, widening like a chasm into the earth. My strength, weaker. "Screw... you..."

The last thing my mind registered was fire flying at my face.

Chapter Thirty-One

Trevor

They locked me in my quarters when Thompson deemed the station safe enough for now. I spent an hour pacing between my door and bed, going over everything that'd gone wrong so many times. Everything blurred together. This had to be a dream.

My aching ribs testified for reality.

A clicking drew my eyes to the door to my quarters. The door shouldn't make that sound. *Didn't* make that sound. Unless—

The door swung open and Freddy entered in quick, direct movements. He spun and locked us inside. The gash above his eyebrow had stopped bleeding, but it looked terrible. A new shiner mirrored the gash on his other eye, which was puffy and in the process of closing.

"What happened to you?" I asked him.

"It's not about what happened to me," he said. "There's been a casualty. Weyland wants to move ASAP. I told him to hold off for another hour."

Oh god. A thousand weights sunk onto me. Here it came. Official confirmation. "Who?"

"Michael."

I stumbled backward, like his name alone was a physical blow. I collapsed into my desk chair, unable to breathe. This was my fault. All of it.

"I'm sorry, Trevor, but we don't have time for mourning. Weyland's moving soon. He wanted you to have this." He pulled a gun out of his waistband and held it out to me, tapping a small knob on the side with his thumb. "Safety's here. Flick it off, point and shoot. Just in case."

I swallowed hard. Shooting guns was not what I'd signed up for when I'd agreed to work for the Navy. I hadn't signed up for any of this. I should never have come back. And when I had, I never should've tried to protect this station alone. I should have taken Dr. Hill's offer and left with Chelsea for TAO.

Freddy left without another word. I slipped the gun into the front waistband of my pants. I doubted I'd use it, but it ushered a blanket of safety over me. At least I had a weapon.

I backed up to the edge of my bed and sank into it. Something poked out from beneath my pillow. I dug underneath and my fingers brushed a cylindrical object, a note rubber-banded to the outside. I pulled the object out, slid off the paper, and read the cursive script.

You know what to do. Help Chelsea.

For Abby. —V

I held up the bottle and read the label. Some type of topical medicine for third-degree burns.

"*Third* degree?" What the hell did they do to Chelsea? And more importantly, why was Valerie helping me sort it out?

<hr />

Sneaking over to Valerie and Chelsea's quarters was way too easy. For one, Freddy had left the door ajar, so all I'd had to do was wait until no one was outside. A few vents later had found me outside their door. Except the door to Chelsea's room was warped.

What the hell? I touched the metal gently. The hinges had been melted and the window kicked out. *Valerie.* My heart in my throat, I peered into the small window on the door. No one was inside. That couldn't be right. I pried the casing off the card reader and punched in an override code. It blinked green, but the door didn't budge.

I tried it again. Nothing. Great. Valerie had freaking destroyed the frame, too.

An air vent opening was inlaid on the wall a few paces away. I crawled into it, weaving through a maze, grunting through the pain in my chest, until I perched at an opening above Valerie's bed. I kicked the cover hard and it clanked to the floor. Chelsea didn't even startle. Where was she?

I jumped down. She'd turned the lights down low, and everything was impeccably neat. No clutter, beds made, not a speck of dust to be seen. *She's keeping busy.*

Light peeked from under the bottom of the bathroom door. Water ran from the faucet on the other side, the only sound in the room.

I approached the door with slow steps and knocked lightly.

"Go away." Her voice was so soft, so defeated; the door almost blocked the noise completely.

"Chelsea, it's me. Open up."

She snorted. "Screw off."

"I have something you need. It's from Helen." She didn't need to know the truth—that the medicine came from the same person responsible for the station being hijacked.

She turned the faucet off and opened the door. The bags under her eyes had deepened since the last time I saw her.

"What do you want?" she asked.

I stepped toward her. "I have something for you."

She backed away, lips twisting into a scowl. "Stay away from me."

"Helen said to give you this." Another step.

She responded in kind, bumping into her sink. She held out her hand. "Hand it over and leave."

"What happened?"

She rolled her eyes and snatched the medicine tube. She winced as her arm swung and cradled it to her chest. "Shit."

My eyes narrowed. "What did he do to you?"

Chelsea crossed her arms at her chest. "Nothing. Go away. How do you even know something happened, anyway?"

"Helen saw it with her powers." Another lie.

I grabbed her left wrist and jerked it aside. She shot a hand up to cover it, but hit too hard and she cursed. I moved her fingers out of the way and revealed what she wanted to hide: a large, white bandage.

"I'm not trying to hurt you," I said.

"My ass," she spat. "First you and Valerie work with them, then they send you in here like some kind of medicine-delivering Trojan horse."

"I'm *not* working for them."

She laughed once, harsh and disbelieving. "Please. Valerie told me everything. You two have always had some sort of *thing*, and I knew it. I fucking knew it. Helen's in on it, too. I fell for it, for the dream of Atlantis. Then you let them do *this* to me," she pointed at her bandage. "I can't believe I ever trusted you. How much of this, of us, was ever real?"

Her implication that I used her as nothing more than a *tool* snapped something taut inside me. My jaw twitched. "Will you calm the hell down for one second?"

She flinched. Three seconds of mixed anger and sorrow washed over her face before she reeled back her left hand. It crushed my cheek. My head rang and warmth seared my skin straight to the bone.

"Your lies killed Michael. Almost killed everyone onboard," she said. Her words pushed a serrated knife through me with every whispered syllable. "How long have you known they'd come? How long have you been planning this?"

I had no words. No response to the girl I loved accusing me of planning the hijacking, the loss, of everything I held close.

"You're one stupid son of a bitch." Her voice was venomous. Sharp as steel. "As soon as we're rescued, I hope Captain Marks throws you in jail to rot where you belong."

"Chelsea, no."

Her words shattered me, and any strength I had left, sent my entire being through a grinder. Every part of me *hurt*. She really did believe I was working with Thompson, that I'd worked with him and Valerie to endanger and capture the very thing I'd fought for the last two years to protect. She thought I'd betrayed her, and that hurt most of all. All I'd wanted from the beginning was to help her, to be there for her. To keep her and SeaSatellite5 safe.

I couldn't breathe, couldn't move. I held her glare. Let it rip me to shreds.

I needed to see. I needed to know what they'd done—what *I'd* done—to her.

I reached out too quickly for her to deflect, got my fingers around the bandage, and tore it off. Chelsea yelped and shoved me away. My back slammed into the corner of the doorframe, but before she could cover it up, I caught a glimpse of the damage. Her skin had changed colors, fried. Inflammation marked her from above her low-cut tank top almost to her neck. She'd been burned. Badly. Also very carefully. The area surrounding the marking was angry though not destroyed.

My gaze zeroed in on the brand—and bile shot straight from my stomach into my mouth. Thompson had burned the logo for my mother's company onto Chelsea's skin. It was the same design of the tattoo on the guy who'd attacked her months ago. I brought my hand to my mouth, my knuckles resting under my nose as I gagged.

"Yeah, I know it's gross," Chelsea mumbled. "It's looking a lot better now than before. I think I broke another record for number of powers in Helen's stupid research." She waved her hands around. "Yippie, I'm fast-healing."

I stepped forward, took the tube from her, and opened it. She tried to take the medicine back, but I held it out of her reach.

"Let me help you," I said. "Please."

"Why? You hate me."

"I—" Was she serious? "Why would I hate you?"

"That's the only reason I can think of for you stringing me along. I interrupted *something* the night we met. That's why you were there. You weren't running from your family, you were doing their bidding."

"That's not what happened." Who'd fed her these lies?

Her fists clenched at her sides. "I know what I saw."

No, she didn't.

"The situation got messed up. They played us. Valerie played us. *Dammit, Chelsea.*" My fingers tightened around the medicine tube. "I'd do *anything* to save you, to get you as far away from this station as possible right now, but I *can't.* I don't have powers; I can't teleport. I'm me, Trevor. That's it. Just like the night you were mugged, the most I can do is *attempt* to tackle the bad guys, but I would lay down my life to save you, Chelsea. I love you."

It sounded like pleading to my ears, and maybe it was, but every word rang true. I needed to her listen to me, and if it meant baring my soul, then here my soul was for viewing.

"You've been everything to me from the moment you saw me in the Franklin," I continued. "You gave me sanity when I thought I'd lost mine, gave me a reason to continue fighting. I could have run. I *wanted* to run. But I didn't because I wanted to save you. Protect you. That's all I've *ever* wanted, Chelsea. For you to be safe, and to be with you, because you're everything to me."

She didn't respond for so many long moments that I didn't think she would at all.

"I love you," I said again. "Please, let me help you. I lied, yeah, and I'm so, *so* sorry. But I'm not the enemy."

Her lips pursed as she looked at me, her eyes reaching somewhere deep. She stared down my soul, and my soul was too hurt from battle to look away.

Tears welled up in her eyes and threatened to spill over. "I already did let you help me, once. Look where that got me."

"Chelsea, please." My fingers sought hers, and I was surprised when she let me take them. "I shouldn't have lied, but I didn't know what to say. I didn't..." None of this was supposed to happen.

I swallowed. My eyesight blurred. "I didn't want to accept you were Atlantean," I continued, "or what that meant for me. For SeaSatellite5. Because of Abby and where she is now, and how close Valerie and I were to being right there with her: lost, *insane*."

Her eyes saddened, her fire drifting away. "When you lied to the Captain, disowning me in front of him, I thought I was done for. Crazy. Headed for the Brig or the loony bin. You left me to flounder. But you didn't know me then."

I leaned in toward her. "I do now."

"You still let all of this happen. You didn't say *anything*. Not a single warning."

An invisible hand wrung my chest, twisting my heart dry. I was frozen in place for all of eternity.

"I'm sorry." Sadness ripped through me like a tidal wave. I tried to swallow it. Couldn't. Tears seeped out, and I couldn't stop them. "I didn't know what to do. I still don't."

She hiccupped her own sobs and raised a hand to my face. Her warm palm cupped the same cheek she'd slapped minutes earlier. "Then let's just take it one step at a time. What do we do now?"

I pulled myself together with a steadying breath and held up the medicine. "Let me put this on you. Then we plan. I know Weyland wants to make a move."

"Took him long enough," she said, quiet.

"Too many people in the crossfire."

She sucked in her bottom lip, tears brimming all over again. "Mich—" She coughed to stop herself from crying and shook her head. She hoisted herself up onto the sink counter. "Just put this crap on me so it stops hurting, okay?"

Just as Freddy had, she didn't pause to mourn Michael. Maybe she wouldn't, not until this was all over. Or maybe she already had. In either case, I swallowed my own knot of feelings before they closed up my throat for good.

I twisted off the cap of the ointment and squeezed some of the lotion onto my fingers. "This will probably hurt."

She looked at the wall. "Just do it."

Gingerly, I spread the medicine. She flinched at first, but there must have been some kind of numbing agent in it because she stopped moving and let me finish. I capped the tube and washed my hands.

"We're gonna get out of this. Help is on the way," I said.

Her eyes glossed over when they met mine. "Did you talk to the Admiral, too?"

"No, but someone's coming for us. You have to hang on a little longer." As long as TAO got the message and didn't take our non-response as a bad sign, anyway.

"For how long? Because they kind of opened the chaos door when they killed Michael." Her voice broke on his name, and a hand flew to her mouth. Her body shook, slowly at first, then in fits.

"Trevor, I killed him," she got out between sobs. Her face grew red, and she slapped a hand over her mouth like it'd stop the crying. "I stood there… and d-did nothing. They k-killed him right in front of me."

I wrapped my arms around her, careful to avoid her burn, and held her tight. My chin found a home on her good shoulder. I cupped the back of her head, holding her to me, hoping she'd find any strength I had left and use it as her own. "No, Thompson killed him. You didn't hurt anyone."

"I was *there*. I let them kill him without saying a single word. All these stupid powers, and I did *nothing*." She pulled back, and what I saw in her eyes nearly killed me. Guilt. Guilt that ran so deep it stained her soul. "Michael might still be alive if I hadn't egged on

Thompson. He could still *be here*." Her face tightened, tears streaming relentlessly. I brushed them away with my thumbs. "He's dead, Trevor. He's dead."

"It's okay," I said, still wiping away every new tear. "It's going to be okay."

<hr/>

After the sobs had stopped and the burn medicine had taken full effect, I'd snuck to my quarters to grab a letter from my mother. A logo in the same design as Chelsea's burn had been printed in the top left corner. I returned to Chelsea on quick, but weighted, feet. If I showed her this, if Chelsea reacted to the letter, I'd have to explain everything.

I pushed open the door to her quarters and sat next to her on the bed.

"Trevor, I don't know about this," she said, leaning away. "He said they were Lemurian, and that this mark was meant to keep me under control."

"They told you about Lemuria?" Did he tell her the truth Valerie had twisted? As far as I knew, Valerie and Thompson talked about the war, not why they wanted SeaSatellite5. Not that Valerie and I got placed here in case we found Link Pieces. From what I knew, Chelsea only had half the story. And a warped half at that.

"I don't get it. Even if Lemuria is real, Atlantis and Lemuria wouldn't have existed at the same time. But then he said something about time travel…"

"I don't know either," I lied and held the paper out to her. "Touch a finger to it."

Chelsea eyed the letter like it would jump up and attack her. "Why?"

"Because I want to see something." If the letterhead was a mark meant to deter Atlanteans, then I would tell her the truth.

"Fine." She touched her fingers to the letter and they immediately sizzled and smoked. She recoiled, flinging her hand away. "Shit!" She waved her hand in front of her face. Her fingers scorched bright scarlet. "What was that?"

I couldn't form words. Thompson had burned her, sealed away *something* inside of her. Probably her Atlantean powers. He might've even taken them away for good.

Her eyes darted from mine to the letter faster than a humming birds' wings. "You… you don't just work with them, do you? You're related to them." She pointed to the letter. "Are you *kidding me?*"

Hesitation stopped me from answering right away. I knew I had no choice. "Thompson and his guys work for my parents. Valerie, too. I chose not to side with them a long time ago. That's why I ran to Boston. I don't believe in what they do."

"But they're family."

"Some, yeah. Others are relatives so distant, it doesn't matter."

"But you let them take the station." She looked down to her burn. "You knew they wanted it. Since when?"

"Chels—"

"Oh, my god," she said and stood. "This all started with the outpost, didn't it? Thompson killed Michael over an artifact he said was Atlantean. Was a… a Link Piece or something." Her mouth opened wider with all the words she left unsaid. I didn't need to hear them.

"I didn't know they'd take SeaSatellite5," I told her. "I wasn't sure they'd actually come at all. Chelsea, this isn't the time for this conversation. We need to figure out how to end this."

She gritted her teeth, her next words a growl. "But you knew. You knew this entire time that we'd found something more than Atlantean. Something greater." She paused, her brow furrowing around narrowed eyes. "That's why you were so anxious in the outpost and around the weird wardrobe. You know that really is?"

"Maybe, but—"

"No! I can't believe this. You sold us the hell out."

I rose in a quick motion, swiping the air at the same time. "No. Valerie told them about the artifacts. I didn't. I haven't worked for them in months, and when I did, it wasn't willingly. My parents—" I didn't want to talk about *this*. "They oppose what Atlantis stood for, and they have a plan to destroy Atlantis at all costs. To use the military's resources to find all possible Link Pieces and build a path to the city through time."

She shook her head, biting her lip. "So... what? Atlantis and Lemuria still exist? They're... at war? And I'm important to it?"

"Yes. But it's complicated, and I don't know all the answers. You have to believe me."

She didn't. The blame for the hijacking and Michael's death gyred in her eyes, fueling a spiral of darkness that twisted my lungs and tangled my gut. It was over. This. Us. Even if we survived this, our relationship wouldn't. Because I tried protecting her the same way I'd tried with Abby—by lying—and I'd never learned that lesson.

"All I know is that Lemuria wants Atlantis wiped out, and that they're willing to do anything to see that happen," I continued. "I got caught up in it, but I ran to Boston to get away from it all. I don't agree with what they're doing. At all."

"And how do you plan on getting us out of this?" she asked.

"Help is coming." We just had to wait it out until TAO got here. "Until then, you and I need to work together the best we can. We're the only ones who know what's going on right now."

She crossed her arms over her chest, her next words slicked with sarcasm. "Us and Dr. Hill, I'm assuming. Mr. I-Can-Read-Atlantean."

"Yes." No more point in lying.

She considered me for a long moment, her eyes softening. "Fine. But my powers are out of commission."

I nodded and pointed to her mark. "I know. That's why Thompson burned you." I risked a step toward her. She didn't retreat, so I wrapped my arms around her. "I'm sorry."

"Me too," she whispered, and it fucking broke my heart. No

matter what happened next, this was a black mark on our relationship forever.

"I don't understand, but I'm sorry you didn't think I was capable of handling the truth," she said.

"Chelsea, I—"

"No," she spoke into my shoulder. "We can figure us out after we get out of this alive. Until then, I'm willing to set it aside. Can you?"

"I'm willing to do anything that will save the crew." And if it meant dying for them, too, I'd do it. "Anything."

She relaxed into my arms, and I rubbed her back. I inhaled the smell of her shampoo in case it was the last time, ran my hand through her hair so I'd remember how it felt—soft and full. If this was the end of us or me, then so be it as long as she was safe.

"Can you fix whatever's blocking my powers?" she asked.

"Maybe. It's a combination of that seal he burned into your skin and malfunctions with Humming Bird." I paused for a moment, thinking it through. "I can probably get Humming Bird adjusted next time Thompson drags me to the Bridge, but I don't know what to do about that burn."

Chelsea looked down at her collarbone. "You're saying I have to get rid of it?"

I shrugged. "I honestly don't know, Chelsea. I don't know how that stuff works."

She locked eyes with me. "If you can fix Humming Bird, I'll do what I can, whatever I have to, to take care of the rest. I—"

The door to her quarters burst open. Chelsea and I jumped apart as Thompson and two of his guys stormed the room. I reached behind me and tugged the gun Freddy gave me out of my waistband.

Chelsea gasped. "What the hell?"

Before I even had the safety off, Thompson gathered fire in his palm and shot a ball at me. It soared, seeking out the gun like a bird of prey might snatch a rat, and knocked the pistol out of my hands.

"What the hell is going on in here?" he demanded.

I stepped in front of Chelsea, the last small measure of protection I thought she'd accept from me. "I gave her medicine for her burn," I said.

"She'll heal. You won't. Get him out of here," Thompson ordered his men, waving the gun around. "If you leave your quarters without permission again, I kill another crew member."

I held up my hands in defeat as they marched me to my room. I didn't bother looking back.

Chapter Thirty-Two

Chelsea

Tensions skyrocketed after Trevor had been yanked from my room. With Valerie no longer trusted to be my guard, Georgie accompanied me everywhere. The only time I had to myself was when either of us went to the bathroom. I used it to hack into the communications system again via Emma's instructions, to update the Admiral on my and Trevor's plan.

Hour after hour passed as I waited for Trevor to lift whatever held my powers down. I sat in my quarters, on the Bridge, on the dinning decks—wherever Georgie wanted me. Trevor's radio silence near killed me. My eyes darted to every clock I could find, watching the minutes tick by as I waited, trying to figure out how to get rid of the Lemurian seal Thompson had burned into my skin.

That's when I looked at the mirror in the bathroom off my quarters and cringed. Thoughts swarmed my mind—hopeful, painful thoughts— as I took what was left of my guitar case and smashed the mirror with it. *Seven years of bad luck, here we go.* As long as it gave me back my powers and got us the hell out of here, I didn't care.

I'd gripped a large shard of glass tight between my fingers and stared at my reflection, at the nasty-as-hell burn mark. Did I need to cut away the whole thing, or just disturb the mark?

Thompson had made it sound like he *really* needed my powers intact, but that he didn't want me to have them right now. If that was the case... what were the odds that this mark to block my powers was temporary? If it was, disturbing it should enough, right?

I took a deep breath, counted to ten, and prayed this would work. I brought the glass shard down onto my tortured, still-burning skin, and sliced open a gash in a vertical line down the Lemurian seal. God, it hurt so bad. Like the seal was being seared from my skin. All the pain from the actual burning swam back into focus, but I swallowed it down, finished the deed, and dressed the new injury as best I could.

It bled a lot. It re-angered the wound. But when warmth rippled up my arms an hour later, followed by goose bumps, I knew it'd been worth it. That it had worked. Like sunshine on a rainy day, my powers returned to me. Light and uplifting and warm. My powers were back. For how long, I wasn't sure. I thought of Trevor, of his kiss and his embrace, the safety I felt around him, and—

A cord snapped taut inside me, narrowing my vision. I teleported onto the Bridge next to Trevor and spun around, gathering water from the air—unaware that was even a source option.

Was this the super soldier part of me that Thompson was so scared of?

Up, like a hydra, my arms went, trailing large waves of water from seemingly nowhere. They knocked one of Thompson's men unconscious and soaked stations that fizzed and shorted out. I grunted through the pain in my shoulder and chest. I'd never been this powerful, this in control. It was like before in the artifact room; this wasn't me. This was the Atlantean soldier inside of me that Thompson wanted.

Flames descended on my waves, dousing them, then flew at me. I ducked and tried responding but my untrained powers failed me.

Thompson's flames danced around me, caging me in heat and flashes until his hand clamped around my arm and the show ended.

No one moved an inch. Thompson's men had fallen on various members of SeaSat5's crew during the display; they hadn't even gotten a chance to act on my distraction. *No.*

Searing pain scorched the skin around my burn wound. "Fuck!" I shouted.

Thompson growled as he examined my wound. The cut I'd made. "What did you do?"

"Ended your stupid seal crap," I snarled.

He yanked me forward a foot. His cheeks grew an impressive shade of red and purple. Maybe he'd stroke himself out, so we could retake the station before the Admiral's soldiers got here. "I thought you were going to cooperate."

"Cooperate, *yes*," I said through gritted teeth. "Completely surrender? I don't think so."

But even as I said it, I felt my power fade. Someone had re-adjusted Humming Bird to block my powers again.

Thompson wrapped his other large hand around my forearm and pulled it behind me. I yelped and cussed. The motion stretched the skin around my wound, tearing healed portions and setting the rest on fire. Blood seeped from the cut I'd made with the glass from my mirror.

Freddy's venomous words filled the Bridge. "Hit her again, I dare you."

From the opposite corner of the Bridge, at Communications, Weyland's jaw muscles clenched. The both of them would be killed if they acted on Freddy's threat.

"I'll do you one better." Thompson held his hand out to one of his thugs, who reached into their pocket and pulled out a syringe.

Get out now. I squinted my eyes, trying to refocus and gain control of my teleportation through the haze of electromagnetic field fluctuations and the burn mark. Again, we stood apart. Again, nothing.

My eyes darted to Trevor's, beseeching. He only shook his head, sadness darkening his eyes. He had tried but couldn't fix it for good, couldn't keep them from overriding his fixes. Thompson handed me off to the thug while he filled the vial. I fought against his hold the best I could, but to no avail.

"Don't!" Trevor shouted. His eyes bugged with anger as he stood from his station, a storm of blue and green unlike anything I've seen before. "She was following orders!"

"Not the ones I gave." He trained his eyes on me. "You know what this is."

A statement. Not a question.

"Please," I begged. My life could end right here, right now. I didn't sign up for this—any of this. A hijacking, finding Atlantis. All I'd wanted was a job after graduation, and Trevor. And now, my love for both would kill me.

"Goodnight, then," Thompson snarled. He bared my neck. I kicked out at him, hitting him square in the groin. He dropped, cursing.

"Goodnight yourself!" I hissed.

His thug shifted his grip on me, yanking both of my hands behind me and slamming his free hand around my mouth. His ability to fling me about like a ragdoll rolled nausea through my stomach.

Thompson stood, cracked his neck, and then closed in on me. "I will enjoy this, you little bitch."

My eyes widened at the sight of the needle so close. This was it. *No! No!*

Trevor ran toward me. Someone tackled him to the ground. I saw Freddy and Weyland also move, but the needle pierced my skin before they could take more than a few steps. It slid through skin and tissue right into my veins.

The liquid spilled into my body. I felt each drop as it left the syringe. I waited for it. For the convulsing, the pain. For the end. I closed my eyes, fearing the worst. Moments slid by, slow at first but quickening. When I reopened my eyes, I found a grinning

Thompson, a tearful Trevor, and the other two stopped dead in their tracks.

Thompson laughed heartedly. "If you could *see* yourself right now!"

His thug let me go. I stumbled a few feet and then swung at Thompson. He caught my punch and pushed me backwards.

Thompson's mouth contorted into an evil grin, spanning to either cheekbone. "Of course you're still alive—what super soldier wouldn't be?"

My head spun, fear and the remnants of Thompson's poison making the world blur and dance. I took a step toward a console and leaned against it. My insides churned.

"Bring the Captain in so he can witness the fate of his crew," Thompson said.

My skin chilled and slicked with sweat as the poison attempted to work its way through my system. My face remained feverishly warm. The poison wasn't killing me. It was throwing a rave in my body, contaminating my blood but not finishing the deed.

A memory of an empty bottle of tequila surfaced. I could drink a whole bottle myself. Poison and alcohol were both toxins. But if it took a whole bottle of tequila to get me worse than tipsy, what the hell was this poison that it had me almost on the ground?

"Don't worry," Thompson cooed. "It'll make your world spin, but it's not enough to kill you, soldier."

The Bridge doors opened. Two guards escorted Captain Marks inside. At least two-thirds of Thompson's crew now haunted the room. Except Valerie. Ever-present for all the other big moments of the last twenty-four hours, she was now suspiciously absent. My stomach rolled again.

I was still half-bent over a console when the Captain finally spoke. "What did you do to her?"

"She'll be fine," Thompson said. "Here's the part where we make a deal. I need your satellite station and all the artifacts downstairs—and the girl."

"Piss off!" the words left my mouth before I could stop them. I braced myself for another attack. It didn't come.

"Why Chelsea?" the Captain asked calmly.

Thompson's men had guns trained on the Captain's Head of Security and his top Navigation and Analytics Officer. Two of his youngest civilian crewmembers stood directly in the line of fire. Pawns, doomed for death in this ridiculous game. His was a position I wished never to be in.

"Her power," Thompson said. "What Ms. Danning is, regardless of inexperience, is of interest to my employers. The poison was for show, but I will not risk her any further. She is the key, one of the last soldiers in existence. They are the few who can read the Waterstar map in its entirety."

There was that damn map again.

Thompson stepped toward me. The other guards mirrored him and inched toward the SeaSat5 crew. *Not good, not good.* The poison seized me. I reached behind me for purchase, the reassurance of a station within grasp. My fingers slipped over keys and buttons. I tried not to push any.

"Here is your choice," Thompson said, pinning me with a stare. He gripped the handle of the gun at his side. "You come freely with us, along with all of the artifacts, once we dock at my employer's location, or I start killing off members of this crew."

The Lemurian mark beneath my collarbone burned, reinforcing his once-threat. He'd taken my powers once, and he'd do it again to me, or worse.

My gaze darted between Captain Marks and Thompson. "Why didn't you capture me hours ago? If you knew this entire time, why not just take what you need?"

"We needed to be sure," Thompson said. "And we need the satellite station." Which made no sense.

"Then what will you do with the crew?"

"They'll be sent to home-port in shuttles," he tugged his gun free from its holster. "What is your choice?"

So, I either save my own ass and have to live with the death of Michael but sacrifice my freedom and maybe ultimately my life, or watch him kill everyone else one by one. Those were my choices. My life or theirs. My freedom or their lives.

Tears streamed down my cheeks and into my mouth. My throat coarsened and dried, and the world spun a dizzying dance. I could barely focus through the spin and fog. I sobbed. I knew what my decision would be, but was too cowardly to make it. How did it come to this? Months ago, everything was so *normal*.

I can't do this. My body shook, and I couldn't form words to answer him.

"Well?" Thompson asked.

"I—I—" Nothing else came out. My eyes darted around. The choice was so easy: me or them? But I couldn't make it. I couldn't.

"How about this," Thompson said, yanking my hand upwards. He plopped his gun in my open palm. The metal's weight was heavier than I expected. He lifted my hand and stepped back.

I looked up from the gun, through the haze of poison, and found myself staring straight down the barrel at Captain Marks. "No."

"Shoot him," Thompson said. Another gun cocked. I risked a glance and found he had his pistol trained on me. "Or I shoot you."

Sweat caked my back and arms. There had to be a way out of this that didn't involve someone dying. There *had* to be.

My mind spun as I tried to think my way out. But your brain doesn't listen to reason when staring down the barrel of a gun. "You need me." The plea was weak. I had nothing more to offer.

"Fine," he said and re-aimed. "The Captain or Mr. Boncore. You choose."

"No!" I shouted. *Oh god, oh god, oh god.* "Kill me instead."

Weak. Defeated. If he wanted me, Thompson should just take me, dead or alive. My life didn't mean this much. *I* didn't mean much. I hadn't done anything worth living for. But Trevor, he built this station. He would change things. Invent things, incredible things. If it'd save Trevor or Captain Marks, Thompson should just kill *me*.

"It's okay, Chelsea," Captain Marks said, like he could read my thoughts. His eyes begged me to take the shot and kill him, despite the consequences. Him or his crew—it wasn't a question for Captain Marks. There was no contest.

What made me such a damn coward that I couldn't make the same sacrifice? That I couldn't turn the gun on myself and make that choice for Thompson? For everyone here?

"This will happen one way or another," Thompson assured me. "You've failed to take me seriously from the get-go. Now, you have a choice to make. Shoot the Captain, or I will kill Mr. Boncore. If it is any consolation, if this scenario happened a thousand years ago, you'd kill Trevor immediately for his heritage."

He's Lemurian. How had I been so stupid? Thompson played us, and Trevor played *me*. A few hours ago, I agreed to help Trevor end this, and now I could—with his death. And a part of me, ever so small and ever so hidden, wanted me to do it. It inched my finger closer to the trigger. Because Trevor was Lemurian. Because Thompson's behavior flipped another switch in me, made my body reach for something ancient inside itself, this super soldier Thompson kept going on about. She called inside of me, begged me to follow through.

My focus narrowed on the gun, on Trevor, and I zoned out everything else. I couldn't breathe. My lungs simply wouldn't take in air. My hand shook violently with the effort of not giving into that super soldier temptation; I almost lost grip of the gun. Bile rose in my throat. Thompson was right. I wanted to kill him, and I hated it. *Hated* it. I hated all of this.

Trevor struggled against his captor, unwilling to hold eye contact with me. "Why are you doing this?" Could he sense the change, too? This Atlantean presence inside me?

My fingers twitched around the trigger, not shooting but not moving away, either.

Thompson cut his eyes to Trevor. "It would be wise for you to be silent."

"Just kill me and end this," Trevor pleaded. "Then all your loose ends are tied up, and no one will know the difference."

My blood burned. I couldn't tell if it was poison or betrayal fueling the fire.

"Make your choice, soldier," Thompson ordered me.

My fingers froze, my mind playing a million and one scenarios over and over in my head. If I shot the Captain, Thompson could shoot Trevor for fun. Despite whatever his true loyalties were, he didn't deserve to die. Not like this. Not when a part of me *yearned* for it. But if I shot the Captain, I could end this. It'd be over so quickly. Or I could shoot myself, but Thompson could still kill both of them—and the whole crew shortly thereafter.

My eyes flitted across the room. Each SeaSat5 crewmember had one or more guards on them. This Atlantean super soldier inside me—whatever that was, and whatever that meant—she flipped the same switch when Thompson charged me with fire. I closed my eyes and focused on the emotions playing in my system. Aligned them. *Used* them.

Arms shaking, I lifted the gun and re-aimed it at Thompson— and fired.

The blast doors of the Bridge exploded in a shower of fire and metal at the exact same moment. I continued to pull the trigger. Five bullets left my gun before pain ripped through my stomach, tearing my skin and organs. Blood splattered across my vision, and I fell to the ground. The pistol tumbled out of my hand.

The gunfire of a dozen or more weapons ricocheted throughout the room, lighting up everything from Lemurian soldiers to SeaSat5's control stations. Sparks from electrical fires lit up the Bridge in a haze of white light.

Someone fell over me, shielding my body. Dark skin, darker hair. Freddy. He turned me onto my back. All I managed was a small smile. Freddy was pretty handsome, now that I looked at him.

He didn't return the smile. I frowned.

His torso moved into view as gunfire echoed behind him, muffled and out of focus. Then the room fell silent. This must have been dream or a hallucination.

A constant white noise thrummed through my ears, echoing my throbbing pulse. I couldn't hear what Freddy said, but his face was frantic, wracked with chaos. He was yelling at someone. Hands pressed down on my abdomen. It hurt. Why was Freddy hurting me?

Trevor's face came into view, then the Captain's. Then Hill's. *Dr. Hill?*

Confusion sunk in, more intense than the white noise or bright lights. Before I could make any sense out of anything at all, my world fizzled into unconsciousness.

Chapter Thirty-Three

Trevor

They'd kept Chelsea in surgery for what felt like forever. I slumped in a chair with my feet bridging another one, waiting for her to wake up. I wanted her to stir so I could prove to myself she made it out alive. Dr. Gordon and her staff were optimistic about Chelsea's recovery, but even getting that prognosis had taken three hours.

My feet slipped against the chair as the image of Chelsea getting shot played across my vision. The echo of that gunshot, the utter silence that encapsulated the Bridge as it rang out, would haunt me forever.

I retrieved the chair and propped my feet again, rubbing my face. Stubble scratched my hand. Chelsea would wake up to some scruffy-faced stranger; one who she may not want anything to do with anymore. If Captain Marks even kept me on SeaSat5 after this debacle.

Captain Marks was currently trying to secure the station. He'd informed me the only thing he wanted me to do was wait for Chelsea to wake up and then sit with her until he could figure out what to do with me. I didn't blame him. While I wasn't the person who dropped the ball on this mess, I hadn't exactly stopped it from happening.

They'd never found Valerie. I doubted Valerie remained on board. With the ability to teleport, she'd be long gone by now. She'd been missing since before I found her note—another reason Captain Marks wanted me out of the way. My loyalties, however screwed up the ties, were clear. If I'd wanted to take the station down for Lemuria, I could have done so anytime within the last year. But I'd chosen SeaSat5. Having me out in the open while they vetted the rest of the crew and searched for Valerie was dangerous. Though looking at Chelsea right now, her hooked up to IVs and other monitors… being taken out by Valerie wasn't something I didn't welcome. I may not have done the work, but I'd said nothing.

Valerie.

I pulled a piece of paper from my pocket. Construction paper. Red. A wish had been scribbled onto it, the paper folded up on my tenth birthday, the night of my indoctrination into modern Lemurian society. They'd done it as this weird ritual, and, supposedly, if you'd nurtured the wish with enough thought and work (and magic, I assumed), it'd come true. It was supposed to stay inside a dreambox until that day.

Valerie had a dreambox too. All Lemurians did. But I'd never found out what her wish was, and was too chicken shit to read my own. I'd opened my dreambox before Captain Marks had condemned me to the Infirmary, but I'd done nothing but stare at it out of nostalgia, or fear of what had happened, since.

I got a feeling I already knew what the wish was.

My fingers obeyed the unspoken command and unfolded the paper. I drew a deep, steadying breath to prepare myself for whatever was written inside. I pushed up the corners of the paper and held it out straight.

I wish for someone to end the war. A savior, Lemurian or Atlantean. It doesn't matter. Just end it.

My eyes closed on the words, lips tightening around what they meant. Emotion clogged my throat so tight, I couldn't breathe.

A moan sounded from Chelsea's bed. I looked over at her. Was she that person? Did she randomly pop into and disrupt my life so completely and thoroughly, just to end the war?

Chelsea stirred and, before I could tell her not to, she sat up—and immediately fell to the recovery bed with a whine. "Ow."

"Relax, Chelsea." God, her name felt like a curse now, like something I didn't have the right to say. She probably hated me for this. Because of my wish. Because of every damn thing that'd happened since we fucking met.

My chest tightened when her eyes met mine, collapsed by an unseen source. I should have gone to her side, but I couldn't, not knowing if she even wanted me there in the first place.

"Why am I in the Infirmary?" Her voice was soft, laden with lasting grogginess.

My hand formed a lazy fist in front of my mouth, constricting in self-loathing. "You got shot."

"Well, that explains my inability to sit up."

Her indifference struck a nerve. My jaw worked side to side. How could she be so cavalier about this? "It's not something to joke about."

"Did I laugh?" She winced and ran a hand over her abdomen. "Whatever pain meds they've got me on, I don't think they're working."

I stood and paced toward an intercom by the door. "You may have torn something by sitting up. I'll call Dr. Gordon."

"It's fine. Don't."

My thumb hovered over the CALL button. I searched her eyes for any evidence of pain or discomfort. "Are you sure?"

"Yes." She pressed a hand to her forehead, not in pain. Trying to focus. "What happened?"

I should call Helen. In the very least, she'd want to know Chelsea woke up.

I pulled up a chair beside her recovery bed and sat down, relaying the scene to her piece by piece. She'd pointed the gun at Thompson and fired. Hit him square in the heart, actually. One of Thompson's guys had fired at the same moment and a single bullet had sliced through her. Freddy had broken free of his captor, slugged him hard enough for the guy to drop his gun, and pistol-whipped him.

"I don't remember being shot," she interrupted, staring at her hands. "I don't remember firing the gun, either. It's all a big blur. But I do remember Freddy's face." She glanced at me. "He protected me, didn't he?"

I nodded. "He covered your body with his. A military rescue team stormed the Bridge moments after you fired the first shot."

Bullets had whizzed by my head, sticking themselves into stations and walls and human flesh. Screams and shouts had inundated the air alongside barked orders, yelped and cried. I had ducked behind my station as soon as Freddy had shielded Chelsea.

The firefight had ended almost as fast as it'd started, but the damage had been done. Weyland had suffered a bullet to the arm, Chelsea had been shot in the abdomen, and the entire Bridge had been decimated by gunfire. Thank god Thompson had flipped the station vertically after the flooding incident, or who knew what would've happened.

With the Bridge secured, Captain Marks had called for the senior staff to do what they could to reset the ship's systems so we wouldn't be dead in the water. He'd relieved me to come here after Humming Bird was stable.

Chelsea stayed quiet after I finished. I reached a hand out to her. She took it.

"I killed him, didn't I?" Her voice was sad and small. It fractured my heart into an infinite sea of tiny pieces. She wasn't a soldier. She didn't deserve any of this. Not the war, not the pain. And I could have saved her from it, either by telling Captain Marks what might have happened, or by doing what Dr. Hill had wanted and handing her over to TAO.

"Don't think about that right now," I said. "You need to concentrate on healing. Your burn already looks better, so the bullet wound should heal fast."

Her glare cleaved my heart in two.

"I don't care about what's happened to me. I care about killing a person," she said.

"A person who already took a friend's life and threatened others'. It's called self-defense for a reason."

"Self-defense… That's so not the point." She ripped her hand away. "I killed him. Guess it's a good thing I chose archaeology over straight-up anthropology. I'd never get into grad school. Like, 'Oh, ignore the pesky murder charge. Really, I love people.'" She rolled her eyes then looked away. "Did anyone else not make it?"

I swallowed hard. Her way of dealing with things (i.e. not actually dealing with them) wasn't going to work this time. She would spiral; it was only a matter of when. "All other crewmembers are fine. Weyland's arm is in a sling, but he'll survive."

"And Thompson's crew?"

"The ones who survived are being held for questioning. Eventually, they'll be imprisoned in some military compound."

"Is Valerie one of them?"

I shook my head. "She's been missing since before the Bridge incident."

"What about Emma Rose?"

My eyebrows furrowed. The name wasn't familiar. "Who?"

"The Chief Engineer who told me how to reconnect the communications buoy."

I wracked my brain for an engineer by that name. There was no Emma Rose. "I don't know who you're talking about."

Chelsea glared, determined to fight me on this. "Well, she's real. She messaged me in *Mega Rush 2*. Gave me instructions."

In my game? Only people with a profile could get—

Emma. Rose. Valerie and Abby's middle names. My heart twisted. Why would Valerie help Chelsea reconnect the buoy?

"Uh, Emma isn't a real person," I said. "Emma is Valerie's middle name."

"Then who's Rose?" she asked.

I squeezed the bridge of my nose, a headache forming behind my eyes. "It's Abby's middle name."

Silence sat uncomfortably between us. All I could think about was the dreambox. Chelsea, the "savior" I'd wished for nine years ago.

She shook her head. "I don't understand. Why would she help if she sided with Thompson, then disappeared?"

"I have no idea." I didn't think Valerie had wanted anyone to die, and that could have been why. Or maybe she thought Thompson would go off the deep end and botch their collective mission. "I wonder if we'll ever know."

"I don't care. She stood by and let too many things happen." She turned to me with a frown. "And what about you?"

The quick subject change confused me. "Excuse me?"

"You knew exactly what we found, when we found it," she said, her words striking like rocks from a slingshot. "You knew those artifacts were something more than art."

Time for the truth.

"I assumed what we found may have been something of interest to people beyond our chain of command, yes. But I wasn't sure any of them were Link Pieces. I can't see them like you can. They're just artifacts to me."

"But there was a strong possibility we had found whatever the hell a Link Piece is?"

"There's *always* a possibility. Anything could become a Link piece. That journal you write in, your guitar, your cell phone, the Empire State Building—anything man-made. Anything touched by humans. It's a giant puzzle, that's all it is."

She closed her eyes and breathed deep. "I can't believe you knew all of this and lied."

I balled my fists. "I didn't have a choice, Chelsea. I'm not a soldier like you. I'm an engineer. My only weapons are ballast systems, not powers and strength. When those systems break, I have no other choice."

"Thing is," she said, her voice low, "you had every choice in the world because you're *not* a soldier."

My heart cracked around her words. She couldn't know how painful they were, to know it was the absolute truth. I wasn't a soldier. I didn't have powers. And because of it, she'd almost died. Because of *me*, she'd taken a bullet to the gut. She might even be here *because* of me.

"I have no idea what's going on anymore," she continued. "Six months ago, my day consisted of classes and rock shows. Now, I've killed someone, found evidence for Atlantis *and* Lemuria, and can make a light-show spectacle of myself." She rolled her head onto her shoulders. "I think I want to go home."

"For good?" I almost didn't want to ask. Our relationship may be in shambles, but her work with the Atlantean outpost was something she was meant to do. Practically her birthright.

I didn't want her to leave for my own selfish reasons. When I was with Chelsea, freedom had finally come. Even during the hijacking, even in spite of it all, she was everything. And here she sat, ready to take that all away. I'd thought I'd lost her, but here she was. I couldn't bear the thought of her walking away from me. From us. From everything we had on SeaSatellite5.

"This isn't my life, Trevor," she said, her voice breaking. "I go to school or work, come home, do homework. Then I go on stage. That's it. That's what I do. I don't travel the world's oceans in search of Atlantis." She swallowed hard and looked down at her hands. "This was an internship, Trevor. It wasn't meant to be permanent."

In other words, neither was I.

Chapter Thirty-Four

Chelsea

Maybe before I was shot, before I murdered someone, I could have handled things. Before then, it was just death. Not caused by me, but witnessed nonetheless. I'd been there before. Death wasn't new. But I'd *killed* someone. Self-defense or not, I couldn't stay here. Couldn't talk to Trevor without space to run away and figure out what I'd become since meeting him.

By the time Captain Marks had escorted me from the Infirmary to the Briefing Room to meet with Dr. Hill and his team, I could stand. Wincing for every second of it, but I stood nonetheless. I didn't understand my healing abilities at all. The burn mark Thompson had given me still hadn't healed, but my gunshot wound was on its way to full—but scarred—recovery just two days later. Dr. Gordon said the burn mark would take weeks or longer to fully heal, if at all. The poison Thompson had used on me was meant to slow down Atlanteans. And slow me down, it did. At least my active powers were back.

Dr. Hill's crew conducted my briefing without the presence of any SeaSat5 officers or science staff. My pain quickly turned to annoyance, but it softened at the sight of Dr. Hill, whose right arm was in a sling. Lacerations marked his cheeks and neck, and dark bags hung under his eyes.

"Are you okay?" I asked. A dumb question. Clearly.

Dr. Hill shed a small smile. "I've been better."

I pointed to the closed door. "Why all the secrecy?"

"This is Army Major Howard Pike and Sophia Burns," he said, introducing me to the other two people in the room. "We owe you an explanation, one which is highly classified."

"I'd say that's an understatement." He'd come aboard SeaSat5 all those weeks ago, knowing exactly what we'd found, like Trevor had. Then he'd lied to me, like Trevor had.

I took a deep breath. "I'd like to hear it, if you're up to it. Are you sure you're okay?"

He nodded. "Dr. Gordon took good care of me. Another day with the Lemurians, and it might have been a different story."

Satisfied with his answer, I glanced at his companions. Howard Pike looked more like a movie star than an Army Major. He had a young face free of wrinkles, but the traces of grey in his otherwise jet black hair betrayed his age. Sophia's dark-caramel skin was a shade lighter than her hair, a combination that made her bright green eyes stand stark against the darker colors. Both of them wore the same military fatigues Dr. Hill had worn when he'd first boarded SeaSat5, except, this time, TAO patches stood out against their black uniforms. My brain, muddled by painkillers, couldn't make sense of it all.

"Do you want me to explain things or would you rather ask the questions yourself?" Dr. Hill said.

"Am I really from Atlantis?" At least that question sounded saner than *what is an Atlanean super soldier?*

"Your ancestors were," he said without hesitation.

"My sister doesn't have powers. Neither do my parents."

"It's possible the active powers skipped a generation," Dr. Hill said. "Some of the other traits must be there, though."

I snorted. Sarah could barely drink three beers without hitting her limit, versus my one bottle of tequila to maybe get buzzed. And I'd never noticed anything weird about my parents. "I really don't think so."

Dr. Hill shrugged. "It's something we would like to look into, if you'd let us. From our understanding, people like yourself had ancestors who stole their children away through Link Pieces that allowed them to escape a fate they couldn't—to escape fighting a war they didn't support."

So, that story in the journal was true. My ancestors saved their kids with time travel. *That dream.* Was someone trying to send me a message?

"And Atlantis is at war with Lemuria?" I asked.

Dr. Hill nodded. "Yes."

"Lemuria exists?"

"Yes."

"And so does Atlantis?"

More nodding from Dr. Hill.

"Then where are they?" I asked. "The evidence we found in the Sargasso Sea doesn't mean Atlantis was ever there, and all the other hypotheses seem ludicrous." Antarctica. America. A missing continent in the Pacific.

Sophia answered this time, an Irish accent wrapping thick around her words. "They are not exactly on Earth. Not as you know it."

"What, like separate dimensions?"

"No."

I rubbed my eyes as if it'd help clear my mind. "Why are they at war?"

"We don't know for sure," Dr. Hill answered. "We do know it's tearing Earth's core apart in time and space. We know they use what are called Link Pieces to travel through time, an action that destroyed their home-times. Your ancestors escaped before the Atlantean Destruction."

Of course they did.

Trevor's words haunted me. *They oppose what Atlantis stood for.*

"Did the Greeks really stand against them?" I asked. "Wait—don't tell me. The Athenians supported Lemuria and waged the war for them."

"Yes, actually," Dr. Hill answered.

"You've got to be kidding me." I let out a long breath and fell into my seat. My abdomen contracted with the movement, sending a shooting pain crackling up my side. I winced. "What's a Link Piece?"

"Objects in time, usually man-made, and sometimes full-on structures," Dr. Hill said.

"So, like Stonehenge to Excalibur?" I joked. Their silence said at least one of those were true. I didn't want to know which. "How do you know what's a Link Piece, then?"

"You and I can see them," Sophia said. "Others, like Dr. Hill and the rest of the TAO staff, need special equipment."

"TAO? You and I?" I asked.

"The Ancient Operation," the Army Major finally spoke. Until now, he'd remained quiet, arms crossed at his broad chest. "Stupid name, don't ask. We have to use scanners and the like, but Sophia can see them. She's an Atlantean super soldier, too. Apparently Link Pieces shimmer or sparkle."

Like the journal. The one telling my ancestors' story. It'd shimmered on and off since day one. I'd thought I'd dreamt it. Maybe not.

"I guessed the journal was a Piece given the way it entranced you," Dr. Hill said. "Was I correct?"

I nodded. "Should I not read it or something? Do I need to keep it contained?"

"No," he said, shaking his head. "But I have a list of other artifacts that I believe are also Link Pieces."

"Why do you say 'link'? Trevor said something about it all being a giant puzzle," I said. "And Thompson said the Lemurians needed the artifacts to create a pathway to Atlantis."

"Through space and time. You can use them to time travel around Earth."

"*Just* Earth?" I wasn't sure I wanted to know the answer. Atlantis and Lemuria? Okay. Aliens? Hell no.

Dr. Hill nodded. "Only Earth, but all of its pasts and futures. We've traveled quite the spectrum so far, from the Stone Age to the far future."

"So, what would the journal link to?" The time traveling part didn't interest me. The journal was far more important.

"Probably the Atlanteans who owned it," Dr. Hill explained. "The connections are formed, usually, between the creator and the time and place of the objects' creation. Or sometimes a strong emotional link can be formed between a time and a place and an object."

"And the others? What else do you think is one of these Link Pieces?"

"There was a unicorn mirror we found. Do you remember it?"

Yes, actually, I did. The mirror was beautiful, albeit aged. It had a unicorn engraved on the center—more of a decorative piece, I imagined, than a functional one—encased in a halo of straw. "Yeah, but I don't remember it shimmering like the journal does."

"You have a stronger connection to the journal," Sophia said. "Therefore, you noticed it first. The same happened with me and the first Link Piece I found."

Right. A thought occurred to me then. I looked to Dr. Hill. "Was there more to the mummy than you admitted, too?"

His eyes narrowed in guilt. "Uh, yes. It looks like she was Atlantean and indeed your officer's 'sci-fi' ideas were probably correct. It appears you opened a stasis chamber of some sort, and, at the time the woman placed herself inside, she thought she'd survive."

"There was a crack at the bottom," I pointed out. "She never would have made it."

"No. Hence mummification," Dr. Hill said.

I dropped my gaze, feeling sorry for the woman. She was only trying to survive whatever she'd run from and ended up a dried up husk.

"Is there anything else you didn't tell me about? Like what's up with this super soldier nonsense? Is that why I have powers?" I looked at Dr. Hill. "Why didn't you say something when I plugged the leak?"

"I couldn't. Not until I knew for sure you were an Atlantean super soldier," he said.

"And you didn't know until *after* SeaSat5 was hijacked?"

"Unrelated," Major Pike said. "When Dr. Hill didn't check in before we arrived, we suspected something went wrong. Then Mr. Boncore tried contacting TAO."

"So SeaSat5 became the center of everything because of the outpost," I guessed.

"Yes," said Dr. Hill. "Although, it's more of a lab than an outpost. A museum of sorts."

"Figures," I mumbled. *Outpost* implied war—which Atlantis was in the middle of, sure. But the way all the artifacts had been preserved and displayed *had* suggested a different scenario.

"And I'm important because I'm some jacked up human?" I asked.

"Aside from Sophia, you are the only super soldier we know about right now," Dr. Hill said. "You both also have direct ties to Atlantis. Your power and ancestry are more important than you know."

That jogged my memory. I glanced at Sophia. "Thompson said he needed me because I can see some map. I think he called it the Waterstar map?"

Sophia perked up, leaned over the table. "Can you see it?"

"I don't even know what it is."

"When I time travel through Link Pieces, a map takes over my mind," Sophia said. "It shows the links between the Pieces. Where they go, where they don't. It looks like a giant snowflake connecting everything with dates and times."

A legitimate water star. At least it made more sense for a name than TAO did.

"So he wanted me because I can see it and he couldn't?" I asked.

Dr. Hill and Major Pike shared a look before the Major answered my question. "There must be something specific they wanted, and figured they could take the station's artifact cache in the process."

"So you're saying they weren't after the artifacts at all? That they wanted me, and me alone?"

"There's no way to know unless your security detail can get it out of the prisoners," Sophia said. "The Lemurians' world is a complicated one. They're not an organized society anymore. Their factions hold too many different beliefs and values to be coherent. It's possible Thompson belonged to a sect that wanted the Waterstar map instead of the cache."

Great. That meant they might come after me again.

"So now what?" I asked. I wanted to go home, but could I leave this find behind for good? No. I couldn't. "I don't want to stop working on this site," I continued. "I mean, I don't think I will. Everything's a bit too crazy right now to make a decision."

"No one's asking you to," Dr. Hill said, leaning forward. "But, if you're willing, I would like to—again—extend an invitation for you to come with us, so you can learn more about who and what you are. We want you to know about this war and how to use your powers to defend yourself."

"And learn how Link Pieces work?"

"That, too. That's what I was getting at when we spoke before the hijacking."

I rubbed my forehead. This sounded completely absurd. "Say we are fighting a war, and say I am this soldier, and SeaSat5 is the new center of it... wouldn't I be better off here?" Not that I'd done a spectacular job of protecting it thus far.

Sophia spoke up. "You need training. You have no idea how to use your abilities to their full potential. I can help you with that."

"I can also train here."

Why did I have such an attachment to this place after what had happened? It's like… whatever was pushing me to leave wasn't strong enough to fight my connection to the station. And it sure was a connection. A powerful, protective one that gripped my mind and wrangled my rational thoughts away.

"Wouldn't you guys want to come here to protect this station, too?" I asked.

"All that's needed to protect the station is for you to remove yourself and all remnants of the artifact cache," Sophia said. "And you would be better off learning your abilities from me than Helen."

"You know Helen?" I asked her.

"I first learned about my abilities from her," said Sophia.

Sophia must be the other student with multiple powers that Helen had mentioned. It all started to make sense now.

I gestured her way. "Does she know what you're up to these days?"

Sophia shook her head. "Not really. Though she was happy to see me earlier."

I bit my lip. This was too much information, too quickly. "Can I have some time to think about it?" The question was directed at Dr. Hill. "A few days or weeks?"

He looked like he expected me to say yes and not question anything, but he hid it with a graceful smile. "Sure. Of course."

"It's a lot to take in," I offered in place of a positive, enthusiastic response on my end. "Especially after everything. I need time to mentally recoup." Not to mention heal the rest of my body. I'd ask for a two-week leave from this ship—from everything. That would be enough time to decide.

Dr. Hill nodded. "We'll be in touch, then?"

"Yeah, absolutely," I said. "We still have an outpost to catalogue."

And, apparently, a war to fight.

Chapter Thirty-Five

Trevor

The Briefing Room threatened to swallow me whole. I deserved every bit of the good cop, bad cop routine being forced upon me. Dave sat across the table, smiling an encouragement as though what happened here didn't matter, while Lieutenant Weyland paced behind him. Every few steps, he'd stop and ask a question, and then resume walking until another relevant inquiry came to mind.

All I could think about was Chelsea. After whatever had happened during her meeting with Dr. Hill and his archaeology team, Captain Marks had granted her a two-week leave for some reason, and she'd left that same day. I wanted to know why—why she'd left and she didn't tell me.

Who was I kidding? I knew exactly why.

Lieutenant Weyland reiterated a question with wild hand motions.

"I've told you everything I know," I said. Or what I could tell them. Dr. Hill's team made it clear they didn't want any SeaSatellite5 staff knowing about the time traveling end of things, or what Link Pieces were, or what TAO did in the background. Good thing

Lieutenant Weyland's main focus was on my involvement with Thompson and not on what I knew but wouldn't say.

"I think the Lieutenant's issue is that you worked with us for a year and didn't once give the suggestion that we're in danger because of what we do," Dave supplied.

"I honestly never thought we'd find anything of value." That was the god's honest truth.

"Did Ms. McAllister think the same?" Weyland asked.

I heaved a sigh. Valerie again. She'd never turned up, meaning she'd definitely left the station before TAO had arrived. "Val thought we'd find something. She's been loyal to them from the day they put us through school with aims of getting onto a satellite station."

"Were you aware she had powers like Chelsea?" Dave asked.

My eyes narrowed. "God, no. I'd never asked her, but after what happened with my cousin, I never…" They didn't know about Abby. "My cousin thought she kept running into people with strange abilities. It didn't end well. After that, I refused to believe anything my parents or Thompson said was true about abilities—Lemurian and Atlantean alike."

"What happened?" Dave asked.

I shook my head. "I don't want to talk about it." Especially if Valerie's guesses were correct. Not only had Abby run into super soldiers, the Atlanteans likely had tortured her too, all for information she didn't have because our parents had lied to her about it all.

"I need to know," Weyland insisted with arched eyebrows. He expected an answer regardless of my feelings on the subject.

Crossing my arms at my chest, I said, "She's in mental hospital in Tennessee. Blissfully unaware of the truth."

They both frowned and fell silent.

Weyland recovered quicker. "Where has Valerie gone?"

"I don't know," I said. "But she was the one who helped Chelsea contact Admiral Dennett."

"Why would she do that?" Dave snapped. The words were more of a bark.

I eyed him, but his bandaged hand stole my attention. Just the other day, he'd had his wrist cast off while playing poker. I thumbed toward it. "What happened?"

His eyes darted to the bandage, fist tightening.

Weyland interjected before Dave could answer me. "Don't change the subject, Trevor. Why would Valerie help Chelsea if she was working for Thompson all along?"

Eyes still lingering on Dave's hand, I said, "My guess is Valerie thought Thompson wanted to destroy the station before they completed their mission. In that case, her loyalties changed to the collective, not him. It's how she works."

Dave's jaw worked, muscles popping.

Weyland either ignored his weird reaction or didn't see it. "If you had to guess where she went, what would that guess be?"

My fists clenched in my lap. "Look, I know you need to worry because you're Head of Security, but Valerie knows as much about SeaSat5 and Humming Bird as I do. The only reason she's not on the senior staff is because our former employers knew you'd catch on quicker if the two of us showed up together. If she wants to get onboard, she will. There's nothing you or I can do about it. And no, I have no idea where she went. My guess is somewhere foreign and urban, like Paris or London. Somewhere she can blend in and hide for a while."

"So, we may never see her again," Dave said.

"It's as likely as her showing up tomorrow with another Lemurian contingent. I can attempt to rework the shield, but she knew the whole time it couldn't block out Thompson's crew when I thought it could." My shoulders drooped. "I didn't know as much as I thought, and that's why we're here right now. I'm sorry."

Dave frowned again, leveling his eyes with mine. "It's okay."

"Not really," Weyland said. "Thanks to these events, the world knows about SeaSatellite5."

My eyes snapped to his. "What?"

"Thompson's crew destroyed the station's cloaking system. It was down the whole time. When we flipped vertical, after Chelsea fixed the hull, word got out. The U.N. managed to keep people from panicking, but everyone knows the United States owns the most advanced piece of submersible technology ever created."

"Financed by the U.N for allied global research purposes," I countered.

"Except, it's manned by more military officers than civilian scientists and has impressive weapons systems. And a nice shield, to boot."

My chest gave out and the world spun. Not good. Not good at all.

Weyland cleared his throat. "I need to speak with the Captain. I'm placing you in quarters confinement until he makes up his mind. Until then, you'll have no access to the station's systems. Dave, make sure that holds."

"Aye, sir," Dave said.

"Think about ways to improve the shield, Trevor," Weyland said, "in the event Captain Marks wants to keep you."

Defeated, I pulled in a deep breath. "Okay."

I spent my time in quarters confinement making a game that would be destroyed upon Captain Marks discovering it. The game detailed everything I knew about Lemuria and Atlantis, an RPG based on what it might have been like to be there the night Lemuria ordered the Athenians to destroy the famous lost city.

The game was stupid and would never sell, so after one play-through, I relaxed into my chair and rubbed the fatigue out of my face. Nothing I did here would see the light of day. Ever. Not anymore. Except possibly Humming Bird. Thanks to Thompson's ridiculous actions, the whole world now knew about SeaSat5.

The whoosh of an incoming email exploded through my computer's speakers. I jumped a foot out of my chair. No one should be messaging me right now, and everyone except Chelsea was here. My heart leapt nearly out of my chest. Chelsea messaged me?

I opened my inbox, and my hope plummeted. An email from Emma Rose waited for me.

Valerie. Where was she?

I clicked on the email.

Trevor,

You'll probably never see me again, and that's fine. I lied, and I know you're angry and confused right now, but please understand: I never thought Thompson would risk the station. SeaSatellite5 is more important than you know, and if I, for one moment, thought he'd risk it just to take the Link Pieces inside, or that TAO would interfere, I wouldn't have helped him. That's why I acted, and why I now need to disappear.

Take care, Trevor. And take care of Abby for me. Visit her.

—V

"Valerie." The word came out more like a whine than anything else. What had she gotten herself into? What attention had she put on SeaSat5 in the process? And where would Valerie go to hide? Not back home. Betraying Thompson in the end put her on the same no-fly list as me. Our families wouldn't take us back now. Guess we both had issues with blind loyalty.

Should I try to find her, trace her cyber footsteps? I didn't know why I suddenly cared what happened to her or where she'd went after leaving SeaSat5, but now that the thought had implanted itself into my mind, I couldn't let it go. I balanced the laptop on my knees and tried following her hack, but she'd covered her tracks well. Three routers, two countries, and seven different IP addresses later, a weight sunk deep in my stomach. She was much better at this than me, and I'd never find her. Ever.

It'd been two weeks since I last saw Chelsea. Since I last spoke to her. Since she nearly broke me with her words. *It wasn't meant to be permanent.* Now, some of SeaSatellite5's crew had packed a tiny shuttle to see Phoenix and Lobster's end of the summer show. To see Chelsea. Anxiety wracked my body, and I couldn't sit still. How was she? Would she okay with me being in the crowd tonight? She'd only invited Freddy, really. Hopefully I'd blend in better at tonight's show than at the one where we met. *Pointless wish.* She'd pinpointed me in a crowd on the night I'd most wanted to stay hidden.

Heavy traffic into Boston forced us to miss their opening band, which didn't matter to me. I wasn't there for them. I was there for Chelsea, just like I would be no matter how many pieces she shattered me into.

While the rest of the guys headed to the bar at the rear of the Franklin, Freddy and I fought our way into a good standing room spot. Did she even want me here? Not like I could have asked her to find out. She hadn't returned any of my calls. Hadn't talked to me since she woke up after her surgery.

Phoenix and Lobster's set started minutes later. Chelsea and their other singer, a guy, took the stage. The first song rode quick and heavy, enough to get the crowd warmed up and cheering. Strobe lights streaked across the stage and crowd. They disoriented me as much tonight as they did the last time I stood here. Chelsea's sister hopped in on bass, followed by their third guitarist and drummer, and the lights broke out into a dizzying, multi-colored array.

The first two songs they played were heavier than anything I'd heard in March. The rifts grew solid, the baseline lower. At one point, I swore one their male singer tried something akin to screamo. I'd be lying if I said the music wasn't good. In fact, they were great. Yet, it wasn't Chelsea. She dressed like a punk rock princess but danced around like something else. She hopped up on amps to wildly play breakdowns and flirted with their main guitarist as lyrics rolled out of her mouth, like it was all part of the show. All part of the new Phoenix and Lobster experience.

But all of that was nothing compared to what she did in the middle of their last song.

Chelsea grabbed her mic off its stand, and the band played lower background music.

"Thank you all for coming out tonight," she spoke as she sauntered to the side of the stage. She nodded to someone behind the curtain with a huge smile across her sweaty face. "We've missed playing more than we can express, and we're sorry for missing the Battle of the Bands a few months ago. To make up for it, we're gonna close out the show tonight in a very special way."

She shoved her bright, fire engine red guitar behind her, the neck running along her legs. The guitar was new, probably bought while she was on leave. Someone off-stage handed her something, and she returned to center stage with it in her hand. She held up the beer can for the crowd to see.

"I don't know about you guys, but I've had one hell of a summer." She placed the mic on her stand then reached into her pockets and pulled out a set of keys.

No. She was not going to shotgun a beer on stage.

She held up both the beer and keys to either side of the stand. "So, this one's for all of us!"

The band came back in with the song, repeating a few chords of the breakdown. Seconds before the last chorus started, Chelsea punctured the beer can and shot-gunned the entire thing in one swift gulp. Then she held the prize out for all to see as she finished the song in full rock star form, barely a drop of beer anywhere on her shiny gold tank top.

I glanced over at Freddy, whose lips pressed together into a thin line, apparently about as amused as I was. Chelsea danced around in her red converse and skinny jeans as she rocked out the rest of the song, hopping from foot to foot in time with the dropkick on the drums. She ended the set with a fist in the air, standing on top of an amp—grinning from ear to ear.

After the show ended, Freddy and I fought our way backstage through the crowd to try and find Chelsea and the band. We both thought the beer stunt was for more than fun. We wandered without direction around the labyrinth that was the Franklin's artist-only area. Freddy wanted to check in on Chelsea, and I didn't argue with him. I'd heard enough stories from Chelsea's mouth about wild parties and her ridiculous alcohol tolerance to know that's all she did on break. But on stage, she looked more than tipsy. Somehow, someway, she'd managed to get drunk. Which meant she'd spiraled, just like I'd been afraid of her doing.

A young woman with long blonde hair and green eyes rounded the corner and paused, her brows furrowed. "Can I help you?" It was Chelsea's sister, Sarah. I'd seen her picture on Chelsea's wall in her quarters.

"Hey, can we see Chelsea?" I asked.

Her cheeks filled with air, which she slowly blew out, a definite Chelsea-ism. Her eyes darted between us, deliberating. "Um, now's not the best time. You're Trevor, right?"

"Yeah. It's nice to meet you, Sarah."

She nodded. "Yeah, uh, Chelsea's… unwinding." She cringed, biting the inside of her lower lip.

"Unwinding, how?" Freddy asked. His fist curled and uncurled at his sides, a nervous habit. Weird, since he and Chelsea weren't really friends until we'd found the outpost. But ever since the hijacking had started, he'd formed an overprotective streak.

Sarah clicked her tongue. "All right, fine. But I'm only showing you this because I don't like it, either."

Sarah waved us on, leading us to a room three hallways over. Chelsea knelt over a coffee table, next to the other singer of their band

and surrounded by people I didn't recognize. Chelsea poured a haphazard line of liquor into shot glasses. Everyone around the table grabbed one and dunked it upright into their solo cup filled with a tan-colored liquid. Chelsea counted to three, then they all chugged the concoction. She finished first and laughed, falling against the couch. The male singer lifted a hand, and they bumped fists.

Freddy cleared his throat, and they all stopped to stare.

"Hey, Chelsea," he said.

The sight of Freddy shut most of them up. He was a stocky, muscular dude, definitely out of place in a hangout full of bands and their groupies.

Chelsea stood up, brushed off her hands on her pants, and danced over wearing a lazy smile. "Freddy! Did you like the show?"

She embraced Freddy. He looked over her shoulder at me. She let go and turned to me with a shrug.

"Oh, come on." She hugged me, too.

"Everything all right?" I asked her.

Chelsea's face grew hard. "Way to go and ruin the moment by being a worrywart." She frowned.

I glanced at Freddy, my jaw hung open. His expression confirmed the same thought. Sarah came over to us, and I asked her if Chelsea was, by original guess, actually drunk.

Sarah cringed. "You don't want to know how."

"No, I think I do," I said.

Sarah pointed to a ratty chair where an empty bottle of whiskey sat. I then followed her gaze to where someone poured another round of shots. "She mumbled something about painkillers and whiskey. My guess is it mixed together poorly. How she's even still standing, I have no idea. But our friend Logan's on speed dial, just in case."

I closed my eyes, disappointment coating every thought.

Freddy stiffened, strode to Chelsea, and grabbed her by the arm. "We're leaving before you do something you regret."

She pushed against him. "No. Get your hands off me. You know nothing."

"Now." His words were firm, ordering.

They stared each other down. Freddy wouldn't budge. Chelsea wouldn't hurt him trying to extricate herself, either. Finally, she huffed, ripped her arm out of Freddy's grasp and grabbed her stuff. Sarah mouthed a *thank you* as we left.

Chelsea. Mixing pills and alcohol... to what, forget? To feel numb?

My heart sank, quick and deep. This wasn't right. And that fire, that blaze of freedom I'd felt when we met outside this building months ago, it died as we walked her out to the car.

Neither of us would ever be free again. Not from these memories, and not ever from the war.

Chapter Thirty-Six

Chelsea

I awoke to a massive headache beating the insides of my skull. I cradled my head. Everything was damn foggy and slow and sensitive, and I couldn't for the life of me remember why. *Did I get drunk?* The blankets I found myself cocooned in weren't familiar. Neither was the bed. The beige colored walls encasing the room didn't belong to me. *Shit. Where am I?*

"I'm glad to see you're awake."

I jumped at the voice, setting off the jackhammer in my head again.

Freddy sat at his desk, wrapped in a navy-issued blanket with his feet propped up.

I swallowed hard. What the *hell* happened that I ended up in a room with Freddy?

I swung my legs over the bed. "Um, I don't know wh—"

"We're not sure what happened in between the end of your set and finding you doing Jägerbombs with your buddies, but Trevor and I scooped you out of there and brought you home to SeaSatellite5." He leaned forward, dropping the blanket off him, and reached for my purse on the side of the bed. He dug around for something then lifted the pill bottle up for me to see. "Don't ever do that again."

I gulped, drowning in guilt. No one was supposed to find out about that. *How* did Freddy find out about that? "I... I won't."

He relaxed, seemingly satisfied with my answer. "You're welcome."

I didn't know what to say or where to look. My cheeks warmed and anxiety rushed my heavy chest. My head pounded so hard that I thought it'd explode.

"I'm sorry," I said. "Thank you for looking out for me."

A half-smile quirked his lips. "Someone has to." His radio beeped, and he answered it. "Olivarez."

"It's me." Trevor's voice filled the other end. "When Chelsea wakes up, can you bring her to the Artifact Room? I want to talk to her."

Freddy glanced my way. "She's awake. Give us fifteen minutes, and we'll be there."

I looked down at myself again. I couldn't show up wearing the same clothes from last night. That'd be too close to a Walk of Shame for my liking. And if Freddy knew about the pills, odds were Trevor did, too.

Freddy noticed my distress and threw me one of my own uniforms. "You can thank Trevor for thinking ahead. He went into your quarters and got you a uniform this morning."

I gulped. I forever owed those two for saving me from myself and then covering my ass on top of it.

"Thank you," I said again. "What time is it?"

"Ten-thirty."

I hung my head. *Ten-thirty?*

"The bathroom's in the corner. Go shower and get dressed."

I changed in record time and washed my face to take off all the heavy makeup I wore. I looked so different without all of it on; it jarred me. What had happened to me in just two weeks?

Freddy escorted me to the Artifact Room and left me with Trevor, who stood behind my desk, tossing a stress ball from one hand to another. My eyes trained on the movement, despite the hammering in my skull. It rolled my stomach. The hangover wasn't lost on Trevor.

"I didn't think that happened to you," he said.

I shrugged. "Guess there's a first time for everything."

He stopped the ball's movement and squeezed it. "That's kind of what I wanted to talk to you about."

"Can we do this later?" Like when I wasn't hung-over and guilty as all hell.

"You're mad, and I understand."

Guess not.

"Hell, I understand why you're freaking out—you killed Thompson. Even if the bastard had it coming, it shouldn't have had to be you. And Michael—that wasn't your fault, either. So, stop blaming yourself."

My breathing came shallow and fast until I was forced to take in longer breaths to squash feelings of queasiness. I leaned against the countertop for support. I'd killed a man, and I'd have to live with that forever, even if I forgave myself for not saving Michael.

"You can't keep doing this to yourself," he continued. "Alcohol can't be your answer."

I managed to make eye contact. "It's not my answer."

"It's just easier than dealing?" He came around the desk and placed a hand on my forearm. "I'm worried about you, and I don't care if you hate me the rest of your life because I lied. I want you to get the help you need."

"What I need is for this all to have been a nightmare. To wake up." Because the most fantastic thing to ever happen to me, finding evidence of Atlantis, had been shadowed by the worst day of my life.

"This," he gestured about the room, "is real, but this isn't my life either, Chelsea. My parents may have raised me on those stories, but they're not what I believe. You're a rock star. I'm a videogame maker.

We were in the wrong place when the ship got hijacked. You were in the wrong place on the Bridge that day."

And I knew that. I did. But all of this, everything, from classified military research stations to an Atlantean-Lemurian war for control over time itself, was a fantasy I wasn't sure I could handle. Couldn't I go back to being the college student ready to graduate and get the hell out of Boston? The girl ready to take the Northeast by storm with her pop-punk band?

Looking at Trevor now, his blue eyes as damn captivating as the first time we met, I couldn't fathom a way that would be possible. Too much had changed. Going back to May of this year would never happen. But maybe I could return to June.

I slid his hand off my forearm and moved my hands into his, lifting them up between us. "Can we forget all of this for a while? Deal with it a little at a time?"

"If that's what you want. I just want you better, with or without me. Seeing you drunk like that, watching Freddy take care of you when I didn't know what to do…"

I sighed and placed my head on his chest. "I'm sorry. And I do want you, Trevor… I love you. I do. I-I want to try again. Slowly." And for the moment, I believed it was possible.

Sighing, and unable to hide a small smile of relief, he wrapped an arm around me and placed a hand on my back. So simple a gesture, and yet, somehow, it righted the entire world again.

The entire station rocked severely to one side like someone had flipped it, center included. Amphorae fell off the counter to my right, shattering into a hundred or more pieces. I gripped the countertop, and Trevor crashed into me, digging my ribs into the linoleum. Something *clunked* behind me onto the floor—my cell phone.

The station swayed violently to an upright position, knocking me and my hung-over brain off balance. The world spun in a dizzying, rocking mess. Trevor shoved his hands under my arms and pulled me up through rising nausea. The general quarters alarm went off.

Lights around us dimmed until they emitted a soft, red glow.

Vomit seized my throat and stomach. I clutched my sides and rushed to a trashcan, dry-heaving into it. Trevor stepped behind me and held up my hair. When it passed, I locked eyes with him, and he crossed the room to the intercom and dialed the Bridge. My heart raced in my veins, pulse thudding behind my ears and at my wrists. We just made it through a *hijacking*. What could possibly be happening now?

Seconds passed and no response came from the Bridge.

"Why is no one answering?" I asked.

Christa's voice came over the station-wide communications band. "Trevor Boncore to the Bridge. Trevor to the Bridge."

Oh, that can't be good.

Trevor held a hand out to me. "Come on."

We made it to the Bridge in less than two minutes. Someone opened the door for Trevor's arrival, and the Commander greeted Trevor with a headset. He pointed to a station, and Trevor went to work. I stood out of the way like I had the day we found the Atlantean outpost. The need to hop onto a NANA station gnawed at me. Emma—Valerie—never should have given me those instructions or taught me what she did.

The Commander approached me with a headset. "If you think you can help—"

I put it on and manned the lower NANA station, which spat out readings that made no sense. "We're not in water?"

"We're not in anything," the Commander confirmed.

I shot Trevor a look across the room. He was half-seated in a Helm station, a look of utter disbelief enveloping his expression. I lifted fingers to indicate channel three on the headset. He nodded and complied.

"What's happening?" I asked him.

"We're being moved," he said in a hushed tone, a hand in front of his mouth.

I hid my lips in a similar fashion. "Moved?"

"Through time and space—to a different part in the timeline."

"What are you saying?" I was ever aware of the growing audience our antics garnered. Almost everyone on the Bridge, the Commander included, stared at us.

"Lemuria," Trevor said, tone clipped and breath hitched. "Chelsea, they're taking the station and us along with it."

My head cocked to one side, daring him to confirm his words. He nodded slowly like I was an idiot not seeing something right in front of me.

"How? And how do you know?" I asked.

"The readings say we aren't where we're supposed to be," he said. "That's because in less than thirty seconds, we won't technically exist." He paused, waiting for me to respond. "Chelsea, we have to do something. *You* have to do something. You're a super solider. You can stop this."

"What will they do to us?"

He shook his head. "I don't know. They need us or the station for one reason or another. If Thompson wanted you—"

"We also have all of those Link Pieces downstairs." My heart dropped into my gut, all breath whooshed from my lungs.

I slammed my fingers onto the keyboard. "Christa, open up a secure line to the number I'm giving you."

The Commander stood in front of my station, questioning why I gave Christa orders. I ignored him. Where was Captain Marks? Why was he always missing when this stuff happened?

"Christa, I need that line," I insisted.

"I can't—" she said.

"Never mind." I grunted and opened it myself. I punched in the code to take over her station—*Thank you, Valerie*—and dialed TAO. "Mayday, mayday, this is SeaSat5 calling TAO. We're being taken.

Repeat, the Lemurians have us."

I repeated the message once before the Commander himself cut the line. "I can't authorize—"

"We are being compromised!" I shouted at him.

His eyes darted between me and the station, a painful worry wrinkling his face. Letting a civilian order around the senior staff was one thing. Opening an unauthorized, secured communications channel in the middle of a crisis was another.

Trevor sidestepped the Commander and reopened the channel for me. The station rocked again, forcefully turning horizontal. Gears ground together, the station not ready for such a maneuver. We tumbled from our seats on the Bridge, crashing to the floor.

I ripped off my headset as I pulled myself up and searched for Trevor. I lifted him up and put my hands on his shoulders to steady myself.

Trevor cursed. "There goes Humming Bird. They lost liquid density. It's fucking *stuck*."

"Tell me what to do to save us," I told him.

A wave of *something* fell over the Bridge. It stood all the hairs on my body on end as if electricity filled the room. The station shook in place again, its walls trembling. Adrenaline sparked in my veins and narrowed my vision into focus. The super soldier part of me clawed her way to the surface. I pushed her down as best I could. *Can't lose control now.*

"We need help," Trevor said. "Maybe one of the artifacts—"

"But which one? And how?" I asked.

He dragged me off towards the blast doors. A pipe burst above us, leaking smoke into the room. Electrical circuits blew next to me. I jerked out of the way, narrowly avoiding sparks and exposed wires.

"Commander, life support systems are failing," Christa said. "NANA isn't far behind."

"Chelsea, we need to go," Trevor said.

But I couldn't concentrate. My mind focused in on Lemuria taking us to some place, some *time* unknown. But why?

Silence completely filled the room, hanging heavy as all the shaking stopped.

"Commander," Freddy said. "I'm getting weird readings. The atmosphere outside—it's not normal."

The Commander rushed to his side. "What do you mean?"

"I've got my screen saying we're centuries off of where we should be. I mean, *when* we should be," another crewman said.

If we were in the future, then maybe something from our time could help.

I spun to the Commander, shrugging off Trevor's attempts to drag me away. "I can get help. I can't tell you how or why, but I can get help."

The Commander must have understood. "Do it."

"Commander!" Freddy shouted. "Look at the security feed!"

The Commander ordered him to bring it onto the main screen on the Bridge. Trevor and I froze. There, before our eyes, were Captain Marks and Dave in the midst of a brutal fistfight. Both of them had blood-streaked faces and torn clothing. Dave sported a crooked nose.

Captain Marks. Fighting Dave.

I sprinted out the door with Trevor and the Commander hot on my trail. We didn't bother with the Lift, opting instead to race down the inner maze of stairs. When we got to Engineering, the fight was over. Captain Marks stood above Dave with his gun pointed. Dave's hands were up in the air. A console next to them smoked and sparked.

"No," Trevor gasped. He rushed over to the smoking machine and ran his hands along its sides. "No, no, no."

"Captain?" the Commander asked.

"I found him tampering with Humming Bird." His breath was ragged, his face covered in cuts. Shattered glass littered the floor. I followed its trail to a case where the fire extinguisher used to be.

Trevor cursed and beat the side of the console. "Captain, he's completely destroyed Humming Bird. I mean, it was fucked the second the Lemurians righted the ship. It's gone for good." His face grew red and he bunched his fists like an angry toddler. He kicked the console for all he was worth.

My heart ached for him, for his entire life's work, which had been destroyed in an instant by Dave, one of his friends. Someone he *trusted*. Was there anyone we could trust anymore?

"How?" My eyes darted to Dave. "Why—?" I started to ask, but a mark on Dave's hand caught my eye. A tattoo made of swirling lines and swooping coils. The same design as the burn mark on my chest, the letterhead of Trevor's parents' company. The same tattoo the man who attacked me in Boston had on the back of his hand. I choked on air, unable to speak. My hands shook.

"You *bastard*," I spat at Dave. I charged toward him, but strong hands secured themselves around my forearms and yanked back hard. The Commander held me in place.

"What's wrong?" he asked.

I pointed to Dave's hand. "It was you that night! *You* attacked me outside the Franklin!"

"You've been the one messing up Humming Bird this whole time," Trevor growled. "It wasn't the interns at all. It was *you*."

Trevor's face contorted through emotions—epiphany, betrayal, fear, anger—before he launched himself past Captain Marks and onto Dave. He tackled Dave to the ground, so empowered by my realization and the loss of Humming Bird that no one could stop him. His fists connected with Dave's face one, twice, ten times until Captain Marks finally wrenched him off.

Dave laughed, blood dripping from his nose into his teeth. He looked like a bad horror movie, like a demon laughing manically with a bloody, swelling, multi-colored face. "Took you long enough to figure it out. I had to get the station ready for today, for this."

Queasiness returned, tumbling my insides. This wasn't the hangover. Dave was the first person I met on SeaSat5 after Trevor. Knowing he had attacked me, knowing he had worked for

Thompson the whole time, made my heart burn. First Valerie, now him. How had he managed to get through the hijacking unnoticed?

"Ignore him." Trevor reached out for me. "We need to get to the Artifact Room."

Dave nodded toward the door. "What do you hope to accomplish in there, anyway? You have no idea how time travel works."

Trevor's knuckles were red with blood, but he didn't stop to wrap them or pay them any mind. Snatching my hand, he dragged me from the man who had turned my world upside down. Someday, I would make him pay. Someday, Trevor would also get his revenge.

We sprinted up the inner column of stairs to my office. I threw open the doors to the closet housing the artifacts and texts from the outpost. My eyes darted up and down each shelf. I hoped something we could use would call out to me. The journal sat on the counter, but right now it didn't shimmer at all. Nada. Nothing. Shelf after shelf of ancient, old pieces of cultures that no longer existed as they once did, and nothing freaking *shimmered*.

I paced into my office, my pulse drumming in my ears. Trevor trailed behind me, one hand on my elbow, the other grabbing artifacts to present to me along the way. I shook my head at each one. None glowed like Sophia and Dr. Hill said Link Pieces should. Nothing.

A tightness grew in my chest, building and building, until all I wanted to do was scream.

Again, I could do something. Again, I could make a difference. And again, there was no way to accomplish that. Just like when Michael died.

Then, out of my left field of vision, something sparkled. Shimmered. *Glowed.* My eyes darted to my cell phone on the floor. I watched it twinkle and wave a cerulean flourish, like pavement on a hot summer's day. The mirage called to me, drawing me toward the illusion as though reaching out with loving, controlling arms. I picked my cell phone up off the ground and stared for a moment. A simple cell phone now a Link Piece?

Then I saw it. It encased my full field of vision, ensconcing me in azure hues and cobalt waves. Snowflake-like structures linked to each other with lines housing dates and times, intricate connections I couldn't follow. My phone was there, sporting lines that darted out of it, sliding in and out of my vision, connecting themselves in the distance to an anchor-point beyond the horizon.

"Chelsea." Trevor's voice, hoarse and desperate, threatened to crash the whole scene.

The vision pulled on my body like gravity, dragging me in and holding me under like a riptide.

Trevor's hand covered mine, the one holding my phone. "You see it, don't you? The Waterstar map?"

I couldn't respond to him, only the pull of the map. My body burned a delightful heat. It started in my hands and spiraled outward into every part of me. Every limb, every node. Every single piece of me hummed with warm power, with a surety I'd never before known.

The room around us swirled and tumbled, slowly metamorphosing into something else, something new, until we stood in the middle of the Franklin, surrounded by people jumping and cheering for a band on stage. I couldn't hear them. At first, there was no sound. Silence like an old black and white movie, where little made sense and you couldn't make out what people were saying. Then, like a cymbal at the top of a crescendo in an orchestra, clarity struck bright and loud.

We stood in the exact place I'd first seen Trevor all those months ago, the exact place I'd teleported to SeaSatellite5 from in May.

The silence shattered in an instant, destroyed by a confusing cacophony of lights and noises, all earth-shatteringly different from SeaSat5. My head spun. Audio Striker's lead singer screeched into his mic. The sound pierced my ears and split my head. I cupped my palms over my ears to drown him out.

Trevor tugged on my arm, mouthing something I couldn't make

out. The whites of his eyes looked weird in the light, like he didn't have pupils at all.

"Fuck me!" I shouted. Couldn't Audio Striker stop playing for one *freaking* second? I squished my palms to my ears even harder.

Someone's elbow jabbed into my ribs, then another and another. A mosh pit roared to life behind me. I hurried out of the way as another body soared toward me and plowed into Trevor. He righted the both of us and pointed behind my head. I followed his finger to an EXIT door near the stage and glanced at the mosh pit blocking the way. This would not be fun.

I grabbed hold of Trevor's arm, dug my fingers into his skin, and marched toward the door, shoving people off of us as we went. Someone's arm flung into Trevor's face, connecting with his nose. He faltered for a second, and I pulled him forward as blood streamed over his lips and chin.

I heaved open the door and sucked in huge breaths of fresh air. Audio Striker's music and fans faded, giving way to taxi cabs beeping and brakes screeching. The city. Boston.

I paced almost to the end of the alley before turning to see Trevor rip off part of his shirt to stem the blood flowing from his nose.

"What the *hell* just fucking happened?" I demanded.

"I don't know." He looked up at the sky, like it had answers, then to me. "We're in Boston."

"No shit. But where are they? Where's SeaSat5?"

"I don't know, Chelsea," he repeated with gritted teeth.

Pressure built inside me, constricting my lungs, clenching my muscles, until I spun and sent my fist soaring into the brick wall of the Franklin. I left it there, embedded in stone with bleeding, broken knuckles, absorbing the pain. Letting it clear my thoughts and disperse my confusion. One breath. Two.

Finally, I opened my eyes and noticed another hole right next to it. I'd made it after hearing about Ray, right before Dave tried to mug me.

I swallowed hard. *None of this is real. This cannot be happening.*

"Chelsea, we have to do *something*," Trevor said.

I spun on Trevor. "We tried! We freaking tried, and it didn't work. Why are we here?"

"Why your cell phone?"

"What?"

He pointed to my other hand, still clasping my phone. "Why'd you grab your phone in your office?"

I honestly didn't know. "It called to me." *Connections.* "I dropped it here the night I teleported to SeaSat5. Do you think it's linked to the Franklin because of that?"

Trevor didn't answer. Instead, he closed the distance between us. "We need to call TAO. Now. They'll know what to do."

My fingers and knuckles ached as I dialed the number Trevor gave me from memory. Between the two of us, we were a bloody mess.

"Put it on speaker," Trevor said, and I did.

It rang a few times, then a woman picked up. "Thank you for calling—"

"We need to speak to Dr. Connor Hill right now," Trevor said.

"It's Chelsea Danning and Trevor. From SeaSat5," I added.

The line cut, and Dr. Hill spoke next. "Chelsea! Trevor! We got your S.O.S."

"Lemuria took SeaSat5 to the future," Trevor said—well, more like shouted—into the phone.

"We used my cell phone to get here," I said. "I think we traveled through time."

Trevor leaned in over the phone. "We need to go back. To help them."

A bus drove by, blaring its horn and covering up the first half of Dr. Hill's response.

"—only one-way. We'd need another Link Piece to travel there. Where are you? I'll send a contingent to get you."

"They're only one-way?" I asked. "Are you freaking *kidding* me?"

His voice garbled, the call losing reception. Damn city cell coverage. "Two hours out... Stay put... Tracking call."

Silence encompassed us, save for sirens whizzing by, a plane flying overhead. City sounds. Sounds that used to make me rest easy, knowing I was home. Tonight, the sounds left my body quaking and my lungs gasping for breath.

Trevor and I looked at each other, expressions mirrored. Drawn lips. Shallow breaths. Wide eyes.

"We left them," I whispered.

He shook his head. "There's nothing we could've done."

"You don't know that." My voice broke over the words.

He shook his head, hand rubbing the back of his neck. "We can help them here. If we stayed, we'd be prisoners, too."

Tears welled up and stung my eyes. "You're assuming they're still alive."

His Adam's apple bobbed as he swallowed. "We have to."

Trevor led me over to the wall where we met months ago, and we slid down it. He wrapped an arm around me. I tucked my head under his chin and squeezed him tight. That's all we had to keep us together. To keep us from falling apart.

Acknowledgements

Gyre has been a three-year journey, and I have a ton of people to thank for their help in turning this manuscript into the book you hold in your hands today. This list is long, so please stick with me.

First and foremost: thank you to my critique partners, Talynn, René, Jen, Chy, Emma, and Suzanne. Thank you for always being there, for never letting me give up, and for always believing this day would come, especially during the times when I didn't. Thank you for every late-night freak out, for reading *Gyre* countless times in *all* its incarnations, for making me delete that one "special" storyline, and for NOLA; for everything. This book would be nothing without the six of you, and words can never express my gratitude for the love and the enthusiasm you've given me and *Gyre* over these years. Thank you.

To my editor, Tori, thank you for falling in love with *Gyre* and for championing me throughout this journey. You are seriously an amazing woman. Thank you also to Nikki, Andrew, Clare, Lisa, Christine, and Andy for all that you do. And a big thank you to the entire CQ family, who welcomed me with open arms.

To my friends at #WIPMarathon, you've been along for the entire ride. Thank you for the monthly check-ins and, most importantly, for your friendship. You ladies remind me that writing isn't a lonely hobby.

A big thank you to my beta readers who read all or part of *Gyre*: Heather, John, Kate, Liz, Patrice, and Steph. Many grateful thanks to my contest mentors and the writing community. Thank you all for every bit of advice, every tough critique, and every cheer of encouragement you've given me.

Thank you to my grandparents, family, and friends. There are far too many of you to risk naming individually, and I don't want to forget anyone. You know who you are. You believed first. I started this publishing journey because of you, and I never would have made it this far without you. Thank you for cheering me on every step of the way, and for being patient with me when I needed to bounce ideas or write something down on the back of a Duckpin Bowling score sheet mid-turn.

To my sister, thank you for teaching me to follow your dreams, regardless of anything or anyone else. You're the best sister anyone could ask for, and I'm glad to call you mine.

To my parents, thank you for your unconditional love and unwavering support. For encouraging me at a young age to grow my imagination in every way possible. For introducing me to the science-fiction and fantasy genres, teaching me that amidst all the unbelievable and impossible things in this world, you will find the very definition of humanity and love. For everything, thank you. And sorry for all the BTVS books I read instead of the books they wanted me to read. Guess it paid off?

About The Author

Born in Connecticut and raised on science-fiction and fantasy, it was inevitable **Jessica Gunn** would end up writing novels. She spent most of high school binge-watching a plethora of "old" and current sci-fi shows before diving into fanfiction. Jessica wrote her first novels in high school.

In college, Jessica studied anthropology where she learned enough about ancient civilizations and flintknapping to inspire GYRE, her first published novel. But being honest, daydreams of Atlantis and other ancient mysteries have captivated her for over a decade.

Jessica now lives as a continuous student of the writing craft in small-town Connecticut. She remains an avid fan of stories of the wormhole and superhero variety. Oh, and villains. She loves villains. When not working or writing, she can be found attending to her ever-growing TBR pile and hiking the forests of New England.

To catch up with Jessica, follow her on Twitter (@JessGunnAuthor) or on her website, www.jessicagunn.com.

Thank You for Reading

Please visit http://curiosityquills.com/reader-survey to share your reading experience with the author of this book!

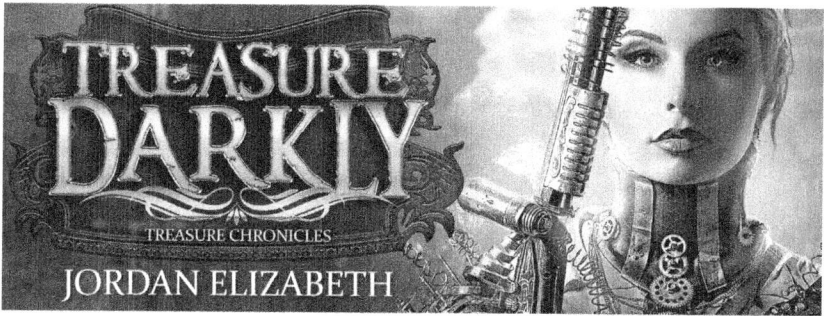

Treasure Darkly, by Jordan Elizabeth

Seventeen-year-old Clark Treasure assumes the drink he stole off the captain is absinthe…until the chemicals in the liquid give him the ability to awaken the dead. A great invention for creating perfect soldiers, yes, but Clark wants to live as a miner, not a slave to the army—or the deceased. On the run, Clark turns to his estranged tycoon father for help. The Treasures welcome Clark with open arms, so he jumps at the chance to help them protect their ranch against Senator Horan, a man who hates anyone more powerful than he.

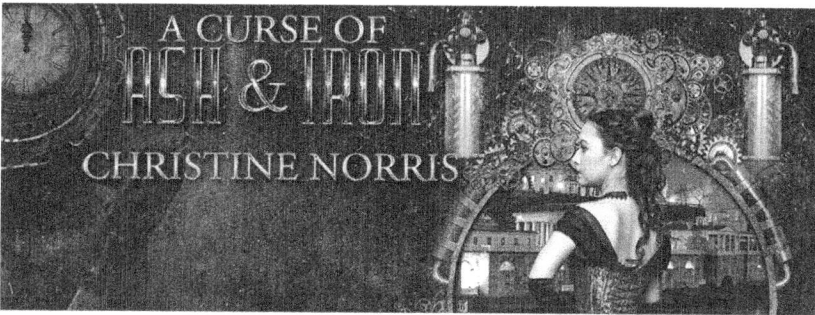

A Curse of Ash & Iron, by Christine Norris

Eleanor Banneker is under a spell, bewitched and enslaved by her evil stepmother. Her long-lost childhood friend, Benjamin Grimm, is the only person immune to the magic that binds her. Even if he doesn't believe in real magic, he cannot abandon her to her fate and must find a way to breach the spell - but time is running short. If he doesn't succeed before the clock strikes midnight on New Year's Eve, Ellie will be bound forever…

Homunculus & The Cat, by Nathan croft

In a world where every culture's mythology is real, Medusa's sisters want revenge on Poseidon, Troy is under siege again, and the Yakuza want their homunculi (mythological artificial humans) back. Near Atlantis' Chinatown, a kitten and her human campaign for homunculi rights. Against them are Japanese death gods, an underworld cult, and a fat Atlantean bureaucrat.

The main character dies (more than once) and a few underworlds' way of death is threatened. Also with giant armored battle squids.

Broken Dolls, by Tyrolin Puxty

Ella doesn't remember what it's like to be human – after all, she's lived as a little doll for thirty years. She forgets what it's like to taste, to smell…to breathe. She helps the professor create other dolls, but they don't seem to hang around for long. His most recent creation is Lisa, a sly goth. Ella doesn't like Lisa. How could she, when Lisa keeps trying to destroy her? Ella likes the professor's granddaughter though, even if she is dying. It's too bad the professor wants to turn Gabby into a doll, too. What's a broken doll to do?

CPSIA information can be obtained at www.ICGtesting.com
Printed in the USA
BVOW08s1243170216

437025BV00004B/56/P

9 781620 070758